THE
MOON
STALLION

THE MOON STALLION

A NOVEL BY JIM BERRY

M. EVANS AND COMPANY, INC.
NEW YORK

LIBRARY OF CONGRESS CATALOGING IN PUBLICATION DATA

Berry, Jim.
  The moon stallion.

  I. Title.
PR6052.E652M6   1982   813'.54   81-19600

ISBN 0-87131-368-5   AACR2

Copyright © 1982 by Jim Berry

M. Evans and Company, Inc.
216 East 49 Street
New York, New York 10017

Design by Diane Gedymin

Manufactured in the United States of America

9 8 7 6 5 4 3 2 1

for all the midnight riders,
      rank outsiders,
      spartan artists,
      freedom fighters, and
      wrong-righters
      who ever dared to take a stand;

      and for my folks and friends—
      as they be few,
      so they be precious . . .

                    London and Pittsburgh
                    1980/81

Go tell the Spartans, thou that passest by,
That here, obedient to their laws, we lie.
—SIMONIDES OF CHIOS

CHAPTER ONE

THE GIANT INDIAN WAS A MAN who needed no one at all. Eight long years of traveling far from his homeland had made him more extreme in the characteristics he had possessed before the banishment: more independent, prouder, harder—more Tehuelche. He had ventured beyond the limits of any of his kinsmen, beyond even their wildest dreams. He had seen many things that even the rich Tehuelche language would find difficult to describe. Yet he would have to try to find the words when he confronted the circle of elders. Upon his broad shoulders would fall the responsibility of convincing the tribe of what was about to befall them. How could he depict the places to which he had been? How could he fulfill the prophecy of the doomed messiah for which he had been singled out? The banishment of the one hundred moons was at an end. His race was nearly run. The nemesis of his people was at hand. Harkana the Orphan had come back, aged twenty-seven, enriched by experience and knowledge; a pauper only in time. If it was to happen in the way that the great shaman Vantempec had decreed, Harkana had returned to die.

The Tehuelche stood at the edge of the great saline swamps with his head full of questions. They alone stood between him and the pampas where he had been born and brought up. As always, he weighed his options carefully. He seldom hurried unless immediately threatened. He was reckless only when circumstances demanded it of him. The scales of survival were delicately balanced.

The route west around the swamps would take him several days longer than if he went due south. When he had first been driven out from his tribe he had ridden northwest. His memory told him how far the marshes stretched in the direction of the sun sleeping. It was too far. One of many dictums in the Tehuelche tongue said that a man without a horse was only half a man. Harkana had been half a man for many moons, ever since a jaguar had taken the bay mare one night in the northern forests.

The route east around the swamps was a vast unknown. He did not know how far. It was a detour of uncertain terrain, food, water, and enemies. The only thing that he was sure of was that eastward lay the white man and his cruelty. For a Tehuelche on foot it was too great a risk. The Orphan discounted the idea of bypassing the saline swamps in the direction of the sun waking. Harkana plunged south, and the swamps soon swallowed him.

His pace was an even, loping jog. Tehuelches were fleet of foot. Harkana could run down a rhea and kill it with just a knife. The large flightless birds were a major food source for the pampas Indians. Looking about as he ran, Harkana saw that the marshes were yet another whole new world to recount in the Tehuelche encampment. How would he describe this pancake of brackish bayous, mud flats, and waving reeds? Perplexed by much of what lay behind him as well as most of what lay ahead, Harkana digested this food for thought as the miles were consumed by the appetite of his running.

Harkana was tall even by Tehuelche standards, over six and a half feet. His build was classically slim-waisted and broad-shouldered. The power which he possessed, particularly in his arms and hands, was prodigious. His stamina, both on foot and in the saddle, was staggering. His supple body suggested leather rather than iron. Like most Tehuelches, he had developed enormous resilience in the face of pain and hardship. Where he came from, survival was granted to those who mastered the adversaries which made living a perilous act. It was a shifting and temporary award.

His world was seen in black-and-white terms. There were very few shades of gray. One lived or one died. One resisted the heat and the cold or one succumbed to it. A Tehuelche broke a wild horse or the horse broke him. Life had hitherto been dangerously simple, hazardously lacking in complexity. The ability to pull through was measured in extremes. There had seldom been a middle road down which one could play games with living; death was ubiquitous. It was the way of the Tehuelche, diamond-hard and bloody. Those who could not follow the way soon perished. Life for the Tehuelches was always underwritten by death elect.

In all these attributes Harkana was a true Tehuelche. Like the rest of the tribe's menfolk, he was born to be a killer, whether in the hunt or in battle. The Orphan had killed his first man at the age of fourteen. In the first nineteen years of his life, the only difference between him and the others of the tribe of Seh Saapelt was that he had been the best. Few could equal his prowess with knife, lance, and boleadoras. As a horseman he was unparalleled. But of all the arts of war, there was one in which Harkana excelled beyond all measure. His ability with the bow had never seen an equal, not in all the annals of legend and myth related around an infinity of firelit circles.

It was as an archer that Harkana first began to separate himself from all other inland Tehuelches. It was the first step on the long road of self-discovery which had culminated in the destiny Vantempec had mapped out for him.

Harkana ran for the rest of the day without stopping. The path was winding and circuitous. Mud sucked at his bare feet, leaving tracks which bubbled briefly and then slimed over with ooze. On the first night, he allowed himself three long swallows of his precious water supply. There was nothing for him to eat. Just another meatless day, no uncommon hardship; there had been too many already. Harkana lay down to sleep on a patch of dry earth. His pillow was a coil of plaited rope, made from the tough fibers found in Paraguayan forests. The poncho which covered him was of thick alpaca from the altiplano. His other accouterments were equally as foreign. The slim steel knife had been taken from a white man when he escaped. The water gourd had been hollowed out of a fruit never seen to thrive this far south. The great bow was fashioned from a wood which had no name in the Tehuelche tongue. It was five feet long and pulled almost ninety pounds. Two arrows were all that he had; he held them in his hand as he ran.

He awoke the way a cat awakes. His black eyes snapped open. There was no groggy interlude. All his senses were instantly alert. The eyes saw great spinnakers of mist drifting past. His ears recorded the foaming insect life, the screech of a bird he could not see, and the distant splash of a larger creature. Into his nostrils came the smell of fetid water, the dank miasmal atmosphere of rotting vegetation and water uncleaned by motion.

The Indian drank sparingly from the gourd. It had a cork cut like a keystone, which he replaced with exaggerated care. Harkana furled the poncho over one shoulder and chested the bow. Then he trotted on south.

Harkana ran on through his second day in the marshland. Except for a loincloth of soft leather, he was naked. In the late afternoon his passage startled a family of peccaries, and he swerved to pursue them. The bow sang, and one of the wild pigs crashed to the ground, snapping the shaft in two. So Harkana had bought meat at the cost of one of his precious arrows. He built a fire, using the friction of an improvised firebow to produce first a smoulder, then a spark, and finally a flash of flame. It ignited the driest wood dust the Indian had been able to scrape from the available kindling. Feeding it with twigs and grasses, Harkana eventually had enough of a blaze to roast a leg of the animal. His hunger satisfied, he drank the gourd down to half empty. Before he set off again next morning he devoured more of the pork flesh. The rest of the carcass he left to the buzzards.

Although the Tehuelche tribes and clans were all inveterate wanderers, they adhered to distinct patterns. The migrations followed good grazing for the horse herds. In the summer the Tehuelches kept to the north of their domain, mostly between the rivers Colorado and Negro. The Tehuelches called them Great River and River of Darkness. Rain was sparse but evenly distributed throughout the year. They began to move south before the brunt of winter set in. This time span allowed the southern grass to grow out enough to see them through the cold season. Triggered by the advent of spring, they returned northward. This had been the way of the Tehuelche for several centuries, ever since Spanish horses had begun to breed wild on the pampas.

It was to the traditional camping ground just south of the Great River that Harkana was heading. He hoped to join with the tribe of Seh Saapelt before they embarked on the migration. This was the white man's month of May. It was known to the Tehuelches as the Moon of the Harsh Wind Blowing.

By the evening of the third day the swamps began to give up their saturation of the land. The deeper mud slicks had been left behind. The ground was dryer in places than anywhere over the last sixty miles. A cascade of twilight poured out the night. Traces of winter became increasingly tangible as the Orphan progressed farther south. The temperature dropped quickly after sundown. The wind rose from its sleeping stillness to shake its head through the clumps of reeds. The land hummed and sighed. Bullfrogs pulsated. The marshes rubbed with eerie vibration. Harkana sipped from the gourd and waited for the moon to rise.

Great changes had occurred in his heart and mind. He wondered what changes had taken place among his people and to the rolling plains country that was his home. The gregarious habits of his youth had left him. Sometimes he seriously doubted that he would ever fit in with his own people again. But Vantempec had begun by telling him that he would return to lead the people to the moon; that they would allow him to take the test denied him by his father. Why should he doubt the wise old doctor of the mind and body? Had he not dubbed Harkana Orphan even before the boy had slain his father? The night was pitch-dark. He needed the moon to ease his burden.

Harkana was burdened by his knowledge. He had learned the white man's tongue. During his three-year sojourn as a prisoner of the whites he had studied the effects of their crossed-sticks religion at close hand. The banishment which had begun as a punishment had ended up as an education in life which no Tehuelche could have purchased for one thousand head of horses. Was it this that crowned him the doomed messiah who would lead his tribe to the moon? Only his god could calm the restless colored wonderings within his mind.

At last the luminous ball began to squeeze itself from the flat

13

horizon. It cast its net of phosphorescence. Peace enveloped the Indian as he bathed in its soothing light. His mind ceased its whirling doubts. The rhythm of his heart became slow and steady. Harkana's soul beat again on the drum of tranquility.

In the new morning Harkana ran on with increased vigor. The fingers of gray brine relinquished their grasp on the earth. Mud dried into clods of soil. Ahead of him spread a great canvas of grassland. And then Harkana caught sight of the tree, a dark speck on the omega of his vision. He launched himself into greater speed. It was an ombú tree, the only tree indigenous to the pampas. The first ombú tree he had seen in ninety-nine moons. He ran toward it with renewed optimism. Then he saw something else as well. Harkana had halved the distance which separated him from the tree. It took shape under the challenge of his stare. High-reaching limbs of silvered bark arced up from a thick torso. This was familiar to him. The branches threw out a wide penumbra of dappled shade, almost the sole natural shade to be found on the plains. But Harkana had been distracted by something foreign, something as out of place on the pampas as the ombú was an integral part of the scene.

He forgot about the tree, significant symbol of his homecoming though it was. Instead, he ran right up to the blemish that had struck both his panorama and his exuberance. He halted in front of it, his chest rising and falling from the exertions of the long sprint. Harkana reached out his strong right arm and touched the wire with his hand. He ran the hand along the wire until it reached one of the barbs. His thumb explored the point of the barb.

As far as he could see, the three-stranded wire ran east and west. Stretched taut between wooden stakes, the wire linked the solitary Indian to twin horizons. He walked over slowly to the nearest fence post. It was made of quebracho, a wood as hard and as heavy as stone. Harkana knew of the wood. It was cut in the northern timber forests, where its tannin was used in the white man's hide industry. Quebracho had no place on the pampas. It had been imported for the express purpose of dividing the plains.

Shock turned to anger in the heart of Harkana the Orphan.

14

There was no need to separate the land into what was yours and what was not. No fences were required on the tribal homeland of the Tehuelche. This was free range: for the white man, the half-breed gaucho, and the noble Indian. Harkana wondered how extensive the fences had become and how many other violent changes he would find after eight years as an outlaw.

He vaulted the yard-high barrier. Instead of continuing south past the ombú tree a quarter of a mile away, he turned toward the east. Patrolling the cutting edge of the fence, he walked for several miles without glimpsing its end.

Another shock awaited him. The wire trembled. A whitish shape shattered his daydream. There in front of him, about eighty yards away, was the most magnificent horse that Harkana had ever set eyes on, a gray stallion. It fought the wire, a length of which held it by the foreleg. The wire must have come loose from a post and the horse ran into it. Horses knew of the dangers on the pampas, but never before had they included the white man's nailed wire. Harkana ran forward, seeing the blood seeping from wounds on the horse's fetlock.

The horse stood still and watched the man approach. The Tehuelche studied the animal's splendid lines. It was an emphatic link in the chain of the prophecy. Upon the greatest gift of the moon would the doomed messiah arrive exultant and unite the Tehuelche nation in an act of total self-destruction. Harkana felt the unique thrill of gut fear rip through him.

The stallion shook loose its mane in shards of silver and waited.

CHAPTER
TWO

IT BECAME HARKANA'S PROUDEST CHALLENGE to pacify the great silver-maned stallion with kindness and patience. He sought control through kinship and affection. He wanted to give as well as to take, to share companionship, to befriend the horse he had found entangled in the white man's wire. Harkana had never known a true friend.

Harkana ceased to think about the time he had been absent from his tribe. Time passing made no difference to him. The stallion meant everything. On this horse the doomed messiah would return to fulfill the prophecy.

A flurry of wind punished his long black hair as he gently lay the single arrow that remained to him upon the earth that no longer did. He fashioned a loop in his rope and stepped gingerly between the top strands of the wickedly barbed wire.

The big horse continued to stare at him the whole time. The Indian was careful not to make any sudden movements, for the trapped animal was nervous from pain and fear. Harkana dropped the looped rope neatly over the horse's neck with one smooth, almost casual swing of his arm. He felt a ripple of the power latent in the stallion when it shifted back half a stride and the rope suddenly swung taut. Harkana waited. Then he eased himself forward and bent to free the horse's leg from the wire. Two of the barbs had made wounds in the fetlock, which had bled profusely but appeared clean. Clotted rivulets snaked down the silver skin. There was no permanent damage. Harkana lifted the great hoof clear, and the stallion took a whole stride back from the fence. Again the rope came up taut, half pulling the Orphan off his feet as the great head tossed and shook. A ripple of enormous strength conveyed itself along the fibers which bound them together, and the Indian wondered at the awesome power that ran down the lasso he was holding.

The horse felt its freedom and jerked its head again, feeling the coarse caress of the rope around its neck. Harkana took a double turn of the lasso around his left wrist as the animal started off. It turned and ran back toward the marsh. The Orphan thought to hold it, but no one man would ever hold that horse. Harkana hung on for dear life as he was pulled off his feet and dragged along the ground at breathtaking speed. If the earth had been hard it would have killed him. He thought fleetingly of how his father had nearly died in the same way. Then his brain held only one thought as the marshes slid under him—he must not let go of the rope. He would not release his grip on the gray stallion.

The wet ground was slick with mud, and the stallion dragged the dead weight of the helpless Tehuelche for over a quarter of a mile. The Orphan clung tenaciously, letting the animal's furious panic spend itself. Eventually it reached an area of treacherously deep mud and pulled to a halt. The man was so covered with filth that he could hardly see. Clearing his eyes, he looked up and found the animal gazing back at him with an almost quizzical expression in its eyes.

Harkana lurched to his feet, taking stock of his cuts and bruises. His left wrist wore an ugly bracelet of rope burn. His other hurts were minor.

He led the stallion gently away from the mud pool, which could have sucked them both under. His bow and his poncho were still in place. He had the steel knife and the precious bridle attached to his belt. The water gourd had been smashed. Only its neck remained on the leather thong. He discarded it, and noticed a cut on his hip. Harkana decided to abandon the last of his arrows, although he knew that he would find no replacements until he made contact with his people. Their arrows were made from southern beeches, whose forests seemed eons away

17

now. The Indian led the horse toward the east, unable to devise a way of getting them both across the fence.

Around midday, with the swampland left behind once more and the fence still visible to Harkana's right, they came upon another ombú tree. It flourished beside a thin stream of clear water. The Indian was able to tether the horse securely and then go down to the water and wash away the caked mud that covered his body. His cuts and bruises surfaced during the washing, but none were more than superficial except for the blistered bangle of skin on his left forearm. Cleansed and refreshed, he drank his fill directly from the stream. He lay flat on his belly, scooping water up to his mouth with his right hand. He paused to listen frequently, like an animal that knew never to trust nature for too long. Life and caution went hand in hand. There were no telltale signs of danger, and the Indian went back to quenching his thirst. The water was painfully cold. He paused again, drops of liquid falling from the sides of his mouth as he raised his head. When he was satisfied, he untied the horse and brought it down on the tether to drink. The stallion drank with the same practiced caution. Harkana crooned in a low, humming voice while the stallion flicked its ears at the sound. Placated by his tone, the horse let the Indian bathe the wounded fetlock and wash away the dried blood to reveal two deep punctures made by the barbs. Harkana fetched mud from the bottom of the tiny stream. He used it to staunch the slow dribble of blood which wept from the reopened wounds. Then Harkana washed his hands and led the horse back to the cantilevered limbs of the tree. There was enough rope to allow the horse to graze in a wide, sweeping arc. Only then did Harkana allow himself to think of his own stomach. It was time to go hunting.

When Harkana walked, there was a coordinated smoothness, an economy of effort that was a delight to behold. He held himself erect with his large hands relaxed at the ends of arms he swung hardly at all in his stride. The muscles across his shoulders and chest moved like beads of mercury under taut brown skin. His long legs bulged at the calves. His feet were laced with a pattern of sinews and tendons which knotted and relaxed in sequence as he loped along in a relaxed and easy rhythm.

18

The Orphan had selected a reasonably straight branch of the tree, which he trimmed of twigs as he moved along. When he had smoothed it to his satisfaction, he lashed the knife at one end, using the leather thong which had secured his water gourd. By the time Harkana was four miles north of the tree he was equipped with a simple lance. He hefted it for balance in his hand. It was adequate. Harkana now stood still, just turning his head slowly through one hundred eighty degress, seeking a snap of movement with his uncanny vision.

The pampas was as flat as a becalmed sea. Movement was difficult to conceal from a hunter's eyes. He studied a flicker of gray which arrested his concentration. Staring hard, he waited for it to occur again. It was a rhea. The Orphan checked the direction of the breeze, which was steady. He peeled off at a tangent to approach with the wind in his face. The bird fed on unaware. It raised its head sporadically, on the lookout for signs of attack. Harkana advanced only when the bird buried its head once more to feed. Each time the bird looked up, he froze every single muscle in his body. When he moved forward, he did so crouched. His eyes never left his quarry. The man oozed ever closer, with great stealth and the unhurried pace of syrup tumbling from a spoon. When he was twenty-five yards away he stopped. The breeze still favored his attack. He readied the spear in his right hand and advanced again. This time the bird sensed his presence. The rhea's head lifted sharply, and for one split second it studied the man through the eye on one side of the cocked head. Harkana had already calculated which direction it was likely to break toward. Rheas relied on speed but usually sought the heaviest cover in the savannah. When the bird broke, Harkana sprinted forward at an abrupt angle which cut off its line to the nearest heavy thicket. In a blur of action the man closed the gap between hunted and hunter, and the lance flashed up and down as the bird blundered past in blind panic. The knife bit deep, and the shock of pain checked the bird's rush; its momentum faltered. A brown arm swept back and then forward again. This time the spear was wrenched forward as the man chased after the wounded bird. The shaft of the spear dragged in the dust. Then the man caught the wounded bird by the neck, just below the throat. He avoided the flailing feet with their powerful hooked toes and managed to extract the spear from the bird's side. With one hand still on the rhea's neck, he drove the blade of the knife into the heart at close range. A shudder ran through the mortally struck animal; Harkana felt it through his hand. The rhea took two more strides, hovering in desperation. It seemed almost to consider the option of further struggle before it collapsed on its side.

Harkana opened the big bird up and cleaned out the entrails. He plucked the bird clean and severed it into great joints, which he shouldered and carried back the four miles to the ombú tree at jogging pace. He was careful to approach the stallion downwind, so the odor of blood did not reach its nostrils. He washed streaks of blood from his body and then gathered just enough wood from the base of the tree to start a meager fire with a rapidly improvised firebow. The bird was soon roasting on the flames some distance from the horse, which showed no signs of alarm. Harkana hummed soothingly until his meat was ready. He extinguished the fire as soon as he had finished cooking, for wood was in scant supply. After he had eaten, the Orphan rechecked the horse's tether before lying down to sleep under the spars of the ombú.

When the first darts of sunrise pierced their target of gloom, Harkana arose and went to drink from the endless supply near at hand. It was a cold dawn, and his breath steamed as he exhaled. He was anxious to begin work with the horse.

He walked over to the stallion, which shied away steadily but without violence. He came toward it again, singing, humming, using the weirding lilt that Tehuelches always produced with their voices when they were trying to gentle a wild horse. Harkana never approached the horse from behind. He always kept himself in full view of the animal. He made no jerky or sudden movements. And always there was the harmonious lullaby of sounds on his lips.

The horse tired of avoiding him, and the Indian stroked its forehead, neck, and throat. The horse worried about the touch of the man's hand at first but soon grew to relish the soft caress and warm dryness of skin on skin. The Orphan threaded his fingers through the long strands of the mane. Within a few days, the horse was whinnying with a pang of pleasure whenever Harkana came close.

The Indian was content to make progress this way. He let the animal sniff at him all it wanted. He fed it clumps of succulent grasses by hand. He touched and stroked the withers and back, especially the back. Later he began to rub the horse's back with the folds of his alpaca poncho, which he let lie on the rippling shoulders like a blanket for minutes at a time. During the day Harkana would walk the horse to fresh ground and let it graze. At night he slept under the umbrella of the ombú tree while the horse dozed on its feet nearby. This went on for four nights.

It was on the morning of the fifth day that Harkana first leaped onto the stallion's back. He vaulted aloft and then immediately back to the ground. He was careful to work from the same side, the left. Training a wild horse was a matter of reducing the surprises to a minimum. He landed again and again on the animal's broad back with an exaggerated and delicate softness. Each time he slid back down again before the animal was even aware of what was taking place. The moment Harkana attempted to remain aloft, the stallion reared mightly, and the Indian would come down in a controlled slide, jumping clear as soon as his feet touched the earth in an effort to avoid the kicking hooves. At last his persistence was rewarded and the horse let him sit astride, soothing the mane with his hand.

Progress became more rapid after that. The stallion took to the bridle quickly, and soon they were exploring new grazing territory together, walking for a couple of hours at a time. Always walking pace. Never any hint or taste of greater speed. Horses reacted to the adrenaline they produced in full flight. The Orphan wanted to restrict that induced excitement until such time as the horse trusted him much more. The horse accepted the bridle with alacrity, but getting it to take the bit was quite something else. The Indian's earliest attempts, even accompanied by much petting and the ever-present lilting lullaby, met with dismal failure. The horse seemed to grow suspicious once more. Harkana eased off when he felt the horse growing resentful of the bar that he needed to push over its tongue and the motives behind something so totally foreign. A week had now passed since

Harkana had first set his eyes on the horse he had to master or die trying.

The Orphan continued to ride the horse without the bit for two days. He killed a pair of peccaries during that time, and his water supply was endless. Time alone made the difference. There was soon enough trust for the stallion to let the bone bar into its mouth. The Orphan began cantering for an hour at a time. The horse learned the meaning of heels and thighs as the man communicated his messages and commands through the whole length of the long legs which clung to its bare back and sides.

Harkana knew then that the battle was almost won. He began to practice all kinds of acrobatics. They cantered together with the man clinging like a lemur under the horse's belly. The Orphan taught his partner to gallop straight as an arrow while he vaulted on and off and back on again. These were great days of exultation for the Tehuelche. He worked with every gymnastic arabesque that he had ever performed with a horse, and a few new manuevers besides.

The time came for Harkana to explore the stallion's full speed. He asked for the gallop and watched their joint shadow skimming over the land. It was so obvious that the horse had much more to give. Harkana clipped it with his hard heels, and the answering acceleration took his breath away. Never had he experienced so much power, so much glorious speed. He gave the horse its head and they catapulted forward for over a mile before the rider turned it round in a smooth, wide arc and they fairly flew together over the unending grass flats. The rhythm of four great hooves drummed on the earth. Their velocity produced a wind that swept Harkana's mop of raven-black hair back across his head. He looked down and saw the air current had buried his hands in the wild flying silver hair of the stallion's mane. Harkana laughed. He cried out for joy in his abandoned exhilaration. This was ecstasy. This was pure pleasure. This was life as it was meant to be lived. This was the way Harkana would have chosen to live forever.

Long raking strides devoured the distance back to the ombú tree. The Indian pulled the horse to a halt with a firm touch on the reins. He hit the ground in an instant, grabbing up his folded poncho. Then Harkana urged the horse on, past the camp that had been his for seventeen days, south at a furious gallop. The Orphan had won his horse and it was time now to go home. For over two miles more they raced, outpacing all but their own shadow. Harkana laughed in the face of his destiny. He laughed at the white man's world. He laughed out loud when he saw the barbed wire fence looming up on the horizon, as if to impede his freedom. The stallion took the yard-high barrier in one soaring leap, clearing it in stride. They seemed to hover over it, transfixed in both time and space. Then they came back down to earth and the Tehuelche eased back on the reins. The horse reacted to the bit with annoyance, slewing to one side but reducing speed not at all. Harkana let it go on, and the mad gallop put yet another mile between them and the fence. A warm, foam-flecked sweat seeped from the pores of the horse's neck. Its mouth brimmed with saliva. It too had found its direction, thought the Orphan. This was the day that it had been meant to live ever since it was a foal. To carry a rider that was truly worthy of it, carry him at a speed none could equal, a speed that had never before been witnessed. This was how a warlord, a prince among his people, should return after one hundred moons of dreadful hardship. Harkana felt his heart beating fast against the slight pressure of the taut bowstring that clung like a band to his chest. Now he was ready for any confrontation. He would meet any challenge. He would accept any test. And still the great horse thundered on, sweating out the frustration, forgetting the anger and pain of the barbed wire.

The moment that Harkana lifted his head and caught sight of the Great River for the first time, his heart was flooded with excitement. Across that meandering stream of the white man's Rio Colorado was the true home of the inland Tehuelches. Their massive territory stretched southward in a great yawn of sparsely grassed plains, dried gullies, struggling streams, and cinder-strewn valleys. It was a poor land, and the white man had so far left it alone. Its soil was lacking in the minerals which gave life to agriculture, pushing up the grain crops and sunflowers in vigorous harvests. The Tehuelches did not sow the seeds of such crops. It was entirely without precious ores and mineral deposits which the white man would have come in droves to locate and dig out, vomiting whole hills of tailings for the precious gems and glittering metals that he craved. The Tehuelches had no use for jewels or gold or silver.

The Patagonian wastelands did not favor cattle, whose appetite was for long, green-shooted succulent grasses, the kind which rapidly petered out south of the Colorado. Here there was only coarse, patchy grazing—a rough stubble of pasture bristling on the chin of the continent. The white man raised his prime beef stock on the true pampas. He drove the Indians south and they adapted, rearing their own herds of tough-bred, resilient horses on a rotation system which accounted in part for their nomadic ways. This was enough for the Tehuelches. They asked no more. Neither had the other tribes, the vanished tribes. They were gone forever now, driven into the mountains, pushed into the sea, hounded, tortured, starved, trapped, murdered, tricked, and crushed into extinction; and all by the white man's hand. They would not be coming back. They were no more. Only the Tehuelches were left to make the great migration in search of winter pasture.

Harkana saw the river's edge bouncing on the horizon. The gap between was closing fast as the horse hurled itself toward it, wagging a tail of dust behind. The Orphan saw how the twisting course of the river had cut deeply into the clay soil. The northern bank fell away steeply. The river was running quite high in this season, but still there were several feet of broken rocks between the lip of the bank and the gray tongue of the water. The signal flashed to his brain and the Orphan pulled on the reins to slow the horse. Again the stallion tugged and slewed half sideways against the nagging pressure of the bone bit on its tongue. It galloped on, and the river loomed frighteningly close.

The Indian leaned back on the reins with every ounce of strength that his arm muscles possessed. The bit dug into the soft flesh at the edges of his mount's mouth. The horse squirmed against it but slowed abruptly and finally pulled up within a hundred yards of the riverbank. The horse tasted blood in its mouth and went wild with fear. It plowed around, bucking and kicking and throwing itself at the sky. Although Harkana held to

24

the animal with every vestige of the strength in his knees and thighs, the horse would not be ridden, not by any man. In the same way that Harkana had shown his control over the horse by use of the bit, so the stallion was now demonstrably rebelling against being ridden. It had always been, would always be, an equal partnership based on respect or it would be no partnership at all. Harkana felt his balance going. He tried in vain to slip to the ground and still keep a hold on the rein. But as he climbed down from that bare-backed mountain of muscle he was bucked backward. He staggered as the horse twisted. The reins were torn from his hand. A giant pair of hooves swept back at his face, and one of them caught him a glancing blow on his cheek. It would have crushed in his skull if it had hit him full on. As it was, the blow tore a huge gash in the side of his face, opening it to the bone. Blinded by blood and shock, the man fell back, striking his head against a rock as he went down. Drumming hooves filled his ears and faded swiftly away into the distance until they were lost along with all consciousness.

CHAPTER THREE

MANUEL DE ROBLES SAGGED BACK into the padded cane chair and wished he could take off his boots. It had been a long and tiring journey all the way down from Buenos Aires to the McClellan estancia near the banks of the Rio Colorado. Sitting there in the living room of the hacienda, he could not remove his boots, but he could reflect that he had not become too softened by the city. He had withstood the three-day ride exceedingly well for a man of forty-two. Including the train, he had traveled almost six hundred miles from his polished desk in the big bad, big beautiful city of Buenos Aires.

Yet Robles had been born in the interior at a time when the interior was a much wilder place than it was now, in the year 1879. Just about as wild as the Patagonian frontier lands were today, he conjectured. A lot of changes had come over Argentina since Manuel was a boy—a lot of changes. Still, he had made the arduous ride down from the nearest railhead without too many problems. Even with the recent track extension south to Tres Arboles, it was still a mighty long and lonely haul on horseback to do the minister's dirty work. It was a godforsaken, desolate corner of the world sure enough, a place where rare men and women came to seek their fortunes.

She was one of them all right, this señora McClellan. Scrubbed clean and shining pink, even as she first appeared on the veranda to greet him when he hailed the house from astride his little chestnut mare. The dour little Scotswoman had promptly presented him with a spotless towel and shown him through to the wash-room. It was more elaborate than Robles had expected for a frontier hacienda; another sign of how times were changing.

Mrs. McClellan had chatted about this and that, explaining that her husband would not be back before twilight. Bruce Mc-Clellan was busy over in the east pasture, erecting the last of the barbed wire fencing they had in stock. Manuel studied her through the doorway she had hooked open while she prepared tea in the kitchen. She was sprightly and quick in her move-ments, scurrying to and fro. Her hair was tied up in a neat bun. Her dress was plain, the apron stiffly starched.

She brought the tray through, bearing a large teapot with a flowered cosy and prim china cups and saucers all properly in place. Robles did not relish English tea, however strong. It lacked guts. But he was parched, and anxious not to offend. He would have preferred a round of yerba maté, but there was no maté inside the McClellan hacienda. Robles had also been offered Scotch whisky, but had declined.

Mrs. McClellan sat down opposite him in the twin cane arm-chair with padded guanaco covers. She placed the tray between them on a low beechwood table and reached forward to pour the tea with precision. The liquid looked quite strong and clean —much like the lady herself.

Virginia McClellan believed wholeheartedly in cleaning. When-ever she was confounded by a rare moment of idleness, she stifled the inactivity by pouncing on any item in the house that she deemed only 99 percent spotless. She was still a traditional Scottish housewife from the western Highlands: God-fearing, stoic, and strait-laced. Instead of adapting her mode of life to her new environment, she had attempted to bend the new world to her view of it.

She has partially succeeded, too, Robles decided, watching how she dealt with her staff, noticing how they squirmed under her plague of foreignness. The poor cook had found it wiser and simpler to adopt the bizarre policies of his señora than to fight them. Young José had been with her for almost five years now, and he was beginning to get used to such strange practices as insisting that Christmas be celebrated at the end of June, to coincide with the snowfall. Virginia could not conceive of a sunshine nativity. Her houseboy, Alejo, who was only fifteen, had been in her service for less than a year. He listened attentively to an endless stream of instructions from the acid tongue of Mrs. McClellan, but he remained a gaucho boy at heart. Alejo loathed waiting on table, for it seemed that he could do nothing right. He was dreading the big Sunday dinner, when all the important local ranchers were to gather under the McClellan roof.

"I am sure my husband will not keep you very much longer, señor Robles," she apologized. Her Spanish was correct but heavily accented. She never felt at ease with the language, although she spoke it well after so many years in her adopted country.

"There's no hurry, señora," Robles told her, hoping to put her at ease. He was still studying her closely as he spoke. It was his way. He had to learn as fast as he could about these English pioneers. Robles made no distinction between English and Scots; to him, they were all "ingleses."

Manuel sipped at his insipid tea and reached for more sugar. He dumped two additional spoonfuls into his cup in an effort to smother the taste, then reached for his pipe. He stuffed the worn old bowl full with loving care and struck a match on the heel of his boot, feeling his tender riding muscles as he lifted his leg.

"Do you object, señora?" he remembered to ask, gesturing with the pipe in his hand.

"Not at all," lied Mrs. McClellan, who hated the odor of strong tobacco. She had been forced to tolerate her husband's mild cigarettes.

Robles saw through her charade but was content to profit by it. He held the lighted match to his pipe and inhaled with deep satisfaction, settling back a little more into the armchair.

"If you will excuse me for a while, señor Robles, I must go and supervise the evening meal. You will find reading material on the bookshelf. If you need anything, just let me know."

"You're very kind," said Robles, rising from his chair as the lady of the house strode smartly into her kitchen sanctuary, unhooking the door as she passed through.

After the kitchen door had ceased to swing on its hinges, Robles became aware of the silence, nudging his thoughts back to the empty land all around the hacienda. The land forsaken by God and just about everyone else. Except for the Indians, of course. They had adapted over centuries, not decades. Not a couple of fast-changing, raw-boned decades, he realized.

It was the Indians who had supplied the reason for his coming so far south. Manuel de Robles was an authority on Indian affairs. He reported directly to the Minister of the Interior. It was a relatively new post, created by the studious Avellaneda and his sycophants. Robles was the first man to hold it. He was supremely qualified for the position. The government wanted more humanity and less injustice. If the Avellaneda administration could not enjoy the majority of public support over the Indian problem before they quit office, at least they would have tried.

"A semblance of what is right, Robles," the minister had reminded him a few days before his departure. "Look deeply into this southern conflict which is brewing on the borders of our country. See for me if there is a solution other than the further extermination of the indigenous peoples of our nation. Bring back the facts. We will implement the policy. Promise nothing at all to anyone, is that understood? Investigate the situation with your usual thoroughness and then file your report. Make your own recommendations, by all means, but I am not interested in snap judgments, is that clear? Take your time. Spend a week or two riding around, visiting haciendas, talking to the men who matter on the peninsula. On no account are you to let your background influence your viewpoint. I have often wondered if prejudice still flows in your veins, Robles."

"I've long wished to find that out myself, sir," Robles had replied, with a hint of sarcasm. It was this fastidious correctness that always infuriated the minister. He could never quite be sure if Robles was being utterly serious or merely condescending with measured politeness. The minister had spent many hours during the past few years since he had met Robles trying to make up his mind on that point. Certainly, he was a strange one. Quiet, discerning, sharp-eyed, easily underestimated. He of the Indian blood. The minister could still remember the day that he had first met him. They had all tried to walk roughshod over him, to make short work of his stay in BA, to put an abrupt end to his career and any ideas he might have for further ministerial advancement. Yet, after seven years, Robles was still there. He had taken a new post that had been especially created for him by the President himself. And a great many of those who would have done the ousting of this quiet quarter-Indian had themselves been ousted in either a reshuffle or under the shadow of corruption. Nothing had ever been pinned on Robles. He had always come through with exaggerated cleanliness. No mud ever stuck to his character. No stigma ever undermined his reputation for truth, integrity, and fairness. No, thought the Minister of the Interior as Robles left him, there was more to this individual than met the eye; a lot more.

As Robles sat alone in the living room of the hacienda, he wondered what McClellan and the other settlers would be like. It had all happened so fast in the new Argentina. The estancieros had made their fortunes too quickly to care about listening to reasons as to why they should not make much more just as fast. What did they care for the native tribes whose lifestyle they were suffocating with the pillow of their own? The Ranqueles were just the last in a long line of examples. Their insurrection had exploded while they had mobility and weapons. It had been easily and ruthlessly crushed. Roca had led eight thousand men armed with rifles against fewer than two thousand Indians with bows and spears. They were not only severely outnumbered but also totally disorganized. Now there were no more Ranqueles. Not unless you counted the few starving stragglers who lived on in the hills, stumbling snowblind, eating roots, dressed in rags, dying slow. If the climate and the famine didn't kill them then they gave up their lives voluntarily, for life held nothing for them without freedom. It had always been that way for the Indians of the pampas and the wastelands of Patagonia. Death alone gave them unmolested liberty.

Robles got up to peruse the McClellan bookshelf. He had always been in love with words. But there was nothing in Spanish for him to read. He heard the kitchen door open, and Mrs. McClellan glided back into the room.

"I'm so sorry to have neglected you, señor Robles, but José can still not be trusted when it comes to seasoning a beef stew."

"Think nothing of it," Robles assured her. "I have been perfectly content just to rest after my journey."

Mrs. McClellan resumed her seat while Robles continued to stand. The houseboy, Alejo, entered the room with an armful of kindling. He bowed curtly to the guest, and Manuel nodded in return. Alejo had a fire going in a matter of minutes.

"Tell me," said Mrs. McClellan, "how long have you been in your present occupation, señor Robles?"

"Less than a year, señora. It was the brainchild of the President himself. He had to fight to get it passed. That took the first three years of his presidency, I believe."

Mrs. McClellan nodded her head in understanding, but Robles could see the wheels turning inside her head. This is a shrewd woman, he decided, not to be underestimated. But there was little fear of that, for Manuel de Robles had learned long ago never to underestimate anyone. He himself enjoyed being underestimated enormously.

"Is it your first time in these parts?" asked the Scotswoman.

"Yes, it is."

"You must find it very barren and extremely dull . . . er, let's say void of life in comparison with the city?"

"Barren, yes, señora McClellan," Robles agreed, "but the interior is seldom dull. I was raised a long way from here but even farther from Buenos Aires, so I am accustomed to the quiet and the emptiness. I see great grandeur in nature. I find it satisfying."

"Is that so? Then you are a country man at heart, like my husband and myself?"

"Indeed. I was brought up near the source of the Colorado, that same river which flows so close to your land. My father grew grapes and made wine. My mother was half Indian— Yamana, in fact. So she was from the extreme south, although I myself never managed to visit the land her people once called their own. My father, fortunately for me, believed in education. Our family was small enough to be able to afford it. I have just one sister, a few years younger than myself. That is quite a rarity among our Catholic countrymen. Anyway, it got me an education."

31

"Quite so."

"Well, I came to Buenos Aires and studied law. The rest is just time and a stroke of luck which made me the right man in the right place."

"You are too modest, señor Robles, I'm sure." She hurried on past the pseudo-compliment. "But how does a lawyer relate to the Indian bureau advising the ministeries, may I ask?"

"Oh, that derived purely from my own personal interest in the tribal forefathers of our land. Having the family connection, so to speak, it was a natural progression to want to see something positive done about the Indian problem. I was always of a belief that there was room enough for everyone in so wide a country as Argentina."

"But surely it is not a matter of space alone, señor Robles?"

"How right you are," Robles said, tugging at one corner of his mustache as he watched the woman's intelligent face brighten perceptibly. "No, besides making room for the Indians we must also educate them. It will be necessary to take steps to see that they are integrated into our society. They must be provided with a toehold in the nineteenth century. Perhaps," he added, "they can even teach us a few things. I believe that the white settlers, especially those that came from Wales originally and have tried to settle on the coast farther south, have found that Indian ways are well suited to bare survival in the first hard years of trying to found a colony in Patagonia."

"That is not quite what I meant, señor Robles," said a crestfallen Mrs. McClellan. Robles watched her unruffled surface dissipate. She appeared anxious to clear up a misunderstanding. Robles wondered why. Was it because she expected her husband any moment and hated the idea of him bursting into the middle of such a misinterpretation? Or was this just a personal issue, colored by strong feelings and embellished with frustration?

"Indeed not," Virginia McClellan added hastily, lest he get the wrong idea. "What I meant was that the land farther south should be taken from the Indians that remain, forcibly if necessary, not given over to them by legal charter."

"But where would you have the Indians live, señora? Where else could they go if not able to remain in the wilderness lands farther south?"

32

"I would not have them live at all, señor. They are merely savages from a bygone era. An era that is dead and all but buried, señor Robles—and there is no alternative but for the Indians to die along with it."

"But, señora, you can't mean that?"

"I can and do, señor Robles," the Scottish housewife said frostily. "This is not 1579, after all. We have been colonizing Argentina for three hundred years now. It is high time we became more modern and more realistic in our approach to the tribes. There is no place for them now, nor will there be so in the new world. Their time is past and ours is just beginning. Señor Robles, for tribes like the Tehuelches, it is already over."

It was the first time that the name of the tribe had been mentioned by anyone he had come into contact with since he left Buenos Aires. The word "Tehuelches" left him rather cold. It was suddenly painful to swallow, and he hardly caught the words that Mrs. McClellan was spouting.

"It's the law of the jungle, señor Robles," she was informing him, "the survival of the fittest."

Robles let the remark go by, although he knew full well just how fit Tehuelches were. There seemed to be little hope left that her husband would do more than endorse the wife's standpoint. As for the others—well, the other gringos would no doubt follow suit. Manuel sucked at his pipe and let his tea get cold.

Virginia McClellan had rested her face into a quiet and falsified smile. She had wanted to make the point quite clear, without alienating a man who could, and was in fact thoroughly expected to, endorse that point. She looked across at this compact man with the weary eyes and wondered what he was thinking. He was hard to fathom, and Virginia had grown used to people who were not at all mysterious. Her puzzlement was interrupted by the sound of approaching horse hooves, which clattered across her compound yard and steadied themselves outside the door of the hacienda.

Robles heard them too. His right hand strayed involuntarily to the worn butt of his Colt revolver. Even his many years in the city could not alter the natural reaction of a man hardened to troubled times. In his forty-two years Robles had found that life was trouble, be it in one form or another. He watched the woman

33

get up and go to the curtained window. She peered out and satisfied herself that all was well.

"It's Bruce," she told him, then hurried to the door and wrenched back the twin bolts.

Robles heard commands being issued in rapid Spanish, accented but very fluent. From the tone of the voice, he got the impression of a big man. It was a deep voice, one that carried authority. The Argentine's sharp ears caught the sound of a horse being led away; detected the jingle of spurs. They came from the few long strides that it took Bruce McClellan to reach the threshold of his front door.

"We have a visitor, dearest," the woman warned him in English. Robles did not know the language. He rose to his feet as McClellan entered the living room, filling it as much with his personality as with his physical bulk. In his left hand he carried a rifle by the end of the barrel. Robles, who knew about guns, recognized it as one of the new Winchester repeaters. The two men met with their eyes and their hands at the same time.

"*Mucho gusto,*" growled the ruddy-complexioned Scot, with a wide grin splitting his face.

"The pleasure is mine," Robles conceded. He also conceded a smile.

McClellan sat himself down in one of the cane chairs. He was big in everything: in body, in appetite, in land, in generosity toward those he approved of, and in hatred toward those he did not. It took Robles time to learn all of these things; but not a long time.

"Seat yourself, señor Robles. We've been anticipating your visit for some time now. The leading farmers and cattlemen in these parts are anxious to know just what is going to be done to rid us of this Indian menace."

Robles watched him place his rifle in the corner of the room, near one of the windows. McClellan turned back to his guest, taking off his sheepskin jacket as he did so.

"I see you are admiring the rifle. Here"—he picked the rifle up and swung it lightly in one hand, offering it across the room, butt first—"feel how she balances. Winchester '73, fifteen-round repeater. Must be one of the few in the whole country. My brother works in the British consulate in Washington. Had it shipped here as soon as they came on the market. If we had a hundred more like them, we'd soon whip those Tehuelches into surrender."

Robles did a wonderful job of ignoring the remark. He studied the craftsmanship that had polished and shaped the walnut stock. He ran his hand over the precision-machined barrel and lever action. What a beautiful piece of workmanship; what loving attention to detail had gone into this instrument of death. Robles took a thoughtful puff at his pipe and watched the look that passed between the McClellans as Virginia glided from the room.

"I hope that I will be able to alleviate the strain of the situation, señor McClellan."

"Oh, do call me Bruce."

Robles learned more about the man from that one short sentence than he would learn all that first evening. It spelled lack of sensitivity to an adopted country. It reeked of a man who clung to his background even in a new world. It revealed McClellan's expectation that Argentina would come into line with his own alien ways, instead of his endeavoring to get into step with the Latin code of life. From that moment on, Manuel de Robles knew that he would forever clash with the McClellans, and most likely with the other Patagonian farmers, too. One simply did not go around calling people by their Christian names when you had met them just five minutes before. Robles like to keep things formal. He made friends with difficulty, with exaggerated slowness, and he made them for life. As far as he was concerned, this was strictly business. To rip that formality to shreds so soon was inherent bad manners. Robles represented the government of the Republic. He could not and would not be compromised. His role was as observer, specialist, and reporter. He bore no prejudice, although his enemies would constantly make unjust references to his mixed blood.

The door to the living room swung on its hinges and Mrs. McClellan came through bearing a tray with two glasses and a bottle of whisky. The whisky bottle was two thirds empty. Mrs. McClellan said something to her husband.

"You do not care to drink whisky, Manuel?" said the man of the house.

"I will take a glass of wine with you, perhaps?"

A man who did not drink whisky. To Bruce McClellan, who had spent more years away from his native Scotland than he had spent in it, that said an awful lot about Manuel de Robles. To him, it was an irrevocable failing. No matter how much of a man you might be, if you did not share a wee dram or two or three, then you could never be much more than an acquaintance of Bruce Harvey McClellan. To him, there was only one kind of man that was worse—and that was a man who did not like to drink at all.

"As you wish, Manuel. Virginia! Bring a bottle of that imported Chilean red for Manuel. I think you will enjoy it. Comes from right the other side of the Andes mountains but travels exceedingly well."

They had their drinks poured and settled down in the two cane chairs. Mrs. McClellan went back to the kitchen. It was dark outside by then. Robles could see a few outrider stars snapping on and off in the indigo sky. He sipped the wine and found it as good as his host had boasted. Robles liked to drink wine. He had grown up with it, for his father had owned a small vineyard. He sipped again from the exquisite cut-glass goblet, trying to keep his mind on the conversation and off the subject of his home near the source of the Colorado River.

"Let's get right down to business, Manuel. I don't know just how much you are aware of our problems down here. But it is imperative that you get to meet the major landowners in the area. Therefore, I have taken the liberty of inviting them all here for dinner on Sunday. I hope you will stay at least a week. Take it easy tomorrow. Rest up after your long journey. It must have been a hard ride down from Tres Arboles for a city man."

Robles heard just a slight emphasis laid on the words "city man." He was not the kind to take offense quickly.

"I shall be busy most of tomorrow," McClellan went on, "but the day after being Saturday, I would like to show you around the farm. Show you just what we have built up down here, what we are trying to protect, to expand and to defend. It was all barren wasteland when we first arrived seventeen years ago. Quite a transition has taken place in that time, as I'm sure you're already aware. It was built out of nothing. So you won't find any of us too proud to seek help. We make no bones about needing the army to come down here and put pay to these Tehuelches. We can defend ourselves, but we need assistance if we are to cross the river and pursue these vermin into the heart of their own territory. I don't suppose that you have any encouraging information as to when the telegraph lines are to be extended this far south?"

"I regret not," Robles said, unsure of how much of his own feelings to divulge at this first meeting. He would prefer to address all the parties involved at one time. Most of what he had to say could wait until Sunday, he found himself deciding.

"Communication," McClellan enthused, leaning to refill his glass, "that's all we really need out here to exterminate these devils. The telegraph and a bullet are about the only two things that can outrun a Tehuelche war pack. Give us the telegraph and a hundred more rifles like that one over there in the corner and we'll blast the last of the Tehuelches off the face of the pampas, just as Roca did to the Ranqueles last year. Perhaps you have brought us news of the Remington rifle shipment which is due to arrive in BA any day now?"

"Unfortunately not," Robles apologized, finishing his glass and declining more. "I have seen one or two Remington repeaters, of course, but they are not available in bulk as yet." Robles had been around guns a lot in his earlier days. He had hunted with his father many a time. He liked to hunt for meat to supplement the diet that an inlander had to put up with. More than once he had waited up half the night to get a cougar that had been taking heavy toll of the stock belonging to a neighbor. He had been a good shot in his day. Robles thought about the freedom he had known in his early years, and started once again to wonder if his education had really been a good thing. He liked to hunt very much.

"Wire supplies have been held up for weeks now. Don't suppose you have any idea when the next stocks of barbed wire are going to reach Tres Arboles, do you?"

Robles did not. "How many acres do you own out here, señor McClellan?"

"Bruce, remember. *Un nombre escocés*—a Scottish name,

37

off a very small part of the perimeter. Big job that is. Can't get Manuel, okay? How many acres, well, fifty-five, maybe sixty thousand. Hard to say exactly. Mind you, we have only fenced the damned barbed wire at present, not in the kind of quantity we require."

Robles was beginning to get something of the full picture, and he did not much like the colors with which it was painted. The situation was more grim than he had thought. His own father had been a freewheeling man of that earlier gaucho generation. He had witnessed the coming of the barbed wire fences on the once untamed and unlimited pampas. It had been like fencing off an ocean and expecting all those who sailed upon it to come meekly into harbor. There would always be some who failed to come to terms with the forces of change. They were outlaws now, wanted men, yet utterly unwanted. Robles wondered what it must have been like for the Indians who had roamed those plains freely not for a couple of generations, but for untold centuries.

McClellan impinged on his wistful wonderings. "You look tired, Manuel, and justly so. Come, let us have something to eat and then you can rest yourself after the long ride. Not quite like Buenos Aires out here, is it?"

"I'll manage, Bruce," Robles forced out, wincing inwardly. "After all, I would hardly classify myself as a city man."

"How so?"

"It has become my home now, true enough, but I was born in Mendoza province. Deep in the wine country, near the source of the Rio Colorado, in fact."

Robles knew he had penetrated McClellan's defenses for the first time. He studied the man himself as much as the effect his words had made upon him. The big Scot reached for tobacco to hide his discomfort. Robles estimated his age at a shade under fifty. His complexion was ruddy rather than tanned. His hair too was reddish, like combed taffeta. He went through the motions of rolling a smoke, feeling Robles's scrutiny. Sun freckles mottled the skin of his face and forearms. McClellan was thick-necked and cold-eyed. He reminded Robles of a tapir with his great hooked nose. The man's fingernails were rusty with nicotine stains. His shirt still bore the traces of having been meticulously

38

ironed before he put it on that morning; such was his wife's living legacy. The heelless boots were decorated with round-wheel spurs.

"Then I would imagine that you are still something of a horseman?" suggested the Scot to break the silence, which had grown ponderous and unwieldy.

"Something," Robles allowed, "for a city man."

"Then perhaps you would care to come hunting with us. The chief of police in Tres Arboles, Alfredo Tossini, will be arriving before nightfall tomorrow and staying the night. We intend to try our luck down by the southeast corner of my land."

"Why not? Perhaps we will be able to supply some pork for the table? I understand that peccaries are hard to find, and even harder to hit."

"Peccaries, Manuel?" McClellan raised his eyebrows. "We are not hunting for peccaries," he said incredulously.

"Oh, really," muttered Robles, embarrassed by his show of ignorance. "I have heard that the occasional mountain lion sometimes finds itself driven this far south. Is it some puma that has been stealing from your herds?"

"My dear Manuel," said McClellan, the humor of the misunderstanding taking the rough edge from his tone, "I can see that you have been away from the wilds for a little too long. Excuse my laughter, I beg you." McClellan sounded almost tender when he said this. "Not mountain lions either, I'm afraid. No, the chief and I are going out after the biggest game of all."

Robles tried to force his brain into action. It made him realize just how truly tired he was, not just from the journey but from the past year's work as Inspector of Indian Affairs. His mind responded sluggishly, reluctantly, until a dim glow dawned at the end of the tunnel of his confusion.

"You don't mean men, McClellan?"

"No, not men." Robles's relief was short-lived. "Tehuelches."

Robles stared at his host, searching the pale gray eyes for a glimmer of jest. He found only genuine blank astonishment.

"Don't come if the idea is distasteful to you."

Robles was thinking furiously. A manhunt! Could he bear to go along on such a thing? Then again, could he afford not to?

39

He was here to look into what was called the Tehuelche problem. This was as much a part of that problem as anything else. The minister had told him to observe and report firsthand on what was going on between the settlers and the last Indian problem left in all of Argentina.

"I'll come," he found himself saying, surprising himself as much as McClellan. He found the level of his own voice disgusted him as he said it.

They ate a brief and laconic dinner.

"How about turning in?" McClellan suggested. "I think I'm going to stay and have a nightcap. Ginny, why don't you show our guest to his room?"

Mrs. McClellan hastened to obey. The couple exchanged a few brief sentences in English. Robles kept his eyes nailed down on the dainty-looking woman, who always gave the impression that she had just stepped fresh from the mold.

"My wife will show you to your room, Manuel. I do hope that you will be comfortable and that your stay proves enjoyable. This is really a very beautiful part of the country once one grows used to the wildness and the isolation. We breakfast at seven, but feel free to come down whenever it suits you. I have things to do which cannot wait, I'm afraid, so why not take the day off, then we'll show you around on Saturday."

"You are very kind," said Robles, using the formal mode of address. He was wondering if McClellan was challenging him to get up early just to prove a point. Robles knew that he wouldn't break the surface before ten o'clock at the earliest, so much did he care about the gauntlet thrown down by the white ranchers of Patagonia. "Good night, señor McClellan . . . Bruce"; he accentuated his indecision. Robles let his uneasiness at the lack of formality show, partly on purpose and partly because he was a lousy actor anyway. He was still cursing his ineptitude as he climbed the steep flight of stairs behind Mrs. McClellan's sensible, square-heeled brogues, which stepped so nimbly before his eyes.

Robles took a good look around the room as soon as he was left alone. It looked more like a hospital room than a bedroom. As he unpacked his saddlebags he started to think about the idea of man hunting man. Robles knew a lot about Tehuelches. They were not just one more tribe of Indians. He wondered if McClellan and this Tossini would agree with him on that point. Every hunt contained the element of risk, the one chance in a hundred that the hunter might become the hunted. Man after man even more so. The intent was so atrociously obvious right from the start.

Robles propped his old Mannlicher rifle up against the chest of drawers and began to think what it would be like to pull the plug on another man's life, to pull the trigger on someone as he had done twice before in his life. But that had been the enemy in time of war. This time they were riding out to look for trouble, to look for somebody to slay. This was killing without reason. At least there was no reason except that the white man thought he had the right. That was it, wasn't it? One man supposing that he was truly superior to another. Well, Tehuelches had their own edge on a large part of mankind, if it were but known. Then there was greed. McClellan owned enough acres to keep a whole tribe of Tehuelches with several thousand head of horses happy all winter long. The land did not belong to any man. If it did, it belonged more to the Indians than some Winchester-handy foreigner who had made good on distant soil. These and other thoughts kept sleep at bay until Robles ran out of strength to run them through his mind another time.

"What do you think of him?" Virginia McClellan asked her husband in the privacy of their bedroom.

"I think we might have problems," he predicted.

"You mean he won't come down strongly enough on the side of sending in the army to wipe out the Tehuelches?"

"I'm not sure about him, Virginia, not yet. I think that he is a man who is somewhat hard to fathom, is this Manuel de Robles. I was taken aback when he agreed to come hunting with Alfredo and me."

"You mean he is really going to go hunting for Tehuelches with you?" the woman gasped.

"He's coming along, at any rate," her husband confirmed. "Let me tell you something that will amuse you. When I first mentioned a hunting trip, dear old Manuel de Robles thought we

41

were going to go out after blasted wild pigs. Just imagine that!"

"And shall I tell you something that is even more amusing?"

Bruce looked up at her. He recognized that triumphant tone. It always heralded an unpleasant shock. He tried to discover it in advance, attempting to do his wife out of her satisfaction. He was still flailing at possibilities when his wife delivered the final blow.

"Robles's mother was a half Yamana Indian!" Virginia began to laugh, slowly at first but gathering momentum like a runaway barrel.

"Sweet Jesus!" McClellan swore.

His wife was still giggling sporadically when they were lying in bed together ten minutes later.

"Really, Ginny, it wasn't all that funny, you know."

"Wasn't it? I thought it certainly was, but then we never have laughed at the same things, have we?"

"Sometimes I don't think I know you at all," he said.

"Sometimes you're right," she retorted, and began to laugh again when she imagined the scene of her husband inviting a man who was part Indian to go hunting his own kind. It really was too funny for words.

McClellan had by this time got other things on his mind, and his wife's laughter was upsetting the new train of desire.

"What has come over you, woman?" he mumbled, then answered his own question by lifting his heavy legs on top of hers and stifling the derision with a mouth which had been soured by whisky.

The men breakfasted early on Saturday morning. They drank milky coffee and dunked oatmeal biscuits while the dawn bit into the darkness outside.

"Going to be a fine winter's day," McClellan, remarked.

Robles said nothing and sipped at the last of his coffee somewhat sulkily. He was thinking about Tossini, whom he had met and taken an instant dislike to the previous evening. Normally it took Robles a long time to get to know someone, whether it be in friendship or in enmity. He never made snap judgments. Al-

42

fredo Tossini proved to be one of the major exceptions in Robles's lifetime.

The chief of police was a paunchy man, flushed with over-indulgence and imagined success. He had ridden in ponderously on an old roan mare which suffered in silence, knowing that its rider was equally anxious to curtail the partnership at the earliest opportunity. Tossini had made heavy work of dismounting. Then he had rolled over to McClellan and shaken the proffered hand limply and for too long. The Scot had introduced him to Robles, who received a clipped version of the same limp handshake. Manuel had immediately noticed suspicion in the closeted brown eyes. Was it the natural suspicion of a policeman, a lawman in lawless times? Or was it Robles's title, which McClellan had given by way of introduction?

The most infuriating thing about Tossini, which everyone found boring to some degree, was that the idiot man said most things twice. It was a verbal tic of repetition.

"*Hola,* Alfredo!" McClellan had called out when first the chief rode in.

"How goes it with you, Broos? How does it go, hombre?"

"Fine, and with you?"

"Not bad at all," Tossini had replied, "not at all bad."

They waited for Tossini to suck up the last of his coffee and then went outside to saddle up. Away from the house, the icy wind dived down to attack their hair. The early morning light painted purple blotches on the eastern sky. Somewhere in the high distance a lone bird of prey emitted a single shrill cry.

Robles kept his head down and saddled his mare in silence, tightening the girth with a gentle hand. McClellan had brought out his own favorite mount, a near-black four-year-old stallion he had broken with his own hands. As he strapped on the light-weight English-style riding saddle, he remembered with pleasure the battle he had subduing this prince among horses.

Stung but still savagely independent after three searing gallops across the pampas, McClellan had told the hands to tie the animal down in the corral. The gauchos who worked for Don Broos trans-fixed the hapless stallion in a web of lariats while McClellan put on the lethal breaking spurs much favored by gauchos short on

43

patience and long on coercion, slim spikes of steel that ran back wickedly from the big man's heels. He had walked over to where the horse stood, wild-eyed, foam-flecked, and scared half to death. McClellan remounted, and the ropes were tossed clear one by one. Set loose, the bucking beast had screamed with pain as McClellan gave it the spurs again and again until its flanks ran with red streams of blood. At last, unable to bear the pain any longer, the horse stood rigidly still, except for a nervous quiver that was a reaction to the wounding. It was beaten in both body and mind. The Scotsman celebrated his gory victory by reaching forward and stroking the horse's neck for the first time.

What remained was still a very strong horse, an extremely speedy horse; but it was not the horse it might have been, for a man to ride with pride. McClellan and his rampaging gauchos had broken the stallion's spirit along with its independence. A Tehuelche warrior, with endless time and gentleness, would have kept that spirit intact and left a gallant beast with a measure of its dignity.

Since then, McClellan had allowed no one to ride the black stallion save himself. The wounds had healed quickly under the practiced hands of the gauchos, who had cheered and waved their hats in the air at the boss's triumph. The horse possessed speed and power to blind the self-satisfied McClellan to the fact that it was terrified of him. Robles noticed it as the man approached the animal this morning.

When all three men were prepared, they mounted up and rode out of the compound. Tossini and McClellan led off, side by side. Robles stayed a few yards behind them. He wasn't in much of a talking mood and preferred to look at the country. It reminded him of a joke his father always cracked whenever he took on a new hand around the vineyard. When he told the fresh employee what the wages were, he would always say that it paid so many pesos and all the scenery you could look at. His father had meant it to be funny and help put the new man at ease, but there was more than a grain of true appreciation of the grandeur of nature in the old man's words. Robles had inherited that appreciation as well as much more of the old man's wisdom. Robles had really loved his father.

Once they were out in the open country, the dawn broke wide open. It was unseasonably fine. As the sun got higher it went on a riotous drunk of reds and yellows, oranges and golds. Manuel de Robles steered his horse across an ocean of waving grass.

They walked their horses for four hours in a dead-straight line southeast and still they were on McClellan-owned land. It took until midday before the Scot announced that they were on open range. Robles rode up abreast of them. They paused. McClellan swept the horizon for a flicker of movement, using big British-made field glasses. Robles had his own binoculars, but he kept them cased. He did not want to locate what they were trying to find.

They rode on for a further half hour. At one point they were particularly close to the Rio Colorado, owing to a large northerly bend the meandering ribbon of water made there. McClellan stopped again, panning the land with the glasses, prospecting for death. Tossini, out of condition, seemed glad of another break in the rubbing rhythm of the long ride.

"We must be almost at the river, Broos," he estimated hopefully, "almost."

"Aye, another couple of miles and we'll be at the bank of the big north bend. Might as well circle out for a couple of miles and then head back. Pity. I'd heard that quite a number of the bastards had been using the big bend area to ford the river and make for that big village they have set up due south of here. Seems like we just struck it unlucky. Wisbey and I bagged a pair of Tehuelches not more than a mile from this spot, but that was over a month ago now. Hey, Robles! You haven't got much to say for yourself this morning. What's the matter, amigo?" McClellan gave him the kind of look that meant he should have stayed home.

"Yes, I'd noticed that myself, señor McClellan. In fact, I was just thinking of remarking on how little I'd said all day when you took the words right out of my mouth. Perhaps that's where they're all going to." To hell with all the first-name stuff, he fumed. I don't like this idea of a manhunt, or the man who suggested it, either. What's the use of pretense? Pretty soon he won't like me either. He's still of two minds as to how to take

45

me, but that will soon sort itself out once we talk over dinner tomorrow night. Why fake a friendship that never existed and never will?

"You're the expert on Indians, Manuel," McClellan said, "tell us what this village to the south represents."

"The winter's almost here," Robles informed them, responding more than he cared to in the face of having a chance to teach them about Tehuelches, "and the Tehuelches have grazed the northern extremities of their territory to its limit during the summer. The various bands come together around this time of each year. They celebrate the change of the season, hold councils and dances, get ready for the great migration south to where the pastures are scraggy but sufficient to see them and their horses through until spring. The village near here would have big toldos, permanent tents, rather than windbreaks and lean-tos such as they erect when on the march."

"Interesting," muttered Tossini, who had unplugged his water bottle. "Where did you learn all that, señor Robles, all that about Indians?"

Robles watched the police chief take a long drink and then wipe the back of his hand across his bedraggled mustache. "My grandparents on my mother's side," he explained.

"Academics?" guessed Tossini, raising an eyebrow.

"Yamanas," Robles said, very coolly and without betraying a trace of the smug satisfaction it gave him to shock someone like Tossini so audaciously.

McClellan and Robles took a couple of discreet sips from their own water bottles and then all three of them turned their horses north and rode on. This was beautiful country all right, Robles was thinking. There was no doubt about that. He scanned the area, taking in the vastness of the canvas stretching taut between the horizons. As the day clouded over, the light became more dappled, splashing the savannah with half shadows. One or two isolated ombú trees stood out like watchtowers. A pair of crows wheeled in the sky. A quickening wind ushered in the latest tidings of a winter about to break.

"Tehuelches!" snapped McClellan.

Robles came out of his daydream with uncomfortable haste.

46

He followed the direction of McClellan's pointing finger. Reaching for his field glasses, Robles discovered that his fingers were shaking. What did he do now? What did he say now? He had no authority down here. The area was out of any man's jurisdiction. Hell! He was totally devoid of authority but burdened with responsibility. He brought the binoculars to bear and identified a single horse with a woman hunched over in the saddle. A young Tehuelche man walked beside her, and the animal was dragging a laden stretcher.

Robles heard the smooth slide of the Winchester rifle coming out of its sheath. It was like the hiss of a snake, and just as deadly. McClellan checked the loading, working the lever action once in a single sharp, decisive move. Tossini fumbled to put a cartridge into the breech of his single-shot Mauser.

"Wait a minute, McClellan!" said Robles urgently.

The other two men turned on him, surprised at the degree of authority he exhibited. They had both reached their separate conclusions about the quiet, unresponsive stranger from the city. In neither case had they credited him with the traits of leadership.

Robles addressed himself to McClellan, knowing that the fat policeman would follow his lead without any fuss.

"They are Tehuelches, of course. No doubt they are making for the camp south of the river, as you suggested. They are just a young couple, probably late teenagers, and I think they may have a child on that stretcher. They mean no harm to us nor to anyone else. They are simply traveling by. This is free range land, you said so yourself, so they are not trespassing either."

"Well?" asked the rancher.

"Leave them be. Let them go on their way."

"They are savages, señor Robles. They have to be eliminated. Women breed warriors and infants grow up into them. A clean, quick death from the barrel of a gun is the best way—more than they deserve, some folk around here would say. Come on, Tossini!"

"Hold on there!" snapped the Argentine. "This is murder, plain and cold. You won't achieve anything by killing them. In fact, this may prove detrimental to your argument. Tossini? For God's sake, hombre, you are a lawman!"

"Not out here I'm not. Out here there is no law, no law at all."

"Except this," put in McClellan, patting the stock of the rifle he was brandishing as if it were a bible. "There's only one rule, Robles, kill them afore they kill you."

"They have no intention of killing us."

"If they were two dozen strong and painted for war it might be a different story. Enough of this! You stay out of it if you have no stomach for it. Let's go, Alfredo. You take the right flank, okay? I'll let you have the first shot."

The two men turned their horses and plunged the riding spurs hard into their flanks. Both animals spurted forward, shifting into a canter on diverging diagonals.

Robles felt useless. A coating of sweat dampened his forehead. He searched for a means to put an end to this senseless slaughter. He was utterly impotent. There was nothing he could do or say that would have stopped these two men. They actually believed that they had the right. Short of shooting them, he was powerless. Robles rode off to his right, where the land sloped into what passed for a hill on the pampas. He watched what happened in horror from that vantage point, intently, with his binoculars clapped over his eyes.

The Indians had seen the two riders fan out and gallop toward them from two separate directions. The man immediately unslung his bow and slotted an arrow into place on the string. Tossini had pulled up about ninety yards away, out of range of the bowman. He was completely safe as he raised the gun to his shoulder and took careful aim. Just as he squeezed the trigger the Indian spun round and gave the horse which bore his family a mighty whack on the rump. The horse set off, alarmed even further by the report from Tossini's rifle. The sudden twist spoiled the police chief's aim, and the bullet meant for the man's chest caught him too high. Robles saw the Indian's jaw blown clean away by the impact of the heavy-caliber bullet. Off to the right the horse was traveling with the Tehuelche woman clinging to its mane and the stretcher bumping along the ground.

McClellan zoomed in after it and gained rapidly despite the woman's efforts to goad her mount into greater speed. Robles took it all in, switching from pursuer to pursued until they were

48

close enough to watch simultaneously. McClellan hauled his stallion to a stop and dismounted. By the time he had thrown the rifle to his shoulder the woman was forty yards away. It was an easy shot from that range. Robles saw the flash of smoke slightly before the crash of the Winchester reached his ears. He flashed his eyes to the woman and saw her pitch forward as if she had been hit by a thunderbolt from heaven. Her body lay still where it landed. Her horse galloped on, riderless.

The wounded Indian had staggered to his feet. Robles refocused his attention on the young man. He couldn't have been more than eighteen years old. The boy's face was a mask of blood. He searched frantically for the arrow that had dropped from his bow, and Manuel realized that he couldn't see. Tossini had by this time reloaded. Taking the initiative from his partner, he too had come closer and dismounted. He did not miss a second time. The boy had pulled out a knife. Tossini drew an efficient bead this time, and the boom of his rifle sent the boy off his feet backward. The recoil jolted the rifleman's shoulder visibly. Robles studied the Indian, but he did not move again. Not ever.

In the few seconds it took Tossini to finish off the boy, McClellan had regained his horse and ridden after the Indian pony, which he soon overtook. He was leading it back by the bridle when Robles put the glasses back on him and took up the rest of the action. There was not a flicker of emotion on McClellan's face as he passed the dead woman. He just looked down on her to make sure that she was dead. It was the lack of expression on Bruce McClellan's face that triggered something deep down in the heart of Manuel de Robles. It was almost as if the rancher considered he had done the world a favor.

Tossini walked his horse over to the prostrate man, rifle at the ready. He kicked the body tentatively, as if it might burn his foot. When McClellan reached his companion, Robles could only watch the mime of their dialogue through his powerful glasses.

And then Robles saw them do something that he never afterward forgot, not in all his life. They inspected the stretcher together. Tossini lifted a small dark bundle from a leather pouch. The policeman held it at arm's length, and Robles felt his fingers slip on the tubes of his glasses. He wiped one hand on his saddle blanket. It was a baby, not even a toddler. Tossini dangled it by one arm while McClellan worked the lever of his rifle and unhurriedly put a bullet into the bundle. A spurt of blood sprang out, and Tossini dropped the lifeless form that had known so little life. Both men returned to their horses, mounted up, and rode across Robles's field of vision, heading back toward whence they had come. The Indian's horse had dragged its trailer away toward the river. Three lifeless heaps were all that remained of the event.

The Argentine replaced his glasses in their battered leather case without really being aware of doing so. Unblinking, he stared after the receding backs of the two killers. They were half a mile away when a slight sound behind him jolted Robles out of his shock.

Robles grabbed for the reins and whirled the mare around. Not over twenty feet away was a solitary Tehuelche Indian mounted on a magnificent gray stallion. He was a giant of a man, rippling with muscles and latent strength. Across his chest was a mighty-looking bow. The man carried a poncho over his neck and swept back over his shoulders to expose his bare torso. His hair was long, jet-black and straight. It had been tied back in a tail with a strip of rawhide. Manuel took in the steel knife on his belt, noticing that it was the kind white men produced in factories.

The two horsemen continued to stare fixedly at each other across an abyss of contrasts. The giant's eyes were as black as the Argentine had ever encountered. Robles could tell that they too had just borne witness to the revolting bloody spectacle that his own had seen. With a certain amount of surprise, Manuel noticed that tears were running from the corners of his own eyes, even as he stared at the Tehuelche. Two large drops of moisture ran down his cheek. He remembered tasting the salt before they reached the stubble on his chin. The Indian's cheek was decorated too, but not with tears. The man sported an ugly wound that was far too fresh to have formed a scar.

Robles noticed the man look past his shoulder and study the backs of the two riders. It seemed that all of this took a long time, but in fact they confronted each other for a matter of seconds. The Tehuelche's face was etched in expressionless stone. Robles also turned to see how far McClellan and Tossini had got. They were just blobs on the periphery of his sight. He heard the Indian's horse take off.

Turning back hastily, he was just in time to see the stallion vanish like a gray wraith amid the tall grasses. Robles noticed that no quiver of arrows adorned the Indian's back, and he couldn't help but wonder if he would still be alive if it had.

CHAPTER FOUR

HARKANA HAD SWUM IN POOLS of consciousness. His face had wept with his own blood. Then a rough, damp cloth came to brush away the darkness and the pain. It was a coarse hand, sticky and rasping. The Orphan flicked his eyes open, but they focused only on a throbbing panorama. His eyelids flickered again, twice, three times; then the Indian was able to make out the form of the gray horse's huge head towering over him, silhouetted against the clouds which seemed to be rubbing his withers. The stallion had come back of its own accord. Harkana lay where he had fallen, thinking hard on that single pinnacle of fact. The horse bent its head once more, and Harkana felt the coarseness of its pink tongue against his own forehead. Despite the pain, he was able to smile at his triumph.

"I will call you Zorkan Rood, the Scarmaker," he said out loud, "for surely you have marked me for life."

The Tehuelche staggered to his feet, pulling himself up on the horse's foreleg while the animal stood motionless. Harkana lurched and tottered down to the river. The horse followed at its own pace, in its own time, as Harkana knew it would always follow wherever he led. He washed away the matted blood that encrusted his split cheek. In a still pool of jade-colored water he saw the boomerang-shaped wound that the hoof had slashed in his flesh. Looming out of the sky came the reflection of the maker of that scar as the stallion brought its head down over Harkana's shoulder to nuzzle him.

"Zorkan Rood," the man breathed again in a whisper.

Marked for life as well as for death, the two savage beings repaired their collective destiny. They rode east, staying north of the Great River. At night, camped beside the swirling magnesium-laced thread which was the Colorado, he would strike up a fire with brushwood and wood dust. Harkana fished in the shallows for river trout and salmon, holding a burning branch in one hand and a club in the other, ready to stun any fish that was drawn by the flame. Harkana was truly happy and ferociously free.

On the third day, he estimated that he was now somewhere near due north of where his people would be camped prior to the winter migration. He sat astride Zorkan Rood, his jet-black eyes fixed on a point across the fording place that separated him from them. What is this of the doomed messiah? he asked himself. What lies ahead for you and the horse if you cross the river? To die bloody on the battlefield. To sacrifice freedom for a legend and the moon.

What did Harkana the Orphan owe to the tribe of Seh Saapelt and the inland Tehuelches? Had they not banished him for one hundred moons? Had they not driven him out in expectation of never seeing his face again? They had nothing to give him, except pain by trial and tribulation. They had nothing he wanted. Harkana the Orphan, mighty hunter, mighty archer, horseman. He was a man who needed no one. Why go back to die young because the wise one's prophecy had preordained it so many moons ago? Here was real freedom. Why not ride north on the stallion, far to the north beyond the reach of the white man's ways and the trappings of his hooked wire fences?

Harkana turned Zorkan Rood around and walked in a dead-straight line away from the Rio Colorado. For over an hour he kept that line, his eyes unblinking as he closed out every thought but that of distancing himself from his people. It was the gunshot that snapped him out of his meditation.

Zorkan Rood shied. The Orphan searched the land ahead, seeing a hill which appeared to screen the cause of the incident. His heels nudged, and they leaped forward. Near the crest of the hill the Indian found a solitary white man with his back to him. The man was sitting a small brown mare. Harkana checked

Zorkan Rood and watched the scene that played out before his eyes. He studied the two white men, the one with flame-colored hair and the fat one. There was nothing he could do as they closed in and picked off the innocent Tehuelche couple, whose only crime was to have been born Tehuelches. And then they took out the infant and held it up like a vegetable to be destroyed. It was over very quickly. The Indians lay dead on the ground, while the wind blew over them like an epitaph. The white men rode away, and Harkana heard them laugh, and his hate was forged afresh.

Zorkan Rood shifted weight to one side, and the white man spun around. Harkana could have killed him long before with the steel knife he wore on his belt. Yet he knew that this was not a time for more killing. He stared at the soft brown eyes and watched in fascination as they filled with tears and overflowed. No word was spoken between them, although the Orphan knew the Spanish language. The Argentine glanced back at the two receding riders, and Harkana lifted Zorkan Rood into one tremendous burst of speed—south.

He never even paused at the river, but splashed on through the fording point, which shelved steeply in midstream. Not panicked, he let the horse swim while he clung to its mane. On the opposite bank the slope was almost perpendicular, so the Orphan let the current carry them in its cold arms until they grounded about half a mile downstream. They rode on until a gully offered the opportunity to plow up onto the plateau and continue the journey.

The following dawn slipped smoothly from the sheath of the night. The life-giving river was behind them, and the land took on a bleak and terrible aspect of desolation. The grassland evaporated. The rocks were cracked and split and strewn in myriad flints and cinders all over the plateau. The wind propelled bracken and tumbleweed in balls that rolled and skated across its pitted surface. Thick wedges of cloud had been driven into the sky, threatening rain. By early afternoon the threat was no longer idle. Needles of moisture slanted down. Harkana pulled the folds of his alpaca poncho around his torso. It grew colder, darker, and more forlorn as the storm brewed and came at last to the boil. By then it was almost sundown once again.

There were three of them, riding abreast. Harkana recognized them as Tehuelche dog soldiers. A small patrol rather than a hunting party, heading back to camp after a day spent checking the boundary of their territory. They saw him after he began to move again, and turned their mounts to cut him off, cantering in at an angle. Harkana pulled his horse to a standstill and waited for them to come on. As they grew closer he reached his right hand up behind his shoulder and unstrung the bow on his back. It was the peace sign of the Tehuelche Indians. As the bow relaxed he laid it across the horse in front of his crotch. The Orphan let his big hands hang loose at his sides when the trio reached him and placed him in the center of their suspicious triangle. These were the elite cavalry of a wholly equestrian people. Their lives were the unquestioned property not of the tribal chief or the shaman, but of the warlord who directed them. He had but to ask and they would fight for the privilege of being the first to die in the pursuit of his bidding.

Their leader, a man in his mid-twenties, rode his horse around to face Harkana and speak.

"Be you Tehuelche?"

"We share the same blood."

"From where do you come?"

"I have ridden out of the north country, the very far north country."

"How far?"

"Beyond the banks of the River of Death" was Harkana's reply. He observed their reaction, the gasps of amazement. A haphazard drizzle was falling.

The leader of the dog soldiers pondered this answer, while the rainfall picked up again.

"The Tehuelche who speaks with bent truth is as rare as one who has traveled so far."

"That is for you to decide." Lying was all but unknown among the Tehuelches of Patagonia, but the River of Death was something which impinged only on the imagination of the oldest of the tribe. They had heard reports of a great river far to the north, festooned in forests thick with lianas, in which swam strange fierce creatures that ate man and beast alive. Yet it was all peripheral knowledge. None had ventured so far.

"I am Tehuelche," confirmed Harkana. "I tell no bent truths."

"And where are you going now?" asked the patrol leader.

"I was once of the tribe of Seh Saapelt. I seek his village and would join him in time for the winter migration. For over one hundred moons have I traveled abroad, making footsteps on foreign lands, breathing the air of my enemies. Now I have returned. I seek only to live again in the land where I was raised."

The rain drummed a relentless tattoo on the four riders. Twilight hovered in the storm.

"Let us take him back to camp, Raganor," suggested the second man to the patrol leader. He was behind Harkana, who did not turn to look at him.

The third member of the trio was a boy of about eighteen. He seemed to have eyes for nothing but Zorkan Rood, whose lines he was devouring while the interrogation went on and the rain stabbed down. "How came you by the gray stallion, stranger?" he inquired, with a furtive glance at Raganor to excuse his impertinence.

"I bought him with my own blood," Harkana replied, using the phrase by which Tehuelches traditionally told of capturing and breaking a wild horse alone and unaided on the pampas.

"He is truly magnificent," the boy said, breathless with excitement.

"Aye," Raganor agreed. "How do you call him?"

"He is Zorkan Rood."

"The Scarmaker," murmured the junior man, whose name was Taapelt. He looked at the fresh wound on Harkana's cheek and fell into a harmony of understanding. The rain continued to strike them, muddying the earth and running in rivulets off the oiled wool of the Orphan's alpaca poncho. The three soldiers wore cloaks made from sewn guanaco furs.

"We will escort you into camp," Raganor decided. "There you will be judged by the elders of the tribe. I must ask for your knife."

Harkana handed it to him, handle first. Raganor looked at it carefully. It was the first time he had seen a steel-bladed knife with a shaped handle made from pine. He looked up at Harkana one more time, searching the stranger's face for more symptoms

56

of his foreignness. The elders would decide what was to become of him, he told himself with a mental shrug.

Taapelt took Zorkan Rood's bridle, and they packed in close on him and set off at a trot. Hemmed in by the three other horses, Harkana rode with his arms folded under his poncho, listening to the lullaby of his native tongue as the three men talked on the way.

The weather worsened. By the time they had ridden the four miles southeast to within sight of the Tehuelche village the storm had broken wide open. Sheets of lightning showered them with grotesque shadows. There were salvos of thunder to salute them as they rode on in through twin lines of black-skinned tents.

At first not a soul was to be seen in the drenched village. Then eyes investigated the quartet of riders that had been allowed access by the guards. A dark face appeared, monklike in the hood of tent flaps. Then another craned forward. Gradually the whole settlement buzzed with the rumor of a stranger in their midst and the spectacle that was Zorkan Rood. Tehuelches knew very little of anything by the standards that were in existence in many parts of the world by 1879, but they knew about horses if they knew about one thing at all. And they knew to a man that this was a rare privilege they were witnessing on this sodden evening in the Moon of the Harsh Wind Blowing. An historic stallion stood in front of their saturated toldos. Eyes were glued on the man who had bought it with his own blood, Harkana the Orphan. The tribe waited patiently in the rain for the wisest of the wise to ask the questions which were in all their throats but were his alone to voice.

"How are you called?" asked Seh Saapelt, although the old man knew full well who the giant stranger was and the name that his own son had bestowed upon him.

"I am Harkana the Orphan, wise one. But you of all men present should know my name, Seh Saapelt; for not only are you the eldest elder of the inland Tehuelche but also the father of my father. Do you not recognize your grandson who has returned to the bosom of his tribe after the banishment of one hundred moons?"

"I know you, Harkana. So you have survived. You are welcome. Be you of a mind to return with us on the migration south?"

"Aye, and I have a mind to regain my rightful place as warlord of the tribe, following in the footsteps of my dead father, who followed in your own, Seh Saapelt. I would take the test denied me by my father, and any other that is decreed by the wisest of the wise."

Most of the tribe were too young to remember how or why Harkana had come to be banished for one hundred moons. Those who could recall how he had come to slay his own father were very few. Life expectancy among the Tehuelches was forty of the white man's years. That was how the seventy-nine-year-old Seh Saapelt got his name, which meant Two Lifetimes. In his prime he had been warlord, then he had achieved respect as an elder, and now he was the chief over all as the oldest and the most venerated.

"Tonight is a bad night for council," said Two Lifetimes, looking at the rain. "Shall we not rest our minds and bodies until the morrow? Then will I call official council of the elders, and we will debate your claim to succeed the dead Vulkana as warlord of the inland Tehuelches. I am aware of the test of which you speak and I will favor it, have no fear."

"I have none," said the Orphan.

"There are few here that can remember the circumstances, few that have memories strong enough to match your wanderings of the hundred moons. Come, rest and eat among us. Tomorrow I would hear your stories of distant lands beyond the River of Death."

Harkana allowed one of the small boys to lead Zorkan Rood away, noticing the way the boy looked up at both the stallion and the only one among them all who could ride it. The boy looked at Harkana as if he were more god than man. It gave the Orphan an almost supernatural sense of his own responsibility. He wondered if ever again he would doubt his and his people's destiny in the same way that he had doubted before he saw the white men kill. There was so much to be done, and so very little time. Even the moon was buried in the thicknesses of cloud overhead. He rode an ice flow of loneliness, the last of his indecision scuttled by untimely fate.

58

"Do not worry yourself," comforted Two Lifetimes, "the boy will tend your horse well. Come," invited the old, toothless chief, "join me in my toldo and I will have food brought for you." The old man issued orders for food "and a cloak to cheat the wind." People scampered off through the drapes of the rainfall to fulfill their tasks. "Raganor, I would have you join us also. Please see that arrangements are made for our guest and then return."

Raganor dipped his head deferentially and hurried off.

Village life gradually returned to normal and its inhabitants to their tents. Only the guards rode out the rain. Harkana followed Seh Saapelt to his large, black-skinned toldo, and was seated there on a softness of furs when Raganor and the food arrived simultaneously.

"What flesh is this?" asked Harkana.

"Is it not to your taste?" Seh Saapelt worried.

"It is good meat but the taste is new to me, that is all."

"This is the new guanaco, which we hunt everywhere in the south and sometimes much farther east of here, close to Great Water," the old man explained.

"The new guanaco? I do not understand."

"A white man's breed, similar to the wild guanaco but slighter of build and with a woolly hide. It is most easy to hunt, being stupid and slow, half domesticated in many cases. It is everywhere on the southern pastures. It crops the short grass plains and has multiplied like a pestilence."

Harkana, who had never seen a sheep in his life, frowned. "Then it uses up much of the winter grazing?"

"Too much," the old man complained. "That is why we do not hesitate to hunt it down, even raiding the white man's lands for it. The meat is succulent, do you not agree?"

"The meat is good, but the source of it leaves a bitter taste in my mouth. How deeply entrenched is the white man in the southern lands? I had no idea that there were whites anywhere south of the Great River."

"A lot has changed since you have been gone from the land of our ancestors," the old man explained, his toothless gums slurring the words. "The whites landed in great canoes and settled on the coast which faces the direction of the sun waking.

Some of the coastal tribes helped them through the first two winters, and now they have repaid those tribes by stealing their land and enslaving their people. They cut the earth to grow tame grasses, but by far the largest industry they have is the raising and breeding of the new guanaco. The white man has spread inland and encroaches farther north with each passing migration."

"Last winter the pastures were poor but adequate," Raganor put in, his hands open-palmed in a gesture of acceptance. "Who knows how hard it will prove to nourish our horses during the winter that is almost upon us?"

"And the lines of hooked wire that tears which I have encountered north of the Great River?" asked Harkana. "Are they widespread in the south as well?"

Seh Saapelt nodded his shriveled old head slowly, staring down at the fur-covered floor of his tent. The fire threw segments of illumination through the slit of the doorway. It highlighted the whites of their eyes. "They lacerate the land everywhere. Each season there are more of them, and the first of the barricades are always found deeper to the north than the preceding migration. Yet, opposition to the Tehuelche is generally not as strong in the south as it is on the territory north of the Great River. It is almost impossible to venture safely over the long grass plains anymore."

"I have seen," Harkana informed them. "A young family of our people were killed by whites with thundersticks just the day before I came. It is time the Tehuelche painted his face for war. I advocate attack on the white man's homes, rather than await his crossing of the Great River. He must learn that we are not as other tribes, to be treated like cattle, herded here and there, surrounded by barricades, starved of our pastures, and reduced to slaves. Are we not the chosen children of the moon?"

Raganor clenched his fists in agreement. "There, wise one, have I not said as Harkana now says? The white man will not stop at the Great River unless we stop him with his own blood spilled in its waters. Observe what he has done to the Ranqueles and other tribes who were once feared, once a force to be reckoned with and now no more. The Tehuelches are all that are

60

left. Hear this son of ours, Seh Saapelt, for he has seen what no Tehuelche has seen, has learned what none of us knows. And remember how he came to us riding on the silver stallion, bought with his own blood. Is it not as the prophecy forewarned?"

Seh Saapelt seemed momentarily to cast off the burden of age and fatigue that had been his for many years. He looked up into the face of Harkana the Orphan, then across to Raganor. "Harkana is my grandson, Raganor, the son of my only son. I know even more than you how much of the prophecy he fulfills. It seemed to end on the day that he slew his father. For that he was banished, and the doomed messiah seemed once again to be a legend of the future, to be passed down to our children and our childen's children. Who among us could foresee that Harkana would come back to us from banishment, come back on the silver-maned stallion to claim himself warlord of the Tehuelche? So I would ask him this. What future do we have if we declare war on the white man?"

"What future do we have if we do not?" Harkana countered. "If we have any choice at all, it is not whether we will keep our lands but whether we will give them up meekly, without bloodshed, or not. Death is the future. There can be no other outcome to this invasion by the whites. I have seen them at close quarters during my travels. Maybe it will happen slowly, but it will happen nonetheless."

Raganor broke in, impassioned by the words he had waited too long to hear spoken. "Seh Saapelt, he is right! You know that he is right! Let us make war on the white man. I would rather die like a man than live like an old woman!"

"Patience, Raganor. All things in good time. Tomorrow we will hold council. There is much to be discussed. I would have Harkana tell us of his one hundred moons in banishment, particularly what he knows of the ways of the whites. Then we will put him to the test to see if he is truly worthy to carry the name of warlord of the inland Tehuelches. We will talk in detail of the white man's presence on our land. Come, the hour is late. Let us rest."

The two warriors rose, but Harkana chose to impart one last line before he retired.

"Wise grandfather, hear my words, I beg you. Raganor and I do not speak with the petulance of youth but with the anger of righteousness. Even if the white man were one hundred times as strong as all the Tehuelches massed together, even then would I advocate war. There is no choice but the choice of when and how to die. I would rather die in battle at the head of our people than be exterminated by hunger and disease. Is this not the way of the Tehuelche? Has this not always been the way of the Tehuelche?"

Raganor looked at the old man with eyes of stone. Seh Saapelt was not one to relent one iota under such scrutiny.

"Tomorrow we will hold council" was all he said.

Outside the tent, Raganor and Harkana walked side by side amid the spokes of the rain.

"Do not judge him too harshly, Raganor. He is wise beyond our dreams. Save your criticism of Seh Saapelt until the day that you are certain that he means to comply with the white man's pressure."

"You think then that he will not?" asked Raganor, who betrayed that his own mind was already made up on that point.

"I know that he will do what he believes is right for the tribe as a whole. He is correct to dilute our sense of urgency. The migration is upon us. This winter poses enough problems without a full-scale war against the whites to add to them. Let us wait and see what tomorrow brings."

"Would you become warlord if the tribe so decrees?"

"Did you not seek that rank yourself, before I came?"

"Yes, before you came. It was my dream. But I see that you are better equipped to carry it than I. You have traveled, you have learned much of the white man's ways, it is hereditary to your line. And then again, there is the prophecy and the stallion."

"What of the prophecy and the horse?"

"I believe the white man's coming is the doom foretold in all the history of legend of our nation. The doomed messiah is something we have all heard of ever since we were too young to pull even the weakest bow. The legend has existed for more generations than even Seh Saapelt can remember. I know only what we all know. Are you he, Harkana the Orphan?"

62

They had reached the tent that had been thrown up for Harkana's use. At its slit opening, Harkana paused to look at Raganor. There was study in his eyes. There was such simple loyalty in this brave man. He was the very epitome of the Tehuelche dog soldier. If the Orphan was to answer in the affirmative, Raganor would unflinchingly accept that it was so. It was a responsibility too shattering to conceive.

"I do not know, my friend," Harkana said honestly, placing his right hand on Raganor's shoulder. "Truly, I do not know."

Raganor changed the subject, feeling the sad warmth of affection for this stranger who clasped his shoulder.

"What test is this that the old one spoke of?"

"It evolved around the death of my father. Do you remember the circumstances surrounding that?"

"I did not fight against the Ranqueles, and I know that he died during that conflict. I was one of the younger warriors who were given the task of guarding the camp against counterattack. I know that you did take part in the last battle, although there are only twenty-five moons between us."

"My father," Harkana explained, gesturing for Raganor to seat himself in the doorway of the toldo, "was Vulkana, a great warlord of the Tehuelches, you may recall. He was a legendary man at arms, and the fables told about him have truth as their origin. I was proud, but rightly so. Despite my lack of moons, I could fight as well as the best, ride like a veteran, and outshoot any warrior in the whole tribe with the bow. I offered my services to my father, in the hope that he would allow me the privilege of becoming the youngest dog soldier to ride into battle against the Ranqueles who were invading our lands. I told him that I had no equal as an archer; that I could send an arrow through the body of a bird in full flight, so great was my prowess with that weapon.

"My father was not to be moved. He was perhaps too proud of reaching all his decisions himself, and he did not take kindly to my suggestion. Alternatively, he may have been trying to protect me from danger, although that is hardly the way of the Tehuelche and my father was nothing at all if not all Tehuelche. He did not reply directly but sent his groom to me with a message, which was soon broadcast throughout the tribe. It became known, to my undying shame, that should my father ever declare war upon the birds of the air then he would send word that my services were required."

"With great respect for your father, who sleeps in the moon's arms, that was an uncalled-for rebuke."

"I, in my armor of pride, took it hard. I rode away that day and for several more wandered alone, save for my horse. By the time I returned to our camping place the great battle had been fought and our forces devastated by the vastly superior numbers of the Ranqueles. My father had been taken prisoner by the enemy. I rode out alone and met the remainder of our men, who were falling back. I rallied them, and we rode back to where the Ranqueles were preparing to put my father to death by having him dragged behind two wild horses."

"The Ranqueles are savages," hissed Raganor, and he spat into the mud outside the tent.

"Vulkana was already lashed to two untamed stallions. There was nothing I could do to save him. I notched an arrow to my bow and sent it through my father's heart, that he might be spared other than instant death with dignity. The Ranqueles rose in uproar and pursued us. For three days we led them on through country we knew like our own hands. They became scattered and dispirited. We fought a rear-guard action as we retreated, until the time and the place were right for counterattack. And then we hit them hard, as only Tehuelche dog soldiers can hit. We had spare horses, while they had pursued us in too much haste to worry about support mounts. With our added speed and mobility, we began to turn the tide of their numbers. By the time they had half recovered from our surprise ambush, we were gone. They re-formed and headed back down toward the lake country, and we picked off the stragglers. One by one the horses tired and died from exhaustion, for we hounded them so closely that they never had an opportunity to graze their stock. Those that were forced to ride double soon lagged behind and were dispatched. Those that were reduced to being half men were killed even more efficiently. It took a week, but none of them ever returned to the camp in the lake country that the Ranqueles had attempted to take from us.

"With just one hundred men we had routed and demolished an army four times our number. We returned and rested before hitting the remainder of the Ranqueles force while they slept. They are sleeping still.

"After an absence of almost half a moon I returned at the head of my victorious little band. The glad tidings spread like a pampas fire, and there was great joy and greater pride. However, the way of the Tehuelche is resolute. I had killed my own father, a crime punishable by death. Moreover, I had acted without the approval of the council, and that could not be lightly dismissed, whatever the reason or the justification. If the council is not consulted then its role is broken. The Tehuelche is ruled by the council. It is the keystone of our way. I had fractured the way of our people. My actions may have been vindicated, and gloriously so, but I knew that I could not go unpunished. I knew it as well as any man. I accepted my sentence as just; I was to be banished for one hundred moons. Now you know why we did not grow up together and serve as dog soldiers in the same force. Now also you are aware of my reason for advising patience with the ways of Seh Saapelt. Tomorrow we will hold council."

Raganor nodded his head slowly. "And what happened to you after you were driven out from the tribe?"

"Ah, that, my friend, is a whole other story. I must tell it to the tribe—will you not listen then? Go and take your rest, Raganor, the hour is getting late."

"Sleep well, lord. May the moon watch over you." Raganor trod through the mud and the darkness, back to his own toldo. Halfway to it he realized that he had called Harkana "lord." It had seemed so natural a thing to do.

Harkana the Orphan closed the flap of his tent and sat meditating on what the morrow might bring. It took an effort to clear his head of the myriad events of the past hundred moons, events which he must now recall and explain and describe. Eventually he fell asleep to the lullaby of the falling rain.

The first thing that Harkana did in the morning was check that all was well with Zorkan Rood. The weather had cleared. It promised to be a dry day made colder by the blows of the wind.

He found the stallion in the very peak of condition, brushed, groomed, fed, and rested. After petting the horse for a few minutes, he grew aware of someone standing behind him. When he turned to see who it was he found a young boy of some hundred forty moons. The boy stood, barefoot, with one muddy little leg trying to hide behind the other in his confusion. The boy had his eyes cast down to the ground, and his lips were trembling.

The Orphan bent to one knee, reducing the awe his stature imposed.

"How are you called?" he asked.

"Pin . . . Pindi, lord," the boy managed to stammer.

"You have groomed the stallion well, Pindi. It must have been hard work after so much rain. Even the mane is free of knots." Harkana leaned forward and tilted the boy's head up.

The boy beamed like a beacon at such lofty praise.

"He was so quiet the whole time, lord. He made no fuss at all."

"Zorkan Rood is like the wind, Pindi. When you respect his power and learn how to ride with its force, he is content to stay calm. But when you dispute his right to freedom and underestimate what he is capable of, then might you be blown away. Would you be groom to him for all time?"

The boy nearly fell over from pleasure. His jaw dropped, his nostrils flared in excitement, and his round little eyes widened while he fought to find the power of speech before the offer was withdrawn.

"Well?" Harkana prompted him.

"Oh yes, lord, I would be the best groom in all the whole world. I promise."

"I have no doubt of it, that is why I offer you the post. The task of caring for my Zorkan Rood is yours and yours alone. I will supply meat for your family. I expect no one to work for me without payment. Go now, run along and tell your father."

The boy quavered, wondering if he should say more. "I have no father, lord. He was slain by the white men soon after I was born."

"Have you a mother, boy?"

66

"She that looks after me is as fine as any mother could be, but she is not really my mother. She is younger sister to my mother, who died on the same day that I first lived. Is that not a sad coincidence, lord?"

"Sometimes, Pindi, the moon leaves us to decide for ourselves which is the sadder, life or death. I am glad that your aunt treats you kindly, for our fortunes are alike in past and linked in future. Run, tell what family fate has bestowed on you that you will groom the silver stallion."

"Thank you, lord." He turned to go, but Harkana put a massive, long-fingered, bony hand on his shoulder. Their faces were very close when the warrior spoke to him again.

"Come, do not be afraid, Pindi. I too am alone. They call me Orphan. Be my friend as well as my groom. What do you say?"

"Oh, lord, I am not worthy," choked the boy, tears staining the corners of his hazel eyes.

"Neither am I," said Harkana.

The boy found himself staring at the space the tall man's face had occupied long after the Tehuelche had stood up and walked away, leading the mystic horse behind him.

The Orphan spent that day as he had spent most of the days of his life: alone. When it was time for the evening meal he rode back in on Zorkan Rood, and there was Pindi waiting to take the horse by the bridle and lead it away for an hour of remorseless care and attention.

For the next two hours the camp was alive with the sounds of the evening meal being served and consumed. As the sun sank, the council gathered. The circle took form with the eldest and most respected huddled together around a space that Seh Saapelt alone could fill. In the center of the circle blazed a huge fire with enough kindling beside it to keep it going all night if necessary. Radiating out from the elders, the warriors and youths had congregated. Only the women remained in their toldos, banned out of earshot. They would receive the news secondhand.

As the fire roared out its blessing and its warning in the same red tongue, silence settled over the assembly. Through the curtain of hushed expectancy came Seh Saapelt. His gait was no longer capable of cutting a path through the onlookers. He was stiff and hunched over to one side, and his feet shuffled rather than strode. Yet his position was enough to open a lane, through which he came at his own pace, in his own time. The gnarled old man took his rightful place at the head of the elders, and the circle closed in tight around the hub of the blaze.

"Tehuelche children of the moon," Seh Saapelt began, "we are called to council in the way of the Tehuelche."

The old man squatted down on the ground where skins had been placed over the mud. The whole tribe now followed suit, leaving the stranger in their midst aloof and alone, standing above them like a spire.

"Among us has come Harkana the Orphan, the only son of Vulkana, the last warlord of the inland Tehuelches and a son of mine. Banned by the law of the elders for one hundred moons, he has returned to claim what was denied him by his own father. Long has been his road, and yet he has survived from the days when Vantempec, the great shaman, was our leader of the spirit. And he has ridden in on the silver-maned stallion, which all of you have seen and all but the youngest will know the true meaning of.

"This land is our land, bequeathed to us by the moon. And for many, many moons have we watched and waited while the white man came and took from us what was not his to take. We have learned how he sells and resells the land among his own tribe. Yet we know that no price can be placed on any land, least of all the territory of the inland Tehuelche. For it is no man's to sell or to purchase. In the face of the white man's force and numbers we have retreated ever southward, saved by the gifts of the moon from annihilation. The barrier of the Great River was set, across which no white man would be permittted to venture. Yet he came in great canoes and landed on the southern coast to settle and proliferate. And we have told ourselves that this should not be so. But the coastal Tehuelches have done nothing. And we have done nothing. The new guanaco has run wild and devoured the best of the southern pasture and we have left the white man in peace. During the last migration we have all seen how the white man repays such tolerance. Not only does he crop the pastures ever shorter, but now he bars them from us with strands of nailed wire, that our horses go hungry and our hunters come back empty-handed.

"Now, once again, it is the Moon of the Harsh Wind Blowing. The migration is upon us once more, and who knows how many pastures of dust we will find this time; or how many barricades of nailed wire be placed across our traditional paths that always we have followed with a happy heart? No man knows. But I would place no limits on the white man's greed, and the time for decision is today and not tomorrow. Do we make war against the white man on the southern front? Or do we allow him to graze the southern pastures out?

"I would have you hear the story that is Harkana the Orphan's alone to tell. This man is young in moons but old in experiences gained in one hundred moons passing. Even beyond the River of Death has he traveled. Hear him well, Tehuelches. Mark his words. For he comes to us as warlord, mounted on the greatest gift that ever the moon bestowed. And he would lead us in battle against the greatest threat there has ever been."

Harkana stepped forward into the center of the circle, close to the fire. The Tehuelche language was rich in vocabulary, but he was untested in the use of its powerful poetry. The Orphan had always been a man of deeds rather than words.

"When first I was driven out from my people, it was the Moon When the Rhea Lays Her Eggs. Hot was the trail. I took the horse, the knife, the bow, and the rope of my possessions and went north, for in those days all land to the south was Tehuelche land.

"You have heard of great saline marshes which lay far away across the Great River. I passed them by in the direction of the sun sleeping."

Harkana spoke for over an hour. He told the council of elders and all the warrior ranks how he rode north, up into the White Mountains and across the altiplano. He told of the thin air and the touchable clouds; the rheas that flew in spirals and ate decaying flesh; the big brother of the guanaco, from whose wool his poncho was made. But most of all he told them about the white man's ways deep in the heart of the land which was known to the whites as Bolivia.

69

He described the mule trains and the loads of silver that were dug from the innards of the mountains with forced Indian labor under threat of the sword and the lash. And he told of the crossed-sticks religion, which he could not even begin to understand himself.

"They drive the men like cattle, work them as slaves, kill them for pleasure," said Harkana, remembering all he had seen and escaped from. "The white man is everywhere in that land, and my horse had died from the thinness of the atmosphere. I made my way down from the heights as the winter came on, stealing a horse from a white camp and riding for days toward the direction of the sun sleeping. Gradually, as the lowlands carried me on, so did the árboles thicken, until I found myself on the brink of a great bosque."

"Arboles?" queried Seh Saapelt. "What means árboles and bosque?"

Harkana realized that he had used the Spanish words for tree and forest, for there was no equivalent in the Tehuelche tongue. The word ombú meant tree to his people, for it was the only tree they had seen. Even the Chilean beeches of the south were known simply as southern ombús.

"They are white man's words. Bosque is a large number of—"

"You have learned the white man's tongue, Harkana the Orphan?" marveled Seh Saapelt.

"I was his prisoner for forty moons, wise one. I was about to tell of my enforced sojourn among the enemies of our people."

"Proceed."

The squatting crowd shifted as Harkana paused in his speech to replenish the huge fire with fresh logs. He glanced up at Seh Saapelt, who nodded his shriveled old head almost imperceptibly, and Harkana knew that his plan to make war would receive the old chief's backing. A spark of emotion ignited in the younger man's heart. It did not stir him to rhetoric, or to heroic gesture, or even to a knowledge of the power that was about to be bestowed upon him. The snatched glance shared unobserved with Seh Saapelt had realized the legend in its full dimension. Unless he turned back now, Harkana was committing himself and all of his people to the fire. And yet he did not hesitate, for the things he had witnessed at the hands of the white man illustrated how bitter and inexorable was the alternative. And so the Orphan went on with the words that would make him warlord to fulfill yet another stanza of the legend of the doomed messiah. He could always turn back, but knew already that he never would.

"In the forest land of heavy heat and strange creatures my new horse soon took sick and died. I was reduced to half a man. On foot I continued to penetrate this land of a million ombús. It was at this time that I discovered the tree from which the great bow is made."

Harkana looked around at this phalanx of gnarled old men, most of whom were in their early forties but looked ready for death. The fire was now chewing at the fresh cud of its kindling, and the flames threw out pools of orange light. It lit the iron features of the warriors' faces, striking shadows out from the corners of their eyes and turning their noses into hooks. To any outsider suddenly stumbling into this menacing council their countenances alone would have been enough to strike fear into the bravest heart. These were the men that Harkana would lead by example and control by a force even greater than their own. It was a terrible aspect that they presented to the world. In all of his travels, the Orphan had never found a people more militarily steadfast to have riding behind him; nor one more suited for the purpose to which he would soon put them. This was the manpower from which he was to fashion the Tehuelche army of the moon.

Harkana had returned to his place in the circle and drawn out the bow. In one fluid movement he stepped through it and strung it as if the tensioning of it were nothing at all. As he had done with the poncho, he handed the bow first to Seh Saapelt, with a gesture that it should be passed all around the circle.

"The white man has erected many camps in clearings cut out from the forest. I avoided them, living off the land, hunting the strange creatures that inhabit the forested world, killing freely with this bow and the splendid arrows I made for it. Eventually I stumbled out onto the banks of the River of Death. It is of colossal size. The far bank was merely a haze of distant greenery. My journey was without destination. It mattered not at all where

I went or how long I stayed in any one spot. And yet the restrictions were becoming clearer. I could not return south. I had left the sun sleeping because of the winter. The farther north that I went, the more I encountered the way of the white man. My path seemed to lead me across the River of Death, and for several days I camped by its swirling muddy waters, wondering how I might traverse the barrier.

"Eventually I saw a woman alone in a canoe. It was not a canoe such as the Yaghans and the Chonos use. This was dug out from the whole trunk of a giant tree, scooped with blades until it was hollow.

"I greeted this woman, who was slim and diminutive, her head reaching to here." Harkana touched his nipple to indicate her height. "She was afraid of my size and my strange language, but eventually she came to trust me, and after I had hunted meat for her she took me across the river. Her people, known as Guaranís, were camped in the forest close to the water. They were a peaceful people, easily frightened. There were seven large families in the tribe. I lived with them for several moons, helping them to hunt bigger game than they had ever attempted to kill. I found my place among them with the accuracy and power of my bow, and the woman became my woman. She was called Keeli.

"One morning, very early, the white men came to attack the camp. The peace of the Guaranís' lives was shattered forever. Many were shot down as they tried to run into the forest. The others were enslaved. I hid the bow and tracked the party all the rest of the day. I might have escaped, but let myself be taken in order to remain with the woman. I was now nearly halfway through the term of my banishment, and the separation was beginning to take its toll. I was drawn to the woman, although I felt suffocated by the forest and its climate. Most of all I missed being a full man. The whites came in on horses. They had cut trails through the forest, and along one such trail they led us back to a stockade. Whites have a passion for enclosures of all kinds.

"For the next forty moons I was their prisoner. I learned their language, which is not difficult, although it is harsh and guttural compared to our own. At first I mixed and confused it with the language of the Guaranís, which I had also made considerable progress with, but in time I could speak both with ease.

"The whites showed great interest in me from the very first, for it was obvious that I was of a different tribe from the rest. I did not divulge the extent of my knowledge of their language, which they call castellano, and avoided many of the questions which they sought answers to. They worked me along with the Guaraní slaves, breaking the earth and planting the yellow grasses just like the whites do to the north of here. Several moons passed and the whites made me a horse handler. I lived with Keeli, and the bond between us grew.

"Here I should explain one thing about the whites that is still partly a mystery to me, though I have given it a great deal of thought since I escaped. The white man has a religion, as I mentioned before. It is bloody and pagan in the extreme. His shamans, who wear nothing but cloaks of black, will stop at nothing to convert outsiders to this religion of the crossed sticks. Yet when they speak of their god it is as if he were invisible and the crossed sticks are nothing but an emblem. It is most strange and quite unbelievably barbarous."

Harkana picked out two twigs from the woodpile and held them up in the crude form of a crucifix to demonstrate.

"It appears to be almost every white man's ambition, not only the shamans', to make nonbelievers worship this invisible god. It is as if every adult Tehuelche would go out and try to make the Yaghans, Alacalufs, and Ranqueles worship the moon, when we all know that the moon is our god alone, for we are his chosen children. More than this I cannot offer by way of explanation.

"Most of the Guaranís accepted the religion without knowing why they did so, apart from the fear of reprisals. I continued to avoid such a confrontation by feigning ignorance of the language. The point of all this is that anyone who rebelled against the crossed sticks was tortured. Those that persisted in refusing were slain. Some were killed with thundersticks, others with spears and long, heavy knives. I saw many hung up from the branches of ombús and strangled with ropes looped around their necks. Those few that openly fought against the religion or were caught trying to escape were burned alive."

Gasps of horror rang out around the Tehuelche council. Even Two Lifetimes could not restrain himself from uttering, "May the moon protect us from such barbarity!"

"What savages!" others exclaimed.

And the shaman Quinkinwa, Vantempec's successor, shook his head and threw out his hands with fingers like tree roots and nails blackened with age. "How monstrous! Burned alive, you say? Why, they are worse barbarians than even the Ranqueles!"

"Keeli was with child," Harkana went on, anxious to finish his storytelling and get down to the serious matters of the immediate future. "The birth went badly. Our daughter was stillborn, and the mother went to the moon one week later; none of the shamans were able to stop the bleeding. I began to think of escape soon after, and my opportunity came when we went on another slave hunt. I was taken along to tend the horses.

"It was easily done. On the first night I led one of the mounts away from the camp while the guard slumbered. Instead of riding directly toward the river, I returned to the Guaraní village, now abandoned and overgrown, and recovered this great bow from where it had been hidden for so long, wrapped in bark and soft skin to protect it from the ants.

"Nothing could stop me then. With a horse between my knees and the bow on my back, I rode through the forest trails toward the river. I had no arrows for the bow and dared not stop to make them until I was across the River of Death. On the way I ran into a small posse of whites, but I outrode them easily. It was at the riverside that I had to fight. There was one white soldier, armed with a thunderstick. He guarded the wharf where the canoes were moored. He had to be eliminated.

"I showed myself from sixty yards away and he fired his thunderstick. I let the horse go at full pace and crossed the space between us, flinging myself from the animal just as the man raised his reloaded weapon. It thundered harmlessly into the sky, and I killed him with my bare hands. It was from him that I took this knife. I will pass it round."

Harkana stopped speaking and silence slashed like a saber through the council, broken only by the shifting of the fire. The moon was rising like a silver scythe. The tribe began to intone a macabre hum, a two-tone incantation of reverence and penitence. It was a remarkably still night, with hardly a breath of wind. For fully fifteen minutes the whole tribe sat with bowed heads and closed eyes. It was Harkana the Orphan who broke the prayer.

"O moon that spins the thread of life, hear the words of your children. In this hour of danger, we seek guidance, ask forgiveness, beseech you to show us a sign. I stand before the Tehuelche people as the bringer of war. Let your people know if they should follow me into battle against the white man or bow down under the yoke of his coming. If I fail the test when morning comes, so be it. If not, let your will prevail on the day of decision.

"My story is at an end. How I recrossed the River of Death and made my way home to the land of my birth is another story. I am come, and I come for one purpose only."

Harkana walked forward to Seh Saapelt, and the crowd of Tehuelches lifted their heads. The Orphan presented the knife, hilt-first, to Two Lifetimes, who feathered the blade with his thumb before passing the last symbol of Harkana's foreignness around the circle.

The stars now jammed the clear sky. The moon had fully risen, three days past full ripeness. Held in the grip of Harkana's words, the whole tribe traveled with him as he went on to describe his journey back across the River of Death, which he swam despite the shoals of flesh-eating fishes which had given the river its macabre name. He finished by telling them how he had come across Zorkan Rood entangled in the barbed wire and had trained and tamed the stallion. Last of all he told how he had witnessed the killing of three innocent Tehuelches by whites, and warned of the thundersticks that shot round after round without needing to be reloaded. Harkana resumed his seat in the inner circle, and Seh Saapelt got to his feet. Every eye was on the old man.

"The decision before us is simple," he began. "As a nation, the inland Tehuelches have existed for many centuries, long before the first white man was ever seen on our lands to the north. We have retreated before his onslaught over the past few generations. The rich pampas have been ceded to him and his herds of cattle. The barrier of the Great River has been set. Are we to go back on that decision? In the south too the whites have encroached heavily on our grazing. And now he kills our people indiscriminately for his pleasure. Our territory shrinks with every passing season. The other tribes of the coast and plains have all but vanished. Only the Tehuelches are in a position to dispute. The nailed wire has split out land.

"Harkana the Orphan comes to us riding the silver-maned stallion, speaking the white man's tongue, bearing foreign accouterments the like of which have never been seen in the land that once the Tehuelche could call his own. I say this. Place upon his shoulders the test which he was denied by his father. Let him kill the bird on the wing with a single arrow. Offer him the diadem of the warlordship of our nation and we will make war on the whites, even by crossing the Great River to strike first. The white man must learn how terrible is the vengeance of the Tehuelche. This is the counsel of Seh Saapelt. Now the elders will decide, as is the way of the Tehuelche."

One by one the elders stood and gave their opinion. They were overwhelmingly in favor of war, some on only the southern front but the majority for total and immediate conflict carried across the Great River before the migration set off. All that was needed was that Harkana prove himself as good as his word by slaying the bird on the wing. Two Lifetimes smiled and began to disperse the council.

But the moon chose that tick of time to intervene. The brightness of the night was suddenly whisked away as a partial eclipse concealed the white disc of their god. They had seen many eclipses of the moon before. The Tehuelches knew to a man what it signified. It was the moon casting the most telling vote of all.

CHAPTER FIVE

THE BITTER MORNING COLD cut like a knife. Harkana the Orphan sat like Buddha in the thick wrappings of his alpaca poncho. Raganor came to him, shivering in a great cloak of rough-stitched guanaco fur.

"It is time, lord," he said simply.

Harkana stood up in the poncho, the great bow already strung in his hand. Raganor watched him pick up three long arrows. He did not bother with a quiver but held the arrows apart from each other, tucked loosely between his fingers. A lot of time had gone into their selection. Dozens of others had been discarded for slight warps in the shaft or tiny quirks of fletching.

The two men exchanged no further words as they walked through the camp. On the way they picked up Keelagut, one of the elders. Seh Saapelt had chosen him to represent the council. With Harkana leading, the trio walked softly out past the line of tents. Raganor nodded to the two guards on the eastern side of the huddle of toldos. They too were enfolded in skins against the brunt of the pre-dawn cold. The hunters continued on past the lines of stock horses and left the village behind them as they went on into the frosted wilderness.

Dawn gradually pushed aside the darkness with a pink hand. The men continued to walk in total silence, as hunters must. Harkana was thinking only of the white men he would kill when this was over. The Orphan hoped that one of them would be the big man with red hair. He wondered how such a man would die.

Across the hard-earthed plain the three men strode. The sun skirmished with the hazy horizon. All was quiet. The wind held its breath. The hunters made hardly a sound, picking their way between the loose rocks on hardened bare feet. When they were about three miles from the village Harkana bid them squat down behind a clump of bushes. He himself knelt with the bow on the ground in front of him. He dug up a small patch of soil with his knife and carefully planted the arrows in it, as if they were rare saplings. Raganor and Keelagut watched him from a few yards away. Harkana waited. They all waited.

There was nothing to observe save the rolling expanse of the cropped grasses, lit up by the sunrise. A full hour went by and the sun ascended to its yellow throne. Broad daylight. Off to the north were mounds of cumulus which threatened rain later in the day.

A second hour crept past. Harkana took one of the arrows with a steady, slow-moving hand and notched it to the bowstring. He got to his feet casually. Old Keelagut could see nothing. He turned to Raganor but received only a blank stare. Raganor had noticed nothing as yet. Following the angle of Harkana's head, they eventually discovered a circling speck in the gray sky. Keelagut cursed his ancient eyes, as he had so often cursed them before. Raganor could not help but wonder just how long before him the Orphan had noticed the bird. It was a gray harrier, patrolling its usual raptorial habitat, skating alone on the rink of cloud.

Nothing about Harkana moved. His eyes were ebony slits of concentration. The bird was no more a dot on his retina, taking shape as it curled closer, hunting. There was no hurry. Tehuelche patience is endless.

The bird glided nearer to where Harkana waited like a statue with his deadly bow. Upon invisible thermals the harrier rose and fell, like a lonesome mariner on unseen waves. It was unaware of being the hunted as well as the hunter, absorbed in a serenely economical glide, punctuated by an occasional effortless wingbeat. All three men could see it clearly, but the bird had failed to spot the motionless men, for it sought only movement with its sharp eyes.

Raganor was thinking that he would not take so fast a target, he would wait for a crow, fat and slow. But then he could see that Harkana meant to kill the harrier, and Raganor at last convinced himself that it was within the realm of this man's regal power. Yet the harrier had found a prey itself—a hare feeding on the ground, out of sight to the men but an irresistible morsel of movement to the bird. It veered and plummeted earthward, straight toward where the men were waiting. No, Harkana, Raganor begged from his heart, not this one, let it go, lord.

Harkana acted. The great bow bent until its gut string was kissing his thin, determined lips. He sighted on the bird and had it cold, but still he let it come on. The harrier backed its wings, hooked at the hare, which had looked up too late into the shadow of death, and rose. The hare kicked and fought in the piercing grip of the talons.

Now, Lord Harkana, shoot now while it is so close and so impeded; but Harkana resisted so easy a moving target.

Suddenly the hare squirmed loose and dropped from the grip of the sharp claws. Harkana led the living lump of flesh and loosed the arrow. Another was on the bowstring in a flash as the harrier, abruptly relieved of its burden, peeled away at speed. Yet, even before the bird had begun to turn on the prey it had lost, Harkana had resighted, and, leading the bird's flight path by just a couple of feet, he loosed the second arrow. The long shaft flashed from the great bow. It met the bird in an explosion of feathers. The harrier's wings crumpled, the body arrested in flight for one split second. Down it came, landing with a soft smack, while two or three small feathers floated after it at the wind's pleasure. Harkana relaxed.

The two men were on their feet behind him, whooping and yelling.

"Har-ka-na!" screamed Raganor in uninhibited exultation.

"A mighty shot," enthused the slightly more sober Keelagut, who could not control the wide grin that split his kernel of a face.

The Orphan turned to them with the slightest of smiles. "Is it done?" he asked.

"Aye, warlord Harkana, it is done," Keelagut answered him.

"It is magnificently well done, lord," confirmed Raganor, aflame with loyalty and pride.

79

The two men stepped past the archer to inspect his work. Raganor found the hare with an arrow right through it but still twitching. He stilled it forever with a light blow from his spear shaft. Keelagut brought in the bird, spitted as if for roasting on the long arrow. They came back to Harkana. Keelagut held the harrier aloft on the arrow. Raganor had the hare drooping over the rims of his fingers. It had lived stiffly alert. Now it was dead, limply delivered from further fear. This was a land where very little ever passed from one world to another without wearing the badge of bloodshed.

The three men ambled back to the village. This time Keelagut led the way. Raganor and Harkana came some distance behind, dallying as they made plans.

"Now let us talk of warfare," said Harkana to his lieutenant.

Raganor flicked a glance at the man strolling at his side. At last real Tehuelche talk, after so many moons of idleness.

"We will raid the white man's land across the Great River," explained the Orphan, almost matter-of-factly. "I will need just twenty-five picked dog soldiers, no more. Pick veterans. There will be no time to train them. Experience will be essential. I expect absolute obedience; select them for that above every other quality, Raganor. Courage and ability are taken for granted. You and I will make up the fighting force. I want the best three horse handlers the tribe can gather; they will have much to do. We will run off as much of the white man's stock as we can safely handle on the path back to our people. It will be a three-horse ride, so there will be many spare mounts for three men to handle while the fighting is done. So, again, only the very best. Later we will spend a great deal of time training the men in ways of war that they have never known until now. For this raid, it will be enough that they obey my every command—make it clear to them. There will be no dispute. I will rely entirely upon your judgment, for my lieutenant has already proven himself in my eyes."

"Harkana is gracious. It will all be done as you request. What else do you require, lord?"

"Pick for us the best firemaker in all the tribe. I need a man who can twist a flame from soaked wood that has already been burned twice over. He will carry his own materials, including preparations for fire arrows, three score of them. As for the rest

80

of the weapons, each man a full quiver, knife, and lance. Half a dozen ropes will be sufficient, no boleadoras needed.

"See that the horses are picked for stamina rather than gallop speed. If Seh Saapelt sends us out tonight, we will feed the mounts well as soon as we get into camp. Make sure the men eat and rest fully during the day. They will carry only water on the raid. Choose one horse for me in addition to Zorkan Rood."

"Anything else, lord?"

"Yes. No man is to wear the marks of war."

"Lord, the paint is the pride of every dog soldier. What reason shall I give?"

"That it is my command that it shall be so. For your own peace of mind, Raganor, think for yourself about the nature of the raid and the nature of the warpaint."

"A night raid, lord—and the paint is white. It would betray our presence. I understand."

"These whites have weapons of miraculous power, Raganor. Why let the men wear paint that would make them living targets? So, it is settled. I shall speak with Seh Saapelt immediately. If it is to be tonight, there is much to be arranged."

Keelagut was the first to reenter the village. He came in slowly, bearing aloft the harrier spitted on the red-streaked arrow; holding it up for all to see, as if it were a banner around which to rally.

The rest of the tribe crowded forward, pressing close to the older man to hear his tale. Keelagut recounted the story in great detail. By the time Raganor and Harkana had walked into the carpet of shadows thrown down by the toldos, it was known by all how he had made true his promise to his father.

"Har-ka-na! Har-ka-na! Har-ka-na!" they cried out. The Orphan's name was on everyone's lips, bursting forth from every throat. "Hail the warlord Harkana the Orphan! Mighty hunter, matchless archer, war leader, lead us against the white man. Now is the hour!"

As Harkana reached the crowd they stepped back from him, chiseling a wide channel through the throng. For now he bore the marks of a supernatural leper. They all shrank from his mystery.

As the sea of bodies parted, Harkana saw the atrophied shape

81

of Seh Saapelt standing motionless at the end of the tunnel of humanity. Raganor peeled off from his warlord, and Harkana approached the old man steadily. His eyes searched the wise old face for some sign of praise or recognition or emotion. There was none. The Orphan's eyes remained hard chips of jet. He did not allow a smile. This was the turning point in the history of the Tehuelche people. Here were the cosmic crossroads down which they were about to blaze a new and heroic trail, which, once taken, could never be reversed. There would be no turning back. Seh Saapelt knew. And Harkana the Orphan knew.

Harkana stopped in front of his grandfather and raised his right hand. The tribe was stilled.

"My grandson," observed the old man, "you left us a rebel and have returned to us as a warlord. Go, form your cohorts of death and destruction. Spill the blood of the white man. There can be no other way. War will be the only way of the Tehuelche."

"Seh Saapelt, if you will undertake to set in motion the first steps of the southerly migration, then I would lead a raid this very night, north across the Great River. The migration should begin in the morning. I will rejoin you by tomorrow's nightfall."

"And your target?"

"The white man's toldos near to the big bend country. We will burn every building and run off the stock. Those that live there will die there. I shall take some thirty men."

"And you can accomplish such a raid with so few?"

"I can. With the insight of the white man's ways and the horses that only Tehuelches can ride, yes, thirty will be ample for what I have in mind."

"So be it," agreed Seh Saapelt.

Harkana noticed the ridges of doubt etched in the old man's forehead. "You do not approve, grandfather?"

"I am troubled, Harkana. This can only lead to death for us all."

"All roads lead to death, Seh Saapelt. It is the time and the manner of our dying that we are free to choose. Does not the doomed messiah come only to lead his people back to the moon?"

"So it is told."

"Well then? What other choice do we have? Of all our nation,

82

you and I are perhaps the only ones who see this for what it really is. You have learned it through the wisdom of time; and I through the wisdom of pain."

A shadow seemed to pass across the old man's eyes. He nodded his head gently, reluctantly.

"And the children who have lived so little, is there no hope for the children?"

Harkana shook his head, clearing it with realism. "Every war has its children, wise one. History draws no lines between ages. War comes to all when it comes. Death leaves its calling card on the toldo of every family, old and young, good and bad, brave and cowardly. The only alternative is to permit the white man to tread us into the earth like grasshoppers; and besides, it is our earth. The moon has decreed it this way."

"For the first time in a long and eventful life," Seh Saapelt mused, "I wish that I might not have lived quite so long that I should bear witness to the total destruction of our race. Come, grandson of mine, let us eat a last meal together in time of peace. The war begins at nightfall."

"I should be honored to breakfast with the wisest of the wise," said Harkana. And he meant it.

The men rode out in the hour before sundown. Like a trampling wave the horses moved through the fading daylight. The hearts of the village all beat now with the tempo of war. Almost one hundred horses thundered north in triangular formation, with the Orphan and Raganor as the spearhead of the wedge. In under two hours they reached and crossed the Great River, whose purple-black waters were sewn with the silver thread of starlight. The hoofbeats broke clear of the river and started up again as the whole troop rode on at a hard canter for another hour.

The orders, when they came, were whispered from Harkana to his lieutenant, who delivered them to the men without fanfare. When Tehuelches spoke of a three-horse ride they meant a nonstop journey which took place at canter speed. Mounts were changed on the move, with scarcely a moment lost or a break in the rhythm. The men simply vaulted from the back of one horse to that of another without breaking stride. The Orphan leaped from the broad back of Zorkan Rood to that of another, lesser horse. The mighty gray ran on at punishing speed, staying up at the head of the pack. Zorkan Rood exuded the wrath of resentment that another should carry its master. But Harkana had calculated his plans down to the very last vestige of detail. At the pace they were moving Zorkan Rood could have borne him all of the way to the ranch of the Red Pig, but the way back was equally long and hard. Something had to be kept in reserve against an emergency or unforeseen pursuit.

On and on through the deepening night, the Tehuelche pack hammered, raising dust behind them. Harkana took them back in the darkness to the hill from which he had watched the destruction of the young Tehuelche family. Pausing briefly to gather his bearings from the stars, he led his troops down the face of the gentle slope and off across the plain in the direction he had observed the two riders take once the shooting was over. After another mile he halted.

"Raganor, I will go ahead at full speed. Bring the men on in a straight line under the twin stars yonder. Come on at a slow canter and fan out across the plain. Tell the men to look for the stallion, and I will link up with you once I have studied the white man's village."

Harkana leaped onto Zorkan Rood, brought up by one of the handlers. The stallion whinnied with pleasure, plunging its head in eagerness to be off. Harkana pulled back from his lieutenant and released the horse like an arrow from his bow. At full gallop Harkana covered the unknown distance toward where the white men made their camp. He knew it could not be very far, for they would have needed to return by nightfall and he judged that they would not be riding at more than a trot. In a little while he was on Bruce McClellan's land, though it was unmarked by fences on this perimeter. It took an hour for him to come in sight of the buildings, all lit up with fire and candle.

A hill jutted up sharply to one side of the compound, rising like a whale frozen above the water's surface. The Indian galloped out around the hill and came in under its lee. The Scot had chosen his land shrewdly. It was a natural hollow into which water permeated. Having skirted the direct approach to the gates of the yard, the Orphan tethered Zorkan Rood to a boulder and climbed quickly to the crest of the hill. Hardly out of breath despite the exertions of the ascent, he crawled forward to peer down on the site he had chosen for his first attack. He took in all the details, drawing a mental map. Working his way twenty yards to his right by crawling lizardlike on his belly, he was able to see not only the hacienda but also the bunkhouse, store, and stable. The main house was a blaze of illumination. Yellow streaks filled the windows, making them resemble some monster's burning eyes. The stable and the storehouse were unlit, but a faint glow emanated from the small buildings where the gauchos were busy gambling on knucklebone, their favorite dice-style game. Harkana was puzzled only by the wind pump which loomed over the single well in the courtyard.

With a plan of the layout fixed in his head, Harkana retreated quickly along the route by which he had come. Within a couple of minutes he was back on the stallion and galloping toward the rendezvous with his men. He found them half an hour out from the hill.

"Raganor, let the men gather around and I will explain the plan of attack. Have them dismount." Harkana looked closely at the men's faces as they came over to where he waited and knelt in a circle as if about to pray. All Tehuelche faces: hungry, lean, weathered, uncomplaining, enduring, vengeful faces. He saw the lust for bloodshed and battle in their eyes and was glad. He wanted them to hate. It would make them reckless. But he also wanted them to understand, for only that would also make them obedient, and it was the obedient ones who would survive. For the Tehuelches this was the beginning of more than just one battle, more even than the beginning of a war against the oppressor who had taken both their land and their heritage. This was the genesis of an epic and almost supernatural journey which would eventually carry them back to their creator. He did not want them to die in ignorance; but they would all die nonetheless. They were to fight on until the last arrow was spent, the last man dismounted and made half a man. This was the way of the Tehuelche. For Harkana, there could be no other.

85

CHAPTER SIX

THE WISBEYS HAD BEEN the last to arrive. They had ridden in just after sundown from the farm adjacent to that of Bruce McClellan, although their hacienda was a good four-hour ride away.

Percival and Mrs. Wisbey were British settlers, and had been in Argentina even longer than the McClellans. When Percy Wisbey was introduced to Robles, the only person in the room he did not know, he bid him the customary "mucho gusto" and asked Robles how long he had worked at the Ministry of the Interior.

"Three years altogether," Robles answered, "but less than one in my present capacity."

"Really?" interjected Fernando Carrioli, who was standing nearby, waiting to be introduced. "And I thought I knew everyone of any note who was involved in any of the ministerial work which affected our region."

Robles gathered the double slight on his position. The younger Carrioli apparently did not consider Indian problems as having much bearing on the future of Patagonia. Robles let the remark go with a shrug, which encouraged Fernando, who was there with his wife and his father, to go further.

"Indeed," he added, with a foppishness that seemed even more out of place in the rugged hacienda, "I don't think I know you at all, señor Robles."

"I have a reputation for being unknown," Robles confided to them all in his naturally quiet voice.

The knot of visitors drew their chairs around the blazing log fire while the servants went about readying the long dining table for dinner. The night soon closed in on them outside the heavy-timbered walls. They would all be staying the night, for the pampas this far south was far too wild a place for them to think of traveling on horseback after dark. There was an aura of comfort, warmth, and safety inside the sturdy wooden building.

Manuel de Robles sipped at his glass of Chilean red wine and listened to the fireside conversation. He enjoyed summing people up by their conversation. He was rather good at it. He began assessing which of the group congregated there to hear what he had to say about their immediate future would offer him the most stubborn resistance. They were all sharply aware that his recommendations would soon go before the minister himself, and that was something none of them could afford to overlook.

The Carriolis were an odd trio. Fernando was in his late twenties. He exuded the air of one who had been born to money and had no conception of life without it. His idea of poverty was a man who was forced to purchase ready-made boots instead of having them handmade, either in Buenos Aires or, preferably, in Europe. Robles studied him with the anonymity of the professional watcher.

He had a thin nose which split his weak-looking face in two. Fernando had never tried to be a strong character, strong as his father had been before he lost a leg and a wife to the Ranqueles and booze took him over. Being strong did not come easily to Fernando; most everything else in life had. Being strong required effort, and effort was one of many things which Fernando Carrioli had in short supply. Instead of rising to new challenges, he preferred to revel in those that had already been met for him. He had few ideas of his own, as Robles would discover before long, for Fernando relied heavily on the ideas of others.

The Carrioli spread was the biggest and oldest in the area. Since the previous year, when his father had lost his leg and gained an addiction, the farm had gone to seed along with its creator. Fernando's soft style of life was suddenly threatened with the disasters of responsibility, the frightening alarums of toil. He let things slip down the slide of waste. He spent more and more of his time in the big city when he should have devoted it to the care and upkeep of the ranch. He had married into one of the most wealthy and respected families of city people. Fernando's dreams revolved around the city of Buenos Aires and a rise on the spiral staircase of politics. He hated farming and everything to do with the outdoors. Yet he needed the revenue that the farm was capable of bringing in, which was plenty if it was properly handled. He undertook the bare minimum of its management. Once Old Man Carrioli died, Fernando and his wife had already agreed, they would sell the spread and move to the city. Unfortunately, the old man was taking a devilishly long time to succumb to alcohol. He must have a liver like a sponge.

Robles had no way of knowing much of this as he shifted his appraisal to the boy's father. In his day, the senior Carrioli had been something of a pioneer and an Indian fighter in these parts. He was plagued with the everlasting misfortune of a useless son. His wife had perished while he was out on a patrol. The farm was saved by the timely intervention of Roca's men. Fate dealt him another mean card a few weeks later when he took an arrow in his thigh and the wound turned gangrenous. They amputated the leg in the field hospital. The bees of bad luck had surged in a swarm through the last years of the old man's life. He had sought to soothe their stings with drink. Robles observed him refill his glass with a third shot of whisky as his daughter-in-law, seated next to him, inserted a smile into her conversation with the other ladies.

An air of exaggerated snobbishness surrounded Isabella Carrioli like a petticoat, thwarting a siege of self-doubts and making her bigotry virtually unassailable. She was attractive in a meticulous rather than a fetching way. Her clothes were fashionable, quietly guaranteeing that few people would talk about what she was wearing. She abhorred the idea of becoming an object of conversation. Like Robles, she was an observer. Unlike him, Isabella saw only the dirt and sweat in the gaucho men who tore a small fortune for her from the bowels of the family estancia. Robles would have called them romantic, footloose emblems of liberty who were undergoing a tragic upheaval. Isabella saw such men as fugitives from the class structure of her world, whose dirt-filled fingernails and swaggering mannerisms were an affront to her femininity. She longed for the day they could sell the estancia off at a top price and move into the city. A house in one of the streets that ran into the Avenida Nueve de Julio was the right home for her to raise a family. She would not even consider children until they were living in Buenos Aires. She wanted them to study music in the drawing room and enter banking or politics, not become brown-skinned little urchins who scampered around barefoot and learned how to ride before they could walk.

In fact, it was the ladies who made the scene appear so thoroughly incongruous to Robles. First of all, far too much of it had an English atmosphere, to which people like the younger Carriolis and Tossini had adapted, rather than the other way around. Percival Wisbey, for example, when he spoke of home, did not refer to the ninety thousand acres which he controlled in Argentina but to the green pastures of Sussex, where he had been born and schooled. It did not matter that Wisbey's parents had moved their lives lock, stock, and barrel to South America when Percy had gone up to Oxford. Neither did he relate the story of how he had flunked out of university at the end of his first term and shipped out to BA one rainy day, never setting eyes again on England's shores from that wistful day in the Port of Liverpool to this evening, thirty-two years later.

As for ladies like Mrs. Wisbey, whose first name was never mentioned throughout the whole evening, they were so utterly English that it was unthinkable that she really could have been born in Rosario, the only daughter of second-generation Anglo-Argentines. Her family was one of the oldest established British families in the country. Although her Spanish was absolutely flawless, she almost never spoke except in reply to a direct question. She armored herself with a battery of nods, gestures, and monosyllables which normally got her through conversation. She inhabited her own private world of taciturnity. Some people said that her marriage to Percy had been the ideal match for her because he was the kind of domineering man who required that his wife be a listener and seldom the mouthpiece. Mrs. Wisbey was an antichameleon, who clung furtively to a vain hope that her background would change hue to conceal her presence. Her opinion was rarely required in her own household. She hated noise and fanfare and the bright midday glare of the sun, under whose scrutiny it seemed there was never a place to hide. Even her small wardrobe of tasteless clothes matched their wearer's total inability to fit any occasion. Mrs. Wisbey had erected a vacuous belljar around herself. She rarely went outdoors. She lived in a hyper-nervous world of candlelight, books large enough to shield her face from onlookers, and heavy drapes which protected her from the world beyond her hacienda's windows.

Robles's thoughts were interrupted by Mrs. McClellan announcing that dinner was ready to be served. It was almost eight o'clock. Everyone rose to their feet—Mrs. Wisbey reluctantly, Old Man Carrioli somewhat unsteadily. Before one became aware of his drinking habits it was easy to be misled by his wooden leg into thinking that his imbalance was due to his crippled state. Apart from Robles, they all knew that he was now four large belts of Scotch whisky to the good and would help himself to a fifth as soon as he had seated himself at the table.

The McClellans took their places at the ends of the long dining table which dominated one half of the big downstairs room that served as both eating place and sitting room. They had designed it without a divider to benefit from the single vast hearth, which now burned merrily. Tossini, being considered the guest of honor, took the chair on Bruce's right hand. Robles sat opposite him, on McClellan's other side.

Manuel stared down the length of the table feeling distinctly ill at ease. They were all there to hear him speak words which would stamp out the Tehuelches once and for all. Yet he did not intend to say anything of the kind. It was the sort of uncomfortable situation which would take any man's appetite away. Robles wished he were on his way back across the pampas. He had really enjoyed the ride down on his little mare. The early winter weather had proved lenient. The rains were sporadic at best. Even the wind had relented somewhat. Robles looked past Tossini's head and shoulders as the thin lace curtains were lifted by a breath of wind. Despite the season, the window was half open, out of respect for the blazing log fire. It threw off such a splendid heat that the room was truly warm with so many people crammed into it.

People of the pampas, thought Robles. Yes, these were the people who populated the pampas nowadays. Fat policemen. Foppish Italian immigrants with drunkards for fathers and supercilious snobs for wives. The Anglo-Argentines who exuded the fact that they were a race apart, who had been given the right to own and control what was theirs by the power of the mighty peso. And the pioneering McClellans themselves, equally divine in their outlook of being superior by the nature of their skin color and the dexterity of their languages. It had come to this. And very soon they would obliterate the last of the indigenous Indians. A couple of years at most, and whatever he did or said or tried would be drowned out in the blast of Winchester and Remington repeating rifles and the screams of the Tehuelche men, women, and children blasted to pieces, just like the three whom McClellan and Tossini had done for the day before yesterday.

It was their world, right enough. Inventive white men with their metal explosive weapons, telegraph talking cables, barbed wire fences, and steel locomotives on forged tracks would see to that. Looking once more up and down the length of the table, Robles couldn't find any one man or woman who seemed to epitomize what the pampas had once been. Maybe over in the bunkhouse there might be a leather-skinned man who held his head high and spoke poetically of life in the saddle in much the same way as Manuel's father had once spoken. Of the life playing knucklebone as the sun went down behind the house, sleeping out under the stars, roasting the tongue of a fresh-slain wild cow, and listening to the guitars laughing in the face of the wind.

The pampas seemed devoid of symbols. And then, amid the burble and chatter of the dining room, Robles remembered the giant, almost naked Tehuelche warrior on his great gray stallion. He was a symbol. He was alive in the true sense. He had not as yet been shot down, imprisoned, or betrayed by the white man's insatiable appetite for land. Who among you, Robles asked silently of that babbling table gathering, who among you could defeat him? Where was he right now? Where would he be eating his roast guanaco? Where would he be sleeping on some flat piece of hard, cold ground with nothing but a temporary windbreak angled around him? And that horse of his. Who among you could ever ride him? For how much longer would stallions such as he be allowed to gallop free across a land that had once seemed so limitless? Soon the fences would cut off the very last avenues of freedom.

Robles's train of thought was once more nudged by reality, this time by the arrival of a big soup tureen. Manuel now took in the boy who brought it. He was young, in his mid-teens. The boy kept his eyes lowered the whole time, as if his vision were an embarassment. Robles noticed how the boy's hands were shaking once they came free of the tureen handles. The boy had placed it between Tossini and himself. For just a moment Robles caught the boy's eye and then he was gone, hurrying back to the kitchen, the unscrutinized sanctuary. Boys like that shouldn't be waiting on table for the ingleses, Manuel continued in his acidly critical theme. They should be taking after their fathers, breaking horses, working cattle, living free and to the full. Why must the white man bend everything his own way? Yes, you are thinking like an Indian, like a Yamana, like the proud and noble savage who was your grandfather. Well, what was so wrong with that when this was apparently the white man's alternative? Aye, but, Manuel, you are becoming an old stick in the mud. You spend too much time finding fault with others. Everything changes. It is only a matter of time. The era of the gaucho has passed by. It has gone forever. It is as sure a fact of life as that which has decreed the end for the Tehuelche horse nomads of Patagonia. They cannot survive, not even if they were offered a life on a reservation, which they are unlikely ever to be offered.

The boy returned bearing two bottles of red wine. Mrs. Mc-Clellan broke off her small talk with the young Carrioli couple to snap at him.

"Alejo! You have forgotten that we also have some white wine to offer our guests!"

"Señora, I am most humbly sorry," faltered the boy abjectly.

"Well," said Virginia McClellan, "don't just stand there, go and fetch it."

"*En seguida,* señora, at once," and the boy began to retrace his steps to the kitchen.

"Alejo! Do not take the red wine back with you. Leave the two you have brought with my husband and then bring two bottles of white."

The boy did as he was told and retired gratefully out of sight.

"Now then, Fernando," Mrs. McClellan said, returning to her conversation, "what were you saying about your most recent trip to Buenos Aires?"

"Well, señora McClellan, in fact I was talking about transportation changes that enable one to go to our future illustrious capital with much greater speed and convenience. The railway extension south of Tres Arboles is due to be finished inside another two months. There is still nothing much by way of a town at the end of it, but that will soon change. At the moment there is just the saladero and the few houses which the workers have erected. However, it is a major step, bringing the railway another seventy miles nearer to us. Both grain and beef prices are rising steadily, and I think it is quite safe to predict that all of us here can look forward to a profitable future.

"But you know, señora, you really should persuade your husband to take you on a trip to BA. After all, next year it is to become the capital of the Republic. How long is it since you were in the city?"

"Did you hear that, dearest?" piped up Mrs. McClellan, projecting her voice the length of the table. "Fernando wants to know when you will take me into our new capital city."

"In the spring, Virginia, in the spring," McClellan assured her, somewhat irritated by young Carrioli's presumptuousness.

"That's exactly what you said this time last year—and the one before that," continued Mrs. McClellan, reluctant to relinquish her advantage. "It has been more than two years since I set eyes on BA."

McClellan turned his attention to the soup and began ladling. As the tomato soup passed around the table it became evident that one plate was lacking. Another of Alejo's omissions, which happened to coincide with the unfortunate teenager's appearance in the room with the two bottles of white wine.

"Alejo!" McClellan bellowed at him by way of welcome. "Bring me another soup plate, you little terror!" Then, in a lower

93

voice, etched with a deep sigh of exasperation: "It's hopeless trying to teach these gaucho brats anything remotely associated with civilized living."

Alejo, now totally flustered, stood gaping at his patrón's command. Robles felt a jab of anger. Civilized living had recently killed three defenseless Indians in cold blood. He himself had once been a gaucho brat. But Robles said nothing. He just leaned around in his chair, reached for the two bottles of wine, and said softly: "Fetch a soup plate for señor McClellan, Alejito."

"Sí, señor." The boy raced back into the cave of the kitchen while Robles busied himself pulling the cork from one of the bottles. He pushed the open bottle down along the table, where Old Man Carrioli straightway snatched it up and poured a glassful. The old fellow ignored his tall-stemmed wine glass and poured the wine over the dregs of his whisky.

The ladies poured a discreet half glass apiece, except for Mrs. Wisbey, who never drank alcohol.

Robles opened the second bottle of white wine and poured off the cork, then filled Tossini's glass. McClellan drank the red with Manuel, who knew a good wine when he tasted it.

They began dinner.

"Tomato soup, why how wonderful," Isabella enthused.

"The very last of my little garden's contribution to a balanced diet," Virginia explained with a modest smile. "Now then, Isabella my dear, do tell me more about BA."

"A lot of European influence, as ever, particularly from your own country. I hardly think you will recognize the city after so long an absence. Almost all of the main streets are now paved, the parks are exquisite, simply exquisite, and the new-style carriages are an absolute delight to ride in. There is such a Parisian air to it all, such a feeling of space even among the crowds. Why, señor Morales at the ministry told us that the city has well over two hundred thousand inhabitants and it is expanding all the time. Can you imagine so many people living in one place?"

Mrs. McClellan thought of London and realized just how provincial some of these Argentines could be, even the sophisticated ones with half an education.

"Unbelievable," she breathed. "My, how this country is growing. There you are, Bruce," she projected, "we really must pay a visit this spring."

Bruce McClellan nodded to his spouse and then turned back to the chief of police, who was sucking up his soup with noisy abandon.

"That's great news about the Remingtons, Alfredo. Why on earth didn't you mention it yesterday?" he whispered. "I think I'll just keep the news to myself for the time being, if you'll play along. I'd like to present that particular piece of information after dinner."

"Certainly, Bruce." Tossini nodded with an understanding half smile. "Kept it to myself so long that I forgot all about it till now, all about it I did. You tell them when it suits you, just when it suits you. I'd do the same thing in my position if I were you, er, the same thing."

Robles wondered what the two men on the corners of his hearing were so intent on keeping to themselves. He drank the soup and sipped his wine. Later in the evening, after the big dinner was demolished, he would be put on trial. At least, that was how it felt. First they would eat, then they would listen to what he had to tell them, and when they had all heard it and grown angry, most of them would get drunk. Robles flicked through his thoughts as he waited for the next course, treating the random ideas which presented themselves as if they were a pack of cards. It was his way of sliding the present and the future to one side. He immediately came across a card labeled "innocent Tehuelches gunned down" and began to regret his card game all at once. The stakes were too high and the cards too wild. His mind's eye kept seeing, over and over again, the way the Tehuelche woman fell forward from her horse when the big bullet smacked into her. And then there was the infant. It took all of his willpower to flick up another card and avoid reliving that particularly grisly happening. It was only after it was all over that Robles had come out of the paralyzing dream of discovering he was being watched by a Tehuelche warrior and then ridden down to examine the dead family. The woman had been at least seven months pregnant. By that time Tossini and McClellan had ridden far ahead. When he finally caught up with them he found them idling along, chatting as if nothing much had happened all day as they dawdled in order that he might overtake them. Robles had ridden past without a word, cantering on alone back to the estancia. It was an obvious and blatant insult. Tight-lipped in his despair, Robles had pondered what he would do and say when the ranchers gathered to hear him. Soon he would know. And so would they.

The next card was marked with questions. Just who was the warrior on the magnificent gray stallion? It was not difficult to imagine him as something more than another luckless hunter who had run out of arrows just when he needed them most. There was something foreign about him; something regal, too. But he was Tehuelche, all right. There was something else about him. He had an almost supernatural presence. Robles turned over yet another card and found that he had come to the end of his pack. Alejo was clearing away the soup plates.

Virginia McClellan caught the boy's eye and signaled for the main course. She was trying very hard to personally groom the boy to serve at table on just such occasions as this. She had achieved only partial success. He performed most of his creased and starched duties with tolerable accuracy, but that fiasco of the soup plate and the wine was typical Alejo. She couldn't turn her back on him for one second without him making a fool of himself, and thus the house management in general.

"That was an excellent soup," praised Alfredo Tossini, "an excellent soup, if I may say so."

Virginia smiled her gratitude as everyone else added their praise.

Alejo came back time and time again, bearing great platters of beef, kidneys, liver, sausage, and ribs that had been charcoal-grilled on the asador. Then came a salad of lettuce, onion, and the luxury of fresh tomatoes. Bread. A refill of wine. The long table was piled high with good food.

Bruce McClellan rose to his feet and proposed a toast to the chief of police. Then Fernando Carrioli proposed a toast to the host and hostess. Uneasy smiles rippled around the table.

The meal proceeded against a background of the crackling log fire, which had been allowed to burn down. The table was lit

with three twin candelabra, and everyone present was well accustomed to the low light level in the room by then. Finally, the
last of the food and drink was consumed. It was just after nine
in the evening.

"A fine meal, Mrs. McClellan," said Robles, and he was telling
the whole truth.

"Yes, Virginia, you have done us proud, my dear," her husband
congratulated her.

Other echoes of praise were murmured from satisfied lips.

"Shall we get down to business, ladies and gentlemen?" suggested McClellan.

"A splendid idea," put in Percival Wisbey, "business first,
brandy afterwards. That's what I always say."

"Right enough, Percy," McClellan agreed in English. Then he
realized the rudeness of speaking a language which only the
Wisbeys and the McClellans understood. "Trust you to know that
I would have brandy even out here," he added in Spanish to make
up for his blunder.

Bruce decided to do his talking sitting down. He simply leaned
back in his chair and took one last mighty swallow of the dancing
liquid ruby in his goblet. "Alejo," he commanded the boy, who
was hovering by his shoulder like a hummingbird, "see that whoever wishes more wine is accommodated, then organize some
coffee."

Robles declined the wine with a slight wave of his hand.
Tossini nodded acceptance. McClellan's glass was refilled without
interrogation. Wisbey asked, "Why not?" of nobody in particular,
and the ladies all declined dutifully. Fernando allowed himself to
be persuaded by Virginia McClellan's comment that "the wine, like
you, Fernando, has just come all the way from Buenos Aires."

Old Man Carrioli was not in a position to decide. He had
fallen into a stupor, with his head resting on the table, pillowed
by his arms. Everyone made an admirable effort not to notice
his state. When it came to not noticing the obvious, there was no
actress anywhere better than Virginia McClellan, who sat next
to the drunken old pioneer.

"Now then," began McClellan in his businesslike tone, the one
that he reserved for serious conversation. "We all know what

we're here to discuss. You've already met Manuel de Robles, Inspector of Indian Affairs. His report will clinch the matter of the Tehuelche problem once and for all, for he reports directly back to the minister himself.

"What is said here tonight will form part of that report. We run the most southerly and therefore the most immediately threatened estancias. This is our golden opportunity to speak and have our voices heard in Buenos Aires. I cannot urge you more strongly to speak your minds and express your hopes and fears for the future in this part of the great country of Argentina. Now is no time to hold back. The chance won't come again.

"You are all people of the pampas. You know the area and own a large part of it. The land is a hard land to master. But I, for one, do not ask the government to assist me against the droughts or the wind or the rinderpest or the mountain lion who attacks my herd from time to time. I accept nature as my adversary. I take a farmer's precautions against pestilence and hope that my stock will survive. I count on my rifle to rid myself of any cat who prowls the stockyards after dark.

"Only last year, the Ranqueles Indians rose in revolt. They killed and they burned and they raped and they pillaged. Their destruction stained the land with blood and tears. We appealed to the authorities, and the army sent down troops under General Roca. Those forces soon defeated the Ranqueles and now they can never trouble us again."

Tell them why, Robles was thinking, tell them why the Ranqueles will never trouble anyone again, ever. Tell them how they were shot down, every man, woman, and child who got in the rifle sights of Roca's heroic soldiers. How those few who escaped went in panic to the high country, barefoot, tentless, without food or weapons. Tell them about the last few hundred Ranqueles Indians, who died from frostbite and starvation in the worst winter to hit southern Chile for thirteen years. Above all, pleaded Robles, tell them that the Ranqueles' insurrection was the only step left to them to avoid total homelessness because their land had been farmed and fenced off by white men who rode out of the north and took it all for themselves and their herds.

"Now," McClellan continued, "a similar threat rears its ugly

98

head. The raids by the Tehuelches have so far been few and far between, but they stand between us and further expansion of the sheep lands which lie unused and empty south of the Colorado River. In other words, a handful of savages separate the great new Republic of Argentina from further progress, from its rightful place in the economic world, from the path of its true destiny. There are more settlers in the area than ever before. And I can tell them, as I now tell you, we shall soon have the weapons to form our own army.

"Our guest of honor here tonight is a man who has grown up along with the country of Patagonia. Don Alfredo Tossini, chief of police of the bustling little township of Tres Arboles, has built his reputation as a law enforcement officer as we have built up our herds and our haciendas: with devotion and hard labor. Alfredo has just informed me that the first shipment of American-made Remington repeating rifles has arrived in the port of Buenos Aires. In a matter of weeks, every able-bodied man on the southern pampas will be in possession of a weapon which will make him a match for five Tehuelches. Banded together, our own small force will be more than equal to the task of protecting our homes and our families from the threat posed by them. In fact, these new rifles should make it possible for us to attack and drive out those Tehuelches who form the large camp a few hours' ride south of the river. Unfortunately, there is still no news of the telegraph link coming on from Tres Arboles, although work is actually progressing on an extension of the railway line.

"Ladies and gentlemen, we have to do more than defend what is already ours. We have to do much, much more. The Tehuelche is no more than *vermin*."

McClellan paused for dramatic effect, giving everyone time to nod agreement.

"Fenceless farms are defenseless farms. This has been the slogan in this neck of the woods for a long time. The fences are springing up, but they are designed to keep our herds in and not Indians out. There has been talk of a reservation for the pampas tribes. Well! I ask you! Would you keep rats upon a reservation? No, ladies and gentlemen, you would not! You would exterminate the rats by any and every means at your disposal. And so it is with Tehuelches. And that, unfortunately, is beyond us, even with the telegraph and the Remington. We need support from the army, for we are too few to rout out this Indian menace and protect our farms in our absence."

Bruce McClellan took a long, slow look around the table, letting his calm gray eyes rest on each face in turn. He satisfied himself that he had the undivided attention of everyone present, with the clear exception of Old Man Carrioli, and then asked, "Are there any questions so far?"

Fernando Carrioli coughed politely.

"Fernando?" McClellan inquired, softening the edge of his voice.

"Have we any idea how strong the Tehuelche is, señor McClellan?"

"In numbers, it is hard to say. Their bands have never been vast, but of late it is said, with considerable justification, they have become much more consolidated in recent years. There was a time once when they roamed around as nothing more than large families. Reports indicate that the encampment less than a day's ride from here could put some two hundred fighting men into the field against us. To the east is an even larger band, but they hug the coastline in their wanderings. Scattered throughout the rest of Patagonia, well, perhaps the same again as those two larger bands. We will get to hear more in detail about the nature of the enemy when Manuel speaks to us, for he is something of an authority on the subject.

"However, before I hand this meeting over to him, I want to refer back to this new shipment of Remingtons. It is essential that every man who works land in this region sees that his gauchos and herd hands are equipped with one of these guns. The railway link with the new saladero seventy miles south of Tres Arboles is due to open in another couple of months. Apart from that, we must press the administration for more prompt action in the matter of a telegraph extension which will connect every farmhouse and hacienda on the pampas. Modern communication is as vital a cog in the wheel of whipping the Tehuelche as rifles and ammunition. Then there is the matter of barbed wire fencing. But I have begun to repeat myself, and have talked for too long as it is.

"Without more ado, I would like to call upon Manuel de Robles, who has made the exceedingly long and arduous journey all the way from BA for this meeting, to speak in some detail about the Tehuelche Indians themselves. Above all, I am counting, indeed we all are, on Manuel's support as an intermediary to the government. My Winchester must not remain the only truly modern weapon in the area any longer. We must learn to defend ourselves, to fight our own battles. Our very lives depend on it, our lives and the lives of our children. We must make our appeal through Manuel. He will, I am sure, put our case forward with his blessing. If half the force that was sent down under Roca could be made available now, coupled with our own men marshaled together and organized, then our troubles with the Tehuelche would very soon be over. Manuel, the floor is yours."

Oh my God, Robles thought, how I am going to disappoint these people? He waited for the scattered applause to die down at the end of McClellan's speech. They were all nodding at each other around the table. Wisbey kept saying, "Hear, hear," whatever the devil that meant. Why couldn't they keep it all in Spanish? This was all hard enough as it was without having to confuse the issues even further with their inane Englishness. The young Carriolis were still clapping with exactly the right degree of enthusiasm. Damn them all, every last one of them! Robles thought. Think of the pregnant Tehuelche woman shot in the back with a heavy-caliber bullet. Think about her infant son, who would never grow into a man. Now, Manuel de Robles, get up and tell them straight what you are going to put into your report —and what you are not.

Robles stood. *"Señores y señoras,"* he started off, "I am not sure that many of you will approve or agree with what I am going to say." His voice was gravelly, but the words were very precise. "However, as a representative of the government, working in an official capacity, here by the specific instruction of the minister himself, I consider that it would be foolish to be other than perfectly frank with you. It would be amiss of me to mislead you, to build up your hopes and expectations. I will tell you the complete truth of the matter, not only as I see it personally but as I shall report it to my superiors.

"The government policy concerning indigenous tribes has

changed a lot over recent years. In the beginning it was based mostly on appeasement. Later it turned to total warfare, the extermination of all tribes who could not be induced or even forced into obeisance or slavery. Avellaneda has altered much of that policy during his term in office. A new system has been worked out, and I was one of its instigators. It is a system which will give freedom to the Indians without causing hardship to the settlers in this part of the country. Tribes such as the Tehuelches of northern Patagonia were here long before we or our ancestors came. They have been here for so long that they were deeply rooted in their habits and customs even before the arrival of the very first white man. The only major change that has taken place in their ways is the appearance of the horse, which spread from the conquistadors. The government, and I myself for that matter, therefore feel that a different outlook on the problem is long overdue. This is not a case of simply protecting your own land, but rather one of continuing to take it from those Indians who still cling to survival. Therefore—"

"Oh, come along, Robles, we're not talking about men and women," said an exasperated McClellan. "We're talking about savages."

"They are human bēings nonetheless," Robles said, very quietly, for McClellan was directly next to him.

"Human beings who paint their faces with ocher and dance to the moon. You can surely do better than that, Robles? Really!"

"Intending no disrespect to our gracious hostess," rejoined the Argentine, "but I notice that she is wearing a particularly fetching shade of lipstick. And señora Carrioli has added just the right amount of rouge to her cheeks for this occasion."

Fernando Carrioli could not contain his agitation. "Now see here," he remonstrated, "are you suggesting that my wife and Mrs. McClellan are about to start dancing to the moon?"

"Not at all, sir. I was merely demonstrating that the different customs between the Indians and the whites are really not quite so different as they appear on the surface. Did you not take your wife to dance the polka or the quadrille during your recent visit to our future capital, señor Carrioli?"

"Well, yes, we were invited by señor Morales himself. It's hardly the same thing as—"

"Isn't it?" interrupted Robles, without raising his voice but using all of his practiced cross-examination style, which now came flooding back. "I put it to you, sir, that if it is not quite the same thing to the white man, then it is not quite the same thing to the Tehuelche. And if it is the same thing to us, then it is equally the same thing to the savage. It is dance and paint whichever way you choose to look at it, no mater how the steps are performed or the make-up applied. Shall I go on?"

"Let him say his piece," McClellan authorized, offering an understanding nod to Fernando. "The rest of you will be able to put forward your views, have no fear of that. But we did invite señor Robles to speak, and I think we should extend him the courtesy of finishing. You have our attention, señor."

Robles inclined his head at McClellan's good manners. So, it was back to "señor Robles" soon enough, Manuel was thinking. Funny how formal a man became when he was hating your very guts for the things you were saying. No matter, Robles had got into his stride by then. He was not there to please them, only to lay it on the line for them.

"You have heard señor McClellan speak of the reservation. This is one of the ideas that will be put before the minister. It may not suit the Tehuelches at all, but it is an alternative to complete annihilation. As there are no longer any tribes still to be found in great numbers, there have been no examples to illustrate the reservation system. However, it has come into use in North America, and the advantages and disadvantages are on record for that part of the world. In theory, it simply involves peaceful overtures being carried out and the offer of a designated area of land that will be set aside exclusively for them to hunt and to wander in. It is appreciated just how difficult this will be to impress upon a people as proud and as historically nomadic as the Tehuelches, but I believe it can be done. There is enough land for all, ladies and gentlemen."

At this remark, there were loud murmurs of disapproval around the table. The younger Carrioli, still smarting from the imagined insult to his wife, threw up his hands in an emphatic gesture of disgust.

"Señor Robles, I really must protest," he said petulantly.

"If you must, you must," retorted Robles mildly.

"You think you can walk across to the Tehuelches and make them remain in some reservation area, just like that?"

"Just like what, señor Carrioli?"

"I beg your pardon?"

"Excuse me, but I thought you were about to come forward with an improved alternative."

Fernando was flustered. He had not expected to come up with new ideas. He was used to simply reconditioning those of others.

"It is not a matter of enough land for all," he fumed, trying to cover his confusion.

"Just what is it a matter of, may I ask?"

"Why, it is, er, a matter of ownership, of, er, possession, of progress, of, of survival even."

"Fernando," McClellan interposed, "perhaps you could just wait a little longer."

"It's all right, señor McCellan," Robles acknowledged. "Let him speak."

Fernando spoke. "My estancia has been in my family for three generations. We have acquired more and more land over the years, put in a great deal of backbreaking labor to build up our herds, diverted streams for irrigation purposes, constructed one of the finest haciendas to be seen in these parts, and so forth. Why," Carrioli lied, "it is everything to my wife and me. It is our rightful inheritance, a part of an enduring legacy. We would sacrifice our lives to hold on to it in order that any children we may be blessed with shall carry it on."

"That," said Robles airily, "may well prove to be necessary."

"A man has a right to protect what is his," continued Fernando, borrowing heavily from what he had heard spouted from so many other mouths, "even if it means killing to do so."

"Quite right, quite right," burbled the pompous Wisbey, entering the joust of dialogue for the first time. His tone bespoke a safe form of echoing the majority verdict. He could hardly be shot down in such supportive company. His Spanish was uttered in the same clipped bombastic self-assurance as his English. "Law of the jungle, what?" he went on, with the relish of knowing that he had said much the same things to a great many men. "Survival of the fittest, don't you know?"

"Listen to me, inglés!" Robles exploded, hissing so venomously that Wisbey recoiled. "Do you really think there is a white man, even a wild-bred gaucho, anywhere in this whole wide country who is remotely as fit as any Tehuelche warrior? Well, do you? You don't really have the faintest idea of what it is you're up against, do you, any of you? None of you even have the vaguest clue who they are, these vermin you would stamp out if you could! Well, let me enlighten you as to what Tehuelches really are. Let me shatter once and for all the misinformed dreams and ill-formed illusions you seem to be nurturing about this tribe whose land you now live on. I think it is high time that you were made to realize just exactly what kind of war you can expect down here once you get your Remington repeaters.

"You, who represent the biggest and most powerful settlers in the region, if you searched your rich estancias and held contests to find your most proficient gaucho for horsemanship and then brought him here; and then you held another contest to elect from that elite cream of men the very top hand of them all; still you would not have found a horseman who was any match whatsoever for any Tehuelche boy of sixteen. Am I making myself clear, young señor Carrioli? Tehuelches can outride anything you've ever seen on horseback, or even imagined existed. They can and do ride all day and night, changing mounts at full gallop, and still fight like hell at the end of it. They adore and worship horses. They eat, drink, sleep, and dream horses. They can cling invisible under the belly of a mount and stick you through the stomach with a spear while you are wondering what happened to the rider. The best of them could plant three arrows in your chest while you are still struggling to reload your single-shot carbines. As archers they have no equal. They are tall, muscular men who have never in their lives slept in a proper bed, or eaten soft foods, or drunk anything more potent than milk. They can run down a rhea on foot. They sleep in a crude tent or a makeshift lean-to against the howling wind of the Patagonian steppe in midwinter and think no more about it then you do about where your next meal is coming from. A Tehuelche dog soldier is—"

"May I say something?" Fernando ventured.

105

"No, young man, you may not!" Robles barked, without a thought for hurt pride. He had the glint of command in his eyes and the tone of enforcing it in his words. "You just sit where you are and learn something that may save your hide one of these days! As I was saying, Tehuelches are something different from any tribe in these parts. The other tribes steer clear of them. They leave them alone. They won't molest Tehuelches unless they are forced to do so. Even the Ranqueles hesitated before invading the border zone around the lakes, until they were driven to it by pressure on their own pastures by white ranchers.

"And that invasion, whether or not you prefer to call it by some other name, *was* an invasion by us of *their* homeland. But let us avoid the morals and the ideals and talk about people. Tehuelches are the toughest spartan cavalry you'll ever meet on this or any other earth. They can go without food, drink, sleep, or friendship for days and nights on end and then kill you with nothing more than a primitive bow and arrow before you are even aware of their presence. Now then, ladies and gentlemen, am I beginning to make myself clear?"

Silence had settled upon the room.

With an effort, Virginia McClellan took it upon herself to break the mood. "Maybe we'd better all have some coffee?" It was enough to dislocate the tension but not to remove it.

"Yes, señora McClellan, I think that would be an excellent idea," Robles agreed. "And while you're arranging it, I will tell the assembled company just what we have going for us in our favor in the advent of a full-scale war with the Tehuelches."

Virginia wafted daintily from the room to supervise the coffee-making personally.

Robles still held the floor. He wasn't finished with them yet.

"Apart from the promise of repeater rifles and instant communication by telegraph wire," he went on, "both of which are still advantages of the future, however imminent, we have two things going for us. First, señor McClellan has quite accurately estimated the Tehuelche numbers within a couple of hundred either way. If all the Tehuelches left on the face of this land, which I again remind you is *their* land, came together, I doubt if they could muster as many as two thousand warriors. A total of four and a half thousand people altogether. Don't discount the women, because they'll fight too if it is a matter of life and death."

"And our other advantage?" asked Bruce McClellan, his interest keen and sincere. He was interested in facts now, not scoring points in the debate with the opposition.

"They will not band together as a single nation, for it is not their way," Robles informed them. "They will not live and fight as one tribe against the threat of the white man taking their land from them—unless . . ." Robles could do nothing to stop the sudden impression which impinged on his brain. His sentence wavered into memory of a near-naked bronze giant on a silver stallion, an Andean poncho thrown back behind his broad shoulders. His thoughts hovered on that lasting image until he was prompted by Tossini, who was staring hard across the table at him.

"Unless what, Robles?"

"Unless they have found a warlord to lead them. They have not had such a leader in almost a decade, and he was only partially successful in uniting the bands against the Ranqueles. That, *señores y señoras,* is what you have on your side. I hope the Remingtons come quickly and the telegraph is laid down before too long, for if you are seeking a war with Indians, the Tehuelches will give you one that you will never forget—those of you that live through it. I have nothing more to say, unless anyone wishes to ask any questions."

"And you are seriously going to recommend to the ministry that peace terms and a reservation are offered to the Tehuelches?" asked an incredulous Wisbey.

"I am, señor."

"But my God, hombre, have you any idea how rich all this land to the south really is? It is a sheep farmer's paradise. And the rest of the land close to the Colorado, it is only slightly poorer than the pure pampas of the north. It boasts almost the same deep, black-soil loam which is absolutely perfect for rearing beef cattle and dairy herds. Agriculturally it could be considered for sunflowers, grain crops, and God knows what else, given sufficient irrigation. The coastal settlers are known to have tripled their sheep herds since they first arrived. They and anyone else who buys the southern plains are sitting on an absolute fortune, I tell you. Yet you would advocate, as the official representative of a government ministry, as a professional adviser, you would recommend that it be granted to a pack of bloodthirsty savages who do nothing but hunt rheas on foot and break horses gently! I say fight! Fight them and kill them off until there's not one left. Total extermination, it's the only way. And with the support of an army unit and these modern rifles, we'll achieve it before the winter's over."

"Well said, Percy," McClellan said.

"My view entirely," Fernando agreed, when really it was Wisbey's.

Alfredo Tossini rose to his feet just a trifle unsteadily as Mrs. McClellan came back into the room with two steaming pots of coffee. Alejo trailed a few paces behind her with cups, saucers, spoons, sugar, and fresh milk, arranged in neat rows on a rectangular tray.

"I would like to say a few words to you all," announced the corpulent police chief, loosening his collar. It was still very warm in the room, although the fire had burned down to a mere glow. The half-open window behind Tossini drew in a welcome current of cool night air. Tossini was perspiring freely, and he reached for the last of his wine, which he put out of its misery in two long swallows.

"I have listened to all that has been said with great interest, great interest indeed. What señor Manuel de Robles has said has shocked me, shocked me very deeply indeed. My good friend Bruce McClellan and my old acquaintance of many years Percival Wisbey, they have the right idea all right, the right idea, Bruce and Percy. Kill the Tehuelches off, kill them all off and have done with it. Remove the vermin once and for all, once and for all."

Fernando Carrioli lit a thin cheroot and blew a stream of smoke into the air, remembering to turn and tilt his head back as he did so. He wished Tossini would shut up. His speeches always amounted to saying nothing at all in a tortuously roundabout way. He shared a knowing glance with his pretty young wife, who sighed under cover of her sculptured left hand to demonstrate her boredom.

Mrs. McClellan kept her ever-available polished smile on her lips as she prayed devoutly that the chief of police would not ramble on all night.

"Now that the new Remington rifles are on their way, it will not be long before the Tehuelches are driven into oblivion, not long at all, I can promise you that."

Wisbey pleaded inwardly for the chief to get on with it. Why in the devil's name did he have to be so all-fired long-winded every time he made a speech? Percy felt exasperated, knowing that as soon as Tossini shut up and resumed his seat at the table McClellan would produce his excellent brandy. Good stuff that was, right enough. Reminded him of the Armagnac his father used to have imported. A very mellow drop indeed.

Even Bruce McClellan was beginning to wonder if Tossini had not had one glass of wine too many. A frown ribbed his forehead below the fringe of his red hair as he considered the most tactful way to dam the flow of almost incoherent repetition.

"Telegraph communication will be here before you know it, ladies and gentlemen, before you know it. Then you'll see improvements, improvements and changes on a scale you can hardly envisage, hardly envisage at present. And those changes will make even the southern pampas a safe place to travel day or night, er, night or day."

Mrs. Wisbey was feeling very tired. She had made her appearance in accordance with her husband's wishes, although she didn't see why it had been necessary. She would rather have remained at home. It had been mostly men's talk anyway. She had had her single cup of coffee; she never took more than one. The thought of brandy horrified her, although, in fairness to those who enjoyed it, she could imagine being driven to strong drink by the meaningless rhetoric of this Argentine oaf from Tres Arboles. She wondered how long she would have to sit it out before Bruce stepped in and put an end to this drivel. She had been very good about the four-hour sidesaddle ride through the dust and wind to get here. Now all she wanted was a decent night's sleep before she had to face the ordeal of the ride back.

Old Man Carrioli blissfully slept through it all. The rest of the gathering by now envied his stupor.

Robles helped himself to another cup of coffee and fetched out his pipe. He was totally submerged in the ocean of his own thoughts as he played absent-mindedly with his drooping mustache.

"The pampas has been transformed into an agricultural garden, a garden of agriculture," went on the seemingly inexhaustible Tossini. "Already we have curbed the marauding lawlessness of the gauchos and seen them become useful members of the community, those marauding—"

So much tedium had been injected into the group of listeners that no one even bothered to look up when Tossini stopped his monologue in mid-sentence. Isabella gave him a mental nudge to get the predictable reiteration of the word "gaucho" out of his mouth. Everyone was either staring at their own hands, or at the story unfolding in the dregs of their coffee cups; or they were absorbed in the fragrance of their tobacco or the yearning for brandy. Robles had lost himself in the embers of the dying fire. Virginia McClellan was the first to look up. She saw a thin trickle of blood crawling out of Tossini's mouth and forming a red line across his lower chin.

"Oh my God, Bruce!" she whispered hoarsely. With that, every sober head turned first to Virginia and then to follow her horror-struck stare in the dim light of the dining room. Sticking out of Tossini's chest, a little below the breastbone, was six inches of arrowhead. The barb dripped blood, which made a spreading stain on the tablecloth. He pitched forward even as they looked across at him. His head struck a half-full bottle of wine, spilling claret over Mrs. McClellan's end of the table. Isabella was splattered liberally with the cold liquid and thought it was blood. She promptly fainted to the floor in a heap. Old Man Carrioli had a rude awakening as Mrs. Wisbey shattered the shocked lull with a piercing scream. He fought hard to remember where he was and why. It was just fifteen seconds since Tossini had uttered his last word.

Robles was the first to react.

"Douse all the lights! Quickly!"

McClellan snuffed out one pair of candles with his bare fingers. Fernando blew the others black.

"Everyone down on the floor and keep away from the windows!"

They all scrambled to the floor, Mrs. Wisbey feeling slightly ridiculous despite her terror.

The kitchen door opened, and a burst of light was hurled into the dining room like a grenade.

"Get down, man!" shouted McClellan, his voice gruff with alarm but under control. Alejo crouched to the floor with the others without knowing why. José, the cook, stepped up to the threshold between the two rooms. Robles leaped for the kitchen door and went through into the outer room in a dive. José looked down at him as though he were out of his mind.

"Kill every light in here! We are attacked by Indians!"

José's face turned white in horror. Robles took care of the lights himself as José sagged to the ground. By the time Robles had made it back to the front of the house on his hands and knees, McClellan had already taken hold of his Winchester. He was squatting in the corner over by the window through which Tossini had been shot. Alejo and José cowered on the floor with the others, their eyes wide and white with alarm. They were both staring at the arrow shaft sticking up from the humped back of the late chief of police at Tres Arboles.

McClellan had never been so comforted by anything as by the touch of the cold steel of his rifle barrel. He snapped a glance out the half-open window, but saw only the night.

"Alejito!" It was Robles's voice, hard and sharp in the darkness.

"Sí, señor?"

"How is he called, the cook?"

"He is José, señor."

"José! Crawl over by Alejo and me; on your belly, hijo."

José heard the command through a mist of panic. He did as he was told, wondering as he crawled what the others would say afterward about the noise his heart was making. Robles saw the two boys were still staring up at the arrow, even while he was talking to them. He would have to do something about the body.

"Alejo, you and José know the house and you also know exactly where the guns were put when the señores arrived. Mine is in the small bedroom, a handgun on a belt, and also a rifle. Listen to me well. Concentrate on what I am telling you!" Robles

111

had reached out and was shaking José lightly by the shoulder. "Get upstairs, both of you, and bring down all the rifles and ammunition, and don't forget my revolver. McClellan, do they know where you keep your spare ammunition?"

"There's a heap of it in one of the cupboards. Alejo knows which one. It won't be any use for the other guns. Wrong caliber."

The other men started to explain to the two youths where their saddlebags were and on which side the ammunition boxes were located. Robles again took command.

"Too complicated," he warned. "Just bring everything, rifles, bags, the lot. Work in the dark, by feel. Bar and shutter all the windows except two, one on the east side of the house and one on the west. Are there any spare guns in here?"

"No," from McClellan, "but you boys be sure and bring Tossini's rifle as well. You take it yourself, José."

"Get going!"

The boys scurried upstairs, and Robles worked his way around the dining table. He pulled the slumped corpse of the police chief to the floor and broke the fletched half of the arrow off where it had entered his back. Then he yanked at the linen tablecloth, sending glasses and coffee cups crashing to the floor. He used it to cover the body. It was a Tehuelche arrow all right. Robles could tell by the way it was fletched. My God, what a bow it must be to send an arrow through a man as big as Alfredo Tossini. Must have been shot from at least sixty yards away. There was no cover nearer than that.

The boys worked fast and well in the dark upstairs rooms. Within a few minutes they were ferrying jackets, saddlebags, rifles, and even hats down the curving ramp of the staircase. Robles took them and distributed the gear around. He felt a lot more in control of himself once he had buckled on the Colt revolver. It was very dark, and he had to lean across to the last embers of the fire to check that all six chambers were loaded. There were just twenty-five more rounds on the gun belt. He was the only one with a handgun.

"Alejo?"

"Sí?"

"Can you shoot a rifle?"

"Yes, señor Robles." The boy was crouched on the landing halfway up the stairs.

"Take my rifle then," Robles instructed, passing his Mannlicher butt-first to the boy. He gave him the only box of ammunition he had for it. "There is a shell in the breech already and the safety's on." Groping through the blackness, Robles noticed that the boy's hands were steady. The young servant was going to be very good. "I want you and José to remain upstairs, one at each of the two windows. Do not show yourselves too openly, but keep a close watch outside. Have you understood?"

"Clearly."

Robles turned back to the big room. Fernando had positioned himself at the other front window, left of the main door, and was looking out. Old Man Carrioli was setting a world's record for sobering up. He had his rifle at the ready by the side window. Wisbey had gone through into the kitchen to cover the back of the house. The ladies, including the now recovered Isabella, were huddled together.

"Stay low on the floor, señoras," Robles instructed them. "If you prefer to be in the kitchen, it is the same." The ladies clung together where they were in one corner of the dining room, alongside the dying fire.

With his night vision now fully adjusted to the gloom, Robles could see the shock in Isabella's eyes as they stared at the shrouded corpse of the dead man. A red stain was welling through the white cloth. Robles thought furiously. Why had he not fired warning shots to alert the hands in the bunkhouse? They might come running and be shot down, but sooner or later guns would be needed. Robles ran ideas around in his mind as he watched Fernando light up another cheroot. The young man blew out the match and inhaled on the tobacco with a deep breath that turned out to be his last.

CHAPTER SEVEN

HARKANA HAD LET A FULL fifteen minutes go by since killing the big silhouette in the window. He was a student of fear. He had seen it take shape and follow patterns in the hundreds of animals and scores of men he had slain. He wanted the fear to instill itself deep into the guts of the whites, as he knew it must.

Now Harkana was ready to give the signal for the fire arrows. It had all been so minutely planned. The Tehuelches who had gathered around him had wondered at the map of the farm that he scratched in the hard earth. They had never waged such detailed and meticulous warfare. Tehuelches were used to a signal, then a wild rush filled with battle cries and whoops and yells. Then the lances couched under their arms and driven low into the chests of the men who stood their ground and the backs of those who did not. Or the uncoordinated volleys of arrows that were loosed as fast as a man could pull a bow.

Now Harkana the Orphan had wrought a whole new way of making war, with a quiet deadliness that his men would soon learn to revere. Every man had been told in detail of the part he would play. It was all so well timed. And the men were not afraid to die. They were not afraid of the white man's thundersticks and the invisible death that they spat. But all save Raganor were a trifle unnerved by their leader's unemotional dealing out of death.

The Orphan had taken three men with him to a position across from the single well which sprouted from the center of the yard. Under Raganor, the old firemaker and all but half a dozen of the rest of the men had ghosted off to the right of the hill. Their bows could easily cover the rear of the hacienda, plus the stable and the storehouse. Six more of them worked their way to the east side of the corral. They led their horses far out from their target, for Harkana had told them that silence was of the essence. These men had got into position by the time the whites rose to begin their dinner. At a given signal, the fire would burst forth and the lighted fire arrows would arc across the whole compound, raining in from all four points of the compass at the same time to bury themselves in the roofs of the two illuminated buildings. Everything was at the ready before one spoonful of soup had been consumed in the main house. The Tehuelches waited on the ground as the wind ruffled the feathers of their long arrows.

Harkana had meant to give the signal soon after the lights went out inside the hacienda. It was then that a tiny pinprick of light caught his attention. A small moving flicker of light that flared momentarily in one of the front windows. Harkana screwed up his eyes in absolute concentration, waiting for the light to move again. He nonchalantly notched up a second arrow. The ember stabbed, flared more brightly, then settled down to a faint glow. Harkana brought the bowstring back to his lips with a sweeping pull of decision. His eyes narrowed to thin slits of black on white. He sighted just below the dull brand of red as it brightened fleetingly for the second time; then he let fly.

Fernando Carrioli made just one sound, like a violent hiccup, before he died with Harkana's long arrow through his throat.

"Fernando!" McClellan could see him lying there by the luminous wand of moonlight which had just risen through the gloom to rest up against the front side of his beleaguered hacienda. "My God, Robles, what's out there?"

"Tehuelches, McClellan. I told you, remember? Shot him by the light from his cheroot." Robles flung himself across the room and was just in time to stop Isabella from reaching the crumpled body. "He's dead, señora. *Lo siento,* I am truly sorry. There is nothing you or anyone else can do for him now. He never felt a thing, I can assure you. Señora McClellan, will you take her? Please?"

Virginia McClellan took hold of the frail body and put her arms around the shoulders of the world's most recent widow.

Isabella was too shocked even to cry. From future's dream she had suddenly and most horribly been plunged into a nightmare very much in the present. The tears would come later.

Robles broke off the barbed end of the arrow which protruded from the back of Fernando's neck. He pulled it out from the front and felt the blood warm the back of his hand. The shaft came out easily, but the sucking sound it made turned Robles's stomach, and he wished he had left it in. He looked around in a daze for something with which to cover the body. He used Fernando's own jacket, unhooking it from the back of the man's chair. It was just as he took Fernando's place at the window, with the dead man's rifle in his hand, that they all heard the sound that those who lived through the attack never forgot all their lives.

"Har-ka-na!"

It was a bloodcurdling, eerie, supernatural wail that came at them, first from a single savage throat and then from all around, reverberating out of the night on all sides of the besieged farmhouse. It made the intensity of their isolation almost impossible to contemplate. Robles smashed the rifle barrel through the pane of glass in the window and fired the gun at nothing in particular, just to break the screaming specter of doom. It would help inform the hands in the bunkhouse as well, he figured. It did. Pandemonium reigned in the gauchos' quarters.

Now all hell broke loose. Small spurts of flame appeared everywhere at once. The lights danced out in a circle. McClellan caught sight of a pair of dark legs running with a flaming arrow. He took hasty aim with his big Winchester '73, fired, and missed. He steadied himself more the second time, muttering words of determination. "Must not panic," he said out loud. He fired again at a moving target. This time he was rewarded by a scream, and the flame was doused immediately. Another straightway took its place. Small bunches of fire now homed in on the hacienda and the bunkhouse. The roof of the vaqueros' quarters was thinly planked and soon caught fire. That of the bigger house was timbered with broad beams and weatherproofed with a treatment which discouraged flames. Inside the bunkhouse, conditions were soon appalling. Smoke billowed from the roof, and the men fought in a curtain of darkness and choking fumes to find their weapons. As the heat became unbearable and the roof started to cave in, they burst out through the one and only door.

Harkana, who had held the great bow at full draw for well over a minute, loosed his arrow. Another man died. His body hit the dust of the yard, and over it thudded a whole volley of well-placed shafts that took a heavy toll of the cowhands. They were plainly lit by flames and the fast-rising moon, while the arrows zoomed in at them from the darkness. They fired off their guns, but there was nothing to take aim at. Six were dead, and the rest made for the corral. They found more Tehuelches waiting for them, but at least these could be seen running off the stock. The gauchos commenced firing as rapidly as they could load and re-load. The gunshots panicked the horses, and two broke loose as an Indian took a bullet through the head. The whites ran for the horses, their route decorated with fallen comrades. A handful of them made it to the corral and through the crisscrossed poles. There was no time for saddles. Two men got up, and a third rode double behind one of them. The fourth man dropped with a lance in his chest, his fall pushing it right through him as he died there in the dust. Then the gauchos were kicking the horses, but the doubled rider took an arrow just as he disappeared into the darkness beyond the flamelight.

The rest of the gauchos were either slain or sheltering behind the stock fences. Harkana picked two of them off from his hiding place near the well. This was enough to completely panic the remainder, who ran toward the hacienda. Fully lit up by the moonlight, they fell as easy targets to waiting Tehuelche bowmen, who shot them down without exposing themselves to the slightest danger. All of the remaining horses from the corral had been run off and were already being grouped by the handlers on the far side of the hill. The Orphan sent the men with him to Raganor, bearing a message which the lieutenant acted upon with alacrity.

Thus Harkana was left in the ring alone, facing the farmhouse, whose roof obstinately refused to burn. It was different with the bunkhouse. As the Tehuelche leader watched, the flames licked up to engulf it in a jungle of heat. The roof caved in, and the walls soon followed suit, buckling in the heat like melting choco-late bars.

McClellan had fired almost continually from his oblique angle.

He was the only man with enough ammunition to risk firing at fleeting shadows. He was pretty sure he had hit another man over by the corral, but he could not be positive. They were devilishly hard to draw a bead on, that much he was sure of. Even when the flames spread their arc of illumination over the battle scene, the Indians just floated back into deeper shadow. And those bows, God, but they were deadly. Quite as effective as any single-shot rifle over these ranges. Robles had been right.

The hooves of the escaping gauchos faded into the distance. The flames from the gutted bunkhouse began to die down. The moon was high now. It was the peak of the night. Nothing stirred. Nothing made a sound. McClellan sagged back from the window, his forehead charred with cordite and smudged with sweat. He wiped a raw hand across his eyes.

"I can't help wondering why we didn't get any warning," he groaned aloud to no one in particular. "What on earth were the guards doing, for Christ's sake?"

Robles looked across at him from the other front window.

"They were busy dying," he said, noticing the tightness in his own soft voice. He had watched the massacre feeling useless, just as McClellan had. He was glad of the silence now. He had to think, to work out what their chances were. God, but this band had been well organized. Someone with a brain behind it, someone out there. A Tehuelche out there plotting their destruction, thinking how to kill them all, just as Robles had to think how to survive. What would their leader do next? What was he after? How long till daybreak?

One way or another, it was all over for the ranch hands. The women were taking it well, but they hadn't seen what he and McClellan had seen. They had only heard the screams and seen the flare of the fire. They had avoided the sight of the gaucho burning alive as he ran from the bunkhouse, running and burning until Robles had put two bullets in him to put him out of his agony.

Robles was calculating. Three men had ridden away. They would head for the Wisbey spread. It was east, but how far east? A four-hour ride at a leisurely pace. They would go hell for leather even bareback. Help might return within five hours. It

118

would be light by then, all but an hour. What if they didn't make it? What of that? Well, there was nothing to do but wait and see. At least they couldn't be burned out. The dawn might drive the Indians off whether help arrived or not. It might and it might not. Daylight gave them targets for their rifles, but what was to stop the Tehuelches from starving them out? No, they wouldn't work that way. Not their style. A quick, highly lethal raid under cover of night and then back across the river and south at full speed on the spare horses. Dawn should save them, if they survived to see it. Robles pulled out his pipe and tobacco pouch; then he remembered Fernando and put them away again. It was going to be a long night.

Following Harkana's explicit instructions, Raganor had set out after the fleeing vaqueros. He rode fast, with his twenty men spread out in a phalanx. The moon illuminated the tracks. One set was a trifle deeper than the other, showing which mount bore the double load.

Tehuelches were master trackers. They could tell not only how many animals had passed in a certain direction but also how long ago, how fast they were traveling, the weight they were carrying, and where they had paused along the way. Tehuelches could track anything over any kind of terrain: man or beast, rock or grass, fresh or wounded, enemy or prey. And they never gave up until they had killed what it was they were pursuing.

This was so easy, for there was a blood spoor as well as the moon to guide them. Three miles out from the estancia they came across the dead body of the wounded man. Then there were but two, and the speed picked up a little. The wings of the Tehuelche posse drew in like buffalo horns. When they knew they were very close, Raganor sent half a dozen on ahead at tangents to the path. He remained with the balance of his troops, riding at a canter behind the tracker, who sometimes loped along on foot, sometimes hung down from the back of his horse. As one man tired, another took over the task. They pursued like a pack of wild dogs, never changing the pace, never varying their intent. They caught them after six miles.

The two gauchos were sweating profusely, but the night air

119

had cooled them, as had their fear. As the hacienda and the dreadful scenes dropped away, mile after mile, they began to breathe more easily. Their faces were blackened by smoke. One of them, McClellan's head man, had been scorched on one side of his face. Part of his hair had been singed away. The pain was intense as he cantered along the rough track which led to the Wisbey estancia.

They stopped just once. Finding that the wounded man was dead, they left him behind. Both of them wondered how he had managed to remain on the horse for so long. They rode with their heads down. The horses needed little guidance. The track was obvious. It was east all the way. The moon shone ever more brightly. The stars melted if you looked at them long enough. The two men let their concentration wander. They had been the only two to get away. Imagined sounds shredded their nerves. Would arrows come out of the darkness to lay a last claim on their hard-bitten lives? Was there anyone out there? Or were the Tehuelches only interested in the big house of the patrón and his fine bloodstock, which they had run off to the badlands farther south?

The men cantered nearly six miles before they found out the answers. The head gaucho chanced to look up and saw a ring of Tehuelche warriors about thirty yards ahead. He had heard nothing. He yanked on the reins of his horse. His companion jerked from his dreams back into the harsh hopelessness of reality. Neither man made a move toward his loaded rifle.

The head gaucho let his gun slide to the ground. His amigo did the same. Raganor studied them closely, like a butterfly collector confronted with a rare new breed. He was flanked by five men on each side. They all had arrows nocked on their bowstrings. Behind the two whites, ten additional dog soldiers had ridden in quietly to surround them. The gauchos looked at each other, then back to the enemy. They raised their hands above their heads. The reason for this strange gesture continued to baffle Raganor long after he had taken both their lives and their horses.

Raganor rode back to find Harkana and the rest of the men. As he skirted the compound his eyes took in the scene of pillage and death. The fires had burned down to a smoulder. The carcass of the bunkhouse stood smoking, the bones of its timbers reduced to charcoal, the ashes of its walls strewn among the dust of the yard. The corral was empty. The only vestige of a hundred hooves were the heaps of cold dung that told of the stock that had been taken and dispatched south.

"How goes it, lord?" Raganor greeted his chief.

"Better for seeing you alive and well, brave Raganor. Tell me of the three who escaped."

"They all now sleep in the bosom of the moon, lord. See, I have retrieved the bodies as you instructed."

"Good, Raganor," said the Orphan. "Come and share my water gourd with me while I tell you how we may yet use the remaining hours of darkness to our advantage. I have a plan."

The roof of the stout hacienda was charred and seared but still held solidly. There was no danger of it collapsing. So Robles was content to sit it out and await help to come galloping in from the east. Another hour went by; and another. They would be in sight of the Wisbey spread by now. If the two of them had ridden hard and kept cool heads they would very soon be explaining what was wrong. In another couple of hours the riders would be there, three at the most. So would the dawn. If they saw another dawn then surely they would survive. Too many ifs, thought Robles. What if the gauchos had been caught? What if they were lying face down on the pampas with the hard stubble of grass stalks threading their hair as they lay lifeless for the birds to find in the morning? It was such a desolate area. And so quiet now after the battle and the blaze had both subsided. The silence was getting to them all. Robles half preferred the clamor of the attack to waiting for something to happen. If the gauchos had failed to get through, well, what then? People didn't just happen by out here. Suppose they were cut off for days? Suppose the Tehuelches really did lay siege to the place and try to starve them out? What was to stop them?

Robles left his post at the front of the house and went upstairs. José spun to face him when he heard the tread of his footsteps on the stairs.

"Easy, hombre," Robles soothed him, "calm yourself. I am Robles. How goes it with you two?" He had groped his way into the door of the main bedroom, the big bedroom that the McClellans used. It was a long, narrow room, spanning the whole width of the house.

It was little Alejo who answered him. "We live," he remarked phlegmatically.

"Who was at the window facing east?" asked Robles, working on taking their minds off the isolation of the situation.

"Me, señor," admitted the houseboy.

Robles felt his way along the wall of the unfamiliar room. Then he could make out the profile of the boy's head in the dimness.

"Let us exchange rifles, Alejo. I feel more comfortable with my own weapon. Here, you take this one instead. What did you see of the men who got away?" He was trying to keep his voice level and his inquiry as casual as if he were asking the time of day.

Alejo was disturbed by the thought of whose rifle it was that he now held across his knees. But he forced his brain away from that topic and worked on Robles's question. It was easy to remember what he had seen.

"They made it, I think. There were two horses, señor Robles. One of them was your own chestnut mare. I recognized it clearly in the light from the fires. Three men rode out. One was Tomás, the head man on the rancho. The others I did not get a good look at. He that rode double behind Tomás took an arrow in the back as they disappeared from sight. Yet I did not see him fall. That is all."

"Did you see any Tehuelches take out after them?"

"No, sir."

"How far is it to the nearest estancia, José?" Robles already knew the answer to that question. McClellan had told him the details earlier on. He just wanted to keep the conversation going, to bring José into it. A plan was forming in his mind. It was a contingency plan; a very risky contingency plan. It would call for a lot of nerve, and the boys might need a boost to theirs, not to mention his own. Yes indeed, so might you, Robles told himself. First things first, Manuel. It may not prove necessary. Aye, but if it is? Time alone would tell.

"Four hours, I calculate, señor Robles," José put in. "Due east to the spread of señor Wisbey, the inglés, you know?"

"I know."

Robles would wait for two more hours; then he would try to get them out of it the only way he could. His plan needed the cover of darkness, so he could not wait longer than two hours. Anyway, if help did not come in that time, then it wasn't coming, not ever. Yes, he decided, looking at his pocket watch, then you will do it, Manuel. And if you are blessed with good fortune, maybe you will succeed. And if you are very lucky into the bargain, maybe you won't get yourself killed, you educated half-breed.

"How about making us all some coffee, Alejito? I will take your place up here for a while."

"Yes, señor."

"How much water is there in the house, my boy?"

"A single full pail. The well is right outside the door, so we seldom keep much indoors."

"And food?"

"The remains of the asado, some cheese, a few potatoes. Everything else is in the storehouse."

"No matter. Off you go then. You may light a candle in the kitchen as long as you keep the shutters and the connecting door closed."

"Sure. Coffee coming up right away. Now then, how many are we?" He began counting on his fingers. "Eight cups, is that correct?" He was asking nobody in particular.

"You have left out yourself and José."

"But we cannot take coffee with the patrón and his guests, señor Robles. It would make the señora very angry."

"You're not servants now, son. Not tonight, anyhow. You're just two more scared fighting men fighting for their lives. Make coffee for everybody. We will all need it before this night gets much older."

"If you say so, señor Robles. Ten cups it is then." Alejo leaned his rifle against the window ledge and started for the door of the bedroom.

"Better make that nine cups, Alejito."

The boy looked not at Robles, but at the rifle he had just put down.

"Who owned the rifle, señor Robles?"

"Fernando Carrioli," Robles said with a shrug, watching the boy's eyes widen. "He got something caught in his throat," the boy heard him say, cynically.

Alejo felt his way downstairs and out into the kitchen.

"Did you ever kill a man, señor Robles?" José asked him as soon as the boy had left.

"Yes."

"Was it easy or was it hard?"

"It was either him or me. There was no time to think at the time, son. It all happened so fast that I shot first and analyzed it later. In fact, I thought about it a lot since then. So I suppose you might say that it was a case of easy to do and a lot harder to live with."

"Are you scared now, señor?"

"Sure. The man who wouldn't be scared at a time like this just hasn't been born. Sure I'm scared. Scared as hell."

"It's just that, well . . ."

"Come along now, you can speak your mind plainly to me. I am not one of the patróns, remember?"

"This I know," José told him, as if it was the supreme accolade. "You are different from the others, Don Manuel. Alejo and I were saying so before the dinner tonight. And, well, I was asking about fear because, well, you don't seem to show it. Not like the others or me or Alejo, I mean. Even señor McClellan, he was real afraid. I could see it in his eyes when I first came into the room after Don Alfredo had been killed. But then I looked at your face and it was under control. I thought then that maybe you had been through a lot of situations like this one. Either that or you are a very brave man."

Robles sat silently, looking out the eastern window. The stars floated across his field of vision. There was not a sound. It was achingly quiet and taut, like an unplucked harp string.

"I was in the army for a while, José. I got used to blood and guns in those years, I imagine. As for being brave, well, one should never sum up a man's courage or lack of it too quickly,

124

eh? Every man is braver than some and less brave than others. You can never quite tell what a man will or will not do until the time comes. You and Alejo are doing just fine, okay?"

"Okay, and thanks. Here he comes with the coffee."

Alejo stepped gingerly into the room with three steaming mugs of black coffee in his hands. He put one on the floor at the feet of Manuel de Robles. Then he went over to sit beside José.

"How are things downstairs?" Robles inquired. He sipped at the scalding coffee and felt the heat warm the pit of his stomach. It tasted very good.

"Quiet, señor. When I returned upstairs, everyone was just sipping the coffee and watching. Even the old man is cold sober now. Is your coffee all right, señor Robles? There is more sugar if you would like."

"It's just fine the way it is, thank you."

"What do you think will happen now, Don Manuel?" asked José timorously.

Robles had for a long time been hoping that no one would ask him that particular question.

"Well, if Tomás and the others made it safely to the Wisbey estancia then help should already be on the way. If they ride hard, they will be here pretty soon, say a couple more hours."

"And if they didn't get away?" the young man wondered out loud.

"Then we have to think of something else. Tell you what, boys, what do you say that we let the time run out for the help to arrive before we start worrying over that. I have something in mind, all right? Let's hope that we won't have to chance it."

"Sure thing" José said.

"Vamos a ver" from Alejo.

All three fell quiet for a while, save for the slurping sounds each made as he sucked up his coffee from the big enameled mugs.

A half hour passed before Robles consulted his timepiece again. He was careful to recede into an unexposed corner of the room before he lit a match, which he cupped in his free hand. There was still over an hour to go before he would make his move. Better get back downstairs, he decided.

"I think I can hear horses!" cried Alejo. He had sharp ears.

They all listened intently. José heard them too. Then Manuel caught on to the unmistakable clop of hooves walking across the yard.

"Back to your posts, you two!" he ordered, grabbing up his rifle. "Keep your eyes open." Robles moved to the door of the room. "Sing out if you see anything," he tossed back over his shoulder. Then he was hurrying down the stairs into the living room.

"Can you see anything, McClellan? We heard horses."

"Two riders, señor Robles!" yelled José from the upstairs room. "And Indians they are not, señor."

"Yes!" echoed the Scotsman. "Just coming out into the moonlight. I think it's Tomás and Julio. They made it back. Must have brought Wisbey's bunch along with them. Hey, Percy, it's going to be all right!"

"Thank God!" Wisbey rejoiced. He seemed elated, and the tension that had amassed during the night oozed out of him.

Robles reached the front window and took in the scene for himself. Something was wrong. The two riders were coming in, all right, riding almost casually across the longest diagonal of the compound. He did not know the men by sight, but he recognized his gallant little chestnut mare. There was no way that the horse had run all the way to Wisbey's place and then back again. It was not in the least lathered up. He had quartered his horse in the main corral along with the working stock. That was where his contingency plan began, for the Tehuelches had overlooked all of the other guests' mounts, which were still enclosed in the stable, as were McClellan's stallion and the little colt that his wife rode when she had to ride something. They had mounts for them all, what with Tossini and Carrioli dead. All he had to do was go get them. He watched the two riders as they wandered haphazardly toward the house, lolling slightly in their saddles.

Saddles! That was it. McClellan moved to the door, but Robles leaned over and put his hands on the plank which barred it.

"Those are my men out there," protested the Scot indignantly. "That man on the left is my head gaucho, Tomás. They got away, remember?"

126

"They did no such thing. They are both dead, McClellan. Look at them closely. The Tehuelches got saddles from somewhere, probably your own storehouse, and tied their bodies in place. If you recall, the men escaped bareback."

"No, they can't be." McClellan just did not want to believe it.

"They can and they are, señor McClellan. I'm sorry. The only place they could have got saddles themselves was at the Wisbey spread. Even if they rode like devils all the way there and back in less than three and a half hours, they certainly could not have done it without fresh mounts. And those are the same horses that they rode out on. I know the mare on the left. I've owned it for seven years."

McClellan half collapsed back against the door, deflated by acute despair. His buoyant mood was punctured like a balloon. "Oh, Christ Almighty!" he breathed. "What on earth do we do now?"

"Pull yourself together, man," said the Argentine. "Get back to the window. We're not dead yet. Hurry up!"

McClellan slid along the floor and pushed himself back up into a sitting position in the corner by the window. Robles took over the other lookout point, his heart and his thoughts moving quickly. A modified plan was taking shape in his head.

"Are you sure?" asked the dazed McClellan, still distrustful of reality.

"Look at the angle of their heads," Robles instructed.

"So—they will starve us out. Is that their game?"

"I don't know, hombre, I just don't know. But it would be a mistake now to wait and find out. That little mare out there knows me well. Will probably come over when it hears the sound of my voice. I'm going to try for it and then get across to where the rest of the horses are. If I can make it to the stable and back again, maybe we'll have a chance to ride out of here. The timing should be perfect. Still dark when I make the move. Light when we make a run for it. If I make it to the stable all right then I'll bring the horses around to the back door. Get everybody in there and tell them to be ready to go. You and I will try to hold off any pursuit, since we have the Colt and the Winchester. I have a suspicion that the Tehuelches won't carry this thing through into broad daylight, but I could be wrong. I wouldn't want to push my luck on a life-and-death matter, but, bearing in mind that they will be saving some of the horses for the return ride across the river, I think it's an even gamble. Worth a try, anyway."

"Let me go," said McClellan. "This is my estancia they are ruining"; then, lowering his voice: "and my wife they will kill after they've raped her."

"You're wrong about that. Tehuelches don't go in for that sort of thing. They treat their own women very well. War is war to them. The only atrocity they would bother to commit is to torture someone who had information that they had to have at any cost. There's no fear of that either, since none of us knows a single word of their language, nor one of them a word of ours. Besides, I can't think of anything that we know which might remotely interest them."

"Then what do they want from us?"

"They want us to die, McClellan. It's as straightforward as that. So I'll go. It's my horse and it'll be skittish already, what with the fire and the smell of blood. Just get ready to give covering fire if necessary. Let them make the first move, okay?"

"Robles," McClellan said thickly, "whatever our differences, you are a brave man."

"It's purely a matter of logistics, señor McClellan."

Robles left him and went over to the remains of the fire. He began blacking his face and hands with ash. By the time he got back to the front window the moon was sinking fast, casting dappled shadows in front of the house. He called to the mare in a low and gentle voice. It responded immediately, pricking up its ears and turning to face the sound. He called it again, and the mare started to approach, bearing its ghastly burden. Robles went out the front door on all fours, knife in one hand, the Colt in the other. His heart pounded like a kettledrum and he felt his hands shaking. Brave man indeed, he mocked himself. If I get through this the first thing I shall do is throw up.

He rolled to where the horse was standing and used its bulk to cover himself. Quickly, he cut the thongs which held the dead man in place, easing the body to the ground to muffle the noise.

Then he mounted the horse as fast as he could and began to drift with just a vague tap of his heels toward the stable. The black shape of the building loomed out of the darkness ahead of him. There was one patch of moonlight on the way, where the shadows thrown by the buildings did not reach. He rode on through it very slowly, resisting the urge to kick the horse. He tried to imitate the lolling head of the dead cowhand. This is it, he thought, trying not to think about what it would feel like to have a three-foot arrow rammed through his chest with the force of a pile driver. Then he was in shadow again, his luck still holding. At the barn door he was able to lift the catch and ride inside without dismounting. Manuel de Robles breathed the biggest sigh of relief in Patagonia for many years when he had secured the stable door behind him.

It was black as coal inside but he was familiar with its geography, having been in there a number of times during his stay. It took him the best part of an hour to saddle all the horses. The dead men's would serve for the two boys. Nobody would have to double up. It just might work.

The moon had now sunk from sight. There was less than an hour to go before dawn. McClellan would have made sure that everyone knew exactly what they had to do. He would be on guard at the front window, with the others packed into the kitchen, ready to come out the back.

Bruce McClellan was at that precise moment wiping the sweat from his forehead with the back of his hand. The hand went straight back to the trigger guard of the Winchester. The man's eyes never left the stable door on the far side of the compound for more than one swift glance around the yard. All was quiet. Was he the only one watching the stable door for Robles to reappear with the horses? Or were the Tehuelches just biding their time out there in the inky darkness that was soon to lift? Maybe they were just waiting for them to be clear targets, their hands full of reins, and then they would shoot them down and steal the last of his stock. Anyway, they were committed now, for there was no way to stop Robles from coming through the stable door.

When the gate did swing back on its heavy hinges, McClellan

saw it happening. Suddenly there were horses ghosting slowly across his field of vision, making for the back of the house. Thank God he had oiled those hinges just last month!

"He's on his way," he whispered to Alejo, who knelt by the connecting door. The houseboy passed the word to the others. Wisbey opened the back door just a crack. He watched Robles advancing across the space which divided them. He was halfway across. The distance halved again and still there was no sound except the gentle clop of hooves on dirt. Robles made it all the way across and knew that no one's luck could be that good. He had been quiet, but he had made a mountain of noise by Tehuelche standards. Either they had pulled out or they were waiting, using the time that was on their side. His nerves tingled on raw ends.

José came out and held the fistful of bridles while Robles got down and tied up his mare very tightly to the hitching rail. Then he did the same with McClellan's black stallion. He signaled for the others to mount up. The women came first. They were doing well, Robles thought. Just as planned, without panic. These people were going very strong. Wisbey and Old Man Carrioli heaved themselves up into saddles and immediately took over their rifles from the boys. José was next up. Mrs. McClellan started to file out. It was two hundred yards to the cover of the high grasses which would swallow their flight. The others followed her. God, they've gone, Robles told himself—they must have. Bruce came through to the back door and nodded for Alejo to proceed. The boy was halfway up into his saddle when the three of them who remained heard a swooping rush of air and the boy came back off the stirrup with an arrow through his heart. Robles caught him before he hit the ground, then let the lifeless body drop and fired his revolver three times into the air. The night broke open with screams and yells.

"Ride on! Ride on out!" yelled Robles, firing another round at the sky. He heard the boom of McClellan's Winchester beside him and saw his wife look back once as she kicked her horse into a gallop. Then Manuel de Robles turned to face the Tehuelches, seeing only empty horses streaming toward him.

"Shoot the horses, man! Shoot them down!"

McClellan opened up and Robles, using his left hand under the Colt for steadier aim, fired off the last two chambers of the handgun as the Indians, screened on the blind side of their mounts, burst from the brush in pursuit of the fleeing whites. McClellan worked the lever action as rapidly as he could, bringing down two horses.

"Reloading," called out Robles, leaning back against the outside wall of the hacienda. McClellan picked off one of the Indians as the man scrambled to his feet with his horse dead under him. Robles fought to reload in feverish haste, noticing that his hands were performing well now that the waiting had broken open into life-or-death action. With three chambers primed, he loosed off two quick shots, and a third horse fell.

Harkana, mounted on the incomparable Zorkan Rood, came at the back of his pack of six men. He cleared one of the dead horses in a low leap and then reached down and plucked one of the horseless men from the ground as if he were a young child. He seemed to give himself so much time to complete this maneuver, but in fact it was accomplished in a couple of breathtaking seconds. The warrior clambered to a sitting position on the hindquarters of the gray stallion just as McClellan fired at Harkana. The warrior took the bullet meant for his leader. It blew away the back of the man's head, and his body crashed earthward. This time he stayed where he fell.

Raganor had by this time reached the tail of the white riders and Old Man Carrioli was done for, though he rode on even with Raganor's spear buried between his shoulder blades.

Harkana called out. Raganor and the remaining two warriors who were still mounted heard the instruction and turned back away from the guns. The last of the whites had vanished into the long grass. Harkana turned Zorkana Rood and exploded back at a gallop to pick up the third surviving horseless warrior. The man was on his feet and reaching for an arrow in his quiver.

Robles rammed two more cartridges into his gun and fired three shots at Raganor's departing trio. He spun to face the Indian on foot, and the gun clicked on an empty chamber as the man drew back the bow. McClellan swore an English oath as he too was forced to reload. The man on foot had them cold.

Several things happened simultaneously. A yell from Harkana and then the warlord was lifting the archer just as the arrow sped on its way. It took Robles in the right shoulder, the impact knocking him back against the house. He dropped the empty Colt. He failed to hold back a loud gasp of pain and shock. McClellan spared him a rapid glance and saw the arrow in his companion. With the rifle fully loaded once more, McClellan threw it to his shoulder, but failed to draw a bead on Harkana, who vanished into the darkness, still grasping the other Indian in his arms. McClellan held his fire.

"Hit badly?"

"Bad enough. Gone right through." Robles reached for the revolver by his side but sagged back with his own mode of cursing as the pain rushed up the right side of his whole body. "McClellan, I think they've finally pulled out, at least for the time being. I counted only a handful, and two of them are on their last journey already. We should make a run for it."

"Can you ride with that?"

"It's either that or die trying. Can you get me on the horse?"

McClellan snapped out of his shocked lethargy, shoved the Colt into Robles's holster, and dropped the last two boxes of his own ammunition inside his shirt. He hated to put the rifle down, but was forced to lean it against the wall in order to hoist the wounded man. It was quite a struggle for the Scot to lift Robles to his feet and assist him, half carrying, half dragging him to the mare. Robles got his left foot in the stirrup and his left hand on the saddle horn. He made it up with a shove from McClellan, but the pain in his shoulder burst like a firework, showering his upper right side with hot needles. He managed to resist vomiting but knew he was losing a lot of blood from the exertion. He could feel it stickying up inside his shirt.

"Should I take the arrow out, hombre?" McClellan needed to be told.

"No, leave it in. I'll bleed to death if you open up the wound."

Robles kicked feebly at his horse and moved out of the compound as the winter sun blossomed above the hard line of the eastern horizon. Is this your last sunrise? Robles asked himself.

McClellan raced back to collect his rifle, unhitched the black horse from the rail, and swirled up into the saddle as the horse shied from him. He kicked it hard in the tracks of the chestnut. He caught Robles at a canter and passed him as they entered the realm of the high grasses, still following the narrowest of tracks single file. Half a mile along, McClellan was out on the open plain. He stopped, craning his neck to see ahead. There was no sign of the others. They had at least a ten-minute start on them. It was broad daylight by then, and there was still no further sign of any Tehuelches. McClellan felt the stress and strain of the night driving him to gallop east, to catch up with the other survivors, to be with his wife. But Robles could advance only at a walk. He was bleeding heavily.

Robles reached him, wincing in pain, breathing in flurries.

"You ride on ahead, McClellan. Get help. Come back for me. I'll follow at my own pace. Nothing you can do for me anyway." The Argentine was all hunched up over the neck of his compact horse. "Go on, do as I tell you. Senseless for you to stick around. If they hit us again we will both die uselessly. Take off, and I'll meet you on the way back. Your place is with your wife. The women only have Wisbey and José with them now."

"Old Man Carrioli's a veteran Indian fighter and a steady man when he's sober. A crack shot with that old gun of his." McClellan, who had not seen Carrioli wounded, was aware that he was trying to convince himself as much as the other man.

"Not anymore, he isn't," Robles stated bitterly. "Look up there."

The shaft of Raganor's lance stuck up vertically through the flattened grass of the trail they were following. McClellan spurred his mount over to the body and jumped down to make a brief inspection. Manuel reached him again with an effort, just as the rancher was climbing back into the saddle.

"He's dead," McClellan informed him, unnecessarily.

"And so might we be if you don't get out of here and get help. It's not heroic, McClellan, just plain common sense."

"If you're sure. Listen, Robles, just keep heading due east and you can't help but meet us on the way out from the Wisbey spread."

Robles nodded, beginning to feel dizzy. His pain was acute, but not obviously so.

"Get gone, hombre. If they come back for you, run for it.

Stop and fight and you're as good as dead, even with that rifle of yours. See you later."

"*Hasta luego,* Robles—*y suerte.*"

McClellan knew that if he thought about what he was doing any longer he would never go. So he kicked the spurs hard into his animal's flanks, and the horse reared ahead. It galloped off with all the speed its fresh limbs could muster.

Robles sat astride his little mare, watching them go until they dissolved among the lapping waves of the pampas.

CHAPTER EIGHT

WINTER WASHED OVER THE Andean highlands, sprinkling the forests below the timberline with a talcum of snow. The wily old mountain lion had lived through many such seasonal changes. Age had taken a heavy toll on both its speed and strength. Its natural camouflage was lost during the snow-filled months, and hunting became that much harder. It managed to bring down only one mangy guanaco as it followed the game along traditional routes through the crystalline conifers to lusher, more sheltered pastures.

A week went by without a successful kill, and the lion pushed deeper into the foothills. Surprising a rival in the act of scent-marking its own territory, the old male was forced to fight a short but furious battle, and was lucky to escape with a bad wound. One of its hind legs had been bitten to the bone. Several more meatless days followed while the scarred old cougar licked its wounds. Forced to travel again or starve, it abandoned its natural terrain and limped on in search of food.

Hampered by the ache that never dulled, slowed by the tendons that never healed, the lion grew thinner day by day. Its frustrated pursuits of fleet game left it panting and ravenous. It ate the rotting remains of a dead rodent, but this was no more than a comma in the long chapter of its hunger.

Moving on relentlessly, emaciated to the point of desperation, the lion eventually broke out of the long-shadowed cover of the trees and entered the plains country. It had been four days without meat when it tried to take a sheep from a pen on a white man's farm. It succeeded in the kill, for the panic-stricken flock had no place to hide or to run. Yet the farmer had come out with his rifle and fired off three quick shots, causing the cat to drop the carcass and clear the stockade in a graceful bound. But it had learned how easily domesticated animals could be slain. From the crest of a singularly defined hill, the mountain lion surveyed another white man's farm, much farther north. The fires made it nervous. The hunger of a whole week without meat made it reckless. Flowing like smoke down the hillside, the cat skirted the blaze and began a circle far out around the area filled with such strange sounds and smells. Then it picked up the scent of blood, fresh blood, and instead of closing in on the corral in search of livestock, the lion followed the spoor eastward as the sun began to rise.

Mingled with the scent of the blood of Manuel de Robles was the heavy man-smell. Normally the cat would have shied away from such a threatening taint, but the madness of hunger was upon it. Ignoring the smells of gun oil, sweat, and leather, the cat fell in on the spoor, crawling low-bellied, crouching and flattened against the earth.

Harkana replenished the arrows in his quiver, then sent Raganor and the remainder of his men south. He gave them orders to overtake the men with the captured horses and to ride nonstop after the migrating tribe. Raganor was too perfect the lieutenant to inquire as to why his lord was not riding with them. Swinging his own horse away, Raganor left the Orphan sitting astride Zorkan Rood, his waving arm signaling the men to follow him.

Harkana set out on Zorkan Rood in the direction of the escaping white men. The first sign of their flight that he came across was the body of Old Man Carrioli, with Raganor's spear still protruding, mastlike, from it. A large bird of prey ejected from the stiffening corpse as the Indian rode up at a walk. It beat its way into the layers of the sky. Harkana did not pause at the dead body. He just looked down as he rode by, noticing that both eyes had already been plucked from their sockets. Soon the birds would return to the carcass and finish their meal.

Robles drifted in thermals of consciousness. The wound was such that it could not be bound with a tourniquet. His right side was so stiff that he was unable to turn his head to see the gaping hole in his back where the arrow had come through. He knew he was weakening fast, and wondered if he was going to die. Passing out briefly for the second time, he slid from the saddle. The fall brought him back to his senses. His loyal little chestnut mare had kept faithfully to the thin trickle of the track which led east to the Wisbey hacienda, and the gallant horse stood over him, perplexed and troubled, waiting for its master to rise. Manuel drifted away yet again until the animal uttered a snort of alarm that brought him back to reality. The mare stood with nostrils flared, disquieted and afraid of the scent it was catching. Feeling useless, Robles could do nothing to stop the horse from taking off, and he was suddenly left very alone. Slowly, painfully, he crawled on his left side to a nearby rock, against which he delicately propped himself in such a position that he could look along both the east and west approaches to the trail. It was a great day for dying, he conjectured. His papa had died on a day full of storm and thunder, with the rain cavorting down the roof of his cabin. Manuel had a sudden picture of his father, riding through the heavy thornbush found in so many places in Mendoza province. The rider had guardamontes surrounding his own legs and the forelegs and chest of his horse. The leather flaps were deeply scratched and scarred, as was the weather-beaten face of the aging horseman. Rafael de Robles had had a good life, despite the hardship and the ups and downs. Sixty years in the incomparable arena of the big outdoors, watching the grapes grow up each season, nurturing them through drought and the occasional whip-lashing rainstorm. Flanked by the enamel teeth of the Andes on one side and the pitiless desert on all others, Rafael had worked hard to produce a sound vintage of wine and family.

Manuel's mother had died peacefully in her sleep a couple of hard and lonely years after her husband's last bout of sickness. Now, only his slightly younger sister remained in the area they both knew as home, married to a neighbor's son. They farmed a large portion of the original Robles holding, while a quarter of the acreage had been sold off. Robles had been thinking that he must pay Carmen a visit. It had been far too many years. Now, lying in the dirt of the southern pampas with his head propped up against a boulder, Manuel was beginning to realize that he had left it too late. What convinced him most of all was picking out the green eyes of the crouching puma in the tall waving grasses that hemmed the narrow trail.

Robles felt his heart begin to pound, and the thought came to him that he would pump his lifeblood even faster from his body as the organ's fist clenched and unclenched in fear. He wondered how long the cat had been there, watching him through those vomit-colored slits. It was twenty-five yards away but crawled in closer as soon as Robles took his eyes from it to reach for his gun.

Using his left hand, the man managed to get the revolver free of its holster. His right arm had completely mutinied by then, disobeying even the orders of pain. With a great effort, Robles brought up his left knee and tried to steady his whole but unpracticed limb against it. He stared down the foresight at the cat waiting to strike. The bead on the end of the Colt's barrel wavered to and fro. Cursing his faintness, Robles controlled his aim more by willpower than muscle. He saw the cat belly-crawl another couple of yards toward him. It was obviously starving, spurred to attack man by the pangs of famine. Robles squeezed the trigger, knowing that even if he missed, which he was very likely to do, the report would probably be enough to frighten the carnivore away. Only there was no report. There was nothing but the snap-click of the hammer falling on an empty chamber. He pulled the trigger again and then a third time. Christ Jesus! How could he have forgotten? Forgot to load your gun, Manuel; a man's mistake in the heat of a battle, your ability marred by pain and blood. Well, you will no doubt pay for that mistake with your life. And a great coldness of purpose came over him as he stared at the small beige head with its flattened ears and jade orbs. The puma bared its teeth under pink-and-black gums, lashing once with its tail as if to give it the courage to advance further under the scrutiny of its wounded prey.

Have to reload, Robles decided. Reaching around his gun belt with the one good hand, he located a cartridge with his fingers and drew it from the loop. He kept his eyes screwed into the cat's all the time. But now he had to avert his stare to slot the bullet home, and Robles felt the animal come closer, fanning the flame of death. His fingers hurried to push the cartridge into a chamber, but he could neither do it blind nor take his eyes from the cat just fifteen yards away. He imagined the raking claws ripping at his abdomen and the fetid breath up over his face before the white incisors sank into his flesh. Robles dropped the bullet in a spasm of clumsiness, and it rolled across his lap and fell into the stubbly grass beneath his crotch.

The cat was so close now that Robles was able to see the muscles of its hind legs bunching for the spring. In one last vision of life Manuel gazed at the clarity of the sky, which suddenly became blocked from his view.

It all happened so quickly. The cat signaled the spring with a low growl, but Robles, gaping in fascinated horror, saw it clawing at its own chest instead of his. It gurgled rather than growled, and failed to stand or to flee. Somewhere between the frantic paws he caught a glimpse of gray and white feathers. Then the overcast sky moved above him and four gray-white legs strode past his line of vision. The giant in the saddle blocked out the sun as he leaped lightly from the stallion, spear in one hand, bow in the other. He sauntered over to the mortally wounded mountain lion and rummaged the point of his spear in its heart, twisting it as it found its mark. The cat squirmed to get at the man behind the spear but then twitched and died, almost gratefully.

When Harkana turned around, Robles recognized him.

"This time it is you that is without arrows," the Indian pointed out in very passable Spanish. Seeing the wounded man's amazement, Harkana nodded his head. "Yes, white man, I speak your tongue."

The Orphan came over to him, leaving the spear and the great bow on the ground. The first thing he did was to kneel next to Robles and twist the gun from his enfeebled fingers. Then the small knife which Robles had tucked away on his belt was removed and tossed aside. The Orphan had not come to save this man's life at the expense of his own.

"You speak Spanish? But how? Where?" Robles could hardly cope with more extremes of living in the same period of twenty-four hours.

"No talk now," ordered the Indian. "You are dying, white man. Let me see."

The Tehuelche lifted the man forward and saw where the arrow had done the worst of its damage. He snapped the arrowhead off where it had come clean through, then leaned Robles back against the boulder with exquisite gentleness.

"No move," he said, looking Manuel in the eyes for the first time. The Argentine saw an expressionless face, but he knew what he was going to do. Harkana placed his left hand flat against the wounded shoulder, the fingers parted around the shaft, which he drew out in one swift pull with his right hand. Robles gasped and vomited down his shirt front. Then he fainted very briefly. When he came to, the Orphan was approaching with the mare led by the bridle. Robles marveled at the complete relaxation with which his mare behaved. Tehuelches know all there is to know about horses and more, he recalled.

Harkana tied the long length of bridle to his ankle while he stooped over the wounded white man and lifted him without even a trace of effort, using only one hand. Robles, who tipped the scales at one hundred sixty pounds, remembered the trouble McClellan had had getting him up into the saddle. The Orphan not only threw him up with obvious ease but also cushioned him against the shock of the movement.

Then the Indian vaulted onto the back of Zorkan Rood and led the mare half a mile to the southeast, where there was a small pool of clear water. On the way, Harkana looked back over his shoulder every so often, checking that Robles was still conscious. Having carried Robles to the water's edge, he broke up the thin film of ice on the surface. The first thing that Harkana did was to cut away the bloodstained shirt and wash off the clusters of clotted blood all around the wound. The water revived Robles like a mild electric shock. Gathering fresh mud on a tuft of grass, the Indian closed the wound, smearing the clay-based mud over the small circular hole where the arrow had pierced and the zigzag gash where it had surfaced. The bleeding was

140

staunched. Robles felt the tension of pain ease as the Orphan continued to wash him, removing the sweat and ashes that coated his face.

"You want to drink, white man?"

Robles nodded. Harkana emptied out his gourd and refilled it with fresh water.

Lifting Robles's head, he cautioned him, "Not too much, just little." Manuel took a sip, then a second. Even swallowing seemed an inordinate effort.

"Was it your arrow?" he asked the Tehuelche, having lost the memory of what happened in the rapid fog of events.

"Harkana's arrow hits you here" was the reply. The Orphan tapped his own heart. "Not in shoulder."

"Harkana," mused Robles, and a cloud lifted in his mind. "Harkana, that is your name?"

"I am Harkana the Orphan of the Tehuelche. It is so."

"And it was your name that they screamed at us." Robles made it a statement of understanding, not a question.

"How are you called, white man?"

"Robles, Manuel de Robles."

"What does it mean, Robles?"

"Es un árbol, a tree."

"Like ombú?"

"A similar size but better timber. There are no oak trees here, Harkana. They are plentiful in distant lands, the lands where my ancestors came from, many years ago. You will not know this tree."

"I have seen many trees. Quebracho, is it like quebracho?"

"A softer, lighter wood. We use it to make furniture, er, chairs and tables. You know these things?"

"I know," Harkana answered with a shrug. "It is a good name for a man. Where do you come from, Robles?"

"I was born in the high country, near the source of the Rio Colorado."

"Which river is that?"

"The same that runs close by us here, just a bit to the south."

"Enough talk. Come, we will go back to where I found you."

Harkana lifted him to the saddle once more, and Robles felt

141

a flush of dizziness mingled with wonder at the casual but ferocious natural strength of the man. They rode back the half mile in silence, and Manuel felt a vestige of his vitality returning. After they had arrived, the Orphan placed Robles back against the boulder.

"You can rest here until your friends find you."

"They are no friends of mine, Harkana."

"They are white men, Robles."

"But all Indians are not Tehuelches," the wounded man emphasized, and for the first time Harkana displayed a slight emotion on his chiseled features. He was obviously interested in the idea that the whites had their separate tribes. Yet he said nothing, picking up Robles's knife from the ground and playing with it while he pondered conversation or departure.

"Why did you take no part in the killing when I saw you that first time? Were you under orders from the Red Pig?"

"The Red Pig—is that how you call McClellan?"

"I cannot pronounce that name. To us he is the Red Pig. I have an arrow anxious to meet with his heart. One day I will introduce them. When I killed the man in the window I hoped it would be the Red Pig. He was of a similar build but I had no way of being sure. It was of little consequence. It could have been you standing exposed aginst the light last night."

"It was the chief of police, the other man with McClellan—er, the Red Pig who did the killing of the young Tehuelche family."

"Already I know that, Robles. We threw his body down the water hole, his and another's. Then we burned all the buildings and ransacked the stores. There was little of any use to the Tehuelche, only knives such as these"—he gestured with Robles's blade—"good bridles, and ropes." Harkana paused. "Chief of police—is that not a maker of laws?"

"Yes, but out here," said Robles, "there are few laws for the white man, and none at all for the Indians."

"He killed a Tehuelche for no reason. Is that the white man's law?"

"Not all of them, Harkana, believe me. His name was Tossini, and he controlled the town of Tres Arboles, north about three days' ride. I mean three days for me on a single horse, not as the Tehuelche rides."

142

"You know much of the Tehuelche, Robles, but you gallop too fast for me with your words. What is town and three trees? I do not understand."

"A town is a place where many white men build their houses together, more than a camp, larger even than the biggest of your villages. We give names to such places, and this one was called Tres Arboles."

"And your knowledge of our people, where does this come from for a man who saw first light in the north country?"

"My mother was part Yamana, but that is not the only reason. I have a job in Buenos Aires which calls for knowledge of the Indians of the south."

"Buenos Aires?" A frown of perplexity furrowed the Indian's brow as he sat calmly on his haunches, spinning the knife with his long, coppery fingers.

"The biggest town of all," Robles attempted, trying to think of a way of explaining to a Tehuelche Indian the meaning of a capital city. "It is located far from here, on the seacoast. More than two hundred thousand people live in Buenos Aires."

"I do not comprehend, but no matter. How can so many live in one place?"

"It is difficult to explain, Harkana, but tell me how you come to speak our language."

"I was prisoner of the whites in the hot northern forests, the place called Paraguay. Held there for forty moons—that is about three of your years. It is an ugly language, no?"

Robles disregarded the unintended insult. "Paraguay," he breathed, "you have been in Paraguay?"

"I was driven out by my people. This too is a long story, and we have not the time now for the telling. Robles, when will the soldiers come?"

Silence jarred the flow of their conversation. It took Robles a full minute to think what to say next. Harkana did not press him for a reply.

"You know about soldiers?" Robles queried, unnecessarily. "Of course, the troops which exterminated the Ranqueles last year. What makes you think that more soldiers will come?"

"Listen, white man. I was not here when the Ranqueles were overwhelmed a few moons past. I had until recently been banned

143

from my homeland for eight of your years. The day you first saw me was the day I returned to my people. No, I remember much further back, when a force of white soldiers pushed the Ranqueles far to the south and west. They were driven into our own lake country. They were hurt but not yet beaten. Needing the land for their own stock, they made the mistake of turning upon the Tehuelches to lay claim to that land. I fought in the battle which drove the Ranqueles out from the lake country. That is what I know of white soldiers."

"But that was all of eight years ago. How old were you then?"

"Let me calculate in your time," said Harkana, pausing. "I had nineteen years. The Ranqueles were numerous, more than the inland Tehuelche. But since the great white army came last year, the elders tell me, less than one hundred now survive, and they are starving and freezing to death. So, Robles, tell me, when will the soldiers come for us?"

"I cannot be sure," Robles answered him, honestly. "Not in the winter. They will wait for you to come north again. In late spring, I suppose."

"Both the winter and the migration are late this year," Harkana informed him. "The season has been soft for half a moon longer than usual. So they will not come before the great thaw is over, at the earliest."

"They will if settlers like the Red Pig get their own way. He is one who will try to get the soldier chiefs in Buenos Aires to act quickly. Listen to me, Harkana. I was sent here to investigate the problem and—"

"What means investigate?"

"To observe and report. To see the problem between Indian and white man in the south and try to find a solution."

"You have seen," Harkana said grimly, laconic at a time when other men might have chosen to be verbose.

"Perhaps I can persuade the Great White Chief in Buenos Aires to make peace instead of war," offered Robles, who was thinking now of how long they had before the rescuers thundered in on their fresh horses. It was mid-morning now and the survivors would have reached the Wisbey estancia for certain. Probably they had already started back, and the ride could be

144

made in less than two hours if they pushed. And they would push very hard.

Harkana sat on his haunches, still playing with the slim little blade that belonged to Manuel de Robles. When he spoke again his tone was different, more resigned, ringing with finality, less inquisitive.

"This land belongs to the Tehuelches, Robles. It was given to our earliest ancestors by the moon. It is not the white man's nor his Great White Chief's to give or to take, to buy or to sell. Tell him that Harkana the Orphan said that. You will try, white man, to do what you have said, but you will fail. This can never be common ground; there is room for everything down here save sharing. For the white man has a hunger for land which can never be satisfied. I have seen it. The elders have seen it. Even you have seen it. That is all."

Robles spoke at length about reservations and what they would mean. He outlined his plans and ideas and told the Indian war-lord how he would present them to the government of the Great White Chief. Harkana said nothing for a long time.

"At least let me try?" pleaded the white man.

The Orphan shrugged. So much was happening to him and his tortured world in so short a time. He wanted to go south and stay in one place for a while. He wanted to be alone to digest the thoughts that crammed his head to the bursting point. There was little point in idle chatter with this white man, although he seemed straight. Tehuelches called such men straight arrows. Good and bad, it was all blazingly irrelevant. Robles could not change what was happening. Harkana had been blessed with a vision that now reached so far that even he himself had become aware of it. An hour had passed. Harkana pronounced the verdict that was his alone to make.

"If the white man stays north of the Great River, the one which you call Rio Colorado, there will be no war. But we both know well enough that he will cross that river to take both our land and our lives. It is the way of the white man."

"And down south," Robles asked, "what of the sheep farmers in the south, beside the sea?"

"Sea? That is Great Water, no? I have heard of whites coming

145

in big canoes. The elders have yet to tell me of their numbers and their ways. What is sheep?"

"How long," Robles wanted to know, "since you migrated south with your people?"

"I was banished for one hundred moons. That is eight migrations."

"You will find great changes in the south," Manuel warned the Tehuelche.

Zorkan Rood stirred. Robles studied the great gray stallion closely. It was grazing serenely, untethered, all its power and speed and strength sleeping while his master conversed. Some men would give all they possessed for a horse such as that. How fitting a companion it was for this iron-hard acceptor of fate. What an immense tragedy this was, in which he, Manuel de Robles, had landed the cameo role of useless arbitrator between two impossible extremes. The craziest thing about it all was that this savage, as McClellan had called him, saw the future the same as Robles did himself.

"The sheep is a white man's animal, domesticated and—"

Harkana interrupted him. "Of course, the new guanaco. Already I have heard how it devours the winter pasture and breeds in its thousands. Tell me, Robles, what has become of the coastal tribes and the fish eaters: the Onas of the islands, the Alacalufs, and the Yamanas?"

"Decimated, slain, intermarried, driven off to the remotest parts of the peninsula. You did not know?"

"Not until now."

"I am sorry. I have Yamana blood myself—my mother."

"Let us hope," remarked Harkana, rising slowly to his feet, "that it was not that blood which you spilled along the trail." The Orphan went over to his horse and ran a large hand through the long tresses of its mane. "I think that war is inevitable, Robles," he decided.

"You will be beaten, Harkana."

"That too is inevitable." He said it with the even ring of a death knell.

"You will die," Robles persisted. "All of you."

"Everyone dies, white man. Only the moon can decide where and when. It is the manner of our dying which concerns me

146

most, since the manner of our living is no longer in our own hands but in those of the enemy."

Harkana appeared to be listening intently as he spoke, but Manuel heard nothing but their dialogue and the sigh of the grasses.

For the first time, a spark of emotion burned in the Indian's black eyes. "If the white man brings his soldiers across the Great River, the pampas will be irrigated with blood. We have no other choice, for the Tehuelche will never allow himself to be herded like cattle or driven like slaves. For those things would kill us more surely than the white man's thundersticks. Dying is all we have left to live for."

"The whites are making thundersticks—we call them guns—that can kill time after time without reloading, faster than the fastest archer."

"I have seen the Red Pig, remember? It did not help them last night."

"Next time all white men will have them. We have a saying in our language, we learn by our mistakes."

"We have a saying in ours, Robles. We die by our mistakes. Who was the target who betrayed himself in the window by the burning brand in his mouth?"

"A young white settler. He was foolish."

"He will grow no wiser."

"Harkana, hear me," Robles requested, conscious of the minutes elapsing. "I will speak with the Great White Chief in the city. I will try to make him see reason, to set aside land for the Tehuelche, to allow you to tend your horses, hunt the rhea and the guanaco, make the annual migration. I will go to him straightway. Do you believe me?"

"You are in need of my belief?"

"Yes, I think I am."

"The winter has come. The ground turns cold. The wind sings a hard song. The Tehuelche will migrate. He will feed off the new guanaco in the south, for the new guanaco crops the pasture that is ours. Those whites which choose to fight will die by our hand. By canoe or by horse, it is the same thing. They have crossed the Great River. That is all.

"Robles, I hope we do not meet again. If we do, one of us

147

will die. Listen!" Harkana raised his hand for silence; then Robles watched him put his ear to the earth. "Horses come. Many horses, from the direction of the sun rising. I think you will live, white man."

He spoke without a trace of concern, unhurried, as if there was all the time in the world.

"I owe to you my life," Robles acknowledged. "If we should meet again, must one of us die? Does it have to be that way, Harkana?"

"It is the way of the Tehuelche," said the Indian grimly. "There can be no other."

Their eyes met again. Even the Argentine could hear the sound of hooves pounding closer. They seemed very near.

"Hurry, Harkana! They will kill you, no matter what you have done for me!"

But the Orphan showed total lack of regard for his urgency, walking nonchalantly to the side of his horse, picking up and placing the big bow across his chest. He lifted himself onto the back of his mount in one smooth, effortless arabesque, then leaned to pluck his spear from the ground.

"He that rides upon Zorkan Rood never has cause to hurry," he explained.

Manuel de Robles saw him spring up into a standing position on the stallion's back, from where, no doubt, he could easily pick out the fast-approaching dust cloud of his enemies. The Orphan dropped back into a riding position.

"This belongs to you," he remembered, sending the knife in an easy spin to embed itself in the ground close to Robles's Colt revolver. And then Harkana smiled briefly at the man whose life he had just saved.

"May you ride always in the light of the moon," he said in parting. He turned the huge horse and spoke one word to it with his heels. Zorkan Rood catapulted forward and vanished almost immediately at a bounding gallop that outpaced all but his own shadow.

CHAPTER NINE

THE WHEELS OF WINTER turned on the axle of time. Patagonia's hard knuckles whitened with snow. The Tehuelches completed the long, arduous migration before the worst of it set in. They camped again in the poor land of the south; but it was no poorer than in previous winters. Not when they arrived. They were tired and the season was fresh. Meadows of snow covered the glacial rock plains. Nowhere was it very deep, apart from the gullies that had filled and the drifts blown up by the wind. In most places its thin white film was pierced by clumps of coarse grasses and small hardy shrubs. Both the vegetation and the meager animal life could handle the snow. So could the Indians. It was the wind that did the damage.

In summer, when the dust lay thick upon the land, the wind would rise and carry it along, like one man forcing a confession from another. The wind bore the dust in whorls and needle thrusts, rubbing, eroding, scoring the terrain year after year, century piled upon century. Glaciers that formed and froze high up in the western cordillera chafed their way down across the steppe, scouring the surface, creating pocks on the face of the earth. Thin, timid rivers and streams ribboned the landscape, wearing away at ever deepening quebradas. Some joined forces, linking fingers in the basin of the Colorado, Chubut, and Deseado systems. It was the coalition watercourses which endured the dry season. The others ran themselves dry trying to make it to the ocean.

Beside a lake ringed by carob trees, the band of Seh Saapelt set up a semipermanent camp. They led out the strings of horses to scant patches of pasture, which became ever more distant as the winter weeks slipped by. Yet it was a good spot to await the coming of the Great Thaw. The hunting parties roamed both east and west. Near the mountains they sometimes came across a solitary maned wolf, hunting much as the Tehuelches did themselves—and for the same prey. The wolf was not above taking vizcachas if it could catch them above ground or dig them out of their burrows. The Indians too were sometimes reduced to killing the little rodents. To return empty-handed was to stay empty-bellied. Hunger sifted pride through the sieve of survival.

The food reserves, mostly charqui, soon became exhausted as the winter thickened. On the Atlantic coast, the Tehuelches combed the beaches for crabs and shellfish, sifting the shallows in near desperation. It had never been a land of easy pickings. Living came hard in the old days. Now it was harder still, for the new guanaco teemed in its thousands, studding the plains where the Tehuelche had once wandered and been satisfied.

It was easy to kill, this new guanaco, and its flesh was tender and succulent. So Harkana issued orders that it should be taken to stave off the pangs of starvation that its own proliferation had instigated. The clashes with the white farmers became inevitable.

The hooked wire fences were everywhere now, measuring the land for the genesis of one people and the exodus of another. The Indians tore down the fences and killed the sheep that fed from the fat of their land. There were so many, and they took only in proportion to their needs. The needs of the inland Tehuelches were few. The white settlers fought with guns and wrote letters of scathing and contemptuous complaint to the ministries in Buenos Aires. They banded together, purchased more modern rifles and ammunition, knowing that the balance would soon be shifting.

In the Moon of the Great Thaw Commencing, the Tehuelches moved east under Seh Saapelt and Harkana the Orphan, camping within one hundred miles of Great Water, as they called the ocean. In sorties they rode on the sea as if it were an enemy. They knew little of how to make it yield its secret fruit. The coastal

150

Tehuelches held the key to such things as fishing, the clubbing of seals, the bow-shooting of cormorants, and the netting of penguins. And the coastal bands had gone north, hugging the edge of the immeasurable blue-gray water. This proved a hard, frugal moon for Seh Saapelt's people.

In the end he ordered another move, this time southwest. They penetrated a zone which the white settlers had come to regard as sacrosanct, for they had been there for five previous winters. Old Two Lifetimes could no longer remember the first winter when his tribe had grazed stock there. It was before the time of his father, and his grandfather, and *his* grandfather before him. Now the white man said it was his land. So they fought.

In the first skirmish, a band of seven Tehuelches came to steal sheep. Five died from gunshot wounds. One was caught and crucified on the barbed wire strands. One made it back to Harkana the Orphan. One was enough. Harkana took a large war party and wiped out the entire settlement. He left no living thing within the fences of the sprawling compound. They rode off the horses and some of the sheep. They even killed the dogs and the chickens. The smoke from the burned-out buildings could be seen on the horizon for several days, a pyre for the dead and a warning to the living.

While the winter played itself out, Manuel de Robles fought a different kind of battle in a different area of conflict. He recovered from his wounds and was soon back in Buenos Aires, lobbying for a Tehuelche reservation. He spoke to a ministry of deaf ears. The government was blinded by insight into the easy fortunes that could be had on the Patagonian peninsula. In the short time that Robles had been away, a major change had occurred: Nicolás de Avellaneda, the outgoing President of Argentina, had nominated his successor. His name was Roca.

Julio Roca, the same general who had whipped the Ranqueles insurrection with a force of eight thousand men. Roca the Conqueror of the Desert. Roca the hero, the Rock, the Indian-hater. Roca believed that his nation had a divine right to all the land to the south. The only frontiers he acknowledged were those of the shorelines.

Robles's pleas and ideals aroused derision. His one face-to-face interview with his own minister was a fiasco.

The minister's office was sumptuous. Stained-wood panels made up the walls. A thick-piled carpet from Isfahan embroidered the floor. A cut-glass decanter and set of eight sherry glasses highlighted one corner, and an ornate lampstand dominated another. The desk itself was made of a wood Robles could not remember the name of, although he had been told more than once. Several other fine pieces of craftsmanship were equally lost on the Argentine from another world. Minister Kurtz was a collector of all things fine. He thought that France made a far likelier mother country than Spain.

Kurtz had spent several years in Paris and spoke the language passably well, although his opinion of his accent was overrated. Kurtz was of German extraction, to complete a trio of connections with Europe. Ice-eyed and corn-haired, he bore a visible Teutonic air. His average height was made taller by his thinness. Hollow-cheeked and wan of complexion, he was easily able to convey an aura of weakness. This gave Kurtz and Robles their only mutual characteristic: that of being underestimated. The causes for this were of course totally opposite. Kurtz had a lot to say but gave the impression of being unable to back it up, while Robles had so little to say that it appeared he had nothing worth backing up.

Replacing his pince-nez on the thin blade of his nose, Minister Kurtz surveyed Robles at length from across the ample acreage of his polished desktop.

"The report is very good, Robles," he said, pronouncing sentence on the sheaf of papers in front of him. "However, the timing is very bad. Great shame. Such a pity, such a waste."

"How so, sir?"

Maybe he really is the country-bumpkin half-breed I hear him described as in all the corridors of power, Kurtz wondered. In all the years I've known him I've never heard him act so naively. But what if it is not an act? What if he really means it?

"Roca," said the minister curtly, as if the President-elect's surname was enough of an explanation.

"Roca?" queried Robles, purposely fixing a bland expression on his face.

"Reservation idea absolutely out of the question now that Roca is coming to power. Military man, you see. No point in pressing for a reservation with Roca's boys. I hear that they are already champing at the bit to march down there and sort the tribes out once and for all."

"Just what does the new government want in Patagonia, Minister?"

"It wants Patagonia, Robles," replied the minister, with exaggerated simplicity. "All of it. Everything it contains."

"Except the Indians."

"Quite so. Anyway, we must adapt, you and I. That's politics, eh?"

"And the Tehuelches?" Robles pressed on. "What of them?"

"The Tehuelches," drawled Minister Kurtz, forever searching for the exact metaphor, the subtle nuance—the *mot juste,* as he preferred to call it—"are the dinosaurs of humanity. History has written them off, you see. New era coming in. End of one epoch, start of another. The tribes simply serve no useful purpose. They can't fit into the future, and stick out in the past like a sore thumb."

"Evidently," muttered Manuel, thinking that this was just about the end of the road not only for the Tehuelches but for himself as well. "I don't see any path left for me to take, sir, other than to tender to you my immediate resignation."

"Nonsense, Robles. This administration has need of men like you. I remember how you used to carve up the prosecution in the courtroom. A great lawyer, one with a future, I said to myself. Why, we all did. Plenty of scope for a man with your talents and qualifications. Roca needs men like you." The minister beamed.

"Yes, but I am not sure that I need Roca," Robles said, watching the smile twitch and die on the minister's lips. He too was thinking back on his courtroom triumphs. He had acted as defense lawyer to a number of accused half-breeds and backwoods provincials. Some of the cases had made front-page news. There was plenty of work for a man willing to lay his career on the line for the sake of defending a mestizo. Robles had made a name for himself, carved a reputation not so much by laying things on the line as by refusing to toe it. He had been very good. The mestizos had sorely missed him when he gave up the law to take on his new position at the ministry. They were the only ones who had: the bullied, browbeaten, humiliated, cheated, robbed, ill-informed, and directionless half-breeds who had found a champion in Manuel de Robles of Mendoza province. Everyone else had been glad to see the back of him, and they hoped it would not be too long before someone stuck a knife into it for real.

"That is for you alone to decide," the minister resolved. "All I can tell you is that the new regime has need of your unique services. The campaign could use a man like you, Robles. And you would be well rewarded, I promise you."

"Perhaps you can explain to me," pleaded Robles, "how one regime can send me south to investigate ways of maintaining life for the tribes and the subsequent presidency can make overtures to me for my assistance in a campaign to wipe them out?"

"Politics is a matter of expediency. One must change with the times. There are no hard and fast rules."

"Señor Kurtz, you yourself were an ardent supporter of the reservation scheme. So where do you stand now, sir, if I may ask?"

"You may, certainly you may," Kurtz allowed, nodding his head swiftly and catching the pince-nez as it fell. "I stand for Minister of the Interior, Robles, that's where I stand. Roca hates Indians. He wants Patagonia, er, how shall I say, contained. The next Minister of the Interior will also want Patagonia to be contained."

"And will the next Minister of the Interior also hate Indians?" For Robles it was the definitive question.

"Only in public" was the answer. It told Robles all he needed to know.

"And what about honesty and consistency and integrity, and what about ideals, señor Kurtz?"

"They are adjusted, Robles, to suit the political climate of the day."

"Mine, unfortunately, are not open to adjustment."

"You know, Manuel de Robles, there are still a good many people in this city, a good many influential people, who would

154

like to see you fall flat on your face. Did you know that I have never been one of them?"

"That's extremely comforting, sir."

"And that tone of yours, Robles. It is not the first time I've noticed what might well be considered a lack of respect." Kurtz showed his annoyance by a flaring of his nostrils.

Robles knew that he was not going to blow up. He had a smoldering temper. It took a lot of bottling up for him to really explode. Now wasn't the time or the place. It was somewhere in the future. No, this was a time for keeping cool and putting a man in his place.

"I'll try to bear that in mind, sir," he said, with the same suggestion of sarcasm.

"There are times when you are too critical by far."

"But at least not hypocritical, wouldn't you agree?" Robles squared up for a showdown.

"Do not try my patience too far, Robles. I warn you. I am not given to—"

"Two centavos, sir, is that what you don't give, Minister?" Robles stood up slowly and deliberately, pushing his chair back over the Isfahan carpet.

"You know, Robles, I never did like you."

"Not even in public, sir?"

"This is too much, d'you hear me, this is too—"

"Two-faced, perhaps?" suggested Robles. "Is that the *mot juste* you were seeking, sir?"

"Get out, Robles! Get out before I have you thrown out!" The minister had also risen to his feet, his tiny hands clenched in fists of frail bone. Sweat seeped from his facial pores. "I've never heard such blatant insolence in my life!" the minister stormed as Robles made his way to the heavy door of the office.

"Not from an Indian, that's for sure. Still, you can always send in the militia and have me wiped out. The new regime would like that, Kurtz, they really would."

Robles swung the door open with tremendous force, letting it crash back against the wall. Not only did it chip the stained-wood panel with its brass handle, but it created such a shudder that one of the Venetian sherry glasses fell and smashed into exceed-

155

ingly expensive pieces. Robles looked down at the smashed glass and then up at the equally shattered face of señor Kurtz.

"I'm so sorry," Robles sympathized, flicking his eyes back to the damage, "we heavy-handed half-breeds have never been known for our appreciation of the finer things in life. Still, you can always buy a replacement with your twenty pieces of silver."

Robles left, went straight to his own office two floors below, cleared out his desk, and departed from the building for the last time.

At precisely the moment that Robles walked out of his job at the ministry in Buenos Aires, thankful to be rid of it all, another man, far away, was equally as grateful at being rid of something. The big shipment of his new invention had gone at last. So many weeks of overtime and late nights. But in the end the export order to Buenos Aires had been dealt with, the numbers had been met, and the cases had been duly dispatched. Mr. Remington was pleased. The new repeating rifle looked like a sure winner, not only in the United States of America but all over the world. He was content. His business was bound to boom. He had left almost nothing to chance. He was not a believer in happenstance. He made his own luck. Remington, inventor of the world's first typewriter, was born to win, for now he had invented a weapon whose killing power had never known its like in the world of the 1870s. Regardless of whether the pen proved mightier than the sword or not, Remington could not lose.

CHAPTER TEN

SPRING CAME SUDDENLY, like an unexpected friend. The pampas grass sprouted fresh plumes of silvery-white inflorescence. The early swallows flitted in. Ice melted into the tinkling cocktails of the streams. Fuchsias broke out in a sweat of color, their red and purple blossoms branding the amber hide of the pampas. Ponderous ombú trees found a green leaf elixir. Resilient little tinamous laid clutches of hard, bright eggs as smooth as porcelain.

While nails were struck into the coffin of the Indians and the railroads stabbed deep into the ribs of the Republic; while telegraph wires fanned out from the soon-to-be capital, linking Buenos Aires with the most remote outposts of a nation bubbling over with youthful dreams of expansion; as unheralded rewards were being realized from the production of beef, grain, wool, and leather, and Mr. Remington was reaping the rewards of his hard winter's labor—so the Tehuelches were put on the move again.

The real guanaco reappeared in numbers. The peccaries multiplied. The hunting was easy once more. The mares dropped their foals and covered their bones with fat. Life was rejuvenated everywhere. It was the season for rejoicing. The Tehuelches held a great feast of thanksgiving and there was much dancing to the moon.

McClellan had not been idle through the winter. His new hacienda was almost complete. It was far bigger and strongly fortified. It had been constructed with defense in mind. The outhouses came next, set out in a ring around the circumference of the original compound like links in a barricade. Two new wells were sunk to replace the spoiled one.

The settlers lobbied loud and long in the government halls of the big city. They were heard. Roca approved. Foreign settlement in the peninsula was being encouraged, not least to keep out the encroachment of the Chileans who sought to lay claim to it. The land was going cheap. The old established families expanded, all but Isabella Carrioli, who sold out and moved into the city permanently. Bruce McClellan bought a third of her spread. Wisbey puchased another sizable slice. New settlers came in with new money. The pampas was plowed, and grain crops planted in the furrows of loam. The Rio Colorado was crossed, and farms and fences sprang up in a flood. In the short interval of one winter the land grabbers changed the face of Patagonia forever. There was risk, but the army had promised action. The pioneers came in the face of danger, but those who turned back were few, and those who stayed were many. And then the rifles came.

After the Tehuelches had been in the spring camp for two weeks, Seh Saapelt summoned Harkana.

"The moon has called my name, Harkana the Orphan," he said weakly from where he lay.

The Orphan looked down on the wasted body of his grandfather. He spoke no words of commiseration. Every man and woman was given one life and one death. Neither could exist without the other. And here was a man who had been blessed with a double cycle of life; favored by the moon itself. He took the old man's withered hand as if it were a sparrow with a broken wing.

"Seh Saapelt, is there much pain?"

"None at all. Only an immeasurable tiredness. But I did not call you here to speak of my last journey, but of yours and that of our people. Bend closer, my voice fails me."

Harkana leaned his ear very close to the old man's urgent whisper.

"The Moon of the Great Thaw Commencing is almost over,"

said Seh Saapelt, "and in two more cycles it will be time to lead the tribe north once more. I have seen you restless of late. I think you need to travel, and clearly there is not much time. The axe of war will fall when the migration gets underway. Go now, Harkana. The tribe faces no threat here and now. I will charge Raganor to take command when I am gone. Ride the gray stallion in search of Juma. We have spoken before of that idea, to unite with our cousins the coastal Tehuelches. Juma is strong in numbers. Bend his ear to your plan; seek to ally his warriors with our own to combat the common enemy. From what I know of Juma, he will welcome a call to arms. If you find him set against you then you have lost nothing. Take one of the women with you if you so desire, but go now, on Zorkan Rood, and live the next two moons for yourself alone. It would please me greatly to know that you have taken something for yourself before the end comes."

The Orphan lifted his head and stared down at the old man who had seen so much. When he passed to the moon, who would he turn to as a sounding board for his ideas?

"There is no woman I would take with me, Seh Saapelt. But I would be alone for a time, it is true. What better purpose could my journey have than to approach Juma? Surely his people have felt the threat of the white man's invasion as much as we have ourselves. The borders of Great Water were ever a region where the white man raided and plundered. Is it not told how he first arrived in the long canoes from across the Great Water? Is not that how the legend of the gift of the moon is explained? If Juma joins with us, then so too will every Tehuelche clan and band in all of our lands. They will follow Juma's lead. I thank you for the opportunity to be alone once more."

"One more thing" the old man croaked, tugging at Harkana's hand with the remains of his strength. "A great battle is coming, and the result of it we both know well. Many a time have we spoken of how there is no longer a choice for the Tehuelche. Those few that survive, those that are taken alive by the whites, will be kept in chains until they die, or forced to work as slaves under his whip. Many will take their own lives rather than allow this to befall them. Soon the Tehuelche will be no more. My

159

dying leaves this last great decision in your hands and yours alone, Harkana the Orphan. It will be harder to bear than anything you have yet had to carry. No one can share it with you."

"I am not sure that I understand you, wise one."

"You could survive. You alone on Zorkan Rood. Take one of the women and perpetuate the children of the moon. Raganor will lead our people to the moon. All you have to do is bid him proceed north without you. Would this not be a victory over the white man? Think hard on it, Harkana. Which is the greater blow to the enemy—that you should die on the last battlefield at the head of our men or that you should escape on the stallion, going where no man can follow? Think of the Red Pig unspiriting Zorkan Rood with the heel blades."

Harkana reeled inwardly. He suddenly imagined the Red Pig mounted on Zorkan Rood, slashing, cutting, stabbing at the silver-gray flanks until they ran with blood and the horse stood still, ready to die. Why had the old man filled his head with this idea at the very last? How would he ever sleep again without the nightmare of this moment returning to plague him? It had never even occurred to him that he might live on beyond the confrontation that loomed on the horizon of his existence. It was written that one would come who would lead the Tehuelches back to the moon; but it was not foretold if he that came would go with them or go on alone. Harkana froze in agony. Yet he maintained control in front of Seh Saapelt. He was unaware of how many minutes ticked past as these visions glided before him, changing him inexorably. He had thought of everything except what would happen to Zorkan Rood.

"I will think on it, Seh Saapelt," he promised, but the old man never heard the words, for he was sleeping already in the cradle of the moon.

They burned the body of Two Lifetimes on a crude pyre. The ashes were scattered by the prevailing wind. The women wailed. The men chanted the death song. They fasted all the following day, and in the evening paid ritual homage to the silver scimitar of the moon. Seh Saapelt was gone.

Harkana did not sleep all that night. At the first light he called Raganor to him and issued his instructions.

"I am going in search of Juma's people, that they might join us in our fight against the white man. If Juma comes with us, so too will every private clan and family that bears the name Tehuelche. If I do not return here before the beginning of the Moon When the Rhea Lays Her Eggs, then start the people north. I will rejoin the migration along the way. Heed well the words and wisdom of the elders in all things save war. Leave the new guanaco alone. There is meat enough now that the season is soft. Do not challenge the white man, but do not run from him either. Live out these next two moons, brave Raganor, for the next migration leads us all to much more than the green pastures of the north. May the moon watch over you until we meet again."

"Farewell, lord. Travel safe back to us, and may the moon favor your mission."

Pindi brought up Zorkan Rood, and Harkana thought that he had never seen the stallion looking in better fettle, groomed, glistening, rippling with muscle and fitness. The sight of the horse on that fine sunny morning brought him a stab of pain as he thought over Seh Saapelt's parting idea for the hundreth time. He had already told himself that he would put it out of his mind until after he had seen Juma.

The Orphan carried a full quiver and a sturdy lance he had fashioned with his own hands, besides the bow and the knife that were so much a part of his legend. A coil of plaited rope dangled from his waistband. As a parting gesture he bent down and plucked the boy groom from the ground, perching him between himself and the huge head of the horse.

Harkana turned back to his lieutenant, Raganor, who stood waiting on his words. "Raganor, summer comes on fast hooves. It will be the hardest of seasons. A dangerous summer of blood and tears flowing. See that our people are happy while the spring lasts."

"I will do all that the Lord Harkana wishes me to do. I look for him in the third span of the new moon."

With a wave of his free hand, Harkana rode out through the camp at a trot, Pindi bouncing lightly on the thick layers of mane. He stopped about half a mile from the rows of toldos and let the boy down.

"Run back, little Pindi," the Orphan instructed. "Play in the

161

meadows. Help the tribe with the chores, have fun with your friends."

"I will, lord, I will." The boy beamed enthusiastically. "And I will practice very hard with the bow, that I may kill many white men in the summer battle."

"Would you fight the white man, Pindi? Would you charge forth against his thundersticks even though the enemy outnumber us many times over?"

Pindi was surprised at these questions. He peered up at Harkana's face, blinking his soft brown eyes rapidly and squinting at the sun. His unencumbered mind saw only one straight path to follow, and he answered as any full-grown Tehuelche would have answered. There was more than a touch of bewilderment in his inflection.

"As the Lord Harkana knows, there is no other way for a Tehuelche."

The boy ran off back toward the camp, leaving Harkana pondering his words and his certainty. How could Harkana even doubt that he would lead his people on the dying day when such was the faith of the tiniest of warriors? He would find a way of setting Zorkan Rood free. The Orphan was glad that he had no woman to consider as well. It was better this way. The warlord of the inland Tehuelches swung Zorkan Rood into the breeze and set off at a canter to seek Juma.

CHAPTER ELEVEN

JUMA NORMALLY WOKE EVERY morning and dressed himself with a smile as readily as he threw on his cloak of guanaco fur. His zest for living seldom left him. His sense of humor was boundless. Every day was the beginning of a new adventure, made more exciting by its uncertainty. His heart was crammed with well-being. His enemies had been few until the white man came.

Yet on the morning of the last day of the Moon of the Great Thaw Commencing, the chief of the coastal Tehuelches wore a frown. He had not slept all night. Flailed by his whiplash tongue, his servants and kinfolk, even his wife of two hundred nineteen moon, steered clear of his ill temper. To the Tehuelche, grief was a very personal commodity. And Juma's grief was like an act of self-immolation. He had passed beyond the point of consolation into infinite despair.

What had happened to her? His one and only daughter; his precious Pandra; what had become of her? Missing all night and still no sign of her in the morning. Half the warriors in Juma's tribe had been dispatched to seek the only child of their illustrious chief. The other half had ridden behind Juma himself for six hours, to no avail. They had searched the clifftops above the ocean, one of her favorite haunts. They had scoured the low grass plains and found her not. They had plowed through the scree-sided quebradas and drawn a total blank. There was no sign of her. Juma had come back to his village a few hours before dawn, hoping against hope that Pandra might have returned in

163

the meantime. She had not. Her father had sent out several hundred more warriors, with instructions to investigate the north country, to leave no stone unturned, to part every clump of grass. They were out there still as the dawn came up like a swelling on the skin of the horizon. Just after the sun first appeared, a cry had gone up from the guards on the southeast corner of the encampment. Juma had heard it, his eyes widening with optimism. He had raced from his toldo and seen his people crowding together. Then, above the throng, he saw the head of the small pinto, Pandra's beloved pony, which went with her everywhere. Clinging to his hope, he stormed forward, for surely she had already dismounted and was hidden from his view by the multitude. Only when the crowd had parted to allow him through did he realize that the pony was riderless. Nothing could have served to confirm his worst fears more than the sight of the pony standing alone.

Now Juma sat once again in the doorway of his large toldo. His eyes were downcast and his hands kneaded the dough of his melancholy between them. And after one more hour the second posse of his dog soldiers returned. They had seen not a trace.

Juma was sure that she had ridden south. The guards reported seeing her head that way on the previous morning. What was left of the pony's tracks corroborated that theory. They led right down to the beach and disappeared, for even a Tehuelche could not follow once all signs had been erased by the tide.

Pandra was headstrong. She took after her father. As was her habit, she had surely ridden off alone toward the seashore, to gather shells and hunt crabs. The twenty-three-year-old Tehuelche beauty was a law unto herself. She had always been that way, Juma reflected. Already she had refused marriage with two of the tribe's greatest warriors. Her father had shown public exasperation with her attitude, but secretly it amused him. It pleased him to have a daughter who was as strong-willed and as self-sufficient as the son with whom he had never been blessed. Now she had vanished on her latest lonely escapade. For Juma, too, it was the end of living.

Perhaps she had been caught by the tide and drowned? No,

164

he decided, that was hardly likely. The girl was as artful as any of the elders, despite her tender moons. And she knew the sea as no other; knew its every mood and sudden change and fickle ways. She outswam anyone in the tribe and loved the sea as if it were one of the family. Pandra had learned to swim before she could even toddle on her feet to reach it. The sea would never have claimed such as she. It had to be a freak fall or the white men. And if a fall, would they not have located the body? True, it could have been swept far out to sea, or returned to shore farther down the peninsula. It was the not knowing that nagged at his brain as he squatted numbly on the threshold of everlasting sorrow. The cold hand of ultimate loss gripped Juma's heart. Nothing would ever be the same again. How could it without Pandra?

By the time the sun went down on that second day, Juma knew that she was dead. Unashamed of his emotion, he let the tears roll down his cheeks. He took neither food nor drink. The light of his life had been extinguished. There was no longer any fight left in the middle-aged Tehuelche chieftain who had carved a reputation second to none in the living folk tales of his people Without Pandra, there could be no Juma.

Had Harkana known anything about the black mood of despondency into which Juma had sunk, he might well have changed his plans and his direction. But he did not know of anything except his own dilemma and the stark beauty of the Patagonian spring. He meandered haphazardly over the land that rolled so richly to the sea. The spring had succeeded in fooling the earth into believing all was well. Harkana was nursing an agony of indecision, the like of which he had always been spared before. Should he heed Seh Saapelt's death wish and ride north alone to perpetuate the Tehuelche strain and give the white man some tiny inkling of defeat? Or should he follow his chosen road, that shared by Raganor and every dog soldier in his tribe, even down to little Pindi? Whatever he decided would bring pain, and this was the period he had set aside to put pain behind him and live only for the present.

Harkana's odyssey took him across the periphery of the humid pampas. He traveled up out of the barren, flint-strewn flatlands of the far south and into a coastal belt lacerated with valleys. The thaw was well underway. Many of the smaller valleys which would dry up in summer now flowed with clear water. The white man's sheep had spilled inland from the many bay settlements and coastal villages which clung to the shoreline. Harkana avoided such habitations as he journeyed on.

His thinking processes grappled with the weight of a true dilemma. At first Seh Saapelt's suggestion had seemed so utterly ridiculous as not to warrant consideration. It was cowardly and unthinkable. How could he abandon his people, his warriors, his kinfolk, his Pindi and his Raganor? How could he leave them to fight the last great battle without spearheading the assault? How could he let them spill their own blood on the homeland while he rode away safe across foreign terrain? This was not the way of Harkana the Orphan. It was not the way of the Tehuelche.

Yet, had not Seh Saapelt been the eldest of the elders, the wisest of the wise? It was not for him to dismiss his advice out of hand. He could not fail to treat the last dying wish of his grandfather, the venerated Two Lifetimes, with the respect which it deserved. Clearly, it was not the rashly spoken utterance of a youth of two hundred moons.

Ay, but where was the decisive black-and-white Harkana now? Was the lance of his purpose broken, or merely deflected by the wisdom he possessed beyond his years? To perpetuate the symbol of the Tehuelche and thus to cheat the white man of the wholeness of his victory; or to seek oblivion in the last battle between all that was new and all that was not? To die or to live for pride? Would not dying be easier than living with the knowledge that he had chosen to flee? Therefore, was it not a greater act of courage to remain alive while others died in his absence? Others such as Raganor and little Pindi. Or would such as they die believing that he had deserted them in their hour of greatest need? The fervent faith of an entire people shattered by his single act of abandonment. Everything they were clamoring to die for suddenly made void of impact or meaning. Could he allow Raganor's lifeblood to irrigate mother earth, his and that of a thousand others like him? And with the blood would flow the sense of betrayal. For Harkana the Orphan had run out on them on the great gray stallion. He had refused to fight and die by their side after all he had vowed to himself, to the tribe, and to the moon. Harkana had split asunder the way of the Tehuelche. No, Seh Saapelt, that can never be. In all honesty, what avenues would remain open to such a survivor? He would be a man without either a future or a past. Without a name, even. Zorkan Rood his only companion.

And what of Zorkan Rood? The horse was not yet in its prime. Such a horse had at least as much value to a Tehuelche as his closest brother; possibly more. In the end, it was better to die living the way of the Tehuelche than to live without the way to die by. If only he could find the means by which to set Zorkan Rood free and yet ride him on the day of the conflict. The Orphan would think on it some more.

But not just then, for at that moment a rifle shot undid the stitches of his thoughts. He snapped out of his daydream and returned in a trice to his warrior role. The horse felt the vibrations of the call to action even before the hard heels asked for speed. They were within half a mile of the coast. They raced to the edge of the cliffs which plunged away to the beach, some forty feet below. Their joint figure became abruptly silhouetted against the skyline, lit by the midday sun. It was all too fine a day for the scene which Harkana saw being enacted on the sands below him. It turned him cold with fury. His mouth twisted in a savage desire to kill. His brain flashed the signals to his limbs, and he raced into action. Clearly there was not much time.

Three white men were dragging an Indian girl from out of the shallows. Their small boat was beached nearby. Anchored offshore was a far larger boat, turned head to wind, its sails furled. The large boat sat very still on the water, riding the bumps of the waves.

The trio of captors were out of range of Harkana's bow. The Tehuelche scanned the cliff face for a place to descend. His eyes lighted on a ledge halfway to the beach. Hammering the very last ounce of speed from Zorkan Rood, he reached it and dropped the coiled rope down the pitted cliff face, dangling it from the stallion's neck. The horse stood like a statue while Harkana

167

lowered himself to the ledge, the bow across his chest and the full quiver strapped to his back. He left his lance embedded in the earth of the plateau. From a height of twenty feet he jumped to the beach, landing with knees well flexed. The soft sand muffled his impact. His anger overcame caution, the danger of being horseless against three men with firearms.

In fact, as Harkana watched the men half drag and half carry the girl up the beach, he saw that they had only one thunderstick between them. Such details could mean the difference between living and dying in the Orphan's world. The girl fought them every step of the way. They were still totally unaware of Harkana's presence one hundred yards away. The Indian heard them laugh lasciviously, and then they began to bicker over who should be the first to rape her.

"By Christ!" moaned Guzmán, who had just felt his left forearm being raked by the girl's fingernails. "She fights like a wildcat, the black bitch!"

He slapped Pandra hard across the face with the back of his hand. The blow shocked her momentarily, but she soon resumed her frantic struggle.

They had launched the jolly boat on orders from the captain. They had been told to bring the girl back to the ship alive. Pandra had been swimming far out to sea when the barkentine had swept into the bay. She had immediately started for the safety of the shore, but the sharp-eyed sailor in the crow's nest had spotted her in no time at all. The current made it hard for her to take the shortest route to land. As the jolly boat smacked into the waves, she had started to swim the longer route with the current at her side. She struck out with every ounce of strength she had, but Pandra had already been afloat for over an hour before the peril had materialized. The three brawny oarsmen gained on her rapidly.

They had caught her in six feet of water. The two men who leaped out of the rowboat had floundered out of their depth while the girl twisted and squirmed. Then the whites found the sandy shore under their feet and were able to take a fierce grip on the girl's waist-length hair, which had come loose in the struggle. The third man beached the boat and came running to assist his

168

shipmates. By the time they all came free of the water, they were out of sight of the mother ship.

"Why don't we have a little fun with her, eh, mates?" suggested leading seaman Grijalvo. "Captain can't see around corners, now can he?"

"Don't suppose he'd have any objections anyway," put in Pérez, a younger boy on his second voyage. " 'Spect he's got much the same thing in mind for himself, anyway." He used the word "anyway" to end most of his sentences.

He was holding the Indian girl by her left arm as she came clear of the sea. His eyes took in the long smooth contours of her naked body, and he grabbed at one of her breasts. It was big enough to offer a firm handhold. "What do you say, anyway, Guzmán?" Pérez added. "You want to ride a big Indian girl before we head back to ship?"

Guzmán was a big grizzly bear of a man, nearly six and a half feet tall and broad to match. He was the ship's bosun and therefore in command of the small shore party. When he spoke, his voice was gruff and sparing, as if he were saving breath for something more worthwhile than conversation.

"Drag her up over there," he instructed, thrusting his full-bearded chin at some rocks that hugged up under the lee of the cliffs. They were large boulders, large enough to shield them from a prying telescope. When Pérez took his eyes off her to follow the big man's gesture, Pandra took the opportunity to sink her teeth in the boy's thumb.

"Aagh!" he yelled. "You little whore!" He wrenched the hand free and sucked at the blood welling in the wound. He then jerked his knee at the girl's head, and the blow glanced off her chin. She felt pain, but it was bearable pain. Pandra let her body hang loose, recovering from the blow, saving her energy for a moment when she could put it to better use than trying to free herself from three full-grown men. Her fear was still under control, but she felt a sick tremor of panic rise inside her each time the bearded giant gripped her. He was able to hold her down easily with just one huge paw. At least she could still wave her limbs about in the hands of the other two men.

Having reached the seclusion of the boulders, they were out of

169

sight of anyone watching from the ship. They had also lost sight of their own small beaching craft. This worried Guzmán somewhat. He was the suspicious kind, never trusting to anything or anyone.

"We ought to leave someone with the jolly," he reckoned aloud. "What if she's not alone?"

"Don't worry, Guzmán, I saw her horse tethered around the bay. Just one pony on its own. This place is as deserted as an ice floe."

"You saw *a* pony," Guzmán chided Pérez. "It may not have been hers at all. You don't know that. And we should leave someone with the jolly. It's our only lifeline back to the ship."

"Stop worrying," cooed Grijalvo, "and let's get on with it before they send out a search party." Grijalvo licked his lips with a snakelike whisk of his tongue.

Guzmán continued to appear unconvinced. His eyes swept the edge of the cliffs above, then panned around to rake the beach in both directions. He was holding the girl easily against the sand now, just using one hand around both of her slim ankles. The other men held her thrashing arms.

Pérez and Grijalvo had brought mooring pegs from the boat. They hammered them into the soft sand with rocks and lashed Pandra's wrists to them. This left their own hands free for other exploration. She struggled, but it was useless now. It had been so from the beginning.

Guzmán wrenched her protesting legs apart and she lay spread-eagled in front of them. Pérez took one leg, Guzmán the other. The big man was still nervous. He continually scanned the shoreline, knowing he could get thirty lashes if he was caught by an officer. For an instant he thought he heard a cracking sound, but it was much more likely to have been just the flop of another wave. He didn't mention it, but all the same he began to regret leaving the jolly so far away and out of sight.

The other two had not even bothered to bring their rifles along, so frenzied was their lust. Grijalvo, whose breath was coming in short rasps of excitement, had dropped his baggy seaman's pantaloons. He knelt between the girl's legs and ran his hands up and down her muscular thighs.

Harkana studied him in this act of rancid prayer. While the men had been dragging Pandra out of sight behind the semi-circle of boulders, the Orphan had been busy. He had circled round and made a dash for their boat. His bare feet made little noise on the sand. When he judged that he was out of earshot, he went to work with his knife. Having holed the boat in two places, he hurled their two thundersticks into the surf and crept inland. The beach was amply strewn with boulders, and he gained the cover of an outcrop about thirty yards from where they held the girl. He could hear their words very clearly. They had heard nothing. The sounds of his destruction had been muffled by the rubbing of the waves over the sand. He watched them tie the girl to the ground while he crouched to draw an arrow from his quiver and notch it to the bowstring.

The Orphan knew that it would have to be done quickly. He bent the bow fully before he even stepped clear of the concealing rock. He took aim almost casually and let loose the long shaft a fraction of a second after Guzmán saw him. The white giant flung himself to the ground. Grijalvo turned on him as both of the girl's legs were suddenly released to kick and thrash at will.

"What are you two playing at?" he howled angrily. He directed his question first at Guzmán, who lay sprawled on the ground, savagely working the bolt of his rifle. Grijalvo turned his head to demand an explanation from Pérez, but he found him lying on his side with an arrow through his neck. Even the slow-witted Grijalvo did not need a second glance before he took cover.

"Did you see anything?" he beseeched, his eyes dilated with terror. His ardor had gone limp in record time. He retied his pantaloons and cursed himself for leaving his rifle in the jolly.

Pandra lay very still on the sand, her eyes glued to the arrow. She did not wish to draw attention to herself, lest they kill her in their panic. It was a Tehuelche fletching, that much she was aware of. Yet who could have shot the arrow? None of her father's people would be here unless she had been followed. In all the years that she had sought her solitude, she had never known her father to send after her. And who among her tribe would take it upon himself to invade her privacy? Whoever it was, Pandra was grateful.

"Behind that rock," said Guzmán, "the big one over there." He pointed. "There might well be more than one of the brown bastards, but I only saw the one. I told you two to bring the guns and keep a watch on the jolly!" He swore colorfully.

"What do we do now?" moaned Grijalvo.

"We wait," snapped the bosun. "We wait until the *San Martín* sends out a search party. We've been gone almost an hour, by my reckoning, and out of sight for most of that. Shouldn't be too long before they wonder what's up."

"Suppose they've just shipped anchor and sailed on?"

"In that case, Grijalvo, you are squatting on your final resting place, 'cause if the Indians don't put an end to you something else in this godforsaken country will. Now keep your mouth shut and give your eyes a chance!"

It was then that a very strange thing happened. It took the Argentine sailors by complete surprise, but the shock of it was even greater to the girl.

The voice came from the center of a cave of silence. Harkana's words rang with the clarity only isolation can evoke.

"Leave the girl unharmed and return to your boat," he commanded in Spanish. His language bore the accent of Paraguay.

Pandra shuddered. It was a kaleidoscope of weird contrast. A man lying dead at her feet with a Tehuelche arrow through him, then the archer speaking the very language of her torturers. Who was this man?

The whites were thinking much the same thing. Guzmán sucked in a double helping of the sea air.

"My God! What's out there? Who is he?"

Grijalvo was too busy whimpering to conjure up an answer.

"Who in hell's name is that hombre?" Guzmán repeated. "I would sure like to know that."

"You saw him, didn't you? You tell me," Grijalvo managed, his upper lip quivering out of control.

"Must have had contact with settlers, I suppose," Guzmán went on, rattled into uncharacteristic verbosity. He was known on board as a taciturn man, taciturn and strong, and the possessor of an ugly temper. Now he was scared, for in all the violence he had witnessed or taken part in, the enemy had been clear and visible. His eyes never left the boulder thirty yards away where he had seen the near-naked brown giant. "All I saw was a tall brown man with a bow and arrow. Nothing more than that. Now how on earth can he know Spanish? You tell me that, eh, Grijalvo?"

"Like you said, he must have had contact with settlers." Grijalvo hardly cared about anything except living to stand on the heaving decks of the *San Martín* once more.

Guzmán was still thinking about it. "Unlikely," he proclaimed after a few more minutes had gone by. "The only contact these Patagonian tribes have with white settlers is war contact. Come on, *mi capitán*. Put out a dozen of the lads in the cutter and come get us off this accursed beach."

Five more minutes passed, and still there was no sign of the cutter.

"Maybe if we leave the girl," blubbered Grijalvo uncontrollably, "and do like he says, maybe he'll let us go back to the boat. It's the girl he wants, isn't it?"

"And just maybe he'll tickle your guts with an arrowhead before you've gone ten paces. Maybe it's us he wants and not the girl. Did you ever think of that? Now shut up, your babbling is making me edgy!"

Harkana had crawled on hands and knees back to the damaged jolly. He could see the crew of the boat launching the cutter. It had eight men at the oars and the second mate at the helm. No cries of alarm rang out, and the Orphan was sure he had reached the beached boat undetected. He was ideally placed, concealed from both the cutter and the two whites ashore. The second mate stood stooped over the tiller, leaning into a quickening breeze. The eight oars bit into the waves in tidy unison. The sun glinted on the metal barrels of their rifles, which lay propped against the gunwale. Harkana watched and just let them come on.

It did not take very long for them to come within easy bowshot. The lone Tehuelche knew he had to hit them hard while he had the chance. He had the girl to think about, tied down and guarded by two ruffians who would slit her throat as soon as spit. Kneeling behind the bulwark of the jolly, Harkana took long and deliberate aim. It was so obvious that the man who stood in

173

the elbow of planks was the man to take out ahead of the rest. Harkana drew an efficient bead and let fly. He did not even follow the arrow to his target; he was busy selecting another shaft and notching it in place.

The second mate teetered in the stern of the cutter, then collapsed backward over the rudder. He disappeared below the waves. The nearest oarsman grabbed the tiller to hold it steady. And the boat came on toward the shore and Harkana's deadly bow. It took two more deaths before the cutter's crew reacted and started to turn about. Another man was hit in the back before the cutter made it out of range. He would take four hours to die, but the end result was still the same. The cutter was remanned with a full complement, under the first mate. Harkana watched it pull away, making for the beach at an oblique angle; it would land at least a mile down the coast. Satisfied, he crawled back to his former position. Now he had a little time to play with—but not much.

"Did you hear anything, Guzmán? I could swear I heard cries."

"Of course I heard them, you halfwit! Do you think I'm deaf or something?"

"What do you think it means? What's happening down there?"

"How the hell should I know?" growled the bigger man. "Do you think I'm clairvoyant? Now be quiet and let me think, will you?"

Harkana had to solve the deadlock with immediate action or he would soon be faced with not one but ten thundersticks. Over to his left his far-ranging eyes found a likely route up the cliff face. He had to get above them, to use his bow to full effect. He could achieve nothing by a headlong charge. Guzmán and Grijalvo had only one rifle between them, but it was one too many.

Harkana stepped nimbly around the rock and sent another arrow into the cliff wall behind Pandra and her captors. It fractured its barbed head into splinters but had the required effect of pinning both of the whites down for several precious minutes. The Orphan used the time to the full. Sprinting from his cover, he gained the face of the cliff and began to climb rapidly with the bow once more across his broad back. He was two thirds of the way to the top before Guzmán caught sight of the movement. He had a clear shot, but the range was lengthy. His first round sent up a spurt of chalky dust three yards from Harkana's unprotected head. The Tehuelche kept on climbing until he ran out of handholds. A second shot missed but rang closer as Guzmán got the range and threw all caution to the winds now that he was sure Harkana was alone.

The Orphan called to Zorkan Rood, and the horse came swiftly. Looming over the lip of the plateau, the stallion was exactly where it was needed, but no amount of calling in the world could communicate Harkana's greatest need. That was achieved by pure luck. When Zorkan Rood answered the call of its master and came to the place on the top of the cliffs directly above him, the rope dangled down from its head. Harkana had to risk his life on a precarious hold, but he got away with the chance and was ascending rapidly once more, hand over hand. Guzmán pulled the trigger for a third time, and the bullet whizzed through the space between Harkana's long legs. Then he vanished.

The cutter had beached. Its crew heaved it on shore close to the place where Pandra had tethered her pinto pony, which took fright and soon pulled free and ran off. The whites let it go, intent on other things. Led by the first mate, the eight-man platoon advanced at quick march along the broad lapel of sand. The rifles that they held in the ready position were Remington repeaters.

Harkana gave them one quick glance from his vantage point on the plateau, then turned his attention back to the two who stood over Pandra. The Orphan rode around to the original point of his descent, above the ledge he had already used once that day. Ignoring the rope burn, he slid down the rope, hardly using it at all to check his fall. He soared out over space in a majestic leap, and Guzmán failed in his one and only chance to pick him off in midair. He would not get another. Grijalvo, whose nerves had tightened like a coiled spring while he fought to locate the exact whereabouts of this deadly native enemy, could take no more. He broke and ran toward the landing party, which was now more than halfway from the cutter. Harkana was waiting on the ground, an arrow resting on the arm of his bow. He wanted Guzmán, for he held the rifle, but now he took the chance to even the odds by sending the shaft slamming into Grijalvo's unprotected chest. Grijalvo's scream was drowned by the blood that seeped into his punctured lung. He did not die all at once, but lay squirming and writhing on the sand as the world shipped its anchor and marooned him in another.

Guzmán had seen him go down and had gauged roughly the position from which the arrow had come. He was still thinking clearly enough to realize that Harkana would have to come to him. All the white man needed to do was repel the attack and wait for help.

Harkana moved like an iguana across the flat ground between the rocks. He could see Guzmán's boots planted over the defenseless body of the girl. Putting down the bow and removing the quiver, he reached for the knife and came up over the last hunch of boulders in one superb leap. Guzmán caught the movement and brought the rifle to bear. There was no way of knowing where the bullet would have caught the Indian, for the white man had no chance to aim. He thought only to blast away from the hip at point-blank range. Yet, at the very instant in which Guzmán's finger tightened on the trigger, Pandra played her part. Her feet came up together, kicking skyward and forcing the barrel of the gun up and out. The Remington crashed, and the bullet whizzed harmlessly past the Orphan's shoulder. Then the two bodies clashed with a mighty shock, and Guzmán felt the ease with which the rifle was twisted from his powerful hands and used to parry the roundhouse right-hand punch he swung at Harkana's head. In all his thirty-four years Adolfo Guzmán had never felt his strength matched. Now he knew real gut fear for the first time, knew he was about to die unless his comrades came up very fast. Guzmán drew his knife frantically, and Pandra watched the two of them cut at each other, Harkana wearing an expression of grim glee on his lips.

It was no contest. Harkana was so much faster on his feet, and his knife hand was a blur that soon scored two minor stabs in his opponent's body. A third slash drew a gasp from the sailor, and his knife dropped from a bleeding hand. Harkana did not bother with his knife, but grabbed Guzmán by the throat with both hands and tripped backward onto the beach. Guzmán flailed once with his fists, and the Orphan dipped his head to take the punches high up on the skull. And then the white man's efforts became weak as Harkana squeezed the strength and the life out of him with his thumbs clamped over Guzmán's windpipe. The eyes bulged, the tongue protruded, the feet stopped kicking for a hold on the loose sand. Harkana held on long after the man went limp and purple in the face. The Orphan had never known such hatred or anger to possess him.

"He's dead!" screamed Pandra. "Let's go before the others reach us!"

With his hands still strangling his enemy, Harkana turned almost absentmindedly toward the urgent young voice. She saw the cruelty in his eyes.

"Come on!" she implored, fighting at the ropes which pinned her hands.

At last Harkana heeded her. He stood, pulling Guzmán up with him and holding the huge white man clear of the ground with his hands still on his throat. He let the body fall.

Harkana retrieved his knife and cut the girl's bonds.

"Follow me," he commanded, and ran over the rocks like a goat, scooping up the bow and replacing the quiver on his back as he moved. Pandra followed fleetly, rubbing at her sore wrists. The men from the cutter were less than four hundred yards away.

Harkana lifted her with his hands under her feet until he was standing with his arms locked above his head. Pandra was tall, nearly six feet. With her own arms outstretched, she found a solid handhold up the cliff and climbed easily to the ledge. Harkana joined her in seconds. Then he pointed out the rope and the route to the top.

"I will toss you up, but you must grab the rope. Fix your eyes on it and concentrate. Think of nothing else. You will not get a second chance, for if the fall does not break your legs then the whites will. Ready?"

Pandra nodded and placed her right foot in the cup of his interlocked hands.

"Now!" he called, and the girl catapulted out from the ledge and found the rope with her hands. She slid back a foot under the weight of her own body, then redoubled her grip to arrest the slide and moved up hand over hand. Harkana watched her using her feet on the rock face. Her long slim legs, taut-muscled and brown-skinned, were like those of a rare gazelle. The Orphan thought of her as a woman for the first time. Pandra gained the clifftop and waved down to him. But Harkana was not looking her way anymore. He had turned both his attention and his bow on the pursuers.

First Mate Fuentes had a cool head on his shoulders. He had summed up the situation and left little to chance. The jolly's crew were all dead. He had sent two men back to guard the cutter as soon as he discovered the holes in the first boat. He was not utterly convinced that the man and the woman were the only Indians involved. He brought up his six riflemen under the lee of the overhang. As the first man peered around the protecting rock, an arrow struck him in the face and threw him back into the arms of a comrade. Fuentes felt a thrill of admiration for the way this single savage fought for his life and that of his woman. He blinked at the eerie deadliness of his archery. Perhaps he should just let him escape.

The next arrow hit another marksman's rifle stock which saved his life. After that, Fuentes found it hard to bring the rifles into play. The men murmured that the Indian could keep them pinned down all day long.

"Until he runs out of arrows," said Fuentes, determined to lead by example, as all tough officers must. He seized the dead man's gun.

"Come on!" yelled Pandra once again, furious that her savior seemed to be electing to die.

Harkana ignored her. He had notched another arrow, which left five in the quiver. He enjoyed killing white men. They were his enemy, the stealers of his land, the killers of his people, the brothers of the Red Pig. The Tehuelche drew back the bow and held it steady at full draw for over a minute. At last the dull metal of a rifle barrel showed very, very cautiously. The whites' situation was such that only one man could place himself in a firing position at a time. The top of a man's head appeared as he squinted to take aim. The man was First Mate Fuentes. Harkana shot him through the eye he had closed to sight the rifle. Fuentes fell back, dead before he touched the ground. And then Harkana was climbing.

The beach party took several seconds to react to the loss of their officer. It was the scuff of falling stones that drew them around the rock buttress to find Harkana climbing with electric speed, defenseless, the bow over his shoulder. Two of them rushed out and raised their guns. Pandra's sinewy right arm snaked back and threw rocks, one after another in rapid succession. The whites flinched from the missiles, but then they fired. One missed; the other hit the moving target in the upper arm, and Harkana was left dangling by one hand, about ten feet from the top. Pandra did not wait for instructions. She was at the horse's head, urging it forward before the white men had even worked the bolts on their Remingtons. One more round was shot, but then Harkana had gone. The white sailors were left below to count the cost of their folly and their failure to slay either of the Tehuelches, who had done nothing so well as refuse to die.

Harkana coiled the rope, ignoring the blood running from his wound. It was late afternoon. He unrolled the alpaca poncho and threw it over his head before mounting the stallion. He lifted Pandra up in front of him and threw the poncho forward to encircle them both. Then he let Zorkan Rood carry them into the future.

Two of the bodies from the first crew of the cutter washed ashore before the sun went down. The captain himself came to supervise the burial. The survivors from the cutter returned to the *San Martín* with many sad stories to tell. Eight little wooden crucifixes, all in a line, were left behind to await the curiosity of the next intrepid beachcomber.

Chapter Twelve

HARKANA TOOK HER BACK to the place where he had spent the previous night. There was a cave, set on the slope of one of the deeper quebradas, rattled by scree. Its deeper recesses twittered with bats by night and was hung with their chrysalid forms by day. But the mouth of the cave was floored with dry earth and shielded from the wind that cuffed the hillside.

They had ridden for more than three hours, and Harkana's flesh wound had bled profusely. The withers and mane of Zorkan Rood were coated with blood. Some had dripped over Pandra's upper thigh. The Orphan ignored the pain, but his weakened state hit him the moment he alighted from the horse.

The girl knew what to do. She wondered if he would allow her to tend him.

She need not have concerned herself. The Orphan's pride was on a whole other level. So she bathed the wound from water in his gourd and wrapped the arm in broad leaves gathered nearby. The bed of the ravine was carpeted with good grass and thick moss. The foliage was lush this time of year.

Harkana felt the girl's long tapering fingers burning his skin with their coolness. He did not look at her. Neither of them spoke. The man watched Zorkan Rood cropping the long grass. "Time beats only in the heart of the moon" ran a Tehuelche dictum. Then he felt the heat of her eyes upon him and looked up at her. He expected her to drop her gaze, but she held it hard upon him. "Take one of the women with you," Seh Saapelt had suggested. There had been no woman to take—until now. What a tragic trio they were. The great stallion and the woman whose name he did not know and himself. Harkana had traveled a hard road, paved with much bloodshed, pitted with pain and milestoned with death. Here was the woman he wanted. Yet, when the summer came they would all die; because of him or in spite of him. It was a hard road.

The girl left to gather kindling, and he watched her lithe form work at ferrying the bundles of twigs and a few substantial logs up to the mouth of the cave. When all this greenness became brindled by the beat of the sun it would be over, for love was twinned with pain. It had taken no time at all for the Indian to realize that he loved her.

He stood up, feeling stronger. He signaled to her with the bow that she was going to hunt. She acknowledged him with a salute of her hand.

Twilight was good hunting. Harkana came across more than one fox which had much the same business on its mind as he did. He walked down the ravine until it sloped up, opening onto the bulk of the plain. The moon rose to keep a curved eye on the world.

Harkana was apprehensive. He had known trouble all his days but had lived largely untroubled because it was so ubiquitous. Here, with a soft and sudden interlude, life had presented him with an alternative he had never dreamed possible. Raw freedom he had known for most of his life, accentuated by the risk to it. The horse had granted him the zenith of that freedom; the girl offered him someone to share it with. By the moon, thought Harkana the Orphan, I hate to leave it all behind.

He killed a rabbit fattened on spring vegetation and carried it back to the camping place still skewered on the arrow that had claimed its life. From far away he could make out the pinprick of firelight that she had lit at the entrance to the cave, like a beacon to guide him home at the end of the day. Happiness, he reflected, had always gone hand in hand with hopelessness.

The distant dot of fire reminded him of the burning brand in the hacienda window and the man he had killed by its glow. He thought back on the battle that night and the mountain lion and

181

Manuel de Robles. "Everyone dies, Robles," he had said to the white man, "only the moon decides." Deep down, Harkana knew that the happiness bound up in the horse and the woman was certain to execute him in the end. It was an interlude only. Soon he would despise himself for it. The realm of life after death was beyond the sphere of his decision. The way of the Tehuelche was not. Harkana climbed slowly up the slant of scree, knowing that the doubts about the future would never plague him again.

He found that she had made a mattress of soft ferns and trussed grasses. The fire was quickly encouraged into life while he skinned and gutted the rabbit. He reskewered it on the arrow and gave it to the girl to turn on the crude spit he had set up. Harkana watched her kneeling in front of the small fire. Her hair hung down so low it almost touched the ground. Her back was straight, her hips were slim, and her buttocks tight and muscular. She had long, slender feet in which the sinews rippled whenever she changed position. Harkana studied her sharp profile as she turned the meat to and fro with a sculptured hand.

Pandra's profile was rim-lit by the flames, as if by a halo. Harkana was looking at her hard when she suddenly turned her face full upon him and gave him a smile that had never before been seen in his world.

"I am Pandra, daughter of Juma, of the coastal Tehuelches," she said.

"You are Juma's daughter," breathed the Orphan very softly. "Yes, you carry yourself with the nobility and confidence that would become a chief's daughter. My name is Harkana the Orphan."

"And you are from the inlanders' tribe, that of Seh Saapelt?"

"I am. But the great Seh Saapelt went to the moon shortly before I left the tribe to seek out your father. His two lifetimes have ended in peace."

"My father spoke of him once or twice that I can remember. They met on one occasion, I believe. It must have been the time of the war with the Ranqueles. I was very young then."

"How is your father? I ask this for I was on my way to see your tribe concerning the changes the white man has wrought on the land of the Tehuelches. Have the coastal Tehuelches suffered at the hands of the white man?"

182

Pandra continued to turn the rabbit as she answered. "Clashes there have been, more than I can remember. The white man's new guanaco has devoured many of the pasture lands which have belonged to Juma's people for generations. We have made raids and been ourselves raided. My father is wary, for the whites have weapons of great power. It is the wire that he hates more than anything else. You know of the wire in the interior?"

"Of course." The Orphan nodded. "It separates the land everywhere. Will your father make war with the tribe that was Seh Saapelt's?"

"You command them now?"

"I do."

"Full-scale war. That is what you are advocating?"

"It is," said Harkana, watching how she took in his words without flinching. "War unto the death, our death. War for the land, our land. War because there is no other way where the white man comes, no way other than the way of the Tehuelche."

"I think my father will understand what you are proposing. Whether or not he will agree to bring his tribe alongside your own and confront the white man totally until death, well, my lord, it is not for the daughter of the chief to say."

"This talk of death destroys the appetite. And we, of all people, have a right to be famished after so long and eventful a day as today. The meat is ready, Pandra, let us eat."

The girl looked closely at the singed flesh, testing it with Harkana's knife. She replaced it over the glowing embers.

"The meat needs a little more time. There is no hurry, Harkana the Orphan, for my father has no doubt already given me up for dead. My pony is bound to have returned to the camping ground without me. The dirges have been sung. The offerings to the moon have already been made. For the moment, we have only each other to worry about. Time is on our side. Tell me of the horse."

Harkana recounted the tale of how he had found and trained Zorkan Rood, but he refrained from talking about how he had come to be traveling alone as half a man so far north of his tribal home.

"There will be enough time to hear the whole story, beautiful Pandra. Come, eat the meat of the great bow. As you suggested, we have time enough to tarry here for a few more days. Then we will ride to seek your father and repair the damage we have done him."

When the rabbit was finished, the Orphan fed the fire another log. Pandra re-dressed his wound. The flow of blood had been staunched. Satisfied, she pressed her lips close to the gash made by the white man's bullet. Harkana felt a cruel gentleness come over him. He bent forward and gathered up her hands. Splashing water from the gourd over them, he rinsed away the last traces of their meal while the fresh log caught and flared, throwing out hoops of orange heat. The inside of the cave came alive with dancing shadows.

Harkana stared into her eyes as he ran his hand through the mass of her hair. She shook her head to free it all, feeling her heart quicken in an unfamiliar tattoo. Pandra let his hands explore every inch of her shoulders, back, and thighs. Harkana's breath came in shorter gasps as he held her more determinedly. His belly was full but hollowed by another kind of hunger.

The girl felt a wave of longing sweep over her, and she sagged against him. The pressure of her palms on his broad back gave her indescribable pleasure. Her blood raced as she felt the labored effort of his breathing. This was the man who had risked his life to save hers; the lord whose blood had been spilled in her defense. She licked at his chest, clinging to him for support as a passionate faintness came over her. Pandra felt herself lifted and carried to the sleeping place she had so painstakingly prepared. He placed her upon it with exaggerated care and knelt beside her for a long moment before he allowed himself to gather her to him.

Their legs entwined like lianas. Crushed together, they discovered how her breasts blossomed against the strength of his skin. Their mouths met and swirled, both tongues searching for a hold. Pandra caught a glimpse of the stars of the universe studding the ceiling of their haven as she gave herself to him. Her whole short but extreme life seemed to flow before her eyes, whether open or closed, as Harkana caressed and kissed every plane and crevice of her long body. Time alone stood still. Everything else moved, melted, flowed, formed, broke, formed again until they became but one body, possessed of two minds, beating with dual hearts.

She felt the initial pain of his hard arrow, Harkana's arrow, the warlord's mighty shaft. Then the pain was erased and there was only a vast galaxy of delight shifting overhead as he rode above her, exultant, triumphant, vibrant as Pandra suffered love for the first time.

The ride was long and every hill plowed with new excitement. Harkana felt scorched by a grinding heat. Its pressure built up but he fought the early volcano, stemming the flow, damming the rush of his ecstacy. Pandra felt it too, that half-controlled urgency thrust within her, curling her toes as it soared to a peak of unspeakable passion which neither could resist. She cried out, but he was deaf to all sounds save that of his pending explosion. Her fingernails clawed at the small of his back, pleading with his body to deliver. The shock of it caused Pandra to stiffen for a second, and then her entire body relaxed into a delicious wafting satisfaction which she had never dreamed existed as Harkana's iron resolve broke asunder and he bathed her with the flood of his loving.

And then they slept.

It was a long night of loving, interspersed with words and stories and past and future and the reconstruction of the fire at timely intervals. It ended with the sun winking at them with its eastern eye.

"How is the wound, my lord?" she asked him.

"It is nothing. Come, Pandra, let us ride on Zorkan Rood, that you may know his magic. We will hunt for peccary during the day and return here again tonight." So he showed her the speed and the power that was the Scarmaker. And she guided him back to a place by the ocean, a place she had known since she was a little girl. She introduced him to the awesome might of the sea, its force and its restlessness. One of the most enduring images that Pandra was to carry with her was of Harkana standing thigh-deep in the crashing Atlantic swells. She would dive through the waves and bob up in the troughs, while he stood there like a statue carved from granite, letting the heavy waves crash down on him, rocking him back on to his heels as he went under, until the waves flowed past to reveal him unmoved.

Their nights burned with acts of loving without rout or surrender on either side. They became one double-hearted body. Her sleep sometimes eclipsed the strength of his arms around her and she would dream that he had left her or been killed. Then she would snap into wakefulness, only to find that such dread had no basis in fact. Like a rock he lay beside her, the contours of his long body dovetailing with her own. At such time their love seemed immortal. Yet the bad dreams always came back. Worries picked at the carcass of her brain. The thought of losing him forever sent a feverish electricity into her body, making sleep a lost cause. Yet he was always there within reach, whether it was the middle of the night or on the morning when she extracted the promise from him.

"Promise me that you will not die and leave me alive," she begged.

"As much as it is within my power to do so, I promise it, Pandra."

"You understand what it is that I am asking you to do?"

"You are asking me to allow you to take your own life, or for me to kill you, when my own death becomes inevitable," Harkana said.

"Yes. And therefore to live after me, no matter for how many days or hours or even minutes that separate our deaths, knowing that I am no more. I could not bear this. I could not do this for you, lord. And yet I am asking it of you."

"I understand."

After five days, they ended their life of seclusion and rode the Scarmaker inland to the north on a path which would take them back to Juma. Harkana kept the pace exceedingly slow, in order that they might spend one more night alone on the way. Pandra seemed to have much on her mind. She had left her father and the tribe as a young girl with a young girl's problems. She was returning as a grown woman with all the violence of heartache that accompanies that transition.

The scouts brought word of their approach. Thus, they rode into the assembled village, with Juma at the apex of the human wedge to greet them.

186

"Father, can you ever forgive me?" Pandra implored him as Harkana brought the horse to a standstill, towering over the smiling face.

"Happily," Juma answered, "forgiveness is one of the few things that it is within my power to grant. Now, come to my toldo. I will have food and drink brought, and in return you can tell me of the adventures which have kept you from your father for so long."

The two riders, sheltered beneath the single garment they possessed between them, rode on to the largest tent in the village. Pandra dismounted with the alpaca poncho to cover her nakedness. The Orphan, wearing only the short leather cloth around his middle, took the horse over to the stock lines. He busied himself removing the bridle and combing the matted mane with one of the crude wooden instruments which the Tehuelches fashioned. He led the horse to water and to graze, fondling it with his hands before he left it and returned to Juma's tent. He had been gone over half an hour.

One glance at the chief was enough. Pandra had already told him of her escape in some detail. Evidently she had mentioned the reason for Harkana's presence on the lands of the coastal Tehuelches. Juma's reply was mirrored in the eyes he turned to face the stranger as the tent flap let in the daylight. They said yes, we will fight. They avowed Juma's intention to bring his six hundred fighting men and all the rest of his people inland to unite with those of Seh Saapelt. Without a word having been spoken between them, Harkana and Juma had become allies. They would work and train side by side. They would live out the rest of the spring moons together. Then they would travel together to rendezvous with Raganor. Harkana the Orphan could see it all in the laughing brown eyes of the warrior chief. When he finally squatted down opposite him, all that was left to discuss was how they would go about it. The rest was just the formalities of respect between one man and another.

CHAPTER THIRTEEN

BRUCE McCLELLAN HAD RIDDEN all the way to the train station at Tres Arboles to personally collect three wagonloads of freight. The Remington repeating rifles came in pinewood boxes, which resembled coffins made for children. The cargo was stacked evenly on McClellan's three flatbed wagons: ten in a box, twenty boxes, together with ammunition enough to fight a long war.

In a matter of weeks every cowhand, gaucho, and rancher was equipped with one of the latest and most sophisticated firearms of his day. McClellan considered the collection and dispersal of the weapons the last link in the chain of effort he had made throughout the spring. The new hacienda was complete, apart from the furnishings and the interior paintwork. His fences now stretched around seventy-two thousand acres of prime land, of which several thousand lay along the southern bank of the Rio Colorado. Not that he owned the most southerly land by any means. In some cases, the estancias reached the Rio Negro, whose waters ensured their success.

Tres Arboles itself had become a bustling little township. It had not happened overnight, or even in the four brief months since McClellan had last been there. It just seemed that way to every man who came twice or three times each year and still remembered it for the stunted ombú struck by lightning long before the railroad came. Now it boasted two hotels, a row of stores, a livery stable, three churches, the telegraph office, and, of course, the station itself. The bigger of the hotels offered a restaurant in which diners could have their steaks cooked to order, preceded by prawns and washed down with imported Chilean wines or even German or French vintages. Yet, no more than two hundred miles to the south, the last of the Tehuelches were eating almost raw peccary flesh and drinking water straight from the river.

The telegraph now linked virtually every estancia, providing Morse code communication in case of attack. And, in returning home at the head of his small military supply train, McClellan and his men rode alongside miles of newly laid railway track. It would connect Tres Arboles with Tossini, the small settlement seventy miles farther south that had been named after the assassinated chief of police. The line was due to open in three more weeks.

Along the southern coast, fortunes were being made in a few years. Sheep were proving the ideal cash livestock to rear on the patchy pastures of Patagonia. Those ranchers who were new to the north were saying that the Indians could have the southern wilderness for their wanderings, but in truth, the whites had already taken that as well. Somewhere lost between these two immigrant worlds stood the vanishing culture of the pampas Indians. Only the Tehuelches had any strength in numbers and horses with which to resist. Their scope of migration had been drastically cut down. At the time Raganor met up with Juma and Harkana they were blissfully unaware of by how much it had been cut during the course of one short springtime.

The game, too, was scarce. Rheas and guanacos and wild pigs had been hunted mercilessly with high-powered rifles. It was sport for the white men. It was life or death for the Tehuelches.

Harkana and Juma had trained more than six hundred dog soldiers. Once joined with the tribe that once had been known as Seh Saapelt's, they numbered over eleven hundred. The total number of horses that mingled their dust and their droppings along the migration route was close to five thousand head. And there were the womenfolk, the children, and the few elders who had somehow lived more than the natural span of life.

The Indians were short of food, compared with previous years, but they were a long way from starving. They were too resourceful for that. They killed sheep and cattle as readily as they hunted down the natural game of their territory. The horses, too, remained in good condition, hardened by the paucity of easy grazing. The Tehuelches, united under Harkana the Orphan as never before in their history, came northward.

News of their numbers, their route, and their whereabouts clicked over the talking wires. McClellan was staggered when he heard. How and why had they managed to form one mass of tribespeople when all of history had shown that the Tehuelches were clannish, a divided people? He wired via Tres Arboles to Buenos Aires itself, asking for army support. Even while the messages, demands, excuses, and conflicting suggestions were issuing to and fro, the Tehuelche horde was increasing. The small, independent groups came to Harkana on the move, asking to be part of the great push against the common enemy. To each of them the Orphan said the same thing—that they would tear down the fences, slay the cattle and sheep, and kill all the white men who stayed to defend them south of the Great River. In the end the chiefs of the white men would send many soldiers and the Tehuelches would die. There could be no other end. The small groups stayed, bringing the stride of their mounts into step with the trained legions of Harkana's people.

Buenos Aires sent three hundred fifty men. They came out by train from Tucumán, arriving in Tres Arboles on what was officially considered on the calendar as the penultimate day of spring. They camped the night on the outskirts of town, then saddled up the horses they had shipped with them in the long gondolas and rode south. They followed the same route beside the new rail track which McClellan had taken two and a half weeks before.

The small army unit was under the command of the youngest lieutenant colonel in the Argentine army. His name was Eduardo González and he came from a well-established military family. González had excelled himself at the military academy, passing every examination with flying colors. He had risen through the ranks with astonishing speed. However, outside two spells of riot control, one in Tucumán itself, the other in Salta, he had never seen action. He had fought many a mock battle situation and commanded platoons and regiments in full-scale maneuvers. He had read the accounts of military commanders all over the world. His knowledge of Napoleonic tactics and Marlborough's brainwaves was encyclopedic. His favorite pastime was war games. Lieutenant Colonel González was thirty-one years old.

González and his men met up with McClellan at about the same time that the Indians reached the most southerly barbed wire fences. The land within those fences was owned by a very tough Italian immigrant who had spent only a year in Argentina. His name was Viglio. In his native Tuscany, he was wanted by the carabinieri on a number of charges, including murder. Things had become so hot that Viglio had bought himself passage on a ship leaving Genoa for Rio de Janeiro. He had intended to settle in Brazil, but he had knifed a whore who tried to steal his wallet while he should have been asleep but wasn't and had got out of the country on yet another seaborne passage, this time to BA. Viglio had managed to extract most of his money from Italy, which would have disputed his ownership of nine tenths of it. He looked at Argentina's capital for a few days, decided that it had a long way to go to compare with Florence, Siena, or Venice, and made off on a three-months tour of the interior. Argentina seemed to have a great deal of land and a dearth of just about everything else. So Viglio had sunk his money into land. He bought a few thousand acres on the north bank of the Rio Negro and paid such good wages, way over the average, that he found no shortage of workers to run the place for him, raising a few cattle, a lot of sheep, and enough food crops to keep him more or less self-sufficient. Viglio was completely unperturbed by the stories he had heard about the savages of Patagonia. He had seen no trace of anyone apart from his own hands and those of his neighbor to the west. Viglio was not the type to be scared by what he had heard about but not set his own eyes on. The day he did finally see Tehuelches, they were ripping down his wire fences.

He gathered up as many of his boys as he could in a short time and rode to the river. Galloping down on the small band of Indians, the whites opened fire. The Tehuelches left the fencing and all but one, who took a bullet in the back, leaped down the riverbank. The whites who followed met such a hail of arrows from the two hundred warriors who had concealed themselves there that they were all dead before they knew what had hit them. Viglio too, pierced with three shafts, smacked down in the dust, having lost not only his land but his life.

Harkana ordered the rest of the wire pulled down and then led a large contingent on to the hacienda. Two of the remaining hands saw them coming. One fled, and the other ran for the house and began to transmit a cable to the neighboring hacienda. Half the message had been relayed when the line went dead. The cables remained intact, for the Tehuelches knew nothing of their function. They simply shot down the cowhand who had been operating the key and burned the hacienda to the ground.

A report of the incident reached Bruce McClellan, and he duly relayed it to the army commander, whose men were camped on his land at the time.

"We will ride south after them at first light, señor McClellan," said the young colonel.

"Wait a minute, I wouldn't be too rash if I were you. You do realize, Colonel, just how heavily outnumbered you are?" McClellan had not yet made up his mind if he liked the young man or not. He appeared fearless, which was a point in his favor; then again, he was obviously naive in many ways, which went against him in McClellan's book.

"I am aware of the enemy's numbers, thank you, señor McClellan. However, it is my duty to protect life and land from the savages, and I cannot do that by sitting around in camp."

"Why not wait for reinforcements, González? Just keep up the patrols across the Colorado and wait for BA to react when they get the news of the latest incident. Remember that Roca came down here with fully eight thousand men to put down the Ranqueles uprising. And they only mustered a couple of thousand themselves, about the same as the Tehuelches in number, by all accounts."

"Militarily, the Roca operation was a bit costly, in my opinion. Could have been done with a quarter of the men. I have three hundred fifty professional soldiers, señor McClellan, armed with the most up-to-date weapons that money can buy. With your vigilantes acting as scouts and guides, that brings my force to four hundred. I am sure we are a match for anything the savages have in mind. One or two volleys and they'll turn and run, you mark my words. I don't intend to annihilate them in a pitched battle, you know, merely to show them who's boss. Need to give them a bloody nose, that will do the trick. Once the main force arrives, we'll move in and settle them once and for all."

McClellan, never a man to hide his feelings, became exasperated.

"Colonel González, with all due respect for your rank, sir, this is not a matter of giving out bloody noses! Tehuelches are, er, are, well, they're Tehuelches, dammit! They are quite deadly for many reasons, not the least of which is their numbers. You talk of my own scouting party—well, think of it like this. We have been down here a decade or so, some of us a bit longer. We know the country well. The Tehuelches have lived here for centuries and know every nook and cranny and fissure between here and the sea, as far as Tierra del Fuego. They are organized for the first time in their history, led by some warlord or other. They believe in what they are fighting for. They are willing to die for it, get shot to pieces, maimed, and blinded for it. Can't you see that? You don't just ride down there and give out a few bloody noses, hombre! You take your life in your hands even if you have several thousand troops in back of you and field guns and cannon as support, which, may I remind you, we do not have!"

"Señor McClellan," sighed González, who had listened out of respect for the civilian, "I appreciate your concern. You and your friends are not under my command. Therefore, while the army would very much appreciate your assistance as scouts, we cannot insist upon it. The maps of the region are none too good, but no doubt we will be able to manage without you. Am I making myself clear? I am under orders to protect the settlers down here. It is my intention to seek out the Tehuelches who perpetrated this raid and deal with them. I shall issue orders for the men to be ready to move out at dawn. Whether or not you and the other civilians care to accompany us is for you to decide. That, sir, is my last word on the matter."

The young colonel turned on his booted heel and marched back to the mess tent, where the cook was spreading a clean white tablecloth over the trestle table.

McClellan watched him go, shaking his head as his own words came flooding back at him. He had sounded just like Manuel de Robles on the night of the raid on his old estancia. You win some and you lose some, McClellan decided; whichever way it goes, you always learn something from it.

The last drop of spring dried in the heat of summer. The land that hardened from the frost and cold in midwinter now hardened anew. Its surface cracked like fresh bread crust. The intermittent seasons of spring and autumn were but short interludes. The summers and winters seemed almost endless. The grasses of the pampas had thickened and grown tall again. The wind was erratic, even muted. The high grass leaned before it almost casually, like men bowing in homage to a king. It was a weird season. There was something not quite tangible in the air, something that vibrated on the earth itself. It infiltrated a man's mind, got under his skin. It was stillness. Its effect was especially noticeable on those new to the region. The stillness made them irritable and irrational. Sometimes they behaved rashly and took decisions they afterward regretted—if they could.

Colonel Eduardo González was furious with the world at large. For an entire fortnight he had ridden his troop up, down, and across the pitiless pampas in search of Tehuelches to fight. Burned by the sun, plagued by lack of water, choked with dust, and they had fought with none at all. They had seen plenty. Always they remained on the horizon, tantalizing mirages of flesh and blood. The Tehuelches melted away like ghosts. The most worrying thing for González was the point made by McClellan as to who was keeping an eye on whom. The vigilante settlers were anxious to return to their homes. They had stock to tend, families to look after. McClellan had acres of wheat to harvest. It was a busy time of year.

"Why don't they just stay put and let me kill them!" moaned

194

the frustrated officer in charge. He directed the nonsensical question at McClellan, who ten minutes before had told him of his intention to return to his farm. He would be taking the rest of the civilian scouts along with him.

"I can't say that I blame you, señor McClellan. We have provisions for another two weeks, so I think we'll circle westward just one more time and rejoin you at the end of another five or six days. My sergeant and I feel we know the ground pretty well now anyway."

"Patience," McClellan advised, "you must learn to have patience. No doubt the order for additional troops has now been passed and a cable to that effect will be awaiting us at my house. Why not leave with us and see for yourself?"

"I hate to leave without at least a skirmish to our credit. Destroys a man's pride to be given the runaround like this. Bad for morale."

"Tehuelches are not easy to pin down," McClellan reminded him soothingly. "Let the summer proceed and keep up the patrols. That is all you can do with your small force. Once the grazing becomes more sparse we will be able to divine more accurately where they will move next."

"That's all very well and good for you to say, señor McClellan," retorted the harassed young colonel, "but I have my career to think about. This was to be my big chance."

"I do sympathize with your predicament, my dear Colonel. I really do. The trouble is that we are facing an enemy who wishes to avoid a pitched battle at all costs. When we have four thousand men at our disposal, instead of four hundred, then, and only then, will we be in a position to force the issue. For the time being, the Tehuelche holds the upper hand because of his superior mobility. Wait until the pasture is hard to find and we will be able to predict his movements like clockwork. Without grass the Tehuelche has no horses; and without horses the Tehuelche is nothing at all. Just give it another month or two. The summer has only just begun, after all."

"Two months!" González exploded. "I can't possibly keep riding around this blasted wilderness for another two months. I shall be relieved of my command inside of three weeks. It wouldn't surprise me in the least if there is a telegraph to that effect waiting for me at your house, señor McClellan. How ironic if, at this very moment, both cables are sitting one on top of the other. The one informing me that I have several thousand men to command instead of this handful. And the other withdrawing that same command. Two months is too late," González repeated for good measure. Additional problems seemed to be presenting themselves like punches.

"You really don't have much choice, Colonel, I'm afraid," said McClellan gingerly. He tried his best to make it sound less like a statement of fact than a gesture of heartfelt commiseration. "Whatever you do," the burly Scot went on, "do not allow your frustration to slacken your vigilance. I have fought Indians ever since I came to Argentina. And furthermore, I underestimated what Tehuelches can do once myself. Most men who make that mistake do not live to repeat it. I was lucky that day. It is paramount to remember that the Tehuelche is a master of changing balance. Keep your wits about you at all times out here, González, lest you become the quarry instead of the hunter. Tehuelches do not play games, not ever."

"I really do not think I need to worry unduly about being able to defend my position. I do have three hundred and fifty fully trained men under me, you know."

"So you keep reminding me, Colonel. However, I shall never ever forget the night when I almost lost my life and that of my wife because I was a mite too stubborn in my pride. As it was, nineteen men died that night and my farm was razed to the ground. Had a man called Robles with me, by chance. We didn't exactly see eye to eye on many things, but I don't mind admitting he saved a few lives that night. Knew all about Indians, did Robles, the kind of knowledge that keeps people alive."

González was smarting with a humiliation it had never been the Scotsman's intention to inflict. The colonel looked him straight in the eye when he spoke again.

"Señor McClellan, I have been a soldier in the Argentine army since I was eighteen years old. It is a profession in which I have done reasonably well, if I do say so myself."

McClellan sighed. "How old are you now, Colonel, if I may ask?"

"You may," González allowed. "I am now thirty-one."

"That's very young for your rank, I believe." González opened his mouth to agree, but McClellan added the bite too quickly: "It is even younger to die."

González reddened, more in anger than embarrassment.

"I have the honor to be the youngest lieutenant colonel in the army, señor," he snapped out.

McClellan was losing patience.

"Ever fought in a pitched battle, González? Ever faced a horde of screaming savages thundering down on you upon superb horses, each one of them intent on taking your life? I'm talking about experience, for which there never has been nor ever will be any substitute, be it in warfare, farming, or anything else."

"Age has nothing to do with it," retorted the younger man, feeling obliged to defend himself when he would have triumphed by ignoring McClellan's criticism altogether.

"I agree, hombre. Thirteen years a soldier and never seen a battle."

"Times have been quiet in Tucumán province. I can't help it if there are no battles to fight. I've fought enough exercise campaigns and night maneuvers to stand me in good stead for the real thing. Can't you see, señor McClellan, that that's the reason why I'm so eager to clash with the Tehuelches while I have the opportunity?"

"Sure, son. I can understand that. But people react differently when blood is being spilled. That's all I'm saying. Normally unshakable types can go to pieces, lose their heads, make the wrong decision. Really, Eduardo," he said with an attempt at affection, "I'm only trying to point out that this is no place to be starting out and Tehuelches are not the sort of enemy one uses for practice. They are very much the real thing. Just remember that many of these Tehuelche warriors killed a man in battle before you and I were into our first pair of long trousers. I learned about them the hard way and was fortunate to survive. Why don't you learn the easy way, then you might do the same."

"I'll run my own affairs, if you don't mind, señor McClellan. I am an officer in the national army, after all, no matter what my age and experience. This is not a civilian operation."

"As you wish, young Colonel," McClellan said with a resigned

197

shrug of his broad shoulders. "For myself, I'm going north in the morning, and the rest of the settlers will either ride with me or pull their gauchos out within the next couple of days. This can be a very remote and isolated region to men who have never been this far south before. The tribe you are facing have lived here or hereabouts for hundreds of years. You are fighting them on their own ground, their own terms. Do not permit them to capitalize on your ignorance. That is all I have to say. I am not trying to belittle you, Eduardo. I am only trying to help."

González burned inwardly but kept his temper. He had been told to humor McClellan as far as possible, for his was a voice that other settlers would listen to. For some reason not yet obvious to the young officer, that was a fact considered significant by his superiors.

Eleven weary, saddle-sore, fruitless days later, Colonel Eduardo González found himself getting a further dose of unwanted advice, this time from his sergeant, Flores.

"With the greatest respect, sir," the sergeant was pointing out, "this is not the best place to make camp." The sergeant blinked nervously. It had taken the best part of a whole month of patrols under the young lieutenant colonel for him to reach the point at which he felt compelled to speak up. Lives were at risk. His own and those of all the troopers under his care.

"Really, Sergeant," González drawled, making each word a drop of acid, "then pray proceed to enlighten your superior officer as to where he should be camping?"

"Almost anywhere but right here, sir," said Flores bluntly.

"Sergeant," sighed the colonel, with elaborate exasperation, "let me remind you of the following. First, the men, you and I included, are both tired and hungry. Second, we still have three very long days of hard riding before we reach the relative safety and comfort of the estancias. Third, one month ago, when we left those estancias, there were no dispatches from headquarters, which makes it pretty damn certain that they will be there this time. I doubt very much if those dispatches will contain hearty congratulations on our success, since we have had no success. I fully expect them to either relieve me of my command or to threaten to do so if the next patrol proves equally negative. The fourth point is that this ravine has a natural stream running through it, shelter from the wind, and a plentiful supply of fire-wood—plentiful, that is, by the stringent standards of this god-awful country. And last, I have not been relieved of my command as yet, and until then I give the orders around here, and don't you ever forget it!"

Flores, a man in his mid-forties, set his lantern jaw grimly and stood his ground.

"Sir, it is precisely because the ravine is so ideal for a camp that it is so lethal. The far end is so narrow that we would have to ride single file through it. The walls on both sides are not higher than thirty feet but are almost perpendicular. It is there-fore a box canyon to all intents and purposes. The high walls and the running water will muffle sounds of approaching enemy, and the night is moonless to boot! The Tehuelches have been seen shadowing our movements for the past four days. They are well aware that fifty men under señor McClellan have left us and are not coming back. Our force has therefore been depleted by one eighth. It would be far safer to camp on the open plain, with room to make a run for it if attacked by vastly superior numbers. In here, all they have to do is keep us penned down and starve us out. Sir, we have no communications open. There is nobody coming to help us out, not in less than a week. And that is only if McClellan starts to worry immediately the next three days are up."

"Sergeant, aren't you overreacting just a little bit? There are no Indians attacking us as yet, or had that fact slipped your mind? We are not besieged, and in the morning we can mount up and ride out of here just as easily as we rode in. Another thing—I did not come down here to retreat but to engage the enemy, something which I have proved myself a total failure in carrying out. We have our guards to warn us of approaching forces, Sergeant, and we will camp here. Good Lord, man, they are only armed with bows and arrows after all!"

"Our movements have been far too regular over the past month, if I may say so, sir. If the Indians have any sense they will have noticed the patterns which we have stuck to. They will have ascertained that we are short of supplies and heading north to reprovision and rest up. If I were their leader, tonight would be the night I would choose for my attack." The sergeant appeared to be on the brink of saying more, then just added a belated "sir" and turned his head to look at the first fires being lit.

"They are savages, Sergeant. They do not, as you put it, have any sense. Otherwise we would not be here in the first place, or, if we were, we would be several thousand strong instead of just a few hundred. Post the guards and get some sleep. I have listened to all I am going to."

"At least," persisted the sergeant, with valorous tenacity, "allow me to double the guards and change them every two hours instead of every four?"

"Sergeant, you are trying my patience too far. I want the normal guard posted, not a double guard. If I wanted double guard I would have told you to post double guard. But I did not ask for double guard, now did I? Why do you think that was, eh, Sergeant? It was because I want the normal guard posted, changed at regular four-hour intervals. See to it!"

"Sir, please listen to me! The men are too exhausted to do four-hour picket duties and remain fully alert."

"Nonsense. They are professional soldiers and they will act as such at all times. Any man caught sleeping at his post will be put on a charge. Make sure the men understand that. I make my rounds as and when it suits me."

"But, sir—"

"I warn you for the very last time, Sergeant. I'll have those stripes of yours torn from the sleeves of your uniform if you do not obey me this instant!" González was glaring at his noncommissioned officer with the knuckles of his right hand clenched white on the hilt of his saber.

The sergeant gave up. "Yes, sir. I hope I'm wrong, sir," he admitted, saluting crisply, "for all our sakes."

The sergeant was not wrong. Harkana had drawn up all of Juma's men, six hundred dog soldiers, and was holding them in readiness about one mile east of the ravine where his scouts had informed him the whites were preparing to spend the night. The Orphan was suspicious. Why had it all been made so easy for him? Natural suspicion was one of the major keys to longevity in the world of the Tehuelches. He had sent out five trios of scouts who circled far out in every direction. They found not a trace of more white soldiers. After the last of them reported in, Harkana was sure that this was not a trap. Unbelievably, the whites had camped in the ravine without a backup force anywhere near to hand. The Orphan waited for one more hour and then gave the order to move in.

The men dismounted and covered the last few hundred yards on foot, leaving the mounts in the care of the horse handlers. By midnight, Harkana had surrounded the twin lips of the ravine crests with his best archers. A phalanx of lancers blocked the entrance down which the white soldiers had come. Half a mile off, another hundred lancers waited for the signal which would bring them charging in, should the whites make a bid to break out from the trap that had been laid.

Harkana himself took up a position at the narrow defile which prevented the ravine from being a total box canyon. He kept a score of archers by his side.

All was inky black. The Tehuelches had moved into position without making a sound. The campfires flickered down and went out as the soldiers slept, apart from the dozen who maintained the vigil of the guard.

Harkana had told them to hold their fire. They had effectively sealed off the ravine. The gray-coated white soldiers were surrounded from on high by six hundred bows. The Orphan rested his men and waited for the first light of dawn.

When it came the Tehuelches stood up all around the rim of the quebrada. It took some minutes for the first soldier to notice them, so still did they stand with their bows at the ready. It was almost as if they were part of the rock itself, so mysteriously had they materialized. The sunrise was just poised to throw in the first splashes of orange light as the word spread like a cholera through the trapped soldiers. By word of mouth and gripped arm and pointed finger, every one of them came to know of the Indians' resolute presence. The rising sun shot a shaft of daylight through the slim defile on the eastern quarter of the ravine. Its rays were littered with particles of dust.

"Will they attack?" trembled Colonel Eduardo González to Sergeant Flores.

"If I was a mind-reader, sir," he replied, no longer having

enough left of his life to bother hiding the sarcasm from his superior officer, "then I would have foreseen this last night and warned you accordingly. Oh, but then I almost forgot. I did utter a warning to that effect, if I am not mistaken, so perhaps I am in a stronger position than most to predict the future. Let's see, sir. I would say that in a few hours every man here will be food for the buzzards."

"But when did they come? We heard nothing, the guards heard nothing," González rambled, tension cracking his voice. "You can't blame me, Sergeant, you can't! How was I to know? How could I have known? Look, should we fight or try to run for it? Give ourselves up as prisoners perhaps? Maybe try to parley with their leader? You're the experienced man here, what do you think we should do?"

The sergeant looked at González and spat a thin yellow jet of saliva onto the ground between them. Real saliva, González thought, at a time like this. It was something, to be able to do that in the face of death. He felt his own parched mouth, grown almost furry by the fear which coated his tongue.

"I think," drawled the sergeant very slowly, scanning the rows upon rows of archers perched above, "that we should all commend our souls to God and prepare to die like men." The sergeant picked up his rifle and prepared to walk away.

"Die?" said the colonel, his voice startled into a higher pitch than usual. "You mean they intend to kill us, all of us?"

"Sir," sneered the sergeant, stopping and turning his head, "what would Tehuelches do with prisoners? What language would we parley in? I am beginning to think that you really are quite as crazy as you have demonstrated for the past month. And to think we all gave up our lives for a man like you!"

The sergeant walked away. This time he did not stop and did not turn his head, even though the colonel spoke again before he collapsed on the ground and commenced to weep.

Harkana watched all of this, totally impassive. He was almost out of earshot but he caught some of the words.

One of the younger soldiers could stand the strain no longer. He made a rush for his horse and began to saddle it feverishly. Harkana allowed him to tighten the girth and mount up; then, as he galloped for the far end of the ravine, Harkana drew back the great bow, letting fly the arrow just as soon as the fletching kissed his lips. The boy died and the war cry rang out all around, made all the more terrifying by the slight echo.

"Har-ka-na!"

Then the arrows rained down mercilessly. The soldiers fired at the heads that appeared, but the targets were small and fleeting. It was a massacre. The whites had hardly a scrap of cover. Their screams filled the whole valley, reverberating on and on. Then those that survived after the first hour of wholesale slaughter found a vestige of cover; it was provided by the heaped bodies of their fallen comrades.

A few Tehuelches had half their heads blown off by the impact of the heavy-caliber bullets, but, all in all, Harkana's casualties were few. In the end, more out of misery and frustration than anything else, Sergeant Flores told the remainder of his men to throw down their rifles. The men obeyed his order and the valley shook with silence, broken only by the groans of the wounded. One of the wounded was Colonel Eduardo González, who had taken an arrow through the calf of his right leg.

Harkana gave the order to cease firing. The arrows had flown like locusts for more than two hours. Harkana called Juma to him and told him of his intentions, then mounted Zorkan Rood and rode down through the defile, alone and unarmed, save for the small steel knife at his waist.

Hundreds of bows with arrows at the ready followed his passage. Every pair of Tehuelche eyes searched the twenty-seven survivors for any attempt to grab for a weapon and harm their leader. Harkana the Orphan rode defenseless through the huddled bleeding foes who had sought to defeat him, knowing that he was as safe as he had ever been in his whole life.

All eyes watched him ride down on the huge silver-gray stallion. When Zorkan Rood stood directly over the wounded colonel, its enormous shadow across the white man's body, Harkana addressed them in their own language. Several of the graycoats recoiled visibly, as if hearing a voice from hell.

"I am Harkana the Orphan, warlord of the Tehuelches. You have sought to find me and to kill me for nearly one moon passing. Now you have found me. Now you have died. This is the land of the Tehuelche and you trespass upon it in violence."

Harkana spoke without a trace of emotion in his tone.

"I, I am in command here," began the cracked voice of the colonel.

"No, here no one commands but me, white man."

"Look," González whimpered, sweat rolling down his face, "don't kill us. There's no need to kill us. What purpose does it serve to kill us?"

"What purpose does it serve to keep you alive?" asked the Orphan, genuinely puzzled. He lifted his voice away from the wounded man and shouted one short, staccato phrase in his own language.

"What! What did you say?" cried out the colonel, frightened beyond belief at not understanding.

"I simply called for one of the reasons why to ride down here," said the Orphan. He looked down at the pitiful young officer, his eyes balloons of pleading. This is not the way a Tehuelche would die, the Orphan thought. The white man does not even know how to die. "You are a fool," Harkana told him. "To make things so easy for us. You wanted a battle, but this was not a battle, it was a massacre. You crossed the Great River, the one you call Rio Colorado. You are too few. Your men and your mounts are tired out. You are as conspicuous as ombú trees when you ride. And as predictable as the sunrise. You camp in a hole from which there is no escape, guarded by men so inept that they had to be woken up to die. Last, you grovel at my feet, begging me to save your life, instead of fighting to the death in silence. Well, send your soldiers in their thousands, in their tens of thousands. We will show them how to fight—and how to die."

Pandra appeared on her pinto pony, leaning back as she descended the eyelet of the defile. Then she trotted up to Harkana's side. He greeted her in Tehuelche.

"What did you tell her?" begged González. "Please tell me, what are you saying?"

"I bid my wife welcome, that is all."

"Your wife?"

"Yes, my wife. We met not long ago, on a beach to the southeast. Three white men were trying to rape her. If they had succeeded they would have cut her throat. Instead, they died. That is just one of the reasons why we kill all who trespass below the Rio Colorado."

"No, listen to me. We can help you. We can explain to our commanders that the war is wrong. I will tell them that they are making a mistake. You must listen to me!"

"Can't you see that it is a waste of time?" said Sergeant Flores, disgusted at this cowardly display. "Not only is he going to kill us, but he is right to do so. I would do the same thing if I were him. What is your name, señor?"

"Señor? You address a savage as señor? Why, I am Harkana the Orphan."

"Kill us all, Harkana the Orphan," said Flores, "but let me die with a gun in my hand. That is all I ask."

Harkana surveyed the sergeant coolly. He was finished with discussion. It served no purpose. But this man interested him.

"You are older than the others, wiser, braver. Why do you follow the orders of such as he?"

"I have my orders and that is all I know. I do not always agree with them, but then again, I do not have to agree with them."

"The way of the white man is very strange," said the Orphan. He translated the dialogue for Pandra, and again González asked him the meaning of his words.

"I was saying that all who cross the Great River must die," Harkana lied impatiently.

The colonel's face erupted in fresh lines of panic.

"The guns and the horses, they are all yours for the taking. I will leave you all the silver pesos that I was given to supply the troops."

Flores could see that it was hopeless; González could not.

"I have no need of your money, nor your guns. The horses I have already taken." Then Harkana told Pandra to leave, and she twirled her horse about and cantered back out of the quebrada.

"But we surrendered to your superiority," insisted the colonel, disbelief crippling his face.

"I did not request it." He shouted a curt order to Juma, who waited up above.

Harkana turned Zorkan Rood away, then hesitated and looked down for the last time on the pathetic excuse for a man that was Colonel Eduardo González.

"In case you are wondering yet again what I was saying to my men up above, I told them to kill all of you. It will be done."

Harkana raised his right hand and rode Zorkan Rood at a gallop to the steep incline out of the ravine. Before he had even reached it a thick volley of arrows had thudded down, five of them racing each other to be the first into the colonel's sobbing chest. The whites plunged desperately to retrieve their rifles, but hardly managed to lay a hand on their weapons before they were immersed in death.

Juma's men plundered the bodies, taking knives, belts, and water bottles. The horses were unsaddled and rounded up. Blankets were taken too. When the whites' camp had been stripped of everything that might prove useful, Harkana assembled the men and had Juma lead them home.

He dallied with his wife for an hour or so, leading their horses through the ravine and thinking about what lay ahead.

"Now," said the warlord, "they will send enough to win. So clearly, there is not much time. What would you say if I were to suggest that we ride away alone from the land of the Teh-uelches, never to return? Would you come?"

"My lord, I would follow you into death more readily, but if you were to command me, yes, I would come with you."

"Next to having nothing to live for," Harkana told her, "the hardest thing must be having something to die for. Come, let us go home while we still have one."

CHAPTER FOURTEEN

THE TELEGRAPH WIRES HUMMED until they were hot with the news of the massacre. There was uproar in the city, fueled by the newspaper reports of the atrocities. Blame was handed around like a lighted match. More than one senior official had his fingers severely blistered. The editor of the *Nación* researched and printed a profile of the young Colonel González, and the story of his inexperience and stubbornness was aired in public. Within three weeks the outcry had forced the war ministry to organize a major expeditionary force.

The force consisted of six thousand cavalry and two thousand light infantry, supported by twelve field howitzers and ten 25-pounder cannons. They were mustered in the capital, and special trains were made up to move the troops and their equipment to the interior. Amid great cheering the men and officers were waved off from the main terminal at Buenos Aires. It took four long, slow trains to take the whole force as far as Tres Arboles. The cannons, ammunition, and much of the food were transferred to freight trains and switched to the southern track which had just been opened. This mass of guns and equipment was awaiting the main detachments of troops when they arrived on horseback at Tossini, the last outpost of civilization before the bare ranch land of Patagonia.

The Patagonian Expeditionary Force, as it was called, had been placed under the command of General Emilio Branco. Branco was a soldier on an entirely different level from the young Colonel González. Branco had been one of Roca's general staff in the desert campaign. He had been a soldier since he was fifteen years old. His troopers had nicknamed him Quebracho Branco when he was just a captain, and the name had stuck like moss through a long and distinguished career. When his appointment was first announced, people asked why a man with such a force had not been dispatched in the first place. And the answers that flooded back were many. Who would have thought that eight thousand men with artillery would be needed to quell an Indian insurrection by one small tribe which could put only a couple of thousand primitively armed warriors into the field? Ridiculous, a waste of taxpayers' money! But then came the González fiasco, and people thought again. Branco would settle the matter once and for all. He was well known for his mopping-up operation, after Roca's major battle with the Ranqueles had left a few scattered pockets of resistance. Branco was the man to do it, all right. It soon became a common rumor that Roca had tried to avoid sending Branco because he feared the latter's success would put him on the threshold of a political career, potential competition the new President could well do without. Now it had become mandatory that the Tehuelches be liquidated without further delay. Branco knew his job. No one had ever disputed that fact.

Emilio Branco was a small, wiry nutshell of a man. His head was dominated by an extraordinarily long, thin nose, which made the top part of his body resemble a gun turret. His bright brown eyes betrayed the fact that he had lost his sense of mercy at a tender age. He was in his early fifties when granted the command, and although his hair was thinning, he carried his age well. He was fit and energetic and had remarkable stamina. His whiplash tongue could be used sparingly, for his subordinates knew its power and its sting.

Branco had got everything he wanted in the way of men and equipment. And he had got it with the minister's blessing. Indeed, as the minister had said to him over a private dinner on the eve of the general's departure, Branco had been supplied with everything except an excuse for failure.

"Failure is a darkness neither of our careers will withstand, Emilio," the minister warned over coffee.

"I appreciate that, sir," the general replied.

"Success is a torch with which to illuminate our successful enhancement." The minister enjoyed his metaphors. "I am sure you realize that as well as I do, General."

"I do, sir."

"I have no intention of telling you how to run your army and do the job you have been dispatched to do," said the minister. "However," he pointed out, pausing to clear his throat, "there is one slight thing I would venture to suggest."

"What is that, sir?" Branco felt compelled to inquire, despite his eagerness to leave the minister's home and return to his own, where his wife was awaiting him.

"The leader of the Tehuelches, this, er, Harkana devil—if you find it possible to take him alive, do so. I have a feeling that he could prove useful to us for propaganda purposes. You know the sort of thing, put him on display through the streets of Buenos Aires. Exhibit our humanity and our domination of the savage at one and the same time. A practical demonstration of our superiority in the hinterland would do much to encourage settlement in those regions which are bound never to succeed unless we can populate them. Take this Harkana the Orphan prisoner and we will be able to make a classic gesture of our growing power and our ability to protect all those who head south to mold a new Argentina.

"Remember that, Emilio. This Indian warlord could be infinitely more valuable to us alive than if he were just one more warrior to die in a hail of bullets on some distant battleground. I leave it in your capable hands."

"In war, it is sometimes impossible to determine who will die and who will live," mused Branco. "But I will try."

"Try," said the minister, but Branco heard the word only as one more command. He took his leave after the minister clasped one of those hands in which the delicate matter had been duly left, and rode a carriage through the city. As the hooves of the pony smacked on the dusty streets, Branco started to put together the outlines of his campaign. There were to be no prisoners, save this warlord savage if at all possible. The Republic had no use for Tehuelche prisoners. The men would not work as slaves but would die by their own hand or by starving themselves. The women were not sought after as concubines, and the children were far more trouble than they were worth as house-boys. About all they were good for was work as grooms. So Branco planned not only a battle but the extermination of an entire people. First he would cut down their warriors; then he would raze their villages and slay the noncombatants. It was the only humane thing to do.

The general rested two nights when he reached Tres Arboles and then set about organizing his communications. Trains would supply him as far south as Tossini, where the general first inspected his force and prepared it for the long ride south. The links in his fortified chain would be provided by the estancias of the local ranchers, who were themselves linked by the thin but priceless wire of the telegraph line. The latest reports informed the white soldiers that the Tehuelches had set up a huge summer camp, bigger than anything ever seen before, one hundred and twenty miles south of the last estancia. Branco sent out his infantry divisions in two bobbing gray lines, supported by a single division of cavalry. The rest pulled out the next morning, flanking the artillery units and supply wagons. The army stretched back over an enormous distance.

Scouting parties brought the news of the march to McClellan, who had been instructed of the impending arrival by the new police chief at Tres Arboles. The army bivouacked on several acres of fallow McClellan land, and Bruce McClellan made them sumptuously welcome. The general and his staff were given dinner in the remarkable hacienda which the McClellans had built up in just six months. It became a nightly ritual for the four evenings the officers camped there.

In the daytime, Branco undertook to get his men across the Rio Colorado and en route to the south. When this had been completed, the general rode out himself. McClellan rode with them.

Harkana's spies told him of the time, the direction, and the numbers of their coming. The army of the whites was five times the size of the Orphan's. Even with all the assembled clans and families who had flocked to Harkana's banner, the Tehuelches numbered no more than eighteen hundred warriors. They had not bothered to fortify their village, for their mode of warfare relied on mobility. Horses could not be used behind barricades. Indeed, the horses could be used either to attack or to flee. Running was still an option, but Harkana told his men that there would be no more retreating. There was no room anymore. The wire had won, for it sprang up like a weed just as fast as they tore it down. There were no longer any sanctuaries which could shelter and provide for all the thousands of Indians who had come together as one mighty tribe. The pastures would not support the horses. The game was gone. The streams had gone underground until late autumn. The charqui and maize supplies were running low. It was the Moon When the Sun Cracks the Earth, and all the Tehuelches had left was dying.

Getting his army across the Rio Negro proved to be a tricky operation for Branco. Even in late summer it was a wide, fast-flowing body of water that argued under the twin pontoon bridges constructed by the general's engineers. Branco started his force across at first light, and by the time the sun went down that evening, all but fifteen hundred of his cavalry were safely across. He sent word to the unit's commander, Major Chacón, to rejoin him as soon as possible. Branco was not splitting his force, merely leaving his reserve a few hours behind.

In fact, through no fault of his own, Chacón was delayed nearly seven hours when one of the bridges broke apart in midstream. Three of his men and horses were swept away and drowned in the icy water before they could be rescued. With only a single narrow pontoon in use, the major was considerably encumbered. As a professional soldier, he saw to it that the second bridge was repaired and ready in the event of a swift retreat. All of this took the best part of a day, and Chacón camped that night on the southern bank of the Negro, with a full day's ride separating him from his commander in chief.

By the end of that day, Branco and the main column were pitching camp a good many miles farther on. It would be their last camp on land owned by an estanciero.

"One more hard day's ride should bring us within range of the enemy," Branco informed Bruce McClellan across the officers' mess table that evening. McClellan was the only civilian accompanying the army into Harkana's territory.

"Yes, sir," the rancher agreed. "We should see their village

211

on the day after tomorrow, and if Harkana has a mind to stand and fight, we should engage him there."

Branco was not in the least perturbed by the fact that Major Chacón had not managed to bring up his men that evening. He had great faith in Chacón, who was extremely experienced. He would turn up long before he was needed. Besides, even without him Branco had a three-to-one advantage in numbers. The Indians had never seen field guns and howitzers before. General Emilio Branco was not a worried man.

"One small point, señor McClellan, if you please," interposed the general.

"Sir?"

"We wish to take this leader of theirs, this Harkana the Orphan, alive. I am relying on you to identify him for us, since you are the only man along who has set eyes on him before, and at quite close quarters, I believe. Do you think you would recognize him again through a good pair of field glasses?"

So that was the reason the army had wanted him to ride with them. "Yes, sir, I am sure I will." He was beginning to appreciate some of what was at stake in this campaign. "We can watch for his horse, General. He rides a fabulous gray stallion, one of the finest I have ever seen. Locate the horse and you will find Harkana upon his back."

"Excellent. Then I leave it to you to spot this horse for us in order that I may instruct my men not to shoot him down."

"About this stallion, er, do you have any specific instructions regarding Harkana's horse, General Branco?" McClellan was seldom slow to push an advantage. After all, why shouldn't he get something in return?

"Concerning the horse?" drawled the general, with slow but notable derision. "General Roca, former Minister of War and now our newly elected President, issued no precise instructions to me concerning the Indian leader's horse. Why do you ask?"

"I was wondering, in the event of the horse being captured uninjured, whether I might be able to buy it from the army, or from the government, or from whomever lays claim to such spoils of war? You see, general, such a fine piece of horseflesh would greatly increase the value of my bloodstock. My twin Hereford bulls have considerably enhanced the quality of my beef cattle, and I would very much like to perform the same upgrading with my horses. Thought I might go in for racing one of these days."

Branco had little interest in matters outside the army and his own future in politics. He answered with more than a touch of impatience.

"I cannot be expected to tell my men to preserve the life of one particular horse during the heat of a major battle, McClellan."

"Of course not, General. I was only thinking that since I am to identify Harkana for you by means of his horse, the chances are reasonably good that the horse would not become a casualty itself, and, that being the case, I might be granted first option on making a bid for it. That is all I had in mind."

"I'll tell you what I'll do for you," said Branco expansively. "If Harkana lives and the horse manages to survive along with him, I will take the Indian and you can have the horse to do with as you please. However, I make no promises, and no bargains that the horse will be unscathed; and I still expect your utmost cooperation in picking the man out for me well before battle commences. Is that clear?"

"Certainly, General. You have a deal."

"I do not make deals," Branco reminded him. "But we appear to have reached an agreement."

With Chacón's men catching up but still five hours behind, Branco moved out and rode south at a steady pace all the next day. He ordered camp to be made on a broad expanse of open plain facing a small but pronounced hill to the south. He dispatched four pairs of scouts. The fact that only one pair returned to camp was as informative to Branco as the story the surviving scouts related. The Tehuelche village was situated about three miles away. It was heavily guarded, and the scouts had managed to observe it only from a distance, using binoculars as they hid in the long grass, hoping against hope that the Tehuelches would not see their horses. The Indians did pinpoint the three other pairs, who were destroyed by warriors Harkana had sent out especially for the purpose, mounted on the fleetest horses of his five thousand.

Branco called a meeting of his top commanders. They pored

over a map of the terrain, which was singularly featureless except for the single hill and a clump of trees to the west.

"Gentlemen, this is what I propose," Branco expounded. "I want the infantry lines drawn up here." He indicated a line on the map which lay between the southern extremity of the hill and the trees. "Chacón's detachment will be placed in reserve close by the high ground, here." He pointed with his baton again. "My command position will of course occupy the hilltop, and I shall want two of the field guns located below us. The rest of the artillery will be set up beside those trees, giving them a clear field of fire directly into the village itself and threatening this part of the plain, across which I hope to provoke their charge. The two mounted battalions we have with us at present will occupy a central position, here, south and east of the hill.

"We will commence a barrage at thirty minutes after first light. Inform all gunnery officers that the objective is to shell the Tehuelche village, keep it under constant fire until such time as they receive orders to the contrary. I want that village flattened, blown out of existence. If the savages are stupid enough to tether their spare mounts within the village compound, then we will wipe out the lot within fifteen minutes of getting the range. If the gun crews do their job well, as they are paid to do, as they have been taught to do, we can have this whole operation over in time for lunch. I will hold the gunnery officers personally responsible for any infringement of these instructions."

Branco then turned to the colonel commanding the two companies of infantry. The officer found Branco's baton aimed at his navel.

"Your men will defend the guns and hold their fire in the event of a charge until the range is under a hundred and fifty meters. Usual battle formation. Go over the details of ammunition distribution with your platoon leaders before retiring tonight. Understood?"

The colonel acknowledged his orders, and General Branco stepped back to face all of his officers together.

"Gentlemen, these Tehuelches have been allowed to build themselves a reputation as brave warriors. Their leader, Harkana, has become respected as a strategist. Tomorrow I intend to prove these reputations illusory, undeserved, and unfounded. I count upon all of you. I am not looking for heroics, and I will not tolerate failure. All I require is the methodic annihilation of an opposing army whose only weapon is maneuverability. Should they choose to run, then we will have our work cut out for the next couple of weeks. But I do not think they will get very far. Either way, the end result will be the same.

"Chacón will arrive at any moment. In fact, I am surprised that the pickets have not announced his approach already this evening. The major will remain in reserve, and if, as I expect, he is not forced to play a part in the proceedings, then it is he that will undertake our mopping-up operations. Is all of that clear?"

"What if Chacón has not come up by daybreak, sir?" inquired the infantry officer. He coughed and shuffled his feet as Branco turned his icy stare upon him.

"Then we proceed without him. Or do you imagine that fifty-five hundred trained men and twenty-two cannon will prove insufficient to do the job? I now have quite accurate reports as to the enemy numbers. Harkana will not be able to field in excess of two thousand warriors against us. They have no reserves, Colonel, only extra horses, and horses don't hold lances. Now then, are there any further questions, gentlemen?"

The young infantry colonel parried the glances of his fellow officers somewhat sheepishly. He felt relieved to get away from the general's tent. Facing up to Quebracho Branco was worse than facing up to any horde of Indians, he felt sure. But then, the colonel had never seen a Tehuelche in his life.

Branco and his men were well informed as to the numbers of warriors Harkana had at his disposal. The warlord had placed six hundred each under Juma, Raganor, and himself.

But the whites were wrong in calculating that the Tehuelches had no reserves upon which to call. Pandra would lead a force of almost one thousand female warriors who had been under intensive training for many weeks. Their lances were just as sharp and just as deadly as those wielded by the men. The white

215

enemy soldiers would find themselves equally as dead, no matter who bore the lance against them.

Horses Harkana had to spare. He would keep them under guard behind his lines, spaced out in groups of fifty. The village would be left with just twenty men-at-arms. Every able-bodied male over the age of fourteen would fight an active role in the battle for the preservation of their nation. Only the old women, the small children, and the infirm would remain in the toldos that now flecked a vast acreage of the dun-colored plain.

Harkana called a council with Juma, Raganor, and Pandra to go over the battle plan once again.

"We will not attack the fixed positions of the white soldiers unless we are forced to. The range of their weapons is superior, as is their firepower and their numbers. But we must remain flexible at all times. Speed of movement is our one clear advantage. We will bide our time and wait for them to make the first move before we commit ourselves.

"It is not known how great is the power of these larger wheeled thundersticks that we have seen being hauled across our land, but we can be sure that it warrants the effort of the journey. We will take the field in a wide semicircle, in order to spread our ranks thin before their fire. The training we have done with the firewheels may prove significant. The object is to scatter the men on foot and panic their horses. If it does, Raganor will press home the first charge to make the most of the ensuing confusion. As for their riders, they are no match for us in horsemanship. Only their weapons and their numbers will defeat us. The pincer charge which we have practiced many times will hurt them as much as anything our small force could devise. The rest sits in the lap of the moon.

"Juma, I beseech you to maintain a trio of reliable aides by your side, that you may read my signal to attack and act upon it swiftly." Juma's eyesight was beginning to fail him. "The timing will be of the utmost importance," Harkana went on. "I shall lead against the guns.

"Pandra, you know what you have to do. Keep constant watch for my signal. Keep your riders back until you have judged how the tide of battle runs, should I be slain. If the guns can be

216

silenced and the white cavalry put to flight, then make your charge and drive them to the river. Allow the mounted archers time and space to take their toll on a retreating force. If the thundersticks cannot be silenced and Juma cannot scatter the opposing horsemen, then aim your attack upon the white commanders. I expect them to position themselves on the peak of high ground, but we will know when the time comes. Is each of you sure of what must be done?"

Harkana looked first at Raganor, who nodded grimly; then to Juma, who lifted his shaggy head in understanding; finally across to Pandra, who met his gaze coolly. She was looking at a warlord but she was seeing her husband.

The Tehuelche leaders left Harkana's toldo and walked outside as the sun began its dive into the horizon. Across the broad expanse of plain which separated them from Branco's army they could see the hundreds of tiny cookfires glowing in even lines, crisscrossing the white soldiers' position. The Tehuelches had already noted the formation of the encampment. They had counted tents, horses, cannon, and the nests of slanting carbines as accurately as they could while remaining beyond rifle range. None of them knew what howitzers could do. Even the Orphan could only guess at their purpose, their range, and their killing power. His guesses were wildly inaccurate. Harkana's experience of the ways of the white man did not stretch to witnessing a professional army division in battle. He could only put together a rough estimate of how the whites might fight such a conflict, based on logic and the knowledge of what he would do in their place.

The commanders of the Tehuelche nation took their last evening meal together. It was a silent meal. When it was finished they bid each other good night. Juma retired to his toldo. Raganor went off to make a final round of the guards. Harkana took Pandra with him and strolled over to the long tethers where the Tehuelche horse herds grazed in their thousands. Mustered together, the stock stretched in four straight lines from one end of the village to the other. Pindi was putting the final touches to Zorkan Rood. The boy had been hard at work for over two hours.

"How goes it with you, Pindi?" asked Harkana lightly.

217

"Very well, lord," the boy responded, proudly stepping back to reveal the full quality of his workmanship. The Scarmaker's silver mane cascaded in its full splendor. It seemed to light up their faces in the night.

"Yes, I can see that Zorkan Rood has been well groomed for the battle, but I was asking after you, Pindi."

"I too am groomed for battle, lord." The boy grinned happily.

Harkana had already made the decision to refrain from ordering the boy to remain in camp. In the final outcome it would make little difference to his fate and would make much to his spirit. Once the Tehuelche army had been destroyed, Harkana had little doubt, the whites would systematically kill or capture all who remained alive. He doubted that many prisoners would be taken, and the more he thought about it, the more he disputed who would be luckiest—those who died in battle or those who did not. The Orphan had therefore granted Pindi a position in his own unit, that he might ride close behind the warlord wherever he went.

"Leave us now with Zorkan Rood, Pindi. Take your meal, for the hour is growing late."

"Yes, lord. Until the morrow, no?"

"Until the morrow."

Pandra turned to the man who had been her husband for so short a time.

"Do you wish to be left alone, my lord?"

"No. Stay with me here for a while, then we will retire for the night. You know that it will be our last, Pandra?"

"I know it. You have not forgotten the promise which you made to me in the cave when first we met?"

"I have not forgotten. When the time comes, it will be kept. Are you afraid?" Harkana's brow was knotted with worry, but his voice was soft and level. She could not see the details of his face in the darkness.

Pandra answered him obliquely. "I am more afraid to live without you, lord, than I am to die by your side."

"No man could ask for more," Harkana said in a half whisper, more to himself than to the woman. He petted Zorkan Rood's neck, and the horse nuzzled his arm. The furrows on his brow deepened, but it was too dark for Pandra to notice how his face took on new lines of sorrow. The fate of Zorkan Rood was out of his hands. He wondered if he would not rather see the gray stallion perish in battle than never to know what became of it afterward. Or, worse still, to know that it had fallen into the hands of the enemy. He realized that he was looking at the situation in the same way in which Pandra had viewed hers with him. Tearing his eyes away from Zorkan Rood, Harkana put his right arm around the woman's shoulders. He forced himself not to dwell further on his dilemma as he led her away toward their toldo for what remained of the night.

Dawn rolled up its curtain, and Branco and his officers got their first close look at the Tehuelche army of the moon that had arrayed itself against them, seeking to block the way into their village. The Argentine forces took up their positions as Branco had instructed. Chacón still had not joined them. Branco mounted his horse on the hilltop and waited for the sun to cast its full light upon the enemy tents. Then he gave the signal.

Harkana did nothing. He spotted a small white puff of smoke, which was immediately followed by a high-pitched whistle and an explosion. The shell passed high over the Indians' heads, and then came the second, terrible explosion. The Tehuelches turned as one man to watch the shell burst midway between their rear lines and their village. Many of the horses shied, but there was no loss of control. Another puff of white across the plain under the trees, and this time the range finders came within one hundred meters of the nearest toldos. Harkana was thinking furiously.

Branco was deep in thought as well. His scouts had just reported Chacón still five hours away at least. The general stuck with his plan and watched the third shell overshoot the central area of the village by a mere fifteen meters. The blast ripped through several tents, and the twenty warriors who had been assigned the futile task of defending the encampment against an outflanking movement could do no more than rattle their lances in fury at an enemy they could not even see.

While the fourth shell was in the air, Harkana acted. He sent messengers at top speed to both Juma and Raganor, ordering them to prepare for a wholesale charge against the heavy guns which were about to destroy their village. The fireballs of interwoven bracken were lit and towed out ahead of the main body of the cavalry, which Harkana now ordered to advance at walking pace. All but one of the Indians dragging the fireballs were picked off long before they got anywhere near the artillery. The wounded survivor managed to tie the rope hauling the blazing bracken to his horse's neck before he too was riddled with bullets. The horse careened on toward the lines of white infantry, which broke ranks to let it pass. Two men were scorched before the horse was brought down by rifle fire. The Orphan knew that this was an entirely different kind of warfare that he was facing. In the battles against the Ranqueles, such tactics had caused havoc.

Harkana sliced the air with his hand, and the pincer formation of eighteen hundred mounted Tehuelches picked up into a trot as more and more cannon shells whined overhead. Branco had given the order to fire at will. They had the range now, and the village far behind Harkana's advancing forces was being blown apart. Men, women, children, and horses were blasted into eternity by a rain of metal shelling which split the air and everything that breathed it.

Harkana looked back and saw that the horse handlers were coping well with his instruction to spread the horses over the plain in clusters, taking them even farther away from the settlement. The Tehuelches broke into a canter, an effortless easy striding gait which they could keep up for hours. They held tightly to their line, taking their pace from the warlord. Determination was etched on their faces as they bore down on the artillery batteries. With less than four hundred meters to go, the Orphan signaled the gallop with his hand aimed forward and down. A phalanx of lances were leveled chest high.

Seeing the change in pace cutting down the distance so quickly, Branco sent word to fire a broadside of grapeshot into the charging horsemen. The gun crews worked feverishly to reload and alter trajectory, hoping that the first infantry volleys would be enough to turn the charge away. At one hundred fifty meters they discovered that it was not enough. Half of the cannons were hit before they had a chance to fire. Huge holes opened up in the Tehuelche ranks as grapeshot poured into them from point-blank range. Hundreds of Indians and horses went down, both dead and alive. Those who had not been shot were trampled by those who came behind, but the first wave of Tehuelche lancers drove through the gun batteries, causing heavy damage. A huge cape of dust kicked up in their wake followed them over the guns, obliterating the scene from Branco's watchful eyes. He waited for the dust to die down before he ordered half his cavalry force across to close with the Indians. That slight delay probably cost the white infantry some two hundred men as the Tehuelches brought the brunt of their hatred to bear upon them. Catching sight of the countercharge, Harkana wheeled his men away in a graceful arc which seemed to hover tantalizingly within range of the incoming white riders but never quite close enough for them to make effective use of their sabers and pistols. The curve described by Harkana's force brought them almost full circle. They changed mounts during a short lull, in which Branco's attacking cavalry found themselves between the Indians and their own artillery. The order to continue shelling the village was given. Confused, helpless, and in many cases scared witless, the gunnery officers went about their task. This was the enemy which had no defense, no name, no face, and no chance. The howitzers boomed anew. The 25-pounders threw shell after shell into the midst of the village, where indescribable hell was taking place. Twenty lanyards were pulled, and a score of shells zipped over the parched plain to burst with sickening effect among the last remaining toldos of the Tehuelches. Neither Branco nor the Orphan had any way of knowing that there was no longer any living thing in the village.

Harkana had only his imagination to tell him what must have been happening back in his encampment as he re-formed his riders and tore ahead of them on Zorkan Rood, hungry to get to grips with the white horse soldiers. First one, then another and another and another fell to the swift and accurate stab of his lance. The shock of the Indian attack caused a noticeable shudder in the countering Argentine cavalry. Branco sat up stiff in his saddle, wondering if they would turn tail. He yelled to an orderly to send word for the second force of mounted soldiers to throw their full weight into the conflict. Without Chacón, Branco was using up the last of his cavalry in a battle that would be won and lost on horseback.

"Left of center, General, over by the dense melee. See the gray stallion? See how he turns and plunges in and dodges again and again?" McClellan made it sound as though it was the horse who carried the lance and did the killing. "That, General Branco, is Harkana the Orphan."

"I know, I know, McClellan," said the beleaguered commander.

Harkana felt rather than saw the extra cavalry regrouping with the first countercharge, nearly doubling the numbers arrayed against him. His clear voice rang out, and the orders were repeated echo upon echo. The Tehuelches pulled back to the east at full speed. They opened up a gap of perhaps half a mile over their pursuers. Another horse change. The Tehuelches took bows and quivers from the hands of Pandra's warriors. As the white cavalry came within one hundred yards, Harkana signaled the first volley of arrows aimed up in a curving trajectory. Men and horses went down, bringing others unmarked by the missiles on top of them. Legs and necks were snapped, both human and animal. Screams of agony rang out. The white officers struggled to inform their buglers to sound recall. Another blanket of arrows darkened the sky, then another as the whites withdrew.

Harkana came on again. By now the shelling of the village had ceased and every cannon was aimed at the Tehuelche cavalry. Puffs of white smoke decorated the distance, and men fell in piles all around Harkana. As they closed on the white army lines, a thousand Remingtons spoke, and great holes appeared in the Indian lines. Shells plowed into their ranks. Flesh and bones cascaded through the air. Meantime, the Argentine cavalry, which had suffered heavy losses, was re-forming below Branco's hill, watching for his signal.

Both sides steadied for attack and defense. This time, there were many fewer Tehuelches. Harkana knew that there was no hiding place from the artillery, so he chose to engage the enemy

222

at whatever cost and take shelter in their proximity. The cannons could not shell the combat without killing their own men. Harkana fanned his men thin and wide, cutting down the target he offered to the field guns while the white cavalry closed in on them. The Orphan hammered ahead of his remaining men, the lances couched under their arms. Branco had ordered his infantry forward, and there was time for just one volley before the two cavalries clashed. Juma took five bullets through his chest, which hurled him back. His grizzled old body was pummeled by hundreds of hooves as the battle roared over him.

Never had human bone and muscle hurled itself so recklessly against cold steel and red-hot gunmetal. To Branco's horror, the Tehuelches actually broke through his cavalry. The general clenched his fists as he saw the Indians, led by Harkana and Raganor, racing toward the guns. Branco willed his mounted men to regroup and intercept them, but they were slow to recover. His infantry were out of position. A tremendous thunder came from beneath the trees, and hundreds of Tehuelches went down. Now only a few hundred remained, but they were enough to carry the artillery, whose crews fled before the fanatical lancers. Harkana was high on the back of the Scarmaker, madly signaling his trump card. Pandra brought in her force at a punishing canter.

Branco could hardly believe his eyes. He was staggered by the amount of gray uniforms lying on the dusty plain after the Tehuelches had pulled back once more to unite with the women, who were entering the battle fresh.

"Where the devil is Chacón?" he snarled from between clenched teeth. None of his officers could offer him a solution. They were intent on watching how Harkana swept into the lead on the gray stallion, leading a fresh mounted force onto the field. A mile to the east, the white cavalry were regrouping and riding back into the fray. But their horses were tiring, while the Tehuelches had changed mounts at least twice. Branco issued a command which would put the remains of his infantry back in front of his cannons. He ordered them to hold firm at any cost. As he turned back to the south, he realized that the third wave of the Indian attack was directed at the very hilltop upon which he stood. The two 25-pounders at the foot of the hill opened fire at eight hundred meters. They reloaded. Two cavities appeared in the ranks behind the warlord, and the first of the women died. Still they came on. The field guns spoke again. Their effect was devastating but limited. The Indians closed ranks behind Harkana and hit the two fieldpieces before they could fire again. Not a man belonging to the gun crews was left alive, for the Indians swept them away as if they were matchstick men. As the Tehuelche vanguard sped on up the hill, Branco, much to his chagrin, was forced to flee. The Argentine officers rode down the hill and made for the thick gray lines of massed infantry under the shade of the ombú trees. They were closely pursued, and the Tehuelches succeeded in catching three of the most poorly mounted officers. Branco was in a sweat, as much from the revelation that he was beatable as from the hard ride he had been forced to make. The general muttered a quick prayer, which ended with a plea: "Give me Chacón or give me darkness." It was still only mid-afternoon.

Looking about, Branco could see that his infantry had not suffered the heavy casualties he had at first feared. His cavalry had lost some seven hundred men, but Harkana had lost all but a couple of hundred of his dog soldiers.

The two lines of mounted riders met again, and the hand-to-hand fighting was fierce. The Indians had the upper hand at close quarters. Even though they were outnumbered, their superior riding skills and ability with the short-held lance and dagger made the outcome far from certain. Harkana himself held a three-foot length of broken lance, which he stabbed back and forth with punishing speed. His hands were gloved in blood. He would summon no more retreats. His people would die here on this field of battle or they would rout the white cavalry and then storm the rifles once more, although Harkana knew that such an action amounted to no more than a fantastic suicide. For almost an hour the battle hung in the balance.

And then Chacón reached them. The tardy major plunged forward at the head of fifteen hundred mounted men. They expected the Tehuelches to fall back, but they did not. For a few seconds the close fighting almost ceased altogether as the whites took heart from the sight of Chacón's men galloping toward them and the last of the Tehuelches learned that fate had been toying with them all along.

Chacón's cavalry was surprised to find itself fighting mostly women, for all but about fifty of Harkana's warriors had fallen. The battle quickly turned against the Indians. Scores of them went down under whirling sabers and close-aimed revolver fire.

Pandra fought her way to Harkana's side. Raganor too was close by the warlord. Fewer than one hundred Indians remained alive and still on their horses. There was nowhere left to go, no avenue of escape. Five of Chacón's men swarmed upon Harkana, but a cry went up that he was to be taken alive.

The Orphan heard it and flinched. His heart iced over. In that moment a glancing blow from a rifle butt knocked him off balance, and he rocked back from the pain. He had been fighting and riding for ten hours. Zorkan Rood reared as a saber slashed away a tiny part of one of its ears, and Harkana was dislodged from his horse for the one and only time since he had bought it with his blood.

Thrown to the earth, the Orphan was quickly back on his feet. He shook off a rope aimed at his head. He could see nothing but white soldiers all about him. The stallion had vanished. Then he saw Raganor carving a passage through to him. A pistol was raised against the sky. The gun fired and Raganor spun on his horse, but remained on it and still fought his way step by step toward his leader. The soldier with the pistol aimed again as Raganor turned on him and shoved the blade of his lance through the man's stomach. The revolver went off, and this time the bullet took away most of Raganor's forehead. He went down in a flurry of dust and a rising tumult of hooves as Harkana lashed at the men who surrounded him but held back from the attack. The Tehuelche warlord could no longer see any of his own race.

"Harkana!" Turning, he saw Pandra crashing over a heap of bodies, leading a spare mount. Harkana hurled his lance without waiting to see who died from it and made one majestic, soaring leap to half gain the back of the riderless horse. Hammering with

225

heels and hands, he felt the horse lift him from the press of the fight, with Pandra galloping alongside. One wounded soldier, his leg broken in two places, knelt between them and the open plain to the south. The man raised his pistol and pulled the trigger. Harkana felt the horse stumble, but he held it up and ran the man down. The gallant little horse managed to carry him over half a mile more before it collapsed and died from the bullet in its lung. Swinging himself up behind Pandra, they cantered on toward the remains of the village.

Behind them, the last of the Tehuelches were being systematically put to death. General Emilio Branco breathed a long, hard sigh of relief and allowed himself a swallow of brandy from his hip flask. It was over.

No one attacked Pandra and Harkana, although half a hundred were sent to follow the route of their flight. No gunshots were aimed at their backs. No bullets chased the dust of their passage. Harkana knew for certain then that they wanted him alive. Probably they wanted the woman as well. He recalled the last time that white men had sought to make use of Pandra. It would not happen a second time. Cantering between mounds of the dead, they broke from the edge of the field of battle and came to the place which had once been a sizable Tehuelche village.

No one dwelled there anymore. No one lived or breathed or laughed or screamed or moved in the last village of the Tehuelche nation. Bodies both whole and dismembered littered the ground. Some had died from the blast of the shells. Some had been torn by shrapnel. Others had bled from severe wounds, with no one around to stem the flow.

The Orphan reached around Pandra and pulled back on the reins to halt the horse, which panted from its exertion. She watched him after he dismounted with tears in her eyes. Rubbing the swelling bruise on his left side, Harkana surveyed the scene, stepping a few paces one way, then another, then returning to stand in the shadow of their exhausted horse. The entire area within the circle of smashed toldos was illustrated with dead. In among them the Orphan spotted a warrior, one of the proud twenty whom he had ordered to remain behind. But most of the casualties were wrinkled old women who could have offered nothing but pride as resistance to the invaders. Then there were the children, all dead and gone now; too young to have known the full meaning of life before they had been forced to discover the finality of dying.

Harkana heard Pandra stifle a sob. She breathed his name in anguish, and he turned to see what she had discovered. Following her tragic stare, he picked out the face of Pindi. They never learned how the little groom came to be in the village. But he was there just the same. His eyes gaped open, and a thin red stream of blood adorned his chin. Harkana rushed forward and bent to gather the boy in his arms, but there was no body left to gather. Pindi's head had been blasted from his shoulders by a shell from one of the howitzers. And Pandra looked down at her lord's face when he stood back from what once had been his trusted groom, knowing that she was the first and the last to witness tears in the eyes of Harkana the Orphan.

They rode on in silence, conscious but unheeding of those who tracked them. After an hour, he spoke to her for the first time since leaving the village.

"Pandra, my love, they want us alive. You are aware of that?"

"Yes, it would seem to be that way. What will you do?" She felt numbed rather than broken. Even the loss of her father had only marooned her in a state of meaningless torpor.

Harkana made no reply. About ten miles south of the site of his village there was a tiny mound of earth, an atoll in the ocean of the grass steppe.

"There is no point in running further," he announced, slipping down from the horse, which had reached the limit of its endurance. Pandra let him lift her to the ground and watched as he slapped the pony hard across the rump, sending it off. A cloud crossed the Orphan's face; she had no way of knowing that it was the sight of a free-running pony which had caused it.

"How can it be," he wondered, "that such men exist as would bring this to our land? Let them come and do with us as they wish. I will retreat no more from these child-slayers."

The last few hours of daylight dropped down around them, and Branco's advance party closed in on all sides. The mound where the last of the Tehuelches made their stand was a good vantage point but bare of cover. Only Harkana's bow stood

227

between them and capture. His quiver held fourteen arrows. The light faded fast. Only one hour of twilight remained as Harkana once again tested the pull of the weapon he had carried for so many moons, until this, his last fight. He tried to drive the thought of what had happened to Zorkan Rood from his mind.

Chaperoned by a strong escort, Branco went forward in person to inspect what was left of the village. Finding no one alive, he sent out a patrol to follow the tracks of a few survivors southwest. Then he turned his attention to Harkana. Horrified to discover that Lieutenant Valdés had the Tehuelche leader pinned down with only fifty men, Branco immediately summoned up half of his army. They were told to pitch their tents in a circle around the mound where the dark huddle of Harkana and Pandra could be seen quite clearly through field glasses. Branco sent for young Lieutenant Valdés, who was a favorite of the general's. He had known the boy's father. The handsome twenty-six-year-old officer rode up to his commander and snapped off a crisp salute.

"Sir?"

The salute was returned matter-of-factly.

"Valdés, I want them taken alive at all costs. Is that understood?"

"Yes, sir."

"I want you to have the honor of capturing Harkana and putting him in chains. Take the men you need and bring this accursed heathen to me. You will have to work fast or it will be dark. Drive them off that mound in any direction and they will run straight into our hands. I now have over a thousand men circling that hill. Feel up to it?"

"Most certainly, sir. Just one question."

"Well?"

"Do we take the woman alive as well?"

"If possible; it would be to our advantage. However, if you have to kill her to get at Harkana, then do it. My instructions only concern the safekeeping of their chief."

"I understand, sir," Valdés acknowledged, turning his horse away after another smart salute.

"One more thing, Valdés."

"Yes, General."

"The civilian, McClellan. Have you seen him recently?"

"The last time I saw him, sir, he was over by the field kitchen."

"Send a man to inform señor McClellan that I would like a word with him, then go in and drag that savage out here. And, Valdés—good luck."

"Thank you, sir. I'll see to it straightway."

"Good man. Should that Indian prove to be difficult to dislodge, I think señor McClellan might be of some use to us. Besides, I want him to earn that gray stallion we've captured on his behalf."

Twenty minutes later Bruce McClellan joined Branco, and the two men sat at a trestle table outside the general's tent while an orderly served them brandy and water.

"A satisfactory ending to the day, don't you think, señor McClellan?"

"I'm glad it's over."

"Now it's time for you to earn that horse you're so keen on."

"You have the gray stallion!" enthused the rancher. "Where? Is it injured?"

"Calm yourself. The horse is in fine shape, apart from a scratch on one of its ears. I have it in capable hands, have no fear. You can take charge of it yourself as soon as I hear that Harkana is in chains. I have sent a very able young officer, Lieutenant Valdés, to command a platoon that will drive that savage off his last foothold. Shouldn't take long. He is totally surrounded. There is no possibility of escape this time."

McClellan could not disguise the triumphant glow of pleasure he felt as the new owner of Zorkan Rood. He even forgot to drink his brandy.

"Perhaps, General," he suggested, "it might be better to wait for daybreak. Harkana can still do a lot of damage with that bow of his. If you say he is totally surrounded, why not leave him where he is until morning?"

"You think so? Well, let's see if Valdés can't shift him. I have great faith in that boy. I knew his father well. I'd kind of like to take a closer look at Harkana myself. Do you think he might take his own life when he sees how futile further resistance has become?"

"Hard to say. It's always a possibility, I suppose. Kill the

229

woman with one of your very best marksmen and maybe his will to resist will crumble." McClellan was only half listening. His mind was filling up with thoughts of Zorkan Rood. It was the one thing he had in common with Harkana the Orphan.

Harkana sat back to back with Pandra, watching and waiting, knowing the light would fade inside an hour. They both heard the noise at the same time. Harkana got to his knees, a long arrow already notched on his bowstring. Pandra turned toward the sound of a man crawling through the grass as if she were a pointer scenting game. Harkana had seen him and the four others. The other half of Valdés's platoon were approaching with similar caution from the west, the sun warming their backs as they slithered from boulder to boulder and bush to bush. Valdés joined the four coming up the hill from the south. He had seen all he needed to see through his field glasses. Now was as good a time as any.

Harkana was praying inwardly to the moon. Send me more white soldiers here, that I may kill again before this day is done. He did not wish to die with an arrow in his hand.

Pandra drew his attention to the second group, coming at them simultaneously at an angle of ninety degrees to the others. She whispered to the Orphan, who took all of his arrows from the quiver and put them in her hands.

Lieutenant Valdés had had a good idea, but he had reckoned without the phenomenal speed with which Harkana could pull and loose the bow. The young officer, hungry for glory, crawled right up behind the four men who were closest to the Indian. He drew his pistol.

"Ready?" he asked. They grunted their collective acknowledgment. Valdés fired a single shot into the air.

The first man in front of Valdés made it only as far as his knees before an arrow wiped away his life. It caused another beside him to hesitate. Harkana put the second arrow through his upper chest while he fought to make up his mind whether to charge the top of the mound or hit the ground again. Valdés felt the charge he had ordered beginning to falter and came running in front of his men, leading the remaining pair on up the incline.

The plan might have worked except for one thing. The five men on the western slope were fifteen yards farther away from Harkana than the men who surfaced from the grass with Valdés. Reacting to the same signal, they could not all reach the warlord at the same time. That gave him the opportunity of choosing whom to fight first. Harkana bent the bow again, and his third shaft took the young lieutenant's life. The loss of their officer was enough to stop the two men with him in their tracks. They halted in their advance, and the Orphan, taking another arrow from Pandra's hand, waited to see what they would do. They leaped to the ground and buried themselves in the waving grass.

Harkana now spun to face the five coming at him from the direction of the sun sleeping. One of them cried out a warning, but it came too late to save the life of the man Harkana had chosen to take with his fourth arrow. Pandra passed him another without taking her eyes off the two men lying in the grass.

With just ten arrows remaining, Harkana made an unprecedented move, one which even the late but brilliant Valdés could not have foreseen as an option open to an archer trapped on an exposed piece of high ground. The Orphan went on the attack. Pandra followed him like a gazelle as he sprinted down the hillside toward the two prostrate men who had abandoned their assault. Seeing him rushing toward them, they fled, and Harkana plunged to a halt and sent an arrow into the back of the slower from thirty yards. The other did not stop, and the only thing which saved his life was his swinging water canteen, which deflected Harkana's next arrow. The soldier did not stop running until he reached the main lines a quarter of a mile away.

None of this was visible to the quartet who remained pinned down on the blind side of the mound, out of earshot of their support. In the near dark they became half paralyzed by fear and uncertainty as to what to do next. Their corporal had been killed and they had opted to stay put. Harkana did not. He sent Pandra back up to the top of the mound while he circled around lower down and came up on the four unfortunates from below.

Trying to pierce the gloom from a quarter of a mile away, the whites watching the attempt to capture Harkana were no longer sure who was who on the mound. They had no way of communicating with the men trapped on the hillside. Messengers were sent to Branco, but he could make little sense of what they told him was happening. No one knew the details except Harkana. By the time Branco had interrogated the survivor, the last four men in Valdés's ill-fated platoon were all dead, killed by arrows that rushed up at them from the gloom, each launched from a different location. The last two had been firing blindly with their revolvers, confused between the silhouette on the hill and the mysterious foe beneath. They perished in bloody ignorance.

Reunited on the hill, Pandra and Harkana stared at the last four arrows. Darkness enveloped them.

"It is time to die, lord."

"Not while I yet have arrows."

They stared at a hundred pinpricks of light surrounding them. Harkana was thinking, yes, this would be the time to die and cheat the whites of their intention—if not for the horse. If he had set Zorkan Rood free, seen it galloping untamed across the pampas, then this would be the time to go humbly to the moon. Neither of them spoke, and two more hours passed. Then Harkana told Pandra that he would try to find a gap in the lines. She hated for him to leave her. He knew that it was hopeless. She knew it too. But she just clasped his hand for a moment and then watched him swallowed up by the pitch-black night as he loped off down the slope with the great bow across his chest.

Harkana found no way out, but he claimed four more lives around the cookfires of those who had laid siege to him. Near panic riddled the troops, each individual wondering who would be next to feel the long shaft driven into his body. Pandra heard their screams as they died. The Orphan made every arrow count, returning to his wife weaponless save for the slim steel dagger on his hip.

The white camp had become a nightmare of tingling nerves and imagined enemies. Branco got up and made a tour of inspection. He prayed for daylight. McClellan had been right. The last man to die in the general's army was shot by one of his own men, who thought he had seen Harkana creeping up on him from behind. They had no way of knowing that the great bow was now impotent; that it had been used for the very last time. When the sun rose, then they would know.

The last few hours of darkness sifted through the sieve of the night. Like a nocturnal animal, the Orphan sensed dawn's arrival before the first pink light flushed the sky. He slipped the knife into his right hand and crushed Pandra to him. Over her shoulder he could see the first cautious soldiers advancing on them from four hundred meters away. Time had run out for the warlord of the Tehuelches. Lifting Pandra's head with his free hand, he kissed her mouth very softly while he killed her with the blade pushed fast through the side of her neck. She gasped once. Then the pain left her and she hung in his mighty arms, looking up into his face, now masked with unparalleled tragedy.

"I love you, Harkana," she managed to breathe before life abandoned her.

"And I shall always love you," although he knew as he said it that she was already dead and no longer had ears to hear his words.

He held her for five full minutes without moving a muscle. The soldiers were closing in as the dawn broke wide open. He laid her body on the ground with exquisite gentleness. It was all over. The white man had won. His own people were now and forever more in the bosom of the moon. Only he remained alive. He and Zorkan Rood.

Harkana stood tall as the first rays of sunshine blessed him. He picked up the great bow and unstrung it. Placing the weapon across the back of his shoulders, he stretched out both his arms along its curve. The white soldiers were less than a hundred meters away.

As they closed in on him with rifles at the ready and hearts in their mouths, they saw this magnificent man standing like Christ the Redeemer ahead of them. A sergeant ordered them to advance and take him, and the Indian bent the bow across his back until it snapped in two. He dropped the pieces of wood as the men reached him. The bloodied knife still lay on the earth. He left it there. Picking up Pandra's lifeless body, he held her for one last time before the soldiers laid hands on him. Then the sergeant ordered them separated, and they put the Orphan in chains and led him away.

CHAPTER FIFTEEN

A SCORE OF TEHUELCHES managed to escape the holocaust, four of them warriors mistaken for dead in the confusion of battle. They escorted a handful of walking wounded away from the annihilated encampment and went south on foot. In a matter of hours they were overtaken and the men were slain. Three of the younger women ran off and hid. They were never located, and lived on to intermarry with men from another tribe who lived offshore on the islands. Three of the boys were sold off as grooms to rich families in Buenos Aires, but despite their natural ability with horses, they proved disappointing. Two of them wound up their lives in the island prison of Martín Garcia. The other fathered a child by a mestizo woman in the city and later died of smallpox. Thus was the pure Tehuelche blood diluted beyond recall, but neither Pandra nor the Orphan would ever learn how the few survivors of the battle fared.

In chains, they took Harkana the Orphan by train to the capital of the white man's Argentina. A whole platoon of Branco's men were assigned as guards to the prisoner, while another company rode the same glory train. The officer in charge of the guard unit was Lieutenant Arostegui.

Arostegui was a young man of Basque descent, with a kind heart to go with his soldier's courage. He did not like to see the prisoner shackled to the wall of a cattle car, but he was under very specific orders. On no account, for whatever reason, was the prisoner to be released from his bonds. His bread and water were to be pushed through the doorway to him. No one was even to go within reach of him; no one at all. The two guards at the doorway were to be alternated every four hours. They were to remain alert and awake at all times. The prisoner was a very important instrument in the general's armory. The general was Emilio Branco, a hero of the Republic since his victory over the Tehuelche Indians, the last tribe that would ever resist the ways of the whites in Patagonia.

Branco had gone ahead a day earlier. The rest of his divisions had also pulled out. The man of the moment would be there at the terminal to meet the train when it pulled into Buenos Aires. Lieutenant Arostegui wondered what kind of reception awaited them in the central station of the capital.

There were no windows in the cattle car, only slats through which a little fresh air could enter. The atmosphere was fetid. It stank of cow dung. Harkana sat on the floor of the car, dressed only in his chains and a loincloth. He gazed out across the pampas as the train rattled eastward to the big city of the white man. He stared unblinking at the lattice-framed horizon.

Where was Zorkan Rood now? When would the whites execute him, and how?

Harkana had not touched the hunks of bread that he was offered. The water he drank. His ankles were chafed raw by the clasps of iron that linked the threads of heavy chain to large bolts on the wall behind him. His wrists were bleeding from the friction of his hand irons. He could neither stand nor lie flat. The ceiling of the rail car was too low and the tether of his chains was too tight. He could not pace like a wild animal in a zoo, although his captors were transporting him exactly like a wild animal. He had not eaten for three days, so he had no need to defecate. His urine sprang from his crouched body and ran backward against the motion of the train until it found a route through the slats in one corner of the car. Harkana could just make out one thin wafer of sky between the top of this planked wall and the distant slash of green horizon.

He thought about Pandra: tall, lithe, supple, hard-bodied Pandra. Images of her flooded his brain: how he had found her, how he had loved her, how he had killed her. How he had

235

killed them all with his terrible purpose. Harkana the Orphan watched his life flicker by through the slats of the cattle car as the train rumbled on through the white man's world. He saw the herds of cattle like acne on the green skin of the pampas. The plowed land was gutted now with grain crops cramming the furrows. Hectares of sunflowers turned to the sky. Then more herds of beef cattle. A gaucho riding loosely on a piebald gelding, the horse switching at the flies with its untrimmed tail.

The afternoon grew long-shadowed and cooler. His water bowl was retrieved by the young soldier with the long stick. It was pushed back across the stained planks of the car. The soldier stared at the Orphan. The Orphan stared at the sky passing.

The sun sank like a stone, creating ripples of orange light in the sky. Streaks of sun danced briefly through the wooden slats of the gondola, playing with the cobwebs on the inside corners of Harkana's cell. Then it was night.

The passengers and the soldiers slept in comfortable carriages. Lieutenant Arostegui supervised the changing of the guards at the door to the Indian's prison car then he dozed off in his carriage seat facing the locomotive. The guards played dice to pass the time and talked of the whores in La Boca. Harkana did not sleep. He did not talk. He allowed himself one more sip of water, then sank back against the wall, scraping the already raw skin on his wrists. A dribble of blood appeared on them again. He was unaware of the pain, and the blood soon coagulated. Harkana's heart ached for the great gray stallion and the free range of the plains. But he just stared out at the vacant lot of the starry night and let the breeze fan the flames of his hate.

The train first began to slacken speed through the market gardens on the rich fringe of farmland which girded the metropolis. The Orphan studies this growth and wondered at the white man's cancerous agriculture. The free range had been suffocated with a maze of fences. To the whites it was progress and development. To the last of the Tehuelches it was perverted liberty.

But then the train rolled into the packed terminal of Buenos Aires, the pistons exhaled the last of their steamy breath, and

236

the buffers blocked the future. Guards came for him. He let them come. They unshackled the bolts that held him. He put up no resistance. Four rifles were leveled at his chest while soldiers snapped off the wrist shackles and replaced the ankle chains with leg irons, linked by four feet of stout chain. Harkana's hands were bound behind his back with rope. Two further ropes were noosed around his neck, and by these he was led, like a beast to slaughter, down from the cattle car. Under the glass-domed ceiling of the terminus building he was paraded.

Several hundred people had turned out to witness the arrival of the hideous Ogre of Patagonia, the one who had led the massacres of settlers and the soldiers of Colonel González's command, the warlord who had inflicted terrible defeats on government troops until the heroic Branco had smashed his insurrection forever.

The general himself was there at the station, accompanied by an envoy of the President. Bruce McClellan had been invited to be a member of the general's party and had ridden to meet the train in a carriage just behind that of the military leader's entourage.

They pulled Harkana across the gray landscape of cement platforms and yanked him through the press of onlookers. A dozen men with fixed bayonets on their Remingtons surrounded him on all sides. Harkana carried his head high and took in the amazing scene which confronted him. There was no real fear in his mind, for he had long ago resigned himself to death.

As the prisoner was brought closely through the crowd, people called out to him. The words, many of which he understood, struck him not at all. Only Manuel de Robles knew that he understood much of the Spanish language. And Manuel de Robles was nowhere to be seen. The words bounced off his ears while the lieutenant of the guard halted his detachment in front of General Branco and the man from the ministry.

The general surveyed the prisoner with obvious disgust. "He smells," Branco said, wrinkling his long nose.

"It was the cattle car we held him in, General," Lieutenant Arostegui explained.

"Evidently," breathed Branco. "Well, take him away, Lieutenant. You will find suitable accommodation waiting for him outside. The drivers know where he is to be held. Do see that he is thoroughly hosed down before he is put on show. We don't want the upper echelons of Porteño society fainting from the stench, now do we?"

"No, sir. Indeed not, sir. I will see to it myself." The lieutenant saluted.

Branco returned the salute and added: "See that he doesn't die, Lieutenant. He is much more useful to us alive for the time being. He seems thinner than when we first took him."

"He refuses to eat, sir. He has taken nothing but water since his capture. Should we try to feed him forcibly, General?"

Branco seemed to consider this for a moment. The Indian was to be paraded through the city's streets in the morning and then put on display for two more days. Unless the minister changed his mind yet again, which was a possibility, he would then be taken back to Tres Arboles for execution. Something he and that civilian McClellan had hatched up between them in order to demonstrate the unity of the Republic. That made one week in all from capture to execution. No, a fine specimen of a savage like this one could surely survive an idle week without food intake. Anyway, who could imagine going into the same cage with this human gorilla and trying to force him to eat?

"That will not be necessary, Lieutenant; not as long as he continues to take water, at any rate. Tomorrow, you and your detachment will accompany him on the city parade. Afterwards, arrangements have been made for him to be placed under guard at the public zoo. You will be notified of the details later on. Is that clear?"

"Perfectly, sir. I shall attend to it all, do not worry yourself."

"I have not the slightest intention of worrying, my dear Lieutenant. You have all the responsibility and I have all the authority. It is not I that should worry, I assure you."

Lieutenant Arostegui saluted for the second time and marched the prisoner across the station concourse amid cries of "Murderer," "Lynch the black devil," and "Hang the savage" from a score of throats, any one of which the Orphan could have strangled with a single hand. Harkana maintained his mask of utter ac-

238

ceptance. His face betrayed not a single flicker of emotion. Arostegui, who was a sensitive fellow, had begun to take quite an interest in his charge. He possessed a certain bravura, the lieutenant was thinking as they led him out into the harsh morning sunlight of the noisy city. He could hardly fail to appreciate that he would soon be executed and yet, to the lieutenant's eyes, it seemed that the Tehuelche was still clinging to a vestige of life, as if he still had something to live for.

Outside the building, an even bigger, wilder crowd was waiting to view this demon savage who had wrought so much havoc for so long in the badlands. They jeered and threw fruit and eggs. Harkana did not dip his head to avoid the missiles, which soon had his head and upper body smeared with tomato juice and yellow egg yolk. Arostegui, who along with several of his men had received one or two stains themselves, was very relieved once Harkana was all the way through the surly crowd and into the barred cage which had been prepared for him. The crowd was bigger than he could ever have hoped to control with his small force, and he feared that they might get out of control. Unless any of them was thinking of using a gun, the prisoner was safely secured now. The cage was mounted upon a flatbed carriage drawn by two pack horses. Arostegui climbed up beside the driver, took a last look over his shoulder at the prisoner sitting calmly on the floor of the cage, and gave the driver the order to move forward. The carriage cut a slow lane through the seething, jeering pack of humanity, but then the driver flicked his horses with the whip and they lurched into a trot. The crowd parted to make way for them, and soon the party was moving unhampered down the tree-lined avenue.

The cage was high enough for Harkana to stand erect, and as the mob was left behind, he did so. So this was the "Good Airs," the big camp of the white chief and some two hundred thousand of his tribe. He remembered the description given to him by Manuel de Robles. Harkana inspected the cage. Inch-thick iron bars, spaced close together, with a single doorway that was double-locked. The floor, measuring ten feet by seven, gave him a little room to pace, and they had not fastened him to the structure as yet. He still wore the leg irons, and his hands were

239

roped tightly behind his back. Harkana knew that he would be paraded on the following day and then put on view. Then, he supposed, he would have outlived his usefulness and they would kill him.

They took him over a mile through the city, through the select central areas of rich residential dwellings and out past the Italian immigrant slums until they reached the main gate of the jailhouse. The driver exchanged a few words with the gatekeepers and then flipped the reins to encourage the two large cart horses through the double gates and under the stone arch.

The exercise yard was full of prisoners making their evening circuits prior to lockup for the night. Harkana looked at them looking at him as though he were an exotic animal brought in for their entertainment and diversion. Pasty-faced, sullen, underfed, blue-chinned, and with a lot else in common besides, the two hundred or so prisoners stopped to watch the prison carriage come through under the arch, then past the inner gate, and finally halt along the eastern wall. Rapists, killers, army deserters, counterfeiters, thieves, and vagrants welcomed Harkana the Orphan to this end of the earth, men who had sunk so far that they resented the intrusion of one whose only crime was to have been born an Indian prepared to fight to the death for his people's homeland. Harkana squatted down on his haunches and turned his head slowly to one side. He closed his eyes to block out the sight of these dregs of white mankind who crowded in to witness this break in their eternal round of boredom.

"Get away from him!" yelled Arostegui. "Get back to your cells, all of you, do you hear me?"

The lieutenant's men formed a wall around the carriage while the driver busied himself unhitching the horses. He led them away. The soldiers eventually drove back the press of prisoners, and the lieutenant was relieved to see the man whom he took to be the head warden waving to him from one of the upper windows of the main block. Reinforcements soon appeared in the form of a dozen prison guards. The prisoners were quickly herded back to their cells, and the late afternoon air rang with the clash of cell doors and the finality of big keys being turned in the locks.

"Chock up those wheels securely," Arostegui ordered his sergeant. He looked up to find the warden approaching across the cobblestone yard.

"Ah, Lieutenant, I hope everything is in order?"

"I believe so, sir," answered the army man with a crisp salute. "I think we may have to do something about changing the morning exercise routine, that is all. The parade is not due to begin until ten. I will be escorting the prisoner away at nine-thirty. Would it be possible for you to postpone morning exercise until then?"

"I shall arrange it, have no fear. Anything else?"

"I have orders from General Branco that the prisoner is to be hosed down. Might I suggest that it be done forthwith and then again in the morning?"

"Of course. Jiménez!" yelled the warden, looking around for the man he had assigned to tend the new prisoner.

Jiménez had been hovering out of sight behind a pillar. He was disappointed not to have seen the savage pace like a panther or rattle the bars like an ape. Jiménez had already told his family and his associates that he would be in charge of this notorious Ogre of Patagonia during his sojourn in the city. Such a calm and lifeless prisoner was hardly what was expected of a savage who had taken so many lives, burned down the fine haciendas of the rich farmers, and led the massacre of Colonel González's last stand. He would have to find some way of livening him up.

Jiménez waddled over to the warden when he heard his name called. He was a fat man, known to everyone as El Gordo, or Fatso. Arostegui departed with his troops to their billet within the prison walls while the warden gave instructions for washing and feeding the prisoner.

Jiménez soon had the hose attached to the faucet in the yard. He aimed the strong jet of cold water at the Indian's near-naked body. He soaked the Tehuelche from head to foot, moving around the cage with the hose since the Indian could not be persuaded or forced to turn his body. In fact, the only reaction that the jet of icy water drew from the Orphan was the closing of his eyes while he basked in the furious spray that lifted off all the sweat, grime, egg yolk, and fruit juice that had accrued on his

241

coppery skin over the past three days. When the water was suddenly turned off, Harkana flicked open his eyes and studied this fat attendant closely as he recoiled the hose and stashed it away.

Ramón Jiménez was a greasy, unkempt, slovenly man who cared for little save the filling of his abundant paunch. His stomach hung poised over his wide leather belt like a great glob of honey on the end of a spoon. He wore a faded jerkin of brown leather and a rumpled gray shirt with heavily soiled cuffs and threadbare collar.

He filled a bowl with water from the faucet and pushed it and a sizable hunk of stale bread toward his prisoner, using a thin metal rod. Harkana ignored him totally, and this seemed to incite some sort of anger in the fat jailer. He needed to gouge a reaction from those he tended—be it hatred, servility, or insolence. The only attitude El Gordo could not tolerate was indifference.

Harkana sat like a stone, staring unblinkingly. El Gordo touched him with the metal rod, muttering under his breath. The Indian did not move a muscle. El Gordo poked him once more, and would have pursued his taunting had not the chief warden suddenly reappeared in the yard. Jiménez withdrew the rod rapidly and donned his mask of innocence.

"Everything in order, Jiménez?" inquired the chief.

"Sí, señor," replied Gordo eagerly. "I have had the devil hosed down as you ordered. The water is fresh and there is bread for him, which is more than he deserves. He's a lot quieter than I expected. Hope he's a bit more lively tomorrow, or the crowds are in for a disappointment."

"Remember, Jiménez, that not only has he never seen a city before, or a carriage or a cage with iron bars, but he has just watched his whole tribe wiped out and the land that he has roamed all his life he will never see again. Do you expect him to perform for us?"

"Well, jefe, I was just thinking of his reputation, that's all," El Gordo whined by way of explanation. "He doesn't look so ruthless to me."

"Listen, Gordo. My son fought under Branco in the campaign against the Tehuelches. He just got back home the night before

242

last. He was tired out, as you'd expect, but the funny thing was, he needed to talk about it even more than he needed to sleep in a real bed again. My son fought the Tehuelches and survived, thanks to God's mercy. We sat up late into the night, and he told me how the Tehuelches organized their resistance, how they battled for what they believed to be theirs. He told me things you can hardly help but respect, even feel sorry for. They say that this one, this Harkana the Orphan, even killed his own wife rather than let her fall into the hands of Branco's men. No one seems to know why he didn't take his own life as well. He certainly had the weapon and the opportunity. So why don't you spare him a thought beyond your next plate of food, and maybe you'll learn something about why he's so quiet."

"Sure, jefe, but what's an Indian woman more or less, dead or alive?" asked Gordo, thinking of the bife de lomo waiting for him back home.

The warden, who had been honorably discharged from Roca's army with a bullet lodged below his kneecap and a captain's pension, did not bother to hide his disgust.

"Sometimes, Gordo, I find it hard to distinguish between you and the most callous murderer we have in our cells. Do you know that?"

Gordo was unsure whether he was supposed to say yes or no. And he was always careful to say what he was supposed to say. So he said nothing at all, which was what the chief expected from him.

"You just make sure that the ill-treatment of this Indian goes no further than it already has, d'you hear me? In the morning you will hose him and his cage down very thoroughly, understand? You will supply him with fresh water and newly baked bread, not stale bread from two days ago. The fresh bread will be given him regardless of whether or not he shows any signs of eating what he has already been given. Am I making myself clear, Jiménez? I myself will inspect what you do in the morning, and if my orders have not been carried out to the letter—to the letter, mind you!—I will have you up before the board of governors so fast you won't even stop for lunch! Now get to it!"

"Yes, jefe. Whatever you say, jefe. At your service, jefe."

"And another thing!" snapped the warden with a fury he had

seldom demonstrated. "I shall inspect the prisoner's body for bruises, and woe betide you if I find any. So you just make sure that you use that metal rod of yours solely for the purpose for which it is intended. That is all!"

The chief warden turned on his heel and walked briskly away to his office.

"I would like to stick this rod up your ass, my captain," whispered El Gordo once he was doubly sure that the chief was out of earshot.

Harkana had understood most of what had been said. He wondered if the god to whom the captain warden had referred was the same one of the crossed sticks. It seemed paradoxical that some whites could be so soft because of their god, while others could roast a man alive as a sacrifice to him. The Orphan watched Jiménez roll away in his curiously short-stepped gait, and then the Indian closed his eyes but did not sleep.

He thought again of Pandra and was glad that she was dead. He would not speak, for if they found him able to communicate in their ugly language then there was no telling what they might make him endure. They might keep him alive all the longer for his added curiosity value. No, he would not speak, or pace the cage, or rattle his chains, or plead, or get angry. He wanted only to die now, for there was nothing he could do for Zorkan Rood and he would never know what had befallen that most regal of horses. Perhaps when he killed the fat jailer they would decide to have him butchered. Soon he would find out.

They paraded the warlord of the Tehuelches in the van of a great display of military might. General Branco himself led the soldiers, the cavalry, infantry, artillery units, and scouts down the Avenida Nueve de Julio.

The Orphan's cage had met with the chief warden's approval. His stale crust of bread had been replaced by a small loaf still warm from the prison bakery. Harkana spurned it afresh and drank sparingly from the bowl of water. Then they led him out of the prison confines and into the midst of a huge crowd which lined either side of the city's showpiece street. The Porteños looked him over thoroughly as he was wheeled past them. Harkana in turn observed them closely without any easily defined expression betraying what was passing behind his dark eyes. The crowd took delight in pelting him with the refuse from their pantries. He remained impassive and inscrutable. The parade lasted three hours, and then Lieutenant Arostegui and his company escorted the prison carriage to the zoological gardens.

They put Harkana the Orphan on display next to the albino jaguar and across from the recently imported American bison. The jaguar had cost two hundred silver pesos, and the bison was a gift from the United States ambassador to Argentina. Harkana had been paid for with the lives of almost one thousand men.

People drifted in and out to view him all day long. But what was there to see? Just a Patagonian outlaw sitting manacled inside a cage doing nothing but breathing. He never ate, never slept, and sipped water only after the sun had gone down and the doors to the zoological gardens were closed for the night. As a major attraction Harkana the Orphan was singularly disappointing to the fun- and action-loving people of the capital. El Gordo became almost frantic with despair. He took the matter personally. Where was the glory in being the keeper to a man made of stone? Indeed, El Gordo might well have been an attendant in a museum in charge of sculptures and bronze statues for all the mastery he was called upon to demonstrate.

The crowds came again on the second day, but they soon left, voicing their disappointment openly. Jiménez was mortified.

On the first evening he had jabbed and poked at the Indian with the rod as soon as the last spectator had left. It had no effect on the prisoner. Then the night guard had come, and Gordo went home wondering just what it took to light a fire in this man of the iced heart, who had managed to infuriate his jailer by doing nothing at all. The Orphan had succeeded in maddening his keeper to a point past frenzy. When the afternoon crowds came during siesta on the second day, Gordo was determined to force some movement or loss of temper from his unblinking charge. He came forward in front of the audience with the long metal bar in his pudgy fist. Performing for the crowd of citizens who had gathered to see this monster from the badlands, Gordo began to prod at Harkana's bare feet. The squatting Indian paid not the slightest attention. The jailer prodded more viciously. Harkana got up and moved slowly to the far corner of his cage.

"Tickle his cojones, Gordo. Let's see him move a little. They say he is seven feet tall when he stands up. I for one don't believe it."

El Gordo could hardly fail to hear this remark. But it was the fact that he knew that everyone in the crowd had also heard it that prompted him to act. Jiménez was a Latin and had a Latin's temperament. He would show them who was boss. He would show them all. He felt compelled to make his prisoner show some of the fury and wrath for which he was renowned as the supreme warlord of the Tehuelches. He was supposed to be the burner of property, the slayer of white ranchers, the raper of fair-skinned women.

But Harkana sat in his sanctuary corner like Buddha, waiting for the world to know him.

Gordo moved around to the far side of the cage. He leaned through the bars and jabbed Harkana hard in the ribs. The Orphan moved back to the center of the cage. This time he sat on his haunches, watching the crowd, paying no attention to the jailer who menaced him. The fat man came round to the front again and poked at the Indian a second time, turning with a greasy grin to the crowd as he did so, seeking their approval and encouragement. Jiménez grinned puckishly and saw the faces of the audience grin back at him. But then the expressions of all those who stood across from the front of the cage suddenly changed. The grins were replaced by looks of alarm and of horror.

The next events happened so fast that those who told about it afterward lingered far longer in the telling than the events took to happen. Gordo's brain had just registered the signal of those contrasted expressions, but Harkana had moved like lightning. The Indian leaned forward and shot one arm out of the cage, grabbing the fat fist of the jailer which held the metal rod. Before the fat man could even turn his head or cry out, he was lifted backward off his feet and held with his back against the bars. Women screamed. Men yelled. Booted feet came running. It took Harkana just ten seconds to slam the keeper up and off his feet, grab the other end of the rod with his left hand,

246

and force it under the lowest of the helpless man's several chins. Harkana did not strangle his tormentor. He simply pulled back on the rod with both hands, with smooth but tremendous force. El Gordo's neck snapped like deadwood, his grotesquely overweight body hung limp, and then the Tehuelche let it drop, just as the armed guards arrived on the scene.

El Gordo fell in a crumpled heap. He did not move again. He would never move again. His tormenting days were over. His body remained on the grass like a voluminous scarecrow. Pandemonium erupted all around.

By the time the uniformed guards managed to break through the panicking crowd, Harkana was sitting back against the wall of the cage, his forearms resting casually on his knees. The long, powerful hands that had done the killing hung loose from his wrists as if drying in the sun. He was just as still and as watchful as a giant spider in a web of chains.

The crowd rapidly turned into a mob. "Shoot him! Hang him! Burn him!" they screamed. One of the younger guards even went so far as to cock his rifle and bring it to bear, but he was rebuked by Lieutenant Arostegui, who arrived amid the turmoil. He ordered his men to push the crowds away. Arostegui flicked the occasional glance backward over his shoulder at Harkana while this order was being carried out. He had done this killing. This calm young giant had killed a white man as coolly and as matter-of-factly as he might have taken a sip of water. Arostegui glanced back at him again.

The guards had their hands full keeping the incensed crowd at bay until a second detachment raced over to investigate the hullabaloo. The Orphan sat watching those who had once watched him, and for much the same reason—to see how they behaved and just what they might do next. His cage was no longer a prison to prevent his escape; it was iron-barred protection against those who would have torn him to pieces. In ten seconds of cobralike action, Harkana the Orphan had turned everything upside down.

After that, the citizens of Buenos Aires clamored for his execution. McClellan made his voice heard all over the city. He told and retold the story of the night they burned his home to the ground and stole his stock, slaughtered his men, and murdered his friends.

"The only fit thing to do with him is to kill him. Not just kill him," vouchsafed the impassioned Bruce McClellan, "but execute him publicly. Make an example of him, an example that no one who has half a mind to revolt against the Republic will ever forget."

Just why any example should be needed when Harkana was virtually the last dangerous wild Indian left alive, Mr. McClellan did not bother to explain. But the government eventually heeded him.

Politicians in general and the ever ambitious General Emilio Branco in particular were beginning to realize the importance of the southern provinces, not merely as agricultural land but as a political platform. The population might yet be sparse, but it was on the increase. People were voters, and voters chose leaders. Provincial governors were needed. Branco's reputation and his undisputed success in the Tehuelche campaign had made it possible for him to consider running for governor in Chubut province. McClellan carried weight among the settlers and estancieros despite the fact that he was gringo. The foreign investors listened to him. He spoke their language, be it English, Spanish, or the international language of pure profits. The gauchos and ranch hands listened to their patrones most of the time. If McClellan could deliver the voters into his hands, Branco was ready and willing to deliver Harkana the Orphan into McClellan's. And so it came about.

On his last night in Buenos Aires, which Harkana spent back in the prison yard, he ate all the bread that was put in his cage. It was the first solid food that he had tasted in six days straight. Killing Jiménez had whetted his appetite.

On the following morning, soon after dawn, they shipped Harkana back to Tres Arboles. He was to be executed there in public. The barred caged was again assembled inside one of the cattle cars. A platoon of uniformed militia were enlisted as guards for the trip. Branco warned McClellan once more to beware of a suicide attempt.

McClellan, who had decided to ride the same train as the

prisoner, took all of the necessary precautions, but somehow he could not quite envisage the proud Indian leader taking his own life. Not even if a golden opportunity presented itself; and none did.

Even Bruce McClellan understood and appreciated the total isolation of Harkana's position. He had no tribe left to martyr himself for. His people would not even hear of his death or the manner of his dying, for they were almost all dead themselves. The survivors, whether they were imprisoned in the island jail or in the city jail-homes of rich Porteños, would soon perish from white men's diseases and broken hearts. Harkana remained alone in his suffering.

Lieutenant Arostegui was again the officer in charge of the guard party. McClellan was anxious to get the execution over and done with. His wife waited for him at their estancia, where there was a great deal of work to be done before winter set in. And Bruce McClellan had given explicit orders to his head gaucho, Miguel, that the great stallion was to be taken care of as if it were made of solid gold.

When the first night descended on the moving train, McClellan went back from his carriage to look at the condemned man from whom he had now stripped everything. Lieutenant Arostegui accompanied him and instructed the guards to admit him into the carriage where Harkana was being kept, then left. There was a yard of free space between the cage and the doorway into the carriage, and it was here that the two guards and McClellan assembled with two oil lamps to light up the interior. The place stank of cattle. The Scotsman could just make out the silhouette of the Indian giant leaning up against the far wall.

"Leave me alone with the prisoner," ordered McClellan.

The two guards exchanged an uneasy glance in the dim light. McClellan settled their embarrassment for them.

"Of course you must check with the lieutenant, but I think you will find it is in order." McClellan lit up a cigarette for himself and one of the soldiers while the other hurried back through the lurching train to find Arostegui. He returned after a few minutes and nodded his assent.

"On no account go anywhere near the bars, sir," he warned,

accepting a cigarette gratefully. "He killed a man with his bare hands while he was in the city."

"So I heard," mused McClellan. "Just give me ten minutes and then come back."

"Yes, sir."

McClellan studied the Orphan once the guards had left, closing the carriage door behind them. The Indian sat staring out into the night through a grid of vertical iron bars and horizontal wooden slats. He appeared totally oblivious to the white man's presence, even in the narrow confines of the cattle car.

"What a pity, savage," McClellan reflected out loud, "that we do not share a common language. I want you to know what is going to happen to you."

Harkana remained as mute and immovable as a statute. He had regained a little of the lost weight by eating all the food that was offered to him. His body ignored the white man completely, but he heard and understood most of what the Scot was saying.

"You will die screaming, Harkana," the settler continued in Spanish. "They are going to burn you at the stake. I seem to remember that you enjoy arson, so it will prove a fitting departure from the world."

Harkana moved not a single muscle. McClellan took a box of matches from his pocket. He struck one against the rough wood of the gondola framework and flicked it through the bars of the cage. It fell near the Indian's feet, flared briefly, and went out.

"You!" McClellan's voice stabbed through the half darkness of the lamplit dungeon. "This is how we are going to deal with you. Comprende? And the stallion, the silver-gray stallion, I am going to break him to the saddle with spurs like spears. I am going to cut his soft mouth with the metal bit the gauchos use. I will shatter his spirit in a matter of hours, d'you hear me?"

Harkana heard. In broad daylight McClellan might have noticed the slight flaring of his nostrils, the lines of strain that suddenly tugged at the corners of the Tehuelche's eyes. But all McClellan was able to see was the cool, slow way that Harkana turned to look at him. His dark head shifted round until the eyes of the two men met in lances of pure hatred. McClellan saw it and was glad. Something had stirred deep down inside Harkana at last, something that even his unbending will could not keep from showing on his face. The Red Pig had possession of Zorkan Rood! It was the prophecy of Seh Saapelt come true. He fought for control of his anger, won the battle, and continued to let his black eyes bore into those of the Red Pig McClellan.

Encouraged by the suggestion of a reaction which he could not accurately interpret, the white man lit another match. He flicked it between the bars again, and this time it bounced on Harkana's naked thigh before dropping to the straw-strewn floor of the stock car and dying out.

"The gray stallion, Harkana. I have him in chains just like yours. Zorkan Rood! That is what you call him, no?" McClellan jabbed his thumb at his own chest to indicate possession. Harkana would have been further disheartened if he had known that the Red Pig had learned the horse's name from reading the report written by Manuel de Robles. "Your Zorkan Rood will bleed under me on the day I get back from your execution in Tres Arboles. Suffer, you brown bastard. Suffer and die screaming your devilish head off, screaming and friendless. Burn to death knowing that I have taken your horse and your life from you for what you did to my land and my friends. I think you understand about Zorkan Rood, oh yes, you understand that, all right."

There was a knock on the interconnecting door between the carriages, just as McClellan was taking one more match from the box.

"Wait one minute!" he snapped. "I am coming out."

The guards remained outside. Bruce struck the match and launched it in an arc through the air. It fell very close to the prisoner. Harkana picked it up quickly and held it to the skin of his left forearm. He stared at McClellan as the hair on his arm singed away. The skin reddened quickly, and the confined atmosphere of the wagon was suddenly tainted with the odor of burning flesh. Still Harkana held the match to his arm and his eyes to those of the rancher. McClellan began to shake, first with fury, then with impotence. The spot on the Tehuelche's arm had burned almost black before the match reached its end.

Harkana the Orphan smiled. It was the first time any white

251

man had seen him smile. McClellan's pink lips began to tremble. Saliva flecked the corners of his twisted mouth. As the Scot clenched his fists in useless anger, Harkana turned up his arm to show his captor the brutally seared flesh. Then the Tehuelche dropped the arm to his side and turned back to study the emptiness of the night outside. He still wore the ghost of a grin.

Bruce McClellan stormed from the prison wagon, slamming the door behind him and barging past the two bewildered guards, muttering no apologies. When he got back to his own comfortable compartment he summoned the steward and ordered a drink. When the whisky came and was poured for him he clutched at, paid for, and kept the whole bottle. In the morning, there was little left of the liquor and nothing at all of his victory over Harkana, the last warlord of the Tehuelches.

CHAPTER SIXTEEN

MANUEL DE ROBLES HAD LEFT the city of Buenos Aires the day before they brought Harkana in on the train. He had been following the newspaper reports about Branco's progress and ultimate victory. He had read of the capture of the Tehuelche leader. When Robles learned from an editorial in the *Nación* that they were bringing the Orphan into the city to be publicly humiliated, he decided that he had had enough.

Since resigning his job at the Ministry of the Interior, he had made plans to visit his sister back home. She and her husband were expecting him at the end of the month, and he had already forwarded two trunks of his possessions. The trunks were packed with a few clothes and a great many works of literature. His law books and many other city acquisitions had been sold off and turned into cash. Together with his savings, Robles was worth a tidy sum, more than he had realized. Now he hoped to purchase a tract of land near his father's old spread. Manuel had finished with city life for good.

Robles could not stop himself from wondering just where and when and how they would execute Harkana. It occurred to him that he was running out on the man who once had saved his life. The *Nación* initially reported that no final decision had been taken. Rumors abounded. Some said he would be shot by firing squad behind prison walls, others that he would be hanged publicly. Robles heard one man say that Harkana was to be taken back to Patagonia and burned at the stake. Then the *Nación* announced that through "reliable sources" it had learned Harkana was to be imprisoned on the island of Martín Garcia for the rest of his natural life as a demonstration of Roca's clemency. Manuel doubted it. He sought only to distance himself from the whole sad affair. He boarded his chestnut mare on the train and took only his saddlebags, bedroll, and Colt revolver. The train which he rode passed the one bringing Harkana to Buenos Aires a little before 2 A.M. during the first night of the journey inland.

The Argentine had no regrets about leaving.

It was long, lonely ride. He used it to complete his plans. He would buy a pack burro and supplies and travel alone on horseback to his sister's place. Secretly he was hoping that some of his father's former territory might be up for sale. Robles would grow grapes and breed horses. It was enough.

"What kind of life do you call that, Robles?" one of the young Porteño lawyers had asked him while he was looking through the law books that were on sale.

"My kind, hombre, my kind" had come the crisp reply. The lawyer reminded Robles of Fernando Carrioli.

Now Robles was in Tres Arboles with his bones creaking from the long monotony of the train ride. He saddled up the mare, threw the old saddlebags across the pommel of the saddle, and rode into town.

The first call he made was at the livery stable, where he ordered the mare reshoed and paid for three days' feed and care. Feeling in need of a bath, a meal, and a bed, in that order, he headed on down the main street toward the Hotel Paraiso.

My but the town has grown some, he reflected, remembering the days when Tres Arboles was just a line of shacks with but one place to bed down for the night. Now there were no less than four hotels to choose from. He chose the smallest, which was neither the most expensive nor the cheapest. It suited Robles perfectly, for it was set off the main street, and Robles wanted the quietest, not the best. He paid for three nights in advance and took a room with a bath attached.

After the bath and a lunch of steak and salad, Robles retired to bed for the rest of the day. He was going to enjoy the benefits

254

of civilization to the full while they were there to be enjoyed. Soon he would become a wilderness man. It was a long journey to northern Mendoza province. He estimated it would take him about two weeks. He was looking forward to it.

By the time Manuel sat down to breakfast on the morning of his departure, he felt like a new man. Rested, recuperated, relaxed, and ready to go, Robles was tired of Tres Arboles already, good though it had been to him. He ordered another cup of coffee and lit his pipe.

Two men were talking at the table next to his. Robles had seen them come in on the previous evening. They were both from Salta, but one of them had evidently been in Tres Arboles a good many times before.

"Well, José, it was like this. A good few years ago, when this town was founded, there used to be three magnificent ombú trees. Within the triangle made by these three trees they built the town, and of course they could not think of no better name than Tres Arboles," the older man was explaining.

"Sure, Carlo," said the other, with a slight cluck of impatience between his words. "This that you tell me I already know. But why they call the stunted ombú on the northern edge of town Santiago? That is what I am asking you, see? El Arbol Santiago, but why, eh?"

The older man smiled behind his coffee cup, but wiped the grin away by the time he took the cup from his lips.

"José, I will tell it to you, amigo. They used to have a blacksmith in this town and his name was Santiago. Now Santiago was very shortsighted, you understand?" The older man held up three fingers a yard away from José's swarthy face. "Santiago could not even tell you how many fingers at this range, the old mole that he was. Well, when the ombú to the north got hit by one hell of a flash of lightning one night but somehow survived and still grew leaves every season, they called it El Santi. Lightning never strikes twice in the same place, get it?" Carlo guffawed.

José chuckled and nodded his head slowly. It took a while for the point of the story to register in his slow-turning brain.

"Now they reckon it is time to burn the ombú for good, so

255

they have decided to send that damned Indian to his maker at one and the same time. El Santi is getting a bit dangerous to ride under. Must have stood there for a hundred and fifty years, you know. Killing off two birds with one stone. No more crippled tree and no more Harkana the Tehuelche."

Robles spilled his coffee on the table.

"What did you say, hombre?" he asked feverishly.

"Do I know you, señor?" inquired Carlo haughtily.

"Excuse me, señores," Robles put in hastily. "I am Manuel de Robles of Mendoza province. *Lo siento.* I am sorry. Pardon me for interrupting, but I thought I heard you say that they were going to execute Harkana the Orphan here in Tres Arboles?"

"You heard right, señor Robles," José confirmed. "That's why we stopped over, to see the execution. Been a long time since they had a stake-burning anyplace around here. Last one I saw was about twenty years ago. Down around Salta that was, where we come from."

"Yes, yes," Robles hurried on, "but when is this execution to take place?"

Carlo drew out a battered old timepiece from his waistcoat pocket. The chain went down to the wide, coin-studded belt which held up his black bombacha pants. "Train due in thirty minutes from BA," he calculated. "I'd say the Indian has a little less than twenty-four hours to live."

"They are bringing him in this very morning?"

"I think you heard correctly, Robles. What are you so fired up about?" It was José who put the query.

"Oh, nothing in particular. I was just interested, that's all. Kind of surprised, too. You see, I've just come out from Buenos Aires myself, and they told me that the Indian was being brought into the capital on the morning after I left."

"They did. Held him there for three days. Showed him off to all the rich Porteño bastards, with a parade down Nueve de Julio, no less." Carlo was interrupted in his explanation by José, who brought Manuel fully up to date.

"Haven't you heard? They stuck the Indian on display in the zoo, along with all the other wild animals. Then he killed his keeper, strangled the poor unfortunate with his bare hands, so they say, and they decided to give him a public execution right here. About time we went down to the station to see them bring him in, eh, Carlos? You want to come along, señor Robles?"

"No, I don't think so. You see, I was just leaving town myself."

"As you wish. But you're gonna miss a lot of fun. Why not delay your departure till tomorrow? The execution's fixed for seven-thirty in the morning."

"I really have to be moving on," Robles fumbled, toying with the spoon on his saucer.

"Buen viaje. Have a good trip," said Carlo.

"Suerte. Luck," said José.

"Equally to you both," Robles responded, and was very grateful to see them get up and leave the hotel dining room.

Robles dropped a peso on the table and went upstairs to his room. He bolted the door behind him. Reaching for the saddlebags, he began to pack with a haste which he thought he had abandoned forever as one of the ridiculous traits of the city dweller. He had sworn never to have to hurry again, yet here he was rushing to get packed and leave.

Robles caught sight of himself stuffing the saddlebags with two clean shirts, reflected in the tall dressing mirror on the wall of the room. He stopped what he was doing and stared at the man who stared back at him, both of them frozen on the brink of making a mistake that could never be lived down. Going on forty-three years of age, able still to pass for late thirties, he allowed. The mustache still as black as ever, as was the hair on his head, albeit a little thinner in front than in times gone by. The skin of his face and his forearms already beginning to pick up the dark tan that he took on so quickly once he was away from the city. His leather jerkin looking worn but serviceable. The work shirt washed thin but still with some wear in it. The leather of his riding boots supple from a lot of use but soft and splendid from a lot of care.

Robles made his decision. He could not run out on the man who had saved his life. He could do nothing to save him, but he could maybe find some way of letting Harkana know that he had at least one friend among all the hundreds of white

257

people who were gathering to see him die. Robles put down the saddlebags and went down into the lobby of the hotel.

"I'll be staying one more night," he told the hotelier, a small, blue-chinned little weasel of a man who could not look any of his customers straight in the eye, least of all this hard-eyed stranger from Mendoza.

"You've decided to stay for the execution, eh, sénor Robles?"

Robles dropped the required number of pesos on the desk and said nothing.

"Next time you pass through," said the hotelier, as Robles half turned to go, "they will be calling this town Dos Arboles, no doubt, once they burn El Santi along with that savage." The hotelier grinned foolishly.

Robles felt suddenly nauseous.

"There isn't going to be a next time," he said, and went out into the brightness of the dusty street.

Robles ambled through the town on foot in the rough direction of the railroad station. He arrived a couple of minutes too late. He was able to catch just one fleeting glimpse of the back of Harkana's dark head, the head that rode above all of those of the crowd, and then the prisoner and his escort were hastily driven away. Robles stood wistfully gazing after them for some minutes and was completely unaware of the horseman who had approached him.

"Robles, what on earth are you doing here in Tres Arboles?"

It was Bruce McClellan, as Manuel knew from the accented Spanish before he had even wheeled around to face him.

"Even a man of my station in life has to be somewhere, señor McClellan."

"Yes, I heard that you had given up your job at the Indian bureau. How timely that you should be in town for the execution."

"That's right," retorted Robles, seeking to terminate the conversation rather than prolong it.

"Any plans?" asked McClellan with a raised eyebrow to accentuate his query.

"Heading home to Mendoza country. Might look around for a small piece of land to farm." Robles looked up at McClellan, who seemed tired. Manuel wondered if he had just ridden in from the south or if he had come in on the train with the Tehuelche. He didn't let his thoughts press him so much that he had to inquire.

"You surprise me," remarked the Scot, overdoing the act of amazement. "You really do. I thought you were a country boy made good in the city, not a successful city man yearning for the outdoor life."

"Did you?" Robles was not in the mood to give anything away.

"Yes, I did," snapped McClellan, who had grown too used to total respect from his ranch hands and equals alike to care for this sarcasm.

"You got it wrong, I guess, señor McClellan."

McClellan's face hardened visibly. "Been a long haul out from BA," he decided. "If you'll excuse me, I'll be taking a rest in my hotel room." Now it was the rancher who was seeking to curtail the conversation.

"Just one thing before you go," stabbed Robles, seeing the reaction of the immigrant and playing to it.

McClellan stopped and turned back: "Well?"

"I can just about accept," said Robles, "that what happened to the Tehuelches and the other pampas Indians in this part of the continent was inevitable. That if it hadn't been you and Branco in the year of 1880 then it would have been some other power-hungry politician and hotshot gringo sometime sooner or later. I hated to see it happen, particularly in the name of progress, but I can see now that nothing anyone could have done, least of all myself, could have prevented it. The only thing I wanted to ask you is how come you enjoyed it all so much?"

"I like to win, Robles. It's as simple as that."

"And have you won? I mean, really won?"

"What would you call it then, if not a victory? Let's see," calculated McClellan. "My wife is alive and well. My estancia has doubled its acreage in the last fifteen years. I have extended my holdings south of the Colorado River. The Indians who posed the greatest threat are either dead or imprisoned. Their last effective leader has twenty-four hours left on this earth, and I have been presented with his magnificent gray stallion as a token

259

of appreciation by the Republic for my small part in putting down the rebellion. I call that winning. What do you call it, Robles?"

"I call it despicable, señor McClellan," said Robles serenely, looking the Scotsman straight in the eyes as he spoke the blatant insult.

The cold gray eyes tightened with anger but still held their overall stare of triumph. McClellan didn't need a fight just then. It would serve no purpose.

"Don't you own a conscience?" Robles asked him. He was still working on the appalling fact that Zorkan Rood still lived and that this was his new master.

"If I do, then it certainly hasn't made its presence felt of late."

"How fortunate for you. Does Harkana know about the stallion?"

"I tend to think he does, if my powers of sign language are anything to go by. I tried to explain it to him last night, but of course the heathen doesn't understand a word of any civilized language. Pity that I haven't had the time to break the stallion already. Believe me, there is nothing I would have liked more than to watch the Tehuelche burn while mounted upon his gray. Now then, I really must be getting along. Will you stay for the execution?"

Robles's head was pounding with new drumbeats of thought. He did not answer, and McClellan simply shrugged off the latest insolence and picked his way through the remainder of the crowd. Manuel watched the man and the big black horse disappear around a corner in the direction of the main street.

Throughout the rest of that day and all of that night, Harkana was kept in the same cage in which he had been transported from the station. Lieutenant Arostegui was rarely far away from his prisoner. There were to be no more incidents like that with El Gordo. In fact, no one except Arostegui and members of his guard detachment were allowed anywhere near the prisoner. A few of the townsfolk of Tres Arboles had lost friends or family in the recent Indian wars, and there was fear of a lynching or a private vendetta, resulting in the Orphan's being shot or poisoned in his cell. His water and bread were carefully scrutinized before

260

they were passed through the bars to him. Every road led to death, one way or another, as far as the last of the Tehuelches was concerned.

Robles decided on a red wine from Mendoza to ease his mind. The vintage came from a place very near where he was born. He knew the land well. He had played among the vines when he was a boy. He had ridden with his sister and their father around the outskirts of the farm where this good, reliable wine came from. It was not a flamboyant vintage, but it was what Robles needed to remind himself of home and his purpose in returning there. Robles bought a liter of the wine in a stone flask and took it way out on the south side of town. He wanted to avoid El Arbol Santiago and any other reminders of the Tehuelches and the imminent execution, at least until the morrow. Robles wanted only to drink to remember.

He walked three miles from the town, preferring to allow his horse the extra day of rest before they set out on the long journey north and west. Robles sat down in the shade of a large outcrop of boulders, very close to the railroad tracks. It was the new line, he recalled, the one which now linked Tres Arboles to the village of Tossini. Robles pulled the large, wedge-shaped cork from the flask and took a pull, then a second. The wine tasted good in his stomach, and he rolled some of it around on his tongue before swallowing.

Tossini. Named after the chief of police killed on the night the Tehuelches had attacked McClellan's hacienda. Was there no end to the reminders that revolved all around this warlord of Patagonia? Tossini was just a town now, no more than that. McClellan was just another rancher he once fought a battle alongside. He planned never to see him again.

Robles drank again, and the sun felt warmer on him. It was a late summer sun. The autumn storms would begin any day now. A stomach of thunder had rumbled during the night, but it had passed without the wind rising or the rain falling, to reveal a clear, blue-skied morning that looked set to last through the day.

You should have ridden out this morning, Manuel, he thought.

You have made a mistake. It is no longer any concern of yours. It has not been your concern ever since you left the ministry and handed in your written resignation. There is no need to take it so personally.

Aye, but the saving of one's life *is* a personal thing, if anything is. And this Indian warlord, this Harkana the Orphan, *did* save my life. I cannot just run out on him now, *I cannot*. Robles took a long draft from the flask. He heard the buzz of the flies loud in his ears and felt the rapid mellowing effects of the alcohol. Better not drink any more on an empty belly, he reasoned, and pulled out the burlap cloth in which his lunch was wrapped.

Robles sipped at the wine and tugged at his loaf of bread, cutting strips of charqui from the block with his sharp steel knife. Harkana had played with this knife. His hands had touched the hilt, had spun the blade between them. Those same hands that he had used to kill his jailer in the zoological gardens of Buenos Aires less than one week ago. The Orphan was ubiquitous, and the stone jar of wine was less than half full.

The Argentine put away the remains of his meal, satisfied that he had eaten enough. A distant squirt of black smoke was smudging along the horizon. A train was coming in from Tossini. As it moved across his field of vision, rounding the curve made necessary by the escarpment, Robles could see it making slow but steady progress about three miles away. But as soon as it came off the giant bend and was heading straight at him, the locomotive hardly seemed to be getting any nearer at all. Robles stood up, swayed, then shaded his eyes against the sun to watch the locomotive climb up the long ladders of track across the vast iron-hard earth.

The locomotive reached him chugging, pumping, clawing its way up the slight incline which led to Tres Arboles and the long straight tracks that spread out to Tucumán, Salta, Buenos Aires, and Córdoba. Argentina's rail system, sprawling geometrically like the spines of a fan, had finally come of age. The deafening clang of iron wheels and the hot blast of the steam passed on by, dragging a long trail of cattle wagons. Each was filled with beef cattle, ready for butchering and salting for export to the United

262

States and European markets, where they fetched the best price. The saladero in Tres Arboles hummed on almost around the clock these days. Manuel wondered if any of the cattle belonged to Wisbey or to McClellan. They had so much. So much wealth, so much land, so many head of cattle and horses. They and their counterparts had taken it all and left nothing unowned. They had established a dynasty of opulence that Argentina had never known before. No matter how long it lasted, Robles thought, they owned a little too much. "I like to win, Robles," McClellan had told him. And Manuel could see that he had.

As the last rumbling echoes of the train disappeared, Manuel slumped back down to the dusty ground and fell asleep for an hour or more. When he awoke, he expected to have a headache, as much from the sun as from the wine. But he did not. He had only a raging thirst, and he had brought no water with him. So he drank more wine.

It had lost its soothing taste the second time around. The first mouthful was almost unpleasant. Then the alcohol broke through and it became a pleasure to drink again. He finished the liter and slept on until the sun began to sink behind the jagged horizon of the low escarpment. This time it was the cold that woke him.

Manuel de Robles trudged reluctantly back to the town of Tres Arboles. He had even been unable to get drunk. He had failed at that too. And everything was just the same, one liter of rough red wine later. Just as it always was when he drank, be it to remember or to forget or for the hell of it. And it would always be the same afterward. Reality was permanent. He wondered if he had learned his lesson, that nothing can ever be run away from, be it on horseback, by train, or through the ruby red wheels and spirals of too much booze.

Robles put himself together by soaking long and languorously in a bath that left his skin pink from the heat. He went down into the restaurant, but the people who were already eating there were all talking of nothing but the execution. So he persuaded one of the cooks to allow him a pot of black cloffee in his room, and he made do with that and the remains of his lunch. Then he tried to sleep, and he failed in that too.

Robles walked down to the livery stable, where the owner was working late.

"Good evening, jefe," said the liveryman. "A fine night for a stroll, no?"

"I couldn't sleep," said Robles, in answer to a question nobody had yet asked of him. "I will be leaving at seven tomorrow morning. Here's something for yourself. I'd like the horse rubbed down and ready early. Can you manage that for me?"

"For pesos of silver, señor, I can manage miracles to order," chuckled the liveryman, rubbing the two weighty coins on his leather apron. "Care for some maté? I have water on the boil."

"Thank you, yes."

The liveryman went into one dark corner of the stable, leaving Manuel to pet his mare. After five minutes, he shuffled back with a large maté gourd and offered it to his guest. It had a small sprinkling of sugar, like frost, dissolving into the green morass of leaves.

Robles put the boubille to his lips and drew on it smartly. Good maté. What more could a man want than a horse for companionship, a gun for security, a finger of charqui, and a gourd of maté passed around among amigos? Manuel, the only mistake you made in your life is that you took too long to work it out. Better late than never, he said to himself in consolation.

"Have no fear that the horse will not be ready by seven, señor," said the liveryman, taking back the gourd and drawing on the bombilla. "Half the town and his brother are going to be up at first light to witness the execution."

"I suppose so," murmured Robles. Then he had a thought. "What do you think of this execution, compadre? You think it is right to burn a man alive?"

"You know, señor, I've been thinking about it more than some these past days. And it seems to me that all this Indian is really guilty of is trying to protect what he thought was his. Gave it quite a try, too, considering the odds he was facing. He fought his war his way. Sure, he burned and he killed, and maybe his warriors raped a few white women, but then look at what Branco's soldiers went in and did to them. I ask you. Shelled a whole village full of nothing but old folks and kids. Shot down

264

all the wounded, took no prisoners, hounded those that got away, and then, to cap it all, they had to drag this poor chieftain of theirs through the city streets, showing him off like he was some kind of mutant at a carnival show. Ain't necessary, if you ask me. Shoot him and have done with it. Otherwise, well, what's the difference between what they did and what we did? Beats me."

"It beat him too," said Robles dryly.

The maté gourd came back to Robles and he took another long, satisfying pull.

"Yeah, maybe that's so, but then again maybe it isn't. Did you see him come in on that train this morning?"

"No."

"Well, I did, señor. Didn't seem like a beaten man to me, not by a long ride. He had so much damned pride you could almost cut it with a knife. Afraid of nothing that ever breathed or tried to, that was my verdict. They haven't beaten him, señor; all they've done is taken from him everything that he once had. But you can't crush a Tehuelche's pride. He'll carry that to the grave with him, you see if he don't. Indians is like that. Indians is different from us."

Robles took a last short pull on the bombilla and felt the tea soothing his insides. It felt good.

"I'd like to think you're right. Anyway, I think I'll get back to my hotel now. I'll see you around seven."

"Your horse will be ready, señor. I wish you good night."

"And to you," said Robles, signaling his affection with a short handclasp. Then he trudged back to the Hotel Paraiso, feeling the full weight of a weariness that was more mental than physical.

The execution was set for seven-thirty in the morning. Despite the early hour, the crowds had turned out to see it. A fine day lay in the offing. It was a Sunday. The Sabbath allowed almost everyone in town to witness the death of Harkana the Orphan. Those who wanted to flocked to El Arbol Santiago, some sucking at maté gourds, some dressed in black churchgoing suits, others showing the reddened eyes of a late Saturday night. It was considered perfectly acceptable to execute a heathen on the holy day. There were two priests in the town. Both would be present to plead for God's mercy on a heathen's soul. They would even try their hardest to convert the Orphan to Christianity before he lost the opportunity forever.

Robles took more maté with the old liveryman, then saddled up his mare and rode down the main street of Tres Arboles toward the lightning-struck ombú tree. He was amazed by the crowd. Literally hundreds of people had turned out for the macabre event. Even the women had come; a few had even brought their children. If this event marked the passage of the old Argentina into the new nation, then Manuel de Robles, for one, did not wish to make the transition.

Once in the saddle, Robles had made his decision. Fascinated by the old liveryman's words of how Harkana appeared, Manuel had made up his mind that he would leave town just as soon as he had taken one last good look at the face of the man who was about to die. The face of the man who had saved his life. The face of the warlord of the vanished Tehuelche race. No, he would not wait until the torch was lit.

Robles turned the mare, hemmed in by the massing crowd, off the Calle Mayor and down a side street which went north. He could see El Arbol Santiago, stunted and propped up by timbers, like a crumpled trident. Its shadow was forming as the sun rose above the horizon. When he got close to it and placed himself in the rear of the gathering, Robles took in the ropes lying ready and the huge piles of bracken and kindling that had been gathered. A circle of wood had been piled around the tree, save for one small gap, through which the doomed man would pass. Robles felt his heart flutter deep inside his chest, and his hands became clammy. All the wood was crackling, tinder-dry. It had not rained in Tres Arboles for going on two months.

Robles felt nauseous. His head was giddy. His belly trembled. This was the year 1880, for heaven's sake. How could such sixteenth-century barbarity still prevail in the Republic of Argentina, his Argentina? Why didn't they just shoot the man against the wall of the prison, as the livery stable owner had suggested? Or better still, why hadn't they just gunned him down on the battlefield when the rest of his troops had died? Politics even in death. That was what was behind it all. Another man's advancement, another's greed, another's lust for power. Robles attempted to spit his disgust onto the ground, but the inside of his mouth was all caked up with the horror of what he was about to see done to the man who had stood between him and an ignominious death under the talons and teeth of an emaciated mountain lion. Why make an example of this Indian hero when there were none left on earth to heed it?

Sickened by it all, Robles sat astride his quiet-tempered little mare and waited. Very few of the crowd were mounted, but one who was, one who stood out a mile, was Bruce McClellan. He was there on his bold black stallion, halfway around the semicircle of miserable humanity and off to Robles's left. As yet, it seemed that McClellan had not noticed the former Inspector of Indian Affairs for Patagonia.

They brought Harkana the Orphan through the town on foot, along the Calle Mayor and then down the same narrow side street along which the spectators had passed. Robles had his eyes glued on the end of the side street and he saw the Indian as soon as he turned the corner toward him. He was shackled as before, with long leg irons that enabled him to stretch his legs to their full stride. Two guards held the lengthy ropes fastened to his hands, and another held the end of the noose which choked his neck. Lieutenant Arostegui led the procession. His hands were shaking, and he fervently wished that he had a rifle to hold, like the other men in his unit. Authority is a lean companion. Arostegui's hands were shaking so badly that he involuntarily clenched them together and broke the rhythm of his march. It was for but an instant, but it shook him back to soldierly reality. The rest of his squad marched beside and behind the prisoner, each with a loaded rifle resting on his shoulder. To a lesser degree, they too felt the weight of the situation. And perhaps the strangest one there, the coolest of all, was the savage who was to die in the flames.

The sun jabbed out directly behind them as they turned north off the Calle Mayor toward El Arbol Santiago. Each man in the party trod upon the carpet of his own shadow.

Robles saw them coming from a long way off. As they came closer, he saw the straight, calm stare in the eyes of the Tehuelche

267

warlord. The guards, particularly the young officer, looked more ill at ease than the prisoner who had less than an hour to live. A lump was fast forming in the throat of Manuel de Robles.

So great was the calm which surrounded Harkana that the people did not jeer or throw missiles at him. They fixed their eyes on him and waited for some cue. Whenever his own dancing black eyes nailed the gaze of one of the spectators, the onlooker would shuffle his feet and drop his stare to the dust he had kicked up. In an uncanny way, the crowd gradually ceased to stare at the doomed prisoner. Harkana threw off the mantle of being the center of their attention. Instead, some of the crowd began to disperse prematurely, as if an early departure exempted them from the shared responsibility of the proceedings. The rest continued to babble among themselves and look around at their fellows, so as to avoid the off chance of meeting the condemned man's eyes.

The guards took up positions around the dead ombú tree, their rifles pointing at the Indian's chest. The local police ushered him through the gap left in the firewood, and then they retied his hands on a long chain that looped behind the tree stump. His feet were reshackled in a similar manner. There was enough play in the chains to allow Harkana to drop his long arms to his sides, but if he were to go anywhere, he would have to take the tree with him. As the lieutenant drew his men farther back, the local police arranged for the ring of kindling to be made complete. The two priests, hovering like carrion crows, moved from the wings of this death theater to join forces and read prayers from bibles. Harkana grimaced at their proximity. The religion of the crossed sticks was still hard upon him with all its hypocrisy. His eyes lifted away from the two priests and scanned the crowd.

Robles had seen enough. The lump had hardened in his throat. It hurt to swallow. His eyes prickled with emotion. As he turned his mare away, Harkana saw the movement with his falcon eyes.

"Robles!" The word rang out like a bell, resoundingly clear. The word stilled the bubble of the crowd's noise. The priests halted in the middle of their recitation for salvation. The guards raised their rifles as if the single word had been an attempt to escape. Manuel de Robles stopped his horse but did not turn around.

"Manuel de Robles, come here!" called Harkana. His voice was even but penetrating.

Robles turned the horse back, looking not at the Indian but at Bruce McClellan, whose jaw had dropped in amazement. Another triumph for the Tehuelche, Robles thought. Robles walked his mare right past the Scotsman, dismounting at the edge of the crowd. He passed the reins to one of the guards, who held his horse for him. And then he strode very slowly over to where Harkana now had a triumphant smile on his face. But before either of the two men could speak, one of the priests regained his composure.

"He understands Spanish?" he asked incredulously, with a supplicating look at Robles. "Tell him," he prattled on, "that his soul can be saved. Tell him that it is not too late if he will but accept the one true God. Tell him, señor!"

Harkana made his own reply, studying Robles as he addressed the priest.

"I hear you, white father," he began, and his voice was softly searing. "I do not want your religion. Get back from me and take your scriptures and your salvation with you. My soul is yet to be lost, and it is mine alone to save in my own fashion. I would choose to talk with an honest man for the last time on earth."

The priest was not to be put off from his holy mission.

"Indian, I am offering you eternal life. Accept the Christ, take this cross around your neck, and you shall be saved!" The young priest took the ebony crucifix from around his neck. The chain which supported it was made from fine links of silver.

"Leave us, fake white preacher! I have chains enough!"

The second priest, more mature, stepped up to reinforce the pleas of his colleague. Robles spoke to them gently.

"Father, it is better that you leave him to die in his own way. He will never heed you."

Undismayed, the older padre broke in placatingly. "Make him understand," he implored Manuel. "We can save him from the eternal hellfire and grant him everlasting life in heaven if he will only accept the cross and take the vow."

Harkana searched the priests' faces. It was his tone more than anything else which betrayed the depth of his hate.

"If heaven be the place where the white men go that accept the crossed sticks, then I would sooner enter hell. If the eternal life you offer be like the last moon of my own, then I welcome fire today and ever after. If heaven is where the Red Pig goes when he is dead, then I choose hell with open arms. Take the crossed sticks out of my sight!" Harkana spat the last phrase at the two holy men, and they fell back from the burning coals that were the Orphan's eyes. Robles watched them recede. The Indian also waited for them to get out of earshot.

"Come as close as you can, Manuel de Robles," the Indian bid him. The icy calm had again descended on his voice.

The Argentine leaned over the piles of wood that encircled Harkana up to his knees.

"I have a favor to ask," said the Tehuelche.

"I owe you a life. I will do all that I can, but I am no longer the Inspector of Indian Affairs in Buenos Aires. I am only a man with a horse."

"There have been worse things to be, Robles."

"Truly," Robles answered, "but there have been many changes of late."

"Are you thinking that perhaps I crave your former position's power to save my life?"

"That thought never entered my mind, Harkana the Orphan," said Robles.

"Nor mine," the Indian told him. "A man with a horse is all I need to save the life of Zorkan Rood, if he be the right man. Did you know that the gray stallion is in the hands of the Red Pig?"

"I knew it."

"Then I ask you to set him free, that I might die with a peaceful mind. Give me your word that you will do it, and it will be enough. If necessary"—Harkana paused, groping for the right words—"I would ask you to take his life rather than have him live on under the spiked heels of the Red Pig."

Robles half wished that he had ridden away when he heard Harkana's summons, but he knew equally that he had been incapable of it. Clearly, he should have avoided the execution altogether if he was not man enough to grant this favor. Should he not be glad to perform this task for the man who had saved his life?

"Will you do that for me, Robles?" Harkana was very calm again until he saw one of the guards light up a torch, out of the corner of his eye; then urgency pervaded his voice. "We have but a little time. Promise me this, and it will make my journey to the moon but a little thing."

"Señor," interjected the guard, bursting in on Robles's thoughts, "I have been ordered to start the fire."

"One moment, just give me one more moment alone with him," whispered Robles, his voice cracking. The guard who held the burning brand retreated respectfully. "You have my promise, Harkana, but it is not only in return for my life. It is most of all because I believe that what we have done to the Tehuelches, and all the other Indians, was a great evil. I would happily put one small part of it right and cheat McClellan, the Red Pig, of the wholeness of his victory."

"You are a good man, Robles. May the moon light whichever path you choose to follow."

Robles stared at the tall Indian, whose proud bearing had lost none of its majesty during his confinement. To his intense amazement, he saw Harkana smile again. The stone of emotion in the Argentine's throat seemed to lodge in his windpipe. His last words fought their way past it as the guard moved in and touched the torch to the dry twigs in several places around the ring. Manuel stepped back as the heat thrown out by the flames hit him like an ocean wave.

"I think you are the purest man I ever met," he said, blinking as the smoke engulfed him. He wrenched himself away and almost ran to his horse. Tearing the reins from the guard, he mounted in one violent action and rode over to where McClellan sat astride his black stallion.

"Have a nice chat then?" inquired the rancher maliciously. "What did he have to say for himself?"

"He said for you to stay and see how a Tehuelche dies," replied Robles.

"I intend to."

Robles whipped one swift glance back over his shoulder. Harkana was almost obscured by leaping flames, but his face still bore a half smile through the leaping red sheet. The Tehuelche's steady stare of malevolence was fixed on McClellan.

"I," rasped Robles hoarsely, "do not." He jabbed his heels cruelly into the flanks of the mare and carved his way through the crowd, which parted to let him through. He rode at an uncharacteristically violent gallop, whipping the horse's shoulders with the reins as he turned away from the last outhouses of Tres Arboles. On and on he galloped, until both he and his mare were stricken with exhaustion and the town lay five miles behind.

Those of the crowd who watched the Orphan burn to the end were disappointed. Those closest to the scene said afterward that the flesh of his face was seared and stripped from the bones before his sight went out altogether. His chest and shoulders, partially visible above the fence of flames, blistered first scarlet, then purple, then black. And at the very last, the whole body, long since dead, turned and fell forward to hang on the long chains, where it dangled until it no longer held any shape that was even remotely human.

McClellan and the hardest-hearted of his fellows had hoped for screams and pleas for mercy. There had been none. Harkana the Orphan had gone to the moon without so much as a word. Robles could have told them that it would be that way, for he knew better than any man the way that had been the last of the Tehuelche's.

CHAPTER SEVENTEEN

THREE DAYS LATER, Robles was riding away from Mendoza province. He was going in the opposite direction from the place where he had been born, the place where his sister was expecting him as soon as he could get there, the place where he was going to buy his own ranch and settle down. Robles was riding south once more, down into the barren, flinty wilderness that was Patagonia.

He had bought a burro and it was loaded with supplies for the journey. He had also acquired a new Winchester rifle, and he felt it slap against his thigh in the leather pouch under his leg. He was all the time thinking about Harkana as he rode south with the autumn sun beating down on his black hat. He owed his life and a promise to a dead Indian chief whose like would never again tread the sharp rocks of the Patagonian peninsula. So he had to ride down south before he could head north and seek out the peace of mind that he felt he had earned by now.

As he traveled he tried to form a plan of action. McClellan was never going to sell the gray stallion to him. And he was not going to relinquish it for a favor, though he still owed a big one to the tough little Argentine. Zorkan Rood represented McClellan's total and final victory over the Indians. He was the symbol of the Tehuelche vendetta. No, it had to be done another way, either by guile or by force. How would he even explain his presence on McClellan-owned land? He had no earthly reason to be there. The two men hated each other with mutual passion.

Robles would be nothing more than another trespasser. He had to be careful. Bruce McClellan would have the right to drive him off the estancia or worse. A man could disappear in the limitless acreage of Patagonia and never be heard of again. No one would miss Robles, for no one knew who he was and what his business had been on the Scotsman's fine ranch.

Absorbed by what lay immediately ahead, Robles hardly noticed the beauty of the landscape and the richness of nature which surrrounded him on his journey. It took some time before the immensity of the earth and the air could overcome his heavy preoccupation with Harkana, the bloodshed, the dying at the stake, and the enigma that was Zorkan Rood.

Robles was shadowing the railroad track that linked Tres Arboles to Tossini. It was the sound of an approaching train on the line which jolted him out of his thoughts when he was some thirty miles away from the town. A train in the midst of all this flat grassland was something Robles could never quite get used to. It was very far away when he heard its whistle, no doubt warning away some stray head of cattle. He looked up and saw the locomotive on the very farthest boundary of his vision, a smudge of black smoke that moved very slowly on a wide arc of track that curved out from Tossini, following the soft contours of the undulating land. Then the train leveled off and came straight toward the lone rider, hardly seeming to move at all. Robles led the mare a few hundred yards away from the track, so as not to have it take fright from its iron counterpart. Yes, Manuel thought, this is surely the horse of the future, with the tracks spreading out everywhere like a pox on the land. They had even replaced the horse with their inventiveness. Where would it all end?

Eventually the train hustled by, a large steam locomotive pulling eleven stock cars loaded with live beef cattle meant for the frigorífico in Tres Arboles. Later on, hauled by yet another train, it would arrive on the dinner plates of the rich Porteños of Buenos Aires. It was one tiny cog in the huge wheel that rolled out the new Argentina.

Robles encouraged his mare into a trot back to the tracks and then eased it back on course at walking pace. Where were the men coming from? Where were the men who would rule and

274

direct and guide this great country to a worthwhile destiny? Where would they all spring from? And what would happen if no one of the required caliber happened by? What of Argentina then? Those individuals that history had coughed up so far had hardly been statesmen equal to the task; and the task was growing more complex all the time, like a hydra with immortal heads. The ruthless tyrant Rosas, the vacillating bookworm Avellaneda, the misguided zealot Roca. These were the men who had steered Argentina through the course of Robles's lifetime and that of his father before him. In between there had been Mitre and Sarmiento, of whom Robles knew a good deal less. But they were gone from office, and in most cases from life on earth as well. We all die, Robles, Harkana had said, only the moon knows when and where. Back to the Tehuelche; Manuel's train of thoughts had come full circle.

How this country needed a man who told no lies, who was as constant as the sunrise. Robles had known only one man like that, and he had been burned alive for his integrity. Harkana the Orphan, the straight arrow. What had the Orphan ever done to deserve such a fate? What had he done other than to defend with all his might and warrior prowess that which belonged to him and to his people? The irony gathered in Robles's heart and mind as what passes for the autumn season in Patagonia brought the ingredients of a storm together.

Dense gray clouds had scudded in swiftly to surround the last of the blue sky. A lively wind ambushed Robles's long hair and billowed the tails of his poncho. There was no cover on the pampas. If you were caught in a storm, you rode it out. The sparse ombú trees acted as magnets to the harpoon-like lightning. They were best passed by. Rain started to slant down, lightly at first, then quickening to a downpour. The heavens were racked with thunderclaps. Sheets of lightning cut the pale mauve sky.

It did not last long. In forty minutes the storm had passed overhead and a frail sun had reappeared. Robles ached from eight consecutive hours in the saddle and began to scout around for a suitable spot in which to make camp. He was nearly halfway to McClellan's ranch and could easily have made Tossini by nightfall. Despite being wet through, he wanted to avoid contact with people until he got home to his sister's place, so he would camp alone and outdoors until he was there.

Picking out a convenient ombú, Manuel steered the little mare away from the railway. He gathered kindling, damp though it was. The fire fought back against his best efforts to light it, but he eventually coaxed the wood to burn. He put the rest of the firewood close in to dry it out and then set a can of water to boil. Robles carried both coffee and yerba maté in his supplies. But his first drink was going to be something infinitely more warming. He unloaded the mule and set it to graze on a long tether fastened to the trunk of the tree. From one of his precious burlap bags, he pulled half a bottle of white rum. It was distilled from the sugar cane that grew so abundantly in and around Tucumán. Robles rarely drank spirits, but a couple of belts of this after a rainstorm ride was just what he needed. He felt the heat permeate the walls of his stomach, and presently he was humming contentedly, within and without.

He prepared some food: strips of best-quality charqui, a hunk of bread from the first loaf to come from the baker's oven that morning, and a soft membrillo cheese. Manuel thought it a meal fit for a king. He had never sought kingship. This utter simplicity of loneliness and the great outdoors had brought Manuel de Robles to teeter on the brink of a harsh kind of happiness. "Lonely" was the key word. Was he in need of companionship? A woman's companionship, maybe? And why not? Even Harkana had had a woman. Harkana, oh, Harkana, every turn in my mind brings me back to Harkana, Robles thought, feeling the cold, clammy ooze of panic reaching out for him. He had to save that horse somehow, or he would never sleep well again.

Manuel saw the twilight sky belching more clouds and wondered if it would rain again. He busied himself erecting the canvas lean-to that would shelter him through another downpour. Then he lay on a thin ground sheet and drew his blanket and poncho over himself as the sun finally sank and the stars sparred with the thin cloud.

But it did not rain, and Robles did not sleep for a long while. The cloud thinned out, leaving the black cavern of sky bald save for the stars that won through. Robles spent several hours listening to the wind torture the grasses and trying to decide whether any of it, past, present, or future, really mattered.

It was late afternoon on the third day when Robles first caught sight of the McClellan stockyards and new hacienda complex far off in the distance. His heart began to thump disconcertingly. While he had been on the way he had managed to cope with what he had come to do. Now that he had actually arrived on Bruce McClellan's unwelcoming doorstep, it was all suddenly painful and tricky. He was about to steal another man's legal possession, or destroy it. Robles, a lawyer by trade, had never knowingly broken the law of the land.

Something prompted him to take a closer look at the place before anyone at the ranch saw him coming. Against the lightness of the savannah, a rider garbed in black stood out like a trophy on a whitewashed wall, so Manuel guided his horse away to the west, circling far out behind the hill from which Harkana had led the Tehuelche raid. The old, burned-down farmhouse had disappeared almost without a trace. Its charred timbers had long since been removed, and only a brown patchiness of struggling young grasses marked the spot where it had once stood. The other buildings which had been torched on the unforgettable night had been rebuilt in much the same positions as before. Only the spoiled well remained more or less intact, neglected and abandoned like an uncared-for grave. The new hacienda itself, forming the hub of the complex, had been constructed a hundred and fifty yards farther to the north. Alongside it were not one but two fresh well borings, nestling at the foot of the scarp slope.

Robles saw all this in vivid detail as soon as he crested the brow of the hill. He had tethered his mare and the burro and clambered up the steep slope on foot, carrying his Winchester rifle.

McClellan had chosen his land astutely. It was certainly a beautiful spot on which to build a home. In every direction the pampas rolled away—rich, fertile, productive, and immeasurably enduring. Robles was so overcome by this panorama of man's industry that he did not notice the assembled group of people until they began to move across one corner of his vision. They were shaded by a large ombú, which stood like a silvered sentinel over their meeting. Robles flattened himself on his stomach and peered hard at them. They were a long way off but most of them were wearing black, which made it easier to pick them out against the tobacco-colored land. There were also two or three who were just ranch hands. Robles thought they looked like crows gathering around a carcass. Then it dawned on him that they were burying someone. Robles shaded his eyes against the light, fascinated by what was taking place.

He was too far away to hear the prayers being said, but there was no mistaking the meaning behind the battery of bowed heads. After ten minutes the group stepped back, and Manuel caught sight of a splash of color from a mound of flowers. He wished he had his field glasses with him, but they were tucked up in one of the bags on his mule. The ranch hands, four of them, lowered a casket into the grave. After they had put it in its final resting place, all but two of the cowhands joined the mourners returning to the hacienda. As they walked solemnly out into the sunlight, Robles was able to recognize the white face of Virginia McClellan and the stout, waddling gait of Percival Wisbey. As the mourners reached the house and disappeared inside, Robles scrambled back down the hill to regain his animals. He rode around the base of the hill and cantered over to the two men left under the tree.

The ranch hands heard him coming before he came into view. One of them had a Remington repeater in his hands when Robles saluted them from thirty yards.

"Calm yourselves, amigos," he called out. "You will have no need of the rifle unless you seek more labor for your spades." Robles put on an air of exaggerated friendliness.

"Who are you, che?" asked the man with the gun.

Robles reached them, dismounted, and led his horse to the graveside.

"Manuel de Robles," he said evenly, beaming a smile like a slice of watermelon at them. "I fought with señor McClellan in the Indian wars. Tell me, who are you burying here today?"

"Was señor McClellan a close friend to you?" asked the second man uneasily. He dug his spade into the pile of fresh earth as he uttered the sentence, trying to cover up his discomfort.

278

"Not exactly a friend. Just a compadre who shared a tight spot with me when the Tehuelches raided the old estancia on the far side of the hill. You must have heard about that?"

"We heard," admitted the man with the Remington. He seemed satisfied with this explanation and leaned the rifle against the base of the tree. Then he too picked up his spade and dug into the overturned earth. "You fought here the night they killed every hand and the chief of police?" The thinner of the two men threw another couple of spadefuls of earth into the grave. The second hit the triple clusters of fuchsias and knocked them down off the wooden box. He leaned on his spade again. "Not to mention the two Carriolis, and they were the biggest estancieros around these parts," he added.

"I was here that night," Robles admitted.

"You don't say. Hey, Pablo, you hear that? This stranger— er, señor Robles, I mean, he was here the night of the raid. What d'you know about that!" The thin man was obviously impressed.

"It was a bloody night," said Robles, "that's for sure." He tried to maintain a grim expression of tight sadness upon his weather-beaten face as he asked the next question. "And so, tell me, amigos, who do we have buried here that has so recently gone to join Alfredo Tossini and the others in the next world?"

"The patrón, that's who. You tell him, Delgadito."

Robles tried to keep the shock of the news from showing on his features, and he wondered if he had got away with it.

"I knew the patrón should never have brought the crazy horse back here with him," said Delgadito, shaking his head mournfully.

"Crazy horse?" Robles prompted. "I do not understand."

"The gray stallion, of course," Delgadito resumed. "It belonged to that Indian devil, the one they burned last week in Tres Arboles."

"Really?" breathed Robles.

"Sure," Delgadito went on, while Pablo got on with the burial. "Señor Broos McClellan, God rest his soul," the man whispered respectfully, crossing himself, "he brought the gray stallion back here to his ranch. He was obsessed with riding the beast. We tried to tell him, all of us did, that this was a true Indian horse. The kind of horse that will never again be seen on the pampas. He would not listen. We warned him over and over, but señor Mc-Clellan would not have any of it.

"Patrón, I said to him, patrón, a horse like this will die before you can get a saddle on him. And Don Broos just looked me straight in the eye and said, 'Then let him die.' But you know, señor Robles, as if to prove me and the other boys wrong, as if to make a blatant liar out of me, the horse let us saddle him without making hardly any fuss at all. We had enough ropes on him to hold a train locomotive, I don't mind telling you. Miguel dropped the underblanket on his back and dived for cover. The stallion just stood there, calm as you please. Just stood there, waiting; or at least that's how it seemed to me. Then Miguel, he's top hand around here, he came up with the saddle. I saw him cross himself and whisper a dozen Hail Marys as he walked up alongside that horse. I thought he was a killer all along. Yet, it might seem like a lie to you, señor, but he let Miguel put that saddle across his back as if it happened every day of his life. We could hardly believe our eyes. Miguel turned to me, kind of shrugged his shoulders, you know? Then he crept in and tied up the girths. The horse just stood there the whole time and let it happen. We started to laugh about it. Pulled old Miguel's hair a bit, too.

"Miguel had just about expected to get kicked to kingdom come and there he was, standing beside this massive wild stallion with the saddle all cinched up and not even a sign of a buck or a bite. Incredible, I tell you. Was it not exactly as I tell it, Pablo?"

"Sí, hombre, it is true what you are telling." Pablo nodded vigorously and stopped shoveling earth. He was grateful for the interruption, and wiped the sweat from his brow with the back of his right hand. The coffin was no longer to be seen, but the grave was less than half filled. Robles noticed the dirty mark on Pablo's suntanned brow when he took his hand away.

"Go on," prodded Robles, "what happened next? Would you like a swallow of something warming to quench your thirst? That looks like heavy work, no? I have a little cane rum in my saddlebags."

Robles moved to his burro before either of them answered and began to rummage in his supply bags.

"Hombre, I wouldn't say no, would you, Pablo?"

"Why not? Putting a man under is hard work right enough."

Manuel brought the bottle over to them. He offered it first to Delgadito, for he seemed the more willing to talk. The thin gaucho extracted the cork and tossed it into the grave.

"Your health, stranger," he bid Robles, lifting the bottle but pausing before it touched his lips. "And here's to you, Don Broos," he added as an afterthought. "Maybe you will take the archangel's advice where you would not take mine."

He took three mighty swallows from the bottle and passed it over to his companion.

"Where was I?" Delgadito asked himself. "Ah yes, we were having a real laugh at Miguel's expense when the patrón himself comes out from the hacienda. He was wearing the breaking spurs, you know the kind. Metal spikes you can kill a horse with if you lay it on them too hard. Lethal maybe, but very effective if you get across a stubborn bastard. I remember saying to him, *"Buen día,* jefe, I think that perhaps you will have no need of the spikes. He took the saddle more like a lamb than a bronco.' This I said to the patrón, but he was in an ugly mood. 'In that case, jughead, why have you not got the bridle on him yet?' He was really snappy. Someone threw the bridle to Miguel and back he went. He wasn't quite so shaky this time, but we all took a terrific grip on the six ropes that held the stallion down. But again the beast remained calm and sweet-tempered. Took the bit without a murmur. Then señor McClellan strode over, telling us all to stand back and be ready. He tried to make it look like it was just another horse, but I could see that he was nervous. He was just determined not to let it show.

"I remember how it was the time that he broke his black stallion. He was very good that day. But this was different."

"How so?" Robles asked, pulling out his pipe and leather tobacco pouch.

"Well, horses that have been handled by Indians are different. Don't ask me how, they just are. The black was broken the gaucho way. It took bruises and blood but he was broken in a morning, just like always. The gray was another thing. Much more horse, too. Without a doubt the finest I've ever clapped eyes on. What do you say, Pablo?"

"Never seen a better piece of horseflesh in my life, and don't expect to either" was Pablo's appraisal.

Robles offered them tobacco. Pablo declined. Delgadito took out a cracked little pipe, and the other two men waited while he crammed it full and lit up from the match Robles struck for him. Delgadito cupped his bony hand around the flame, holding the bowl of the clay pipe delicately between spindly fingers as he drew deeply to get it going.

"Gracias," he exhaled.

"*De nada,*" returned Manuel. "You were saying, about the stallion?"

"Well, as I was saying," Delgadito continued, "we all held on to that horse like he was one of those newfangled steam train locomotives you see puffing up and down the tracks between Tossini and Tres Arboles. Señor McClellan, he walks up to the gray real slow. Just as he reaches him he lets fly with his fist, cracking the stallion across its nose. The horse shied away, like you would expect. I felt the ripple of power in its muscles come down to me along the rope that I was holding. Fair made me go hot and cold, I can tell you.

"Careful, patrón! I called. But McClellan, er, señor McClellan I mean, he just turned back and glared at me with those terrible cold gray eyes of his. I held my tongue after that. The chief climbed up into the saddle and the horse just stood there and let him. It wasn't till he felt the spurs that he really reacted, and then it was just the pain that he fought against. The patrón called for us to let go, and we slacked off on the lariats. McClellan, señor McClellan rather"—Delgadito hurried to correct his irreverence and then crossed himself once more—"God rest him, he drew off each of the lasso nooses one by one. As the last one came off and hit the ground the horse exploded. It was just as if it had been waiting for that very moment.

"The stallion vaulted into the air without even waiting for the spurs to touch him a second time. By the time the patrón realized what was happening, he was half out of the saddle. His feet slipped from the stirrups, and the horse bolted straight at old Miguel, who dived out of the way just in time; otherwise he would have been trampled for sure. That horse was in no mood

282

to stop for anything, I can tell you. McClellan tried to dig the spurs in, but the horse lifted itself over the corral fence in one great leap. Cleared it with a meter to spare, he did. Spurs hardly glanced him. Doubt if the horse even felt them, all fired up like he was.

"Then they were gone at full gallop across the pampas, with the patrón trying to regain the stirrups. It wasn't a matter of him riding the devil, just the horse taking him wherever it wanted. By the time the pair of them vanished from sight in a great cloud of dust, McClellan was merely hanging on for dear life."

"So it was the horse that killed him?" Robles inquired, wanting to hear the whole of it before riding on.

"Ay, hombre. Killed him is right," affirmed Pablo. "We rode out after a while. There wasn't much point in hurrying. None of us could have caught up with the gray stallion, not even if our lives had depended on it. Miguel found the body. I was riding flank to him and he called me over. About two miles from the hacienda it was. Back was broken by the fall, but that wasn't all." Pablo left the statement meaningfully short of the full story.

"What else was there?" asked Robles dutifully.

"Hey, señor," Delgadito interrupted, "how come you are so interested in the death of our patrón, when you say that you were not particularly friend to him?"

"Yes," drawled Pablo, "I was wondering about that myself."

Robles was taken aback. He thought furiously. The last thing he wanted was a confrontation. What if they suspected him enough to take him into the house where McClellan's wife was? What would he say to her? Then he had the flash of an idea, the perfect salvation of a lie they could hardly doubt.

"He saved my life that night of the raid," he told them. "I was hit by an arrow and bleeding bad." Manuel peeled back his poncho and unbuttoned the rough work shirt enough for them to see the healed scar of the arrow wound on his shoulder. "Señor McClellan got me to a horse and held the Tehuelches at bay with his rifle. Then we rode on to the Wisbey spread and got help. I would have bled to death for sure if he hadn't stayed with me. I was just paying him a final visit before leaving the area and heading north."

"Well, that's different," said Pablo. "He was a brave man right enough."

"Sure," echoed Delgadito. "He saved your life, you say? I can see now why you want to know how he met his maker. But you will never revenge him, señor. No one will ever catch up with that gray murdering stallion, I can assure you of that."

"What happened to the horse then?"

"Well," said Pablo, having finished off the last of the rum and dropped the empty bottle into the grave, "as we were explaining, not only was the patrón's back smashed by the throw, his face was gone as well." Pablo paused, watching Delgadito shake his head, spit, and turn his spade on the pile of fresh earth. "I mean to say that the horse came back for him," Pablo resumed. "Almost as if it wanted to make sure he was dead, see? Ghastly sight, I tell you. Must have come down on him with those great front hooves time and time again. Face was just a bloody pulp, completely unrecognizable. Miguel threw up when he first saw it. We carried the corpse back home but made very sure señora McClellan never saw what that devil horse had done to him."

"And the horse? Did you ever see any more of the stallion?"

Delgadito had finished filling in the grave. Pablo bent to pat down the earth with the back of his spade.

"No, señor Robles," said Delgadito, "and we have no wish ever to set eyes on that *caballo loco* ever again. This happened just yesterday afternoon. We held off on the burial because of the storm. Were you out in that storm?"

"Yes, but it is of little consequence. Well, I thank you for the information. I think I'd better be riding on now. I have a long way to go."

"Will you not offer your condolences to the señora?" suggested Pablo.

"I think not. At a time like this, it is often better to be left alone. Besides, she has her neighbors to comfort her in her bereavement."

"As you please."

"Perhaps you are right," Delgadito considered, sprinkling more fuchsias beside the simple headstone.

284

"Again, I thank you for the news," said Robles, "however hard it was to hear. Adiós, eh."

Robles mounted his mare and took up the rope that held his pack burro.

"*Buen viaje,*" said Pablo.

"Safe journey," from Delgadito.

Robles smiled down at them quizzically, a twinkle in his brown eyes. "May you ride always in the light of the moon," he bid them, in the manner of Harkana the Orphan. He dug his heels in, and the mare took him away from their blank stares of puzzlement.

Riding north for what remained of the day, Manuel de Robles felt a euphoric sense of relief. He made a brief camp for the night and set off once again at dawn, heading northwest toward the source of the Colorado.

He rested for a couple of hours around midday, consuming a good solid lunch before dozing off and dreaming of life in Mendoza province.

Back in the saddle, the afternoon passed by quickly. Robles felt revitalized by the ease with which he had accomplished his mission. He was not in the least bit tired by the time the setting sun dissolved into the western clouds. Summer was gone and the evening air soon chilled. Reaching back, Manuel untied his blanket and threw it around his shoulders, having decided to ride on for a while longer.

The moon rose with a suddenness which startled him. In all his days in the open air he could not remember a fuller, brighter moon. It shone in the clear night sky like a freshly minted silver peso, covering the landscape with luminous light. The effect of the full moon was so vivid that it made Robles faintly uneasy to be walking his horse alone beneath its opal stare. Then the wind ceased abruptly and he felt thoroughly unnerved.

He wondered why his little mare had not reacted, for it was very susceptible to climatic changes. Yet this did not quite feel like another electric storm brewing. The mare had pricked up its ears. Then Robles heard it, too; it was the sound of a horse neighing. Despite the flood of moonlight he could see nothing.

285

The sound came again and his mare turned in the direction of the whinny although Robles had not tugged at the reins. Allowing his mare to walk toward the sound, he located the source of it, hidden behind a clump of tall grass stems. There stood Zorkan Rood, a monarch in his own realm, wearing the diadem of the English riding saddle, bathing in the light of the moon. Robles rode close up to the stallion, noting that the blood on its flanks had dried.

The horse displayed no sign of nerves once Robles had called it gently by its Tehuelche name. Manuel led the stallion back to a small pool that he had just passed. Zorkan Rood bent its huge head to drink. Robles dismounted, tied the mule to his saddle horn, and approached on foot. The gray shook its mane free, like shards of silver bursting from a firework. It pawed the ground and whinnied once more.

"Zorkan Rood," Robles called in a low voice, and the horse immediately relaxed, gazing steadily at the white man across the narrow space which separated them. Robles's mare seemed almost dwarfed by the immense stature of Harkana's horse.

"There, Zorkan Rood, easy," cooed Robles, stepping one pace nearer. The horse responded to the sound of its name. It stood meekly, the strength and speed idling under its peaceful frame.

Robles came to the edge of the pool and plucked a tuft of coarse grass. He smeared the grass with mud, and the stallion let him apply the mudpack to its torn flanks. Manuel sealed the ugly wounds made by McClellan's spurs. It was a poignant reminder to the Argentine of the deed Zorkan Rood's only master had performed for Robles himself, when the blood from his wounded shoulder had threatened to bleed away his life. The horse stood very still while the man cared for it.

Robles looked it over thoroughly as he worked, remembering the incident of the mountain lion, when he had been almost this close to the horse before. Now he had more time on his hands and less blood on his body. He appraised the long lines of muscle and sinew which had kept Harkana ahead of all his pursuers. Harkana, who had never been outfought or outclassed—only outnumbered. Here was the horse which had borne the Indian leader in all his battles. The mount that had carried the

286

Tehuelche warlord on the night of the raid on the McClellan estancia, when Robles had taken an arrow through his shoulder. Robles thought, this is the last of the Tehuelches.

Manuel knew that such a horse was not meant for the likes of himself, as it had never been meant for the likes of Bruce McClellan. This was but one man's horse; and that man was dead. Those Tehuelches who survived their warlord would die in their dank, dirty prisons, or perish as slaves in the big city with hearts broken by melancholy. The gray stallion was the last of the true breed.

Robles unbuckled the girth straps which held the saddle in place. He pulled the slim leather seat to the ground and kicked it away. Then he peeled off the light underblanket and tossed it aside. Going around to the vast gray head, so magnificently hung with white hair, he reached up and unfastened the bridle, removed the bit, and let it all drop into the muddy pool. Both the horse's head and the moon's halo were reflected in the dark water and Robles found them difficult to separate.

"Zorkan Rood," Robles said out loud once more, watching the beast prick up its long ears. "Zorkan Rood, you are free forever."

The man ran his hand down the warm contours of the neck, then came away slowly and remounted his little mare. As he settled into the saddle, the stallion neighed again, a mighty, trembling, shrill cry. The head was thrown up once more, displaying the mane in its prime.

The horse took off quite suddenly, gathering speed with every stride. Nothing blocked its path, save the brilliant orbit of the moon. As it drew farther away, Robles thought that for one warped moment of time, Harkana the Orphan rode upon its back. Tall, unstoppable Harkana, mounted on the horse that only he could ride, one arm waving aloft the mighty bow that only he could bend. Manuel de Robles brushed the mist of emotion out of his tired eyes along with a single teardrop and watched the stallion recede into the distance. And then there was just the endless pampas and Zorkan Rood galloping free.